The hookup type

THE HOOKUP TYPE

Copyright © 2023 by Brittany Wilson

All rights reserved. No part of this book may be reproduced in any form or by any electronic or mechanical means, including information storage and retrieval systems, without written permission from the author, except for the use of brief quotations in a book review.

This novel is entirely a work of fiction. The names, characters, organizations, businesses, places, events, and incidents portrayed in it are either the work of the author's imagination or used fictitiously. Any resemblance to actual persons, living or dead, events or localities is entirely coincidental.

The Hookup Type is a steamy college romance with strong language and mature themes. It is the first book in The Hookup Type series For a full list of content warnings, please visit the author's website.

Proofreading by Sadie @DotTheIEdit

Character Art by Nina @croquith

Cover Illustration by Layla @designwithlayla

ISBN-13 (paperback): 979-8-9882216-1-6

ISBN-13 (eBook): 979-8-9882216-0-9

*For the girl who kept spiral notebooks of ideas and always had a
story in her head.
For anyone who is brave enough to follow a dream.
This one is mine, and I hope you enjoy it.*

Chapter One

MACI

August 2015

I anticipated the long line that stretched out of the only Dairy Queen in Bowling Green, Ohio. The semester started tomorrow, and everyone was looking for that last taste of summer.

"Who told the freshmen about Myles Dairy Queen?" My best friend and roommate, Katie, scrolled through her Instagram feed and sent a look of disgust to everyone around us. "Why can't they go to Sundae Station like the rest of the clueless BG population? They shouldn't know this secret yet."

"It only takes one veteran hookup!" I laughed and crossed my arms, equally annoyed with the long line.

Everyone who had experience on Bowling Green State University's campus knew that Myles gave out almost double the portions for a DQ Blizzard. They always served an extra amount in the lid of the cup, and it felt like you were getting two Blizzards for the price of one. No one understood why this location chose to do this, but no one would dare ask.

"Did Tyler move in yet?" I asked. I knew that she was lightly stalking her hookup from last year.

"Sure looks like it." She smiled, and I heard the giddiness in her voice. "He's at The Edge, across from Falcon's Pointe."

The Edge and Falcon's Pointe were famous for off-campus housing. Each property offered a gym, a pool, a hot tub, and a shuttle that went back and forth to campus.

This year would be a whole different ball game. Since we were juniors, we didn't have to live in the dorms on campus. It was our first year living off-campus in our own apartment. Katie and I got a two-bedroom apartment off Court Street, only a block from the bars. It was the perfect location.

We finally made it inside Myles Dairy Queen. I witnessed another employee slip their hands into a pair of rubber gloves, and the line picked up.

"What are you getting?" I asked Katie while I scanned the menu to see if they had my go-to. Their summer flavors were still out and wouldn't be back until next year. I had to get one last Cotton Candy Blizzard.

"Probably my usual Oreo Blizzard." She slipped her phone into her back pocket and crossed her arms in front of her chest. She bumped her hip with mine and nodded toward the front of the line. "That guy keeps staring at you."

Instinctively, I looked behind me. I learned from past embarrassments that most of the time, it wasn't me that someone was staring at. In this case, I was right again. Behind me stood a beautiful blonde with her hair pulled back into a French braid. She wore a hot-pink tank top and white jeans shorts. Her toenails were painted bright red, and the acrylics typing away on her iPhone matched perfectly.

I wore a BGSU T-shirt, jeans shorts, and Under Armour slides. My dark brown hair was pulled into a messy bun. It wasn't a question of who was getting the cute guy's attention here, but I still gave Katie a playful giggle to entertain her idea.

"Does he fit your criteria?" she asked.

I rolled my eyes. "It's much more than physical, Katie. Not everyone can just dip in and dip out."

"Like a packet of Fun Dip, huh?" Katie and I laughed at her clever comparison.

Last night after we had officially moved in, I told Katie over our favorite bottle of Moscato that I wanted a hookup this year. Someone I could text after going out to the bars and just know they would be available.

I didn't want a relationship. I just wanted sex.

However, my track record with guys didn't present the most robust case. I had a few relationships here and there, including the typical high school boyfriend I thought I would be with forever. But once I left for college, everything changed. I wanted to have a hookup with someone on campus, not with someone back home who was an easy option when I was on break. I wanted someone new that came with a clean slate.

But since I wasn't well versed in hooking up, I needed to tap into a much more positive inner dialogue. College students do it all the time. There was no reason I couldn't be one of them.

While Katie and I stood in a ridiculously long line for ice cream, beds were probably being shared all over campus.

It was finally our turn to order. The girl behind the register couldn't have been older than sixteen. Her face was utterly transparent, letting everyone in line know that this was the last place she wanted to be on a Saturday afternoon.

"Can I help you?" she said and went through the motions.

Katie went first and ordered her Oreo Blizzard. She swiped her debit card and moved down the line so I could go next. I received an equally uplifting expression from the girl at the register before I delivered my order.

"I'll have a small Cotton Candy Blizzard, please," I said cheerfully. I could already taste those little popping candies on my tongue.

"We just ran out of the candies for the Blizzard." The register girl sighed as if she had delivered that answer for hours.

"Seriously?" I whined. She nodded, completely unaffected by my misery. "Who got the last one?"

Color rose to her cheeks as she scanned the dining room. "That guy over there. The one in the black hat." She blushed when she nodded in his direction and gave a small smile.

Naturally, the cute guy who checked out the blondie behind me had snagged the last Blizzard. I completely understood her flushed face. Underneath his black snapback were thick, dark-brown curls. He was laughing, smiling as he put a spoonful of my Cotton Candy Blizzard into his mouth. His cutoff shirt displayed an impressive set of abs and a deep summer tan.

I rolled my eyes and quickly shifted my attention to the register girl. "I'll have an Oreo Blizzard."

Katie laughed when the guy across the counter handed me my ice cream. My look of disappointment must've been that noticeable.

We chose a table in the back, away from the hustle and bustle of the waiting line. We walked behind the snapback guy, and Katie's eyes widened when I tapped him on the shoulder.

"I hope you enjoy every bite of that Blizzard." I giggled. "You got the very last one."

Chapter Two

JAXON

August 2015

She had pretty blue eyes.

It looked like she had just rolled out of bed. Her hair was up, and she wore a faded T-shirt. I could tell it was one she wore often. She stood out from all the other girls who wanted to make a good Opening Weekend impression.

My eyes narrowed, and I swallowed my last bite. "My bad. What did you end up with?"

"Oreo." She shrugged and walked away. Her friend followed closely behind her, laughing as she took a bite of her ice cream.

Without a second thought, I shifted and turned around to face her. "Do you want my lid?"

I finished my question just as she sat down at her table. She hesitated to take my offer, but I could tell she was thinking about it. I studied her body language and met her gaze. I made her nervous but not worried enough that she couldn't hold her own.

I raised my eyebrows, and she rested her chin in her hand. A dimple formed in her right cheek, and I knew I was in. It was a tell-tale sign that girls gave me when they thought I was attractive, which was often. It made for an easy connection if I ever ran into them in the future and wanted to take them home.

"Hey, baby." Heather smiled and sat down across from me.

I got up and didn't even acknowledge her coming to the table. I hated it when she called me that, especially in public. It made it seem like we were together when she was just something I did on the weekends.

Blue Eyes slid her lid to the edge of her table, and I handed her mine. I couldn't help but smile when her eyes lit up at the sight of the pink ice cream.

Her friend looked me up and down. "You were serious?"

"You were serious," Blue Eyes repeated. She sounded much more surprised than her friend. She took a bite and shook her shoulders in a dancing motion. "If I see you out this weekend, I totally owe you a drink."

"Sounds good." I smiled and turned around before she could say anything else. The interaction between us was just enough. Drinks were a common currency in Bowling Green, and now she had a reason to approach me if she saw me out this weekend. It never worked against me to start the night out with options.

I sat down at the table with Heather and heard Blue Eyes laugh with her friend behind me. Heather tugged on her pink tank top and threw her braid behind her shoulder. We weren't the only two at our table, but with the awkward silence that followed my ice cream offer, it sure seemed that way.

"You know her?" my best friend, Bryson, asked. He sat next to Heather, and a girl I didn't recognize sat next to him. Our other roommates, Jared and Connor, were also at the table.

"No, I don't." I shrugged and set the lid full of ice cream on the table in front of me.

Heather's lips formed a hard line, and Bryson laughed, shaking his head.

This was how we both played the game—getting in with girls, keeping some around, and leaving no strings attached. It had been that way since our first year on campus when we lived in the dorms, and junior year would be no different.

Chapter Three

MACI

August 2015

My Journalism and Publications class was the one I was least looking forward to. I didn't want to create a newspaper. I wanted to design curriculums for school districts.

My professor was late, and already this class felt like a waste of time. I couldn't wait to go home and nap. It wasn't even noon, and I was exhausted after Opening Weekend.

Katie and I had done the usual bar hopping. We weaved through Nate and Wally's, Bar 149, City Tap, The Attic, Tiki Bar, and then ended with Brathaus. My liver needed at least a twenty-four-hour break.

I scanned the room for an open seat. Everyone knew that the seat you chose for the first day of classes would be your seat for the rest of the semester. It was just an unspoken way of life in college.

Then, as my focus moved to one of the middle rows, I saw him. At first, I didn't recognize him without the black snapback. His hair was shorter since we spoke at Myles. But the closer I got to the table, I was positive it was the same guy.

He was busy texting when I took the empty seat beside him. I placed my bookbag next to the table and snuck a glance in his direction to see if he even noticed that someone was sitting next to him. He didn't.

I placed my iPhone on the table and leaned back in my chair. "I almost didn't recognize you without that hat on."

He looked up and set his phone down. In return, he narrowed a set of dark-green eyes at me, and a slight smirk crept up in the corner of his lips.

I could tell he had no idea who I was. "You gave me your Blizzard," I added.

"You look different." He smiled and returned to his phone. His fingers were on it the moment the screen lit up. A guy like him had to have all kinds of numbers in his notifications every day.

"I might as well look decent now while I have the effort in me."

"You're just going to assume that different means better, huh?"

He caught me off guard, and my mouth dropped. His laughter was so contagious that a few girls behind us laughed even though they had no idea what was happening.

"I'm just playin'," he said. "I recognize you now that I'm looking at you. It's your eyes."

I went with a basic introduction since I had no idea what to say back. "I'm Maci."

"Jaxon."

Before I could say anything else, the professor introduced herself. I spent the next hour and a half thinking of another question to ask Jaxon. I barely remembered anything from the lecture.

We were given our first assignment. The professor wanted us to work with our table partners to develop a mock article about something surrounding BGSU by Thursday.

Journalism and Publications was also Jaxon's last class, so when he saw I was going to The Union, he followed me to Jamba Juice. I was starving, but I knew that Katie was preparing something delicious in her crockpot, and I didn't want to spoil my appetite. If there was one item Katie Addiman knew about, it was food.

I ordered a smoothie and stepped aside so Jaxon could go next. "On me," I prompted. "I owe you a drink, remember?"

He scanned the menu for a few seconds before his eyes landed on mine. "Get me whatever you got." He grinned.

His smile was consuming, and how powerless I felt when controlling my expressions was borderline pathetic. I smiled back and slid my debit card across the counter.

Jaxon filled the silence effortlessly between us. While we waited for our smoothies, he took it upon himself to put his number in my phone. He then explained how every important contact in someone's phone should have an emoji that describes them.

Since we were partners for Thursday's assignment, I decided not to focus too much on his direct approach. I wasn't expecting him to follow me after class, but I wasn't upset that he did.

Being with him in such a crowded space felt a little weird. I kept waiting for him to see someone else that he knew so he could take off. Every girl who passed us checked him out or smiled at him. I didn't know anything about Jaxon, but I knew I wasn't the only one who thought he was pretty.

I felt his eyes on me as I scrolled through my emoji options. He grabbed our smoothies from the counter and handed me my drink. I waited to see if he would walk in the opposite direction, but instead, he followed me out the side doors of The Union that led toward the parking lot. My thumb hovered over the side-eyes emoji, and I heard a gasp.

"You can't stick me with the creepy side-eyes emoji." Jaxon struggled to open his straw wrapper one-handed. He was attempting to text, walk, and drink at the same time. It was clear he hadn't won a gold star in multitasking.

I sighed and snatched the straw from his hand. He stifled a grin when I undid the plastic and stuck it in the lid of his drink.

"Okay, well, what emoji are you putting next to my name?" I took a sip of my strawberry banana smoothie and glanced at him. If he thought the side-eyes emoji didn't suit him even though we had officially met less than two hours ago, I had no idea what to expect mine to be.

"The ghost emoji, for sure." He smiled with his straw halfway in his mouth.

"The ghost emoji!" I exclaimed. "Why?"

"It's the end of summer, and you look like you've barely seen the sun."

I laughed. "I have tan lines!"

"That's pretty pathetic, then." He slipped his phone into the pocket of his shorts. "There's no going back. You have the ghost."

"Whatever, creepy side-eyes," I said into my straw.

"You're the one who's gonna have to explain it to your boyfriend when some dude's number shows up with some creepy side-eyes." He sounded cocky, like this was a conver-sation he had already had today.

"That won't be hard, considering I don't have a boyfriend," I shot back. I took another sip of my smoothie and glanced in his direction. "But your girlfriend looks upset when you talk to other girls."

He wrinkled his nose at the thought. A look of pure disgust washed over his face, and I turned away to hide my grin. "I don't have a girlfriend. What girl are you talking about?"

I immediately recalled the hot blonde with the tits hanging out of her hot-pink tank top. "The one who was sitting next to you at Myles. She looked really annoyed when you came over to Katie and me."

He continued to sip his smoothie, and I watched him process his answer. "Heather's not my girlfriend. She stayed at my place the night before, and I couldn't get rid of her the next morning. So she ended up following us to Myles."

Initially, I was shocked by how casually he said that statement, but part of me wasn't surprised by his confession.

"Sounds like you've had to deal with that issue a few times." The words left my mouth before I could think them over. I waited to see if that comment was out of line since it came from someone he had only met a few hours ago.

Jaxon showed no signs of being bothered by it. Instead, he nodded and lightly bit his bottom lip, trying to hide the grin that crept up into the corners of his mouth.

Jaxon was hot, carried himself well, and was funny and easy to talk to. He was the type of guy I was attracted to and the type of guy I would sleep with. But regardless of how perfect Jaxon seemed, I needed to narrow down my requirements for a hookup before getting in the sack with the first guy to pique my interest.

There was no way my verbal confirmation of wanting a hookup was that powerful for me to meet Jaxon only a few days later.

Chapter Four

JAXON

August 2015

Maci drove me back to Falcon's Pointe since she was meeting her roommate at The Edge. The complex was right across the parking lot from mine, so it wasn't out of her way. Even though part of me thought she would drive me home regardless of where I lived.

Maci didn't seem like the kind of girl who would stick around if I invited her upstairs. She was cute, and I liked talking to her, but I didn't tag her as a hookup kind of girl. She seemed like the type that needed a few dates first, and I didn't have time for that nonsense.

In our three-minute drive to Falcon's Pointe, I learned that Maci was from Columbus, an education major, and she was also in her junior year. I didn't give her a lot of space to ask about me. From my experience with women, the less they knew about me, the better.

I wasn't sure why I followed her to The Union after class. It made sense to get her number since we had an assignment due on Thursday, but I thought back to how she approached me at Myles and how different her introduction was compared to every other girl who tried to talk to me on campus. It was simple and not at all flirty, like she was genuinely only interested in talking to me because of an ice cream order. There was no underlying goal to try and sleep with me or make an impression.

So when she sat next to me in class carrying the same energy, something about her stuck out. But I had to tread lightly to see if it was even worth trying to sleep with her.

She pulled up in front of my building and stopped so I could get out. "Just text me if you think of any ideas for the article before Thursday's class," she said without looking up from her phone.

I nodded. "Thanks for the ride."

"No worries, creepy side-eyes."

Her eyes met mine, and I forced myself to climb out of the passenger seat. My regular invitation to come upstairs sat on the tip of my tongue. I shut her car door to end the conversation, and she drove across the parking lot.

"Who was that?" I knew it was Bryson Kennedy's voice before I looked over.

"This girl in my class gave me a ride home," I explained.

"Is she cute?"

I shook my head and shut down any other answers that came to mind. "Not sure if she's my type." I couldn't even narrow down a type. I cycled through every category.

Heather was sitting on our living room couch when we entered our apartment. Bryson let out a loud laugh and went right to the fridge for a Gatorade. Our roommate, Jared, shrugged his shoulders and returned to his bedroom. Once his door shut, my switch flipped instantly. There was a particular side of me reserved for girls who wouldn't leave me alone and couldn't take a hint.

"Why are you here?" I sneered at Heather. Just seeing her in my apartment bothered the shit out of me. I didn't feel like having sex; if she wasn't around so I could get laid, she had no reason to be present.

"I'm free for like ten minutes," Bryson said over the counter.

"Yo." I laughed and walked back to my bedroom. My temper rose when she followed me down the hallway.

Heather sat down on my bed. "Jax—"

"For real, get out." My voice got louder, and I avoided eye contact with her. "I have shit I want to do today, and none of it is you."

Color rose to her cheeks, and she looked down at her hands. I hadn't confused her with what I wanted. No feelings were involved, and we only hung out when we were interested in one thing going down. I never felt bad when girls got the wrong impression. If she cried, I was going to lose my shit.

"You're an asshole, Jaxon." She got up and started down the hall.

I peered my head out of my bedroom door and watched her leave. "I'll hear from you soon!"

The front door of our apartment slammed shut, and my shoulders relaxed instantly.

"That leech is wild." Bryson tossed me a Gatorade. "Those girls from City Tap asked to hang out tonight. You down?"

"From Saturday?"

Bryson nodded.

"Just let me know what time," I said. "And I call dibs on the brunette if they're the girls I'm thinking of."

Chapter Five

MACI

September 2015

It was only the third day of classes, and I was already looking forward to the long weekend. Monday was Labor Day, which meant the bars would extend their hours on Sunday, and BG would become a celebration for three solid days. There would be cookouts, bar crawls, and raging house parties. Katie and I could hardly wait to start planning our outfits.

"Are you texting that guy again?" Katie sipped her coffee on the couch while watching The Real Housewives of Somewhere. I couldn't keep up with her bingeing.

I told her how Jaxon, the guy from Myles Dairy Queen, was in my Journalism and Publications class. She poured over the fact that we had been on and off texting since Tuesday night and reminded me how good-looking he was every few hours. Even though I was surprised he started a conversation that had nothing to do with our class together, I repeatedly dismissed her idea of anything happening between us.

"It's not like that," I sang. "Totally just friends. I don't even know if I would label it friends yet. We just have class together."

"Totally." Katie rolled her eyes. "How is the Fun Dip hunt going?"

"It's . . . going, I guess. Maybe this weekend will bring me luck?"

"Or you could just sleep with Jaxon and see if he fits the agenda," she suggested.

My phone vibrated, and I looked down at my screen. Jaxon was calling me, and it was the perfect opportunity to transition out of the conversation with Katie.

I picked up on the third ring. "Hello?"

"Let's get Dunkin." Jaxon let out a sharp exhale, and the sound of weights echoed in the background.

I leaned my elbows on the counter. "Are you at the gym?"

"Yeah, I'll be ready in like twenty minutes. I'm just waiting for my boy, Kennedy, to finish up."

"Jaxon, my first class starts in twenty minutes. I'm just about to walk out the door." I watched Katie pop up at the sound of his name, and I had to turn the phone away so I wouldn't laugh into the microphone.

She started mouthing something I couldn't make out. I muted Jaxon so he wouldn't hear my obnoxious chain of cackling. Katie could make me laugh with just her facial expressions. I had no self-control.

"Fine," he groaned. "I'll see you later."

"Can you please bring me an iced coffee?" I asked before he could hang up.

"And a Fun Dip!" Katie squealed from the couch.

I threw together another comment to distract from hers. "A medium hazelnut iced coffee, please."

"I'll see you later," he repeated, but I could tell by his tone that he was smiling.

"You already mentioned going there," I teased. "I guess we'll see just how badly you want credit for this assignment."

"Bye, Maci." He chuckled, and the line went dead.

"It's fate." Katie smiled once I set my phone on the counter. "I'm so good."

Chapter Six

JAXON

October 2015

The month of September went by fast.

Every Thursday between Social Justice in Sports and Journalism and Publications, I found myself standing in line at the only Dunkin Donuts on campus. I would order two medium hazelnut iced coffees and two everything bagels with cream cheese. The cute redhead with giant tits at the register began to expect my order and always had it ready for me. I made sure to compliment her every time to make sure it was something that continued.

Maci and I would sit in The Union before class, discussing everything and anything that came to mind. She always called me out on my bullshit and was never afraid to tell me how it was. I liked spending time with her, and before I knew it, our texts spread into categories that had absolutely nothing to do with our class.

It was . . . different, being around Maci as much as I was without getting laid. It was the longest I'd ever hung out with a girl and not had sex with her. Usually, I would sleep with them and then like clockwork, they would flip a crazy switch in their head. I didn't want Maci to get all weird if I tried hooking up with her.

Since I took care of food before class, Maci would drive us back to her place for dinner. We usually didn't eat until close to five, but we used the time in between to work on other homework and assignments. Knowing I had that time blocked out in my schedule every week was nice. Normally if a girl mentioned doing homework together, she would easily persuade me to do something much more enjoyable to pass the time. But Maci actually used those couple of hours to get shit done.

This had been our routine since I met her. Her roommate, Katie, reached the point where she expected me to be there. She was cool, and I could see why Maci was friends with her. She was also nice to look at—smooth brown skin, light-brown eyes, and dark curls that she usually wore down.

Connor would be all over her. She was totally his type.

Maci was focused on whatever trashy reality show Katie had on TV. I brushed my fingers along her forearm and drew her attention away from the screen. I was beginning to like how soft her eyes got every time I touched her, like she was checking to see if I was okay.

I gestured toward the bag of shredded cheese in front of her, and she passed it to me. Her eyes flew right back to the screen, and I smiled when she wasn't looking. I liked how my touch didn't make her nervous, but it probably helped that I did it as often as possible. It was just something that came naturally to me.

"Why have I never seen you at the bars, Jaxon?" Katie blew on her chili and added another spoonful of sour cream to her bowl. She was sitting at the small island in the kitchen while Maci and I were on the floor at the coffee table.

I shrugged. "We probably just don't run into each other."

"Would you pretend not to know me?"

I went to answer, but I decided to take another bite of chili instead. Maci's face killed me, and I had to look away to swallow. She looked appalled, but I wasn't lying.

"Jax!" Maci smacked my arm.

I laughed and let her get her hit in. "I would probably ignore Maci, too, if I'm being honest. Taking a girl home is hard when you have other good-looking girls around you. Kennedy and I are always looking for some hoes."

Katie contemplated my response and didn't read into my compliment. She also wasn't offended by how I spoke about girls at the bar.

Maci shrugged and seemed to understand my reasoning. She knew by now how I was with women. We swapped stories and talked about past hookups in some conversations. I knew that she had only slept with five guys; three of them she dated, and two of them were guys she had known since high school. She knew I didn't even know my number and that I'd never dated anyone.

"Okay, then," Maci piped up. Her eyes narrowed, and I knew she was about to challenge me on something. "If you saw me out and a guy was chattin' me up, would you intervene? Or would you and Kennedy be too busy with your hoes?"

"Chattin' you up, huh?" I laughed. It was always funny to hear her try to talk like me. "While I'm busy with hoes?"

She nodded. She was such a dork.

"Depends. What are you wearing?" I moved a little closer to her, and she smacked me again.

"I don't care if I'm wearing a hazmat suit or a thong bikini," Katie exaggerated. "Nobody better intervene if that's where my night is heading."

"I better never get cock-blocked by a person in a hazmat suit." I stood up and walked my bowl to the sink. Katie watched me and made sure I put it in the dishwasher.

Living with females seemed exhausting. Heaven forbid I left the toilet seat up. Maci would reprimand me with, "Ladies live here, Jax. Put that shit back down."

I leaned over the counter and peered into the living room. "I wouldn't butt in." I would love to see Maci in action at the bars. I would've totally hit on her if we had met at the bar instead of in a classroom.

"We should all go out!" Maci's face lit up instantly, and I knew I couldn't say no.

"You guys don't have plans for Halloween?" I ran my fingers through my hair. I couldn't have Maci and Katie with me on Saturday. My guys wouldn't have it if we were all looking to take a girl home that night.

Bryson and I had plans to rummage through at least a dozen house parties on Saturday. We were going as firemen. Connor and Jared were going as cowboys. Both were typical costumes that females fawn over.

"What about tomorrow night?" Maci noticed my hesitation to her original question. "Katie and I have a party on Saturday anyway. We can pregame here tomorrow and then all go out?"

I would have to devise an excuse for why I couldn't go to Ohio State with Bryson, Jared, Connor, and a few guys from the football team. We'd been talking about it all week. I had to see if this thing with Maci was going anywhere. If we went out, I could see if we were better off as friends or if it was worth taking the risk of hooking up with her.

"I'll be here." I made it sound like I was cringing at the thought.

"Aww, I'm excited!" Maci smiled and got up to clean her bowl. "I can't wait to see you drunk." She laughed and wrapped her arms around my waist so she could hug me.

I felt my upper body relax. She turned back toward the living room, and I watched her walk away. Her black tank top hugged her waistline, and her running shorts were tight around her ass.

Even if I didn't sleep with Maci, I could still guess what she hid underneath all her clothes.

Chapter Seven

MACI

October 2015

"God dammit!" I yelled at the steering wheel of my Hyundai Elantra. She usually never did me wrong, but I felt betrayed as I sat in the driver's seat.

Okay, I regularly ignored the reminder sticker at the top left corner of my windshield. I winced at the evidence plastered right in front of me. My dashboard lit up in multiple places. With every blink, I felt more judgment radiate from the tiny little oil can light.

I was due for an oil change a whopping eight hundred miles ago.

While my angry car and I sat helplessly in Lot J, I tried calling Katie. It went straight to voicemail. Katie wouldn't be done with class for another hour or so.

I stuck the key in the ignition and gave it another try. The engine revved, and I heard the effort my little car gave.

"Come on!" My begging turned into a nervous laugh when the engine picked up. My car sounded like it was going to fall apart, but I didn't want to turn it off in case it didn't start again. I quickly searched on my phone and found the nearest auto shop. Al's Auto and Towing was only five miles away.

As I turned out of the parking lot, my phone vibrated in my cup holder. It was Jaxon.

I smiled and put him on speaker so I didn't have to hold my phone. "Hello?"

"What's up?" It was eerily quiet in the background wherever he was. I usually heard the gym, people in The Union, or nearby traffic whenever we were on the phone.

"Well, right now, I'm trying to roll my car into an auto shop to get an oil change," I admitted. "What's up with you?"

"What do you mean you're *rolling* your car? Where are you?"

I pictured his facial expression and laughed. "I'm not actually rolling my car, Jaxon. I'm driving down College Drive. But my car sounds like it could quit on me at any moment, so I'm letting her coast as much as possible." Another round of beeping came from the dashboard, and I did my best to ignore it.

"Pull over and wait for me," he ordered. "I'll be right there."

"Where are *you* at?" I hugged the curb and came to a stop. I turned off the engine and immediately regretted my decision.

"I'm at my place," he shouted. It sounded like I was on speaker. "I'm heading out now."

"*You're* just sitting at home? Did you call me because you were bored?" I teased and reclined my seat.

A door slammed shut, and I was no longer on speakerphone. "You called me this morning, and I was in class." He returned my playful tone. "You don't know my schedule yet?"

"Ah, yes. It is actually at the top of my priority list this week—memorize Jaxon's schedule."

"I wasn't sure if you needed something, and look at this. When I called you back, you conveniently did!"

"Since when do I need a reason to call you?" I snapped. "I didn't plan for this combustion." I gestured toward the hood of my car even though he couldn't see it.

"You don't *need* a reason. There just usually is one. I mean, I get why you call me so often. I'm a very entertaining way to pass the time."

"Well, don't worry. If I'm getting in the way of your sexy phone time, I'll call less often." I smirked and got out of the car. The thought of Jaxon having sexy phone time suddenly left me with a bad taste in my mouth.

"Sexy phone time!" He laughed. "You're something else."

I grinned and leaned against the hood. A few cars passed me on the road, and it occurred to me that I had no idea what Jaxon drove. About five minutes went by before he arrived.

"I see you," Jaxon said and ended our call. He stepped out of a dark-gray Jeep Wrangler and shook his head. I could tell he got his hair cut this morning. "Why don't you have your caution lights on?"

"I mean, I clearly scream caution." I smiled shyly as he closed the space between us. He pulled me in for a hug and brought me close to his chest. He smelled like he was fresh out of the shower.

"Can we talk about this babe magnet of a car you drive?" I stepped back to distract myself from how incredible his arms looked in his cut-off shirt. "Why the hell have I been our chauffeur when you drive this!"

"Parking passes are expensive and stupid here." He shrugged. "You have a pass, and I don't."

He wasn't wrong. I had a parking pass, and there were times I still couldn't find a spot in the morning.

"Pop your hood," he instructed and walked to the front of my car.

I reached in and pulled the lever. As soon as the hood lifted, a light wave of smoke fluttered in all directions.

"For fuck's sake, Mace." Jaxon waved his hand around to try and see the damage.

I bit the inside of my cheek to keep from laughing. He looked completely appalled at the situation.

As soon as he made eye contact, I put on my best straight face and waited for him to continue. He sounded even more disappointed than he was about the smoke. "When were you due for an oil change?"

I couldn't say it. I had never in my life felt more embarrassed to admit that I ignored something so blatantly obvious. "I am a *little* over my miles," I answered slowly.

Jaxon shook his head again and smirked. He leaned in so he could assess the dashboard and looked up at the sticker from my last oil change. "Eight hundred miles ago!" he yelled.

He pushed off of my seat and ran his hands over his new haircut. It had to be a muscle memory thing since he barely had any hair to run his hands through. He put his hands on his hips and stared at me with an open mouth and a face that read, "This bitch."

"I know it looks bad." I laughed, unable to hide how entertained I was by the whole scene. "But do you mind giving me a ride to my place after I call a tow? Clearly, I won't be driving this to the auto shop."

"I can fix this," he said casually and gestured for me to follow him to his Jeep.

I felt a flutter in my stomach as the words left his mouth. Knowing he could fix my car made him even more attractive. I pictured him on one of those rolling planks that people used in movies to slide underneath vehicles with a wrench in one hand and a rag in the other. Auto Repair Jaxon looked pretty hot in that fantasy, especially with the fresh haircut.

I lifted myself into the passenger seat of his Jeep and looked around. It had a black interior, and a faint new car smell lingered in the fabric. There wasn't an object out of place, as if this was his first time driving it since he arrived on campus.

Jaxon rolled down the windows and scrolled through his phone for a song before he took off down College Drive. Somehow even watching him drive made him sexy.

Soon, Rihanna's part in "Take Care" played through the speakers, and I sang along to the lyrics.

"Okay." Jaxon turned up the music. "I wasn't expecting you to know some Drake."

"This album was my life after high school," I said, mentally prepared for Drake's intro. I felt Jaxon staring at me to see if I was going to trip up. I was taken back to late-night car drives with old friends, drive-thru runs for bagels at Dunkin, and walks in the park.

"Alright, I've got one for ya." Jaxon searched his playlist. He tapped a song and turned the volume down so I could hear him. "If you get this one, I'll be impressed. I would've sworn you were all into country and shit."

"Oh, I can get down with some country," I answered playfully. "I am a woman of many tastes in music."

His next song choice played through the hefty bass in the Jeep. He was kidding himself if he thought I didn't know every word of Lil Wayne's "She Will."

A few minutes later, we pulled into the parking lot of Al's Auto and Towing. Jaxon put the car in park and turned to face me. I caught myself staring as his mouth curved into an adorable grin. With one hand still on the wheel and the other resting behind my seat, I had to remind myself that we were sitting in a parking lot because I lacked attention to detail.

"I thought you said you were fixing it?" I asked, eyeing up the beat-up red barn that was the auto shop.

"Oh, I can," he assured me, "but I need the oil, Mace."

And just like that, Auto Repair Jaxon was back.

Chapter Eight

JAXON

October 2015

Maci rolled her eyes and handed me her debit card. I had never seen her so unsure of something. It was cute, and I wanted to keep it going.

I opened the car door to step out and immediately turned back to her. "Do you know what kind of engine you have?" When she narrowed her eyes, I stifled a laugh and continued, "You know, for the oil?"

She propped her elbow up on the dashboard and cocked her head. "I will give you a moment to *really* think about if I know the answer to that question."

I took a mental image of how sexy she looked leaned over in my passenger seat. I laughed and locked the doors since she was alone in the car. She didn't seem alarmed by the action, but the guy lingering in front of the side entrance rubbed me the wrong way.

I bought the oil and parts I needed from an older guy at the register, who I assumed was Al, and made my way back to the Jeep. Maci was talking with someone on the phone when I returned to the driver's seat.

"Mom, I'm not sure, okay?" Maci said. "My friend Jaxon is going to look at it, and he said he can fix it."

I started the drive back to Maci's car, and her conversation continued.

"No, Mom, he is not making me pay him." She shook her head as if she had to explain this a dozen times today. "I bought him what he needs, and we are heading back to the car now . . . Mom! I'm going to try and forget you even mentioned that."

Maci widened her eyes and looked over at me. I raised my eyebrows and smiled, letting her know I wasn't bothered by the conversation.

"Okay, well, Mom, I will throw that out there and see what he says. Okay . . . okay . . . I will. Love you too, bye!" Maci hung up the phone and sighed. "God, my mother is *exhausting* sometimes."

"She sounds kind of funny to me."

"Well, she invited you to a family dinner in case you ever want to cash that in," Maci said sarcastically.

I stared at the road ahead and tapped my thumb against the steering wheel. I tried to picture what that event would look like. Other than meeting them for a brief moment or accidental run–in, I had never spent time with a girl's family. There was never any reason to get to know them when their daughter was only temporary.

I pulled behind Maci's car and turned off the engine.

Maci tried her best to sound interested in what would happen next. "Do you need my help?"

I sucked in a breath. "As tempting as that is, I think you should either wait in the car or watch from the tree lawn."

"Fine." She hopped out of the car and followed me.

"Unlock your car, goofy," I said without turning around. I didn't have to see her face to know she was shooting a half-smile that included her right dimple in my direction. I felt stupid that I was wearing the same expression.

It was easy to be with Maci. It was easy being *friends* with Maci. When I looked at her, I saw someone I could spend all day talking to about anything that came to mind. But I also saw a girl I wanted to fuck at least a dozen different ways. It was a complicated and unnatural back and forth that happened incessantly in my head.

It was exhausting.

I heard the locks shift in her door and went to work. Maci sat on the tree lawn next to the car and scrolled through her phone. She filled me in on photos she liked on Instagram, and I did my best to sound invested in celebrity gossip. This went on for about fifteen minutes while I double-checked a few parts underneath the hood.

"Mace," I called, "bring me the toolbox from my trunk."

She jumped up like she was eager to have something to do. It was obnoxious how much I smiled at this girl when she wasn't looking. I slipped off my shirt and hung it over my shoulder. I had no idea my afternoon would consist of working above an overheated engine, but once I heard Maci's laugh a few feet away, it suddenly didn't matter.

"Would you like your tools with . . ." She rounded the hood of the car. "Or without a side of C-cups."

She held my toolbox in one hand, and in her other, a sparkly blue bra dangled from her index finger. She cocked her head and waited for me to answer.

My eyes narrowed, and I took the box of tools from her hand. I knew she was enjoying this. Part of me was relieved to see she had a sense of humor surrounding her unexpected find. If Heather had found another girl's bra in the back of my Jeep, I would've heard about it for months.

I was also sleeping with Heather. I was *just friends* with Maci.

"So you're a boob guy?" She smiled and held the bra out in front of her to get the full effect.

"I can be," I admitted and grinned up at her. "But I'm a sucker for a nice ass too."

"Girls don't just leave these around," she continued, playing off the sudden change in topic. "They're too expensive."

"Well, it's been in there for a while"—I thought through my timeline—"at least a year. So I think it's safe to say she doesn't miss it. You should see my boy Kennedy's car." I would love to see her reaction to the shit Bryson had lying around in his backseat.

Maci rolled her eyes and flung the bra back in my trunk.

After I double-checked my work and ensured everything was as tight as possible, I wiped my hands off with my shirt. "Start it up."

She climbed in and turned the key. Her car hummed like it was taking a breath of fresh air. I closed her hood, and she smiled at me from behind her wheel.

"Consider me impressed," Maci admitted. "You really saved me today."

"Think you could pay me back with some lunch since family dinner isn't an option right now?"

She grinned and nodded.

"I think I want Pollyeyes," I pondered out loud. "Are you good with Pollyeyes?"

Campus Pollyeyes served giant stuffed breadsticks that were filled with different toppings. Served with a side of their homemade ranch, they were always a go-to food option in Bowling Green.

"Yeah, but we have to be quick," she said. "Katie and I still need to go shopping for tonight."

I walked to her passenger side and slipped my shirt back on. I looked over at her as she scrolled through a playlist. The way she bit her bottom lip told me she was thinking about something.

"What's up, Mace?" I prompted casually.

"Oh, nothing!" she answered quickly and chose a country artist by the name of Thomas Rhett. "Are you still planning on stopping by tonight?"

"That's the plan." I nodded, and her shoulders instantly relaxed. She was afraid I was going to bail. Even though I wasn't sure how tonight would go, I would never do that to her.

My answer had completely shifted her mood, and I would give it over and over again if it kept that sexy grin on her face. I watched as she sang some song about a T-shirt, and suddenly country music didn't sound that bad.

Chapter Nine

MACI

October 2015

Katie and I were notorious for waiting until the last minute to get costumes. Halloween was tomorrow, and we still had to get ready to have people over tonight for pregaming.

The whole situation with my car had set me back a bit. I couldn't clean the apartment or get it ready for tonight, and after Jaxon had fixed my car and we got Pollyeyes, I had to drive him back to get his Jeep at the scene of the car crime. I never complained about spending time with him, but I could complain about having less time to do everything else.

"How many people are coming tonight?" I asked Katie as I sifted through costume options. I laughed at the sexy sloth costume and pulled it out for Katie to see.

"Stop it!" She grabbed it from my hands. "How much would you pay me to wear this out tomorrow at the bars?"

"There isn't a high enough number." I giggled.

She stuck the sloth back onto the rack and tried on hats from the shelves behind her. "I invited Lucas and Sam. I think Sam is bringing his boyfriend, and Trisha is coming with her two roommates."

I counted on my fingers as she read off names. "I texted Pete and Mason, and they both said they would come. Hilary is always a maybe, and if she comes, Brenna will come. Jaxon hopefully comes."

Katie spun around and I paused my list.

"So, including us, thirteen people?" I said innocently.

A smile slowly crept across Katie's face. She stuck a cop hat on my head and sighed. "Can we have a short inter-friend-tion?"

"Here?" I threw my hands up. "In the middle of a costume store?"

"You said you *hope* that Jaxon comes. What's the update with that?"

"What do you mean by *update*?"

Katie took a breath and prepped for her next attempt. "Are you guys still just friends? Why don't you think he will come?"

I shrugged, not knowing how to answer the second part of the question.

The first part was easy. We really were friends, and I liked Jaxon. He was fun to be around, and we didn't have to try when it came to having a good time. We had our Thursday routine of coffee, class, and dinner. I would give him a call just to talk or fill time. He helped me with my car disaster.

But still, I wasn't sure if he felt the same way I did about our blossoming friendship. Not all guys could do the best friend role without expecting more. Given his history, I wouldn't be surprised if I wasn't even on his list of options. I wasn't sure if he saw me like that since he's never once tried to make a move on me.

He was out gallivanting with C-cup chicks who wore sparkly blue bras and probably gave him blow jobs in the back of his Jeep. I was calling him to fix my car, and my roommate made him dinner once a week. It wasn't a hard choice from where I stood.

"I'm not giving him anything, Katie. You're telling me that if he were given a better way to spend his evening tonight, he wouldn't take it?" The words hurt a little bit coming out of my mouth. While I had filled Katie in on his heroic act with my car, I decided to leave out the lingerie discovery.

"What do you need to give him? You're just friends, right?" Her tone was soft and more genuine than before.

I continued to sort through the wall of costumes. I stumbled across a sexy cop and robber set and pulled it for Katie to look at. She nodded in approval, and we headed toward the register.

"We are just friends." I removed the hat that was on my head and set it on the counter with the costumes. "Jaxon has never once shown any kind of interest in me. What if I made a move on him, and it ruined everything?"

I watched Craig, the guy who rang up our costumes, nod his head as if he were a part of the conversation.

Katie took a moment to try and understand my answer. "Mace, you know how he is with girls. He wouldn't want anything serious with you. This could be perfect!"

"You can't have Fun Dip with a person you actually care about losing," I stated confidently.

"If Morgan Freeman had said that line, it would be *iconic*!" Katie laughed and grabbed the bags with our costumes. "What an inspiration! We are totally getting some Fun Dip for tonight."

"If he comes tonight and I get a good feeling, I'll make a move," I promised Katie as we walked to her car.

"Jaxon or Morgan Freeman?" She grinned.

"Either one!" I exclaimed.

Fun Dip, pong balls, and the ingredients for making Blood Orange Sangria. The only thing missing was Morgan.

Chapter Ten

JAXON

October 2015

Bryson and the guys planned to leave for Ohio State around five, which gave me an hour to tell them that I couldn't go. Helping Maci with her car had set me back a little bit with my schedule, and I had just finished up an essay that was due tomorrow morning.

It was kind of nice knowing I wouldn't have to endure the two-and-a-half-hour car ride to Columbus. We were going to stay with some guy named Michael, a friend of Connor's from high school. We'd go out, cause havoc, get some girls, and then wake up tomorrow morning to drive back to BG to do it all over again.

The whole process sounded exhausting as I stared at my blank phone screen. It was now four o'clock, and I was actually looking forward to hanging out with Maci and her friends. It would be low-key and a change of pace from the chaos that happened in my apartment.

I got out of bed and slipped on some basketball shorts. Connor and Jared were in the living room playing Call of Duty while Bryson was laying pizza rolls out on a baking pan and drinking a beer.

"You want some, bro?" He pointed to the bag.

"I'm good." I shook my head. "My stomach has been in knots all day. I don't know if I'm gonna go to Columbus."

"Are you sick?" He pulled out two more beers from the fridge and passed me one. "Drink that." He nodded to the bottle. "See if it helps."

I could tell by his voice that he knew I was lying. We were better friends than that, and I didn't understand why I was lying in the first place.

"J, if you don't wanna come, it's cool. Just promise me you'll get some butt from that broad you've been hanging out with." He smiled and sipped his beer.

I popped the top off of my bottle and took a sip. "It's not like that with her, man." There was only one perspective Bryson could look at for it to make sense. "That girl from high school you're friends with, would you *ever* tap that?"

"Stephanie?" His eyes narrowed, and he shook his head. "Naw, man. I don't see her that way. I knew I'd treat her like all the other leeches I've slept with once I hooked up with her."

Bryson and I shared a very similar process when it came to the morning-after. We simply didn't do it.

"Same concept." I shrugged. "We're pretty good friends. If I try to hook up with her, that's it."

"You haven't slept with her yet?" He raised his eyebrows. "All the times you've hung out at her crib?"

"I've thought about it," I admitted. "I just know how it goes. I have class with her the rest of the semester, and I just don't want to deal with that."

Bryson drained the rest of his beer. "You're running out of time before your window closes. Once she friend-zones your ass, you lose your chance."

He wasn't wrong. There were plenty of other girls to hook up with in Bowling Green. I didn't have to risk ruining things with one I actually liked.

"Yo, man, come on!" Jared screamed from the couch and threw his controller into the cushion.

Connor laughed hysterically and poured two shots of Jack Daniel's. He clapped and watched Jared down both of them. Then he turned to Bryson and yelled, "Kennedy, when are we heading out?"

Jared muttered something under his breath, and Connor snatched the bottle from his hand and poured another shot. Jared switched on the surround sound, and the bass flooded through the speakers.

"Don't come if you don't want to, man," Bryson said over the music. "But I swear if you aren't smashing cheeks tonight, you owe me a bottle of Jack."

"I owe *you* a bottle if I don't get laid?"

"It's for your own good." He took his hat off and ran a hand through his hair. "If this girl doesn't work out, you'll bag another one tomorrow."

Chapter Eleven

MACI

October 2015

"Katie, that's enough vodka! Last time I checked, sangria doesn't even have vodka!" I laughed and watched Katie pour a bottle of Smirnoff into my T.J. Maxx "steal of a deal" glass beverage dispenser. Something about it made me feel like my life was way more put together than it actually was.

"It's the surprise kicker of the beverage," Katie tried to argue without laughing.

"Yes," I said. "The surprise being that you won't remember a damn thing after you have a few glasses."

Just as Katie secured the lid on the dispenser, Lucas, Sam, and Sam's boyfriend, Owen, walked into our apartment.

"What's up, bitches!" Sam exclaimed, leading with a bottle of Fireball and a six-pack of hard cider.

"Owen! Come try my drink!" Katie lit up and ran to the TV to turn on her iconic Drunk Betch playlist. It was always a crowd favorite.

"Damn. I'm officially replaced by my boyfriend." Sam pouted and gave me a hug.

"Consider it a compliment, love." I snatched his bottle of Fireball and snuck into the kitchen for some shot glasses.

"Damn!" Sam threw his hands up. "And you just want me for my shots!"

"Consider it a compliment, love." I laughed, and we clinked glasses. I didn't even react to the familiar taste of fire and cinnamon. It tasted like another Friday night at BG.

Sam and I met in one of my English classes. Our degrees shared an English minor, and once we recognized each other from one of our classes, we realized we actually had a ton together. He made me laugh, and we hated the same people in our minor. It was an instant friendship.

I took a seat at the counter and watched Sam return with two glasses of Katie's vodka-infused sangria. Sam took a swig of his drink and stared at me. "So when does your boo thing get here?"

"Katie!" I whined and rolled my eyes.

She shrugged unapologetically and carried on with her conversation.

"He's just a friend," I spoke slowly and sipped on my sangria. I winced when the mixture hit the back of my throat. "Lord almighty, Katie."

"I'll just wait until he gets here to judge." Sam shrugged. He turned to the door when Hilary and Brenna walked in. Mason and Pete followed in almost immediately after.

It didn't take long for people to make themselves at home. The counter was overloaded with different liquor bottles, and our fridge was packed full of beers and fruity beverages.

A game of Flip Cup began at the dining table. My team was on a three-game winning streak, and I was starting to get a good buzz. I emptied my cup and did one final flip to give us our fourth win. Brenna, Mason, and Owen all exchanged high-fives, and we laughed as the other team sulked.

"Damnit!" Sam screeched. "Sit your ass down, Maci!"

I laughed and shook my shoulders to the music. "Timber" by Pitbull flooded the speakers, and Katie and I immediately pointed to each other from across the table. We sang the words in sync and threw our hands in the air. It was an unofficial end to our Flip Cup game.

"Go dance your way to get us some shots!" Pete pointed to the kitchen. "Let's play Pong." He looked at Mason and asked Owen and Sam if they wanted to play.

"We have winners then!" Brenna screamed and grabbed Hilary's wrist.

Katie and I sang as we made up shots. We chose a mixture of Fireball and green apple vodka. I glanced up at the microwave and saw it was already ten. That gave us another hour or so until we headed out to the bars.

"Everyone, come get a shot!" Katie yelled over the music.

As soon as I grabbed one of each shot, there was a loud knock on the door.

"Come in!" I shouted. I knocked back my shot of green apple, and just as the bite hit the back of my throat, Jaxon walked into our apartment. I had to look ridiculous with the smile that showed up as soon as he did. But I didn't care. He looked *good*.

He was wearing the black snapback he had on the day we met at Myles. He wore a solid white V-neck, dark wash jeans, and red Converse. It was the first time I'd seen him in anything other than basketball shorts and a T-shirt.

I padded across the living room carpet and smiled up at him. "Shot?"

He smiled back at me, and his eyes had a little gloss to them as if he had already had a few shots. He tossed the liquor back with ease. His lips looked soft and were still wet with Fireball when he handed the glass back to me.

Jaxon looked me up and down with a cocky grin. "You clean up nice, Mace."

Chapter Twelve

Jaxon

October 2015

I shouldn't have taken those three shots of Jack with the guys across the hall from our apartment.

Maci looked incredible. She wore a black low-cut, long-sleeve crop top and white skinny jeans. Her hair was curled, and the makeup around her eyes made them even bluer than usual. My eyes trailed down her toned stomach and the cute trail of freckles around her belly button.

I could have that top off in two seconds.

"You clean up nice yourself." She beamed. She was happy to see me, and I could tell she was feeling good.

"Jaxon's here!" I heard Katie yell from behind the counter. Everyone in the apartment cheered, and introductions were no longer needed.

Maci led me to the dining room table and greeted me with a solo cup. I took a sip, unprepared for the bite that came with the fruity drink. "Holy shit."

"Katie's Blood Orange Sangria with a splash of vodka," Maci said and picked up a pong ball. "Play with me."

I took the ball from her hand and looked away before it was obvious that I was staring at her. This was a version of Maci I hadn't seen before, and so far, I was a fan.

Our first game was short. We won the round with only six turns because we kept getting the balls back. Every time Maci made a cup, she cheered and threw her arms around my neck.

With every celebration, I got another whiff of her perfume. She smelled amazing.

I needed to figure out what I was doing before we left to go out. If I stuck with Maci and her friends, I would have to take a shot at sleeping with her tonight. If I wasn't, I could break away in one of the bars.

I finished the rest of my drink and checked my phone. I had five text messages. One was from Bryson, one was from Heather, and the rest were from some random broads.

Katie approached where we were standing and showed us a Snapchat. "Tyler is at 149."

"We can go there first, then," Maci said and gathered up the cups. "Last call, everyone! We are leaving in fifteen!"

"Who is Tyler?" I asked and watched the replay of the video.

"He's my hookup guy. My Fun Dip." Katie looked at Maci, and they both giggled.

I laughed at their reactions. "What the hell is a Fun Dip?"

Katie smacked Maci on the shoulder. "I'll let your pal Maci tell you what a Fun Dip is. Maybe you'll be interested."

Katie immediately took off into the living room, and Maci's mouth hung open. Leave it to Maci to compare it to a gross kid's candy, but it wasn't that hard to guess what she meant. She was looking for a hookup.

Maci sighed and gathered up her hair, only to let it fall again. Her eyes met mine, and neither of us had to say anything else. My mind was made up. For the rest of the night, I wasn't going anywhere.

Chapter Thirteen

MACI

October 2015

I WAS RELIEVED WHEN Jaxon didn't push more into the conversation after Katie threw my Fun Dip idea out there. I knew her intentions were good, and she was trying to be the helpful shove I needed, but I still wasn't sure about sleeping with Jaxon.

We started our evening at 149, and we lost Katie to Tyler as soon as they approached one another. They still followed our party to the other bars but lived in their own bubble the entire time.

Next was Nate and Wally's for fishbowl races. They served up drinks in giant plastic fish bowl cups that reminded me of Kool-Aid. We were greeted by Fetty Wap's "679," and Katie and I burst into the lyrics along with the rest of the bar.

After everyone had a drink in their hands, we raced to see who could finish their bowl first. I wasn't surprised when Jaxon won, and Katie came in second.

Jaxon stuck out his tongue, and it was bright red from his fishbowl drink. I felt butterflies right below the zipper of my white jeans. I had the urge to grab his face right in the middle of the bar just to taste him.

His green eyes met mine, and whatever energy was passing between us couldn't be shoved aside any longer. All our friendship needed was some alcohol to push us into trying whatever this next step was.

"The Attic! Let's go to The Attic!" Sam screamed and threw a hand into the air.

I smiled shyly at Jaxon and turned toward our crew. Just as I went to take a step forward, he slipped his fingers through mine and tugged me back into him. He placed my hand on his hip while his fingers grazed the back of my neck. His eyes trailed up my stomach, and his mouth curved into a grin. I could've collapsed right there in the middle of the bar.

I slowly pulled him closer to me in case he changed his mind. When he didn't hesitate, I parted my lips and gently placed them on his. They were soft and full and tasted even better than I imagined. He drew his hand from the back of my neck and pulled me harder against him. He lightly bit my bottom lip, sending a pulse from my groin all the way down to my toes. He smiled against our kiss and waited to see how I would react. It felt like fireworks were going off in my chest.

I wasn't sure if I could last the rest of the night. I drew back from him and led him out of Nate and Wally's so we were out on the street.

"Tell me about the Fun Dip you're looking for." Jaxon stopped me right in the middle of the sidewalk. A tight smile was on his face, and he was completely oblivious to the hordes of students who were trying to get around us. A few girls openly stared when they caught a glimpse of who was blocking traffic.

"Not here." I took his hand and started back up the street toward Main. From there, it was only a five-minute walk to my apartment.

He stopped me again once we rounded the corner of Wooster. He pulled me back into him and leaned closer, his scent intoxicating all control of my common sense. "I want to hear you say it."

I had to remind myself that we were standing on a street corner. This man in front of me wasn't the Jaxon I was friends with. This was Jaxon on a Friday night, trying to work his magic. I didn't know about this Jaxon yet. My scenario had me sleeping with the version of Jaxon who bought my hazelnut iced coffees and ate chili with me on my living room floor.

I was overthinking. I didn't want to choose this moment to suddenly become logical. Clearly, he was interested. He just needed me to take the next step, and this was him asking for permission.

"Just come with me," I pleaded. "I'd rather show you."

When we finally got back to my place, the apartment was awkwardly quiet. The leftovers from our pregaming were scattered all over the living room, and the lighting was suddenly very unflattering. I felt three shades paler than I actually was.

I pressed play on the Roku remote, and Katie's Drunk Betch playlist continued through the speakers. Jaxon took the remote from my hand and threw it on the couch. He kissed me, his mouth a little more eager than it was in the bar. He held the side of my face with one hand while his other hovered over my bare stomach. I pressed my hips into his and felt his erection through his jeans.

I suddenly became *very* aware of what was happening. If I weren't expecting Katie to return at any moment with Tyler, I would've ridden him right on the couch. I pulled away from him and looked toward the front door.

"Why don't you show me your bedroom?" Jaxon coaxed, taking my hand and lacing his fingers with mine.

I instantly felt weak in the knees. I'd wondered since I met him what this would be like. My head felt empty, but I could feel my heart pounding in my chest. All I saw was a guy I knew I had feelings for, a guy I was falling for. I wasn't sure why that was so hard to admit to myself.

I wanted to feel him on top of me. I wanted to moan his name. I wanted him *now*.

"Come with me," I whispered right before I led him down the hall.

Chapter Fourteen

JAXON

October 2015

Maci's bedroom looked like a typical college girl's bedroom. Photos, frames, and collage boards covered the beige stucco walls. A queen size bed sat in the corner of the room, and a green and gray comforter was ruffled against a pile of matching throw pillows. A decent-sized closet with a full-length mirror was next to her bed. A TV was mounted across from the bed, and a desk with a laptop, books, and random clutter took up the last empty wall.

Our only source of light peeked through the curtains, grazing half of her room. It was just enough. There was nothing worse than having sex in some bright-ass light after being at the bars all night.

Maci slid off her sandals and didn't waste any time. She slipped her hands under my shirt and ran her fingers down my chest. Her lips found the sensitive part of my neck, and my body tensed against her touch.

I placed my thumbs on the waistband of her jeans and started to work on the button and zipper. It didn't take me long. My hands found the backs of her thighs, and I lifted her up. She kissed me, and I felt her smile against my lips. I softly bit her bottom lip, and her mouth parted.

She wanted me, and I wanted her. If we didn't do this tonight, we probably never would.

My tongue weaved against hers, and our pace quickened. I laid her gently on the bed without breaking our kiss and felt her hands going at the zipper of my jeans. I took my time and trailed soft kisses down her neck. I felt her lips part against my ear, and a small moan escaped her throat.

I *loved* when girls made noises. But hearing Maci moan did something different for me. I wanted to hear this girl say my name.

I drew back from her and reached behind me to pull up my shirt. Once it was over my head, I glanced down at her. Her arms were above her head, and her stomach was completely exposed. She lifted her hips, prompting me to make the next move. I pulled on her jeans until they caught around her thighs, revealing a tiny sliver of white lace.

Maci's ass caught my attention the first time I met her. Here I was, getting teased by something I had spent so long admiring. I sucked my teeth, and she giggled. I yanked her jeans off the rest of the way and tossed them onto the floor.

Without breaking eye contact, she sat up and slipped her top over her head. She tugged down on the waistband of my pants and stuck her hand into my boxers, wrapping her fingers around my cock. Her stroke started slow, but once I groaned at her touch, she picked up the pace. I hovered over top of her and pressed my forehead to hers.

"Condom?" I swallowed and kicked off my Converse.

She reached for her bedside table and slid open the top drawer. I watched her pull a condom from an open Trojan box as I dropped my jeans and stepped out of my boxers. She handed me the condom, and I threw it on the bed. She scooted herself up against the pile of pillows and motioned for me to come closer.

I climbed onto the bed and hovered over her, planting a soft kiss on her lips. Her bra and panties were the only articles of clothing left between the two of us. I felt how wet she was through the lace right before I pushed the fabric to the side and slid two fingers inside her. She arched her back and gave me the angle I needed to tease her most sensitive spot. She moved against me, and I quickened my stroke, making quick circles with my thumb against her clit while her hands grabbed the pillow behind her. Her body began to shake, and I knew she was close.

"Holy shit," she whimpered and began to roll her hips.

I pressed the palm of my hand against her clit and let her take the lead. I loved watching her lose control like this, and I loved that it was me making her feel this way.

"Jaxon," she groaned, sending butterflies into my stomach.

My mouth was immediately on hers, kissing her as she came back down with my fingers still inside her, teasing her all over again. Her pussy pulsed around my fingers, and I knew she was coming. My hand was wet from her orgasm, and the sheets were soaked. I bit my lip and exhaled through my nose.

I knew a satisfied grin was plastered on my face. "You're a squirter, huh?" I rolled over to pull her on top of me and noticed the slight shift in her expression. I ran my fingers down her back and reassured her. "That's not a bad thing."

She smiled shyly and tucked a curl behind her ear. I wasn't sure what types of guys she had been with in the past that caused her to look so unsure of herself. There was nothing sexier than a woman letting you know she was turned on.

She placed one hand on my chest and cupped the back of my neck to bring me closer to her. I put my hands on her hips and dug softly into her groin with my thumbs. Her lips found mine again, and my erection pushed against her. She moaned into my mouth and kissed me harder.

I had wanted this girl on top of me since that first day of class together. I had pictured it so many times. She traced the outline of my abs and kissed up the side of my neck, her soaked panties rubbing up and down against my cock.

My head split into two different directions. If this were any other time I tried to bag a girl, she would've already been riding me. But I didn't want to just *bag* Maci and leave.

My mind was a little muffled from the alcohol, but I was thinking clearly enough to know what I was getting myself into. I wasn't nervous about having sex with Maci. I wasn't nervous at all when it came to sex. Sex was the easy part. One body part going into another with some fun in between. The aftermath, however, was messy.

I hated picking up broken pieces. Girls *always* left me with their broken pieces. I didn't want Maci to be like other girls. I didn't want to have to clean this up after we broke the friendship we had. It would happen. It happened every single time.

There was a reason I wasn't reaching for the condom. I cared about this girl, and once I fucked her, I knew it would be over.

"Maci, I can't do this," I whispered and shook my head. I dragged my hands down my face and ran them back through my hair.

I felt all of my instincts go into panic mode. They begged me to continue with the position I put us in. It took everything I had to refrain from reneging on my words. Choosing to be a good guy was completely new territory for me, and so far, I wasn't convinced it was worth it.

Fuck me.

She searched my face for a sign to indicate that this wasn't actually happening. "What do you mean?"

Chapter Fifteen

MACI

OCTOBER 2015

I WANTED TO SHRIVEL up and hide in the mountain of throw pillows that Jaxon was propped up against. And speaking of shriveled, his dick was the opposite. He was still hard.

I didn't understand.

"I want to. I just . . ." Jaxon pulled a blanket across his hips. At least he was polite. If he was going to cockblock us, he could at least cover his balls.

"It's fine." I cut him off before he could say something that might actually hurt my feelings. I rolled off him and padded across the room to get a shirt from the closet.

Once it was over my head, I turned back toward him and saw that he was wearing his boxers and T-shirt. He looked relaxed. His tent was no longer pitched, and I took that as an invitation to go back over to him. I didn't know what to say. I felt way out of my comfort zone.

Maybe I weirded him out, or I looked different in this lighting. On second thought, thank goodness for the lighting. My face had to be a new shade of red.

"I can leave if you want me to," Jaxon muttered, interrupting my rabbit hole of embarrassment.

"Do you *want* to leave?" I sat on the edge of my bed and kept a little distance between us. I couldn't tell if he was mad, disappointed, annoyed, or all of the above. A lump formed in my throat. I just had to have my fucking Fun Dip, and I ruined everything.

"Maci." His voice was almost a whisper. The lines around his eyes were soft, and the right side of his mouth lifted into a small smile.

I tucked a stray curl behind my ear and traced the pattern on my comforter. I felt like I was going to implode. I wished he would just spit it out.

"I'm sorry," he moaned and leaned closer to me. "Cut me a break, and please put on some shorts."

I looked down and realized I was still in my white lace panties. I rolled my eyes and reached under my bed to feel for a pair of shorts. I sat them on my lap and waited to put them on. I had to know. The questions came up my throat like bile.

"What's up, Jaxon?" I tried my best not to sound too pathetic. "Did I do something?"

"Nope." He shook his head and smiled down at the floor. "I loved *all* of that. I actually can't even think about that right now, or else I'll get hard again."

"And you don't want to sleep with me." I stood up and slid on my shorts. I clearly didn't need to be naked for anything else tonight.

He saw the confused expression on my face, and his eyes narrowed. "Mace, I *can't* sleep with you. I actually care about you. I like what we have."

It felt like the Jaxon I knew was in front of me again. I tried hard to stifle the smile cutting into my cheeks but couldn't help it. Out of all the possible answers that ran through my head, I wasn't expecting that one.

"So you just wanted to get me off and call it a night?" I giggled when his eyes widened.

He licked the center of his top lip and laughed. I watched his face relax as sleepiness took over the heated space between us. He shifted his body to one side of the bed and adjusted the pillows behind him. The sight of him shirtless against my sheets was a little hard to look at.

Unfortunately for me, Jaxon was still hot as hell, and my clit still throbbed from his touch. He had played my body like something he had mastered years ago. I'd gotten off plenty of times before, but that was the first time I had ever made the sheets wet.

"Come here," he whispered in a way that sent chills down to my toes.

I crawled over to him and rested my head on his chest. He kissed my temple and pulled me into him. I lifted my head to face him and stopped myself from parting his lips and starting round two.

I ran my fingers through his hair. "I wish we could start tonight over."

"It's for the best," he said and leaned his head into my touch. "Now nothing has to change. If we had gone through with it, you would hate me in the morning."

"You're sure about that?" I joked.

He smirked. "My track record agrees with me."

"Whatever you say, Jax," I whispered. I closed my eyes and focused on the rise and fall of his chest. I had no choice but to trust him.

I fell asleep wondering how the rest of the evening could've gone if Jaxon hadn't stopped us. I was touched that he cared so much about our friendship, but this whole situation sucked.

Chapter Sixteen

JAXON

October 2015

Around seven in the morning, I woke up to a loud-ass train passing right outside Maci's window.

Maci mumbled about it in her sleep and nestled deeper into my arm. I could've spent all afternoon in her bed. It didn't matter if I was hot from all of her blankets or if last night was the first time I had ever shared a bed with a girl and not had sex with them. I just liked being with her.

That feeling was exactly why I needed to leave as early as I did. I left her with a kiss on the cheek and a promise to text her later.

As I stood in her doorway, I watched her roll over onto my side of the bed. I placed my snapback on my head and gently closed her door. I hesitated for a moment before letting myself out of the apartment.

The walk to Falcon's Pointe wasn't that bad. A few townies had their houses decorated and ready to go for Halloween tonight. A few homemade ghost decorations hung from a front porch, and various pumpkins lined the lawns and flowerbeds. It was nice outside for it being so early, and it made me think that I might be able to wear my firefighter costume without freezing my ass off. Last year for Halloween, it snowed, and it was miserable passing from bar to bar.

Once I crossed the main road, I scrolled through my phone and read a few unopened text messages. Two were from

Bryson, who asked if I got the ass I was looking for. One was from Heather, who asked if I would swing by after the bars. One was from Addie, who asked the same thing as Heather, only I had no idea who the hell Addie was. The last text was from an unknown number.

I tucked my phone back into my pocket and felt the lack of sleep kicking in. Maci and I returned to her apartment around two in the morning and probably didn't fall asleep until three. I couldn't wait to get home and crash.

I walked into my apartment promptly at seven forty-eight. An empty bottle of Jack Daniel's sat on the coffee table, and empty beer bottles were scattered around the kitchen counter. The guys must've left right after I did last night. No one had been here since.

I bypassed the mess and headed straight for my room. I unlocked the door and fell onto my bed. I didn't set an alarm or plug my phone into charge, and I didn't wake up until one forty-five that afternoon.

—⁂—

"J, do you have that charcoal stuff?" Bryson yelled from the kitchen.

I smeared another line of black powder under my eyes and rubbed it around. I stared at my bare chest under my bright yellow suspenders and put a few dots of makeup in random spots.

"Let me see how you're doing it." Bryson popped his head into my bathroom.

I handed him the charcoal powder. "Who's all here?"

"I'll give you three guesses." He smirked and took a swig of his drink.

"Is Heather's ass sitting in our living room?" I demanded. I laughed into my Jack and Coke when I saw Bryson's expression.

"After I'm done doing all this shit"—he motioned to the makeup on his face—"and you get your dick sucked by the sexy kitten out there, we can head out."

I took a long sip of my drink and placed my firefighter hat on my head. "Does she have the tail and everything?"

Bryson burst into hysterics and went across the hall to his bedroom.

I slipped on my Timberlands and took a final look in the mirror. I wore dark-wash jeans, a red firefighter hat, and yellow suspenders. Even though my face looked like I had just been on a lifesaving rescue mission, it was the easiest costume I'd ever put together.

"Hey, Jax?" A voice I knew all too well was at my bedroom door. I walked out of my bathroom and was greeted by Heather. She wore a tight black strapless dress, cat ears, and black heels. She sighed, taking in my costume. "Damn."

"What do you want, Heather?" I demanded. I set my drink down on the dresser to spray a few pumps of cologne.

"I just thought I would check in," she slurred, letting herself into the room. "I didn't hear from you last night."

"I was with someone else," I said casually. I could tell her I got married last night, and she would still offer to get me off. I didn't know what this girl's problem was.

"I missed you." She pouted and took a seat on my bed.

I looked over at her and took another sip of my drink. She *did* look hot in her costume. I had no idea that she was a fucking cat, but at this moment, I didn't care. I was buzzed, horny, and ready to have a good time.

Every part of me wanted to reach out to Maci to see what bar she was headed to, but I needed to get my head straight after what happened last night. I was positive that if I ended up in her bed again, I wouldn't be able to stop myself a second time. It was best I didn't see her until tomorrow.

"How bad did you miss me?" I challenged and walked over to Heather.

She finished the rest of her beer and set the can on my end table. "Shut the door."

I felt my phone vibrate in the back pocket of my jeans right before I slipped them off. I quickly locked my door and turned off the light.

Chapter Seventeen

MACI

October 2015

"Did he say anything back yet?" Katie yelled over the music.

I sipped on my Long Island and shook my head. "For the fifth time, Katie, no, he hasn't texted me back."

After I told Katie what happened last night with Jaxon, she insisted that it was because he was a good guy, and I owed it to myself to see where it would lead. I knew she really liked Jaxon and wasn't ready to see me write him off just yet.

We were at Bar 149, and it was completely packed. I texted Jaxon a picture of Katie and me in our costumes right before we left the apartment to head for the bars. It was cute enough to send after what happened last night and just the right amount of casual for two people who almost slept together.

Fuck me. I didn't know what was expected at this point. I checked my phone for the time, and it was one in the morning.

"We can probably hit one last bar before we head home." I laughed as Katie adjusted her bright orange crop top.

"Hey there, Mrs. Officer," someone slurred in my ear.

I swore if I heard that one more time tonight. I rolled my eyes and looked to my left, where a guy dressed as a Teenage Mutant Ninja Turtle was leaning against the bar. He lifted his eye mask and smiled. He was cute and had pretty eyes, but the only face I wanted to see in front of me wasn't responding to my text messages.

"Let me buy you a drink." The turtle motioned for the bartender.

"We were just leaving." I got up from my barstool, tapped Katie's shoulder, and we headed toward the exit.

"Brathaus!" Katie yelled so our party could hear her.

I brushed past her, eager to get outside. I had to get away from the crowd for a few moments.

Dozens of different costumes passed me on the street. I scanned the crowds and pulled out my phone again. There was still no response from Jaxon, and I hated that I was looking for him while I waited for Katie and the others.

Brathaus was around the corner from Bar 149 on Court Street. It was pretty packed since it was a popular place to end the night. It was home to Stop Light shots, Legal Joints, and free popcorn.

We got drinks at the bar and snagged the only empty table left in the back. I set my Legal Joint on the table and leaned on my elbows.

"Let's do Stop Light shots," Katie announced to the table before she dragged Tyler up to the bar.

I watched Sam and Owen dance in an open spot on the floor as "Hey Mama" by Nicki Minaj erupted through the speakers. They were dressed as sexy Mario and Luigi and quickly became a crowd favorite. Other couples started to join them, and pretty soon, I was alone at the table.

I sipped my Legal Joint and tried to get out of my depressing headspace. I didn't want to confuse my ongoing disappointment with being sad. Jaxon was still my friend, and neither of our feelings was hurt, but I couldn't help but wonder if I would've hated him in the morning like he said I would.

An elbow smacked into my arm, and I caught my glass just in time to save my drink. I spun around to confront the idiot who ran into the table, and I was greeted with a drunken smile, an exposed chest, and golden-brown eyes that popped against a light brown complexion.

A six-pack sat perfectly between two bright red suspenders. His arms were incredibly toned, and he had a tattoo that covered his shoulder and bicep. A black firefighter hat sat on top of his head, and his face had black smudges going in random directions. I could tell he applied the makeup himself.

His smile was captivating. This guy had almost taken me out at my own table, and here I was, smirking like an idiot and checking him out.

"Do you wanna arm wrestle?" He was still smiling as he leaned an arm on the table.

I stifled a laugh and set my drink back on the table. "You literally just ran into me, and you want to *arm wrestle?*"

He drew back his arm. "What do you want me to say?" A group of girls dressed as the Power Puff Girls walked past us, and his glossy eyes followed.

"You don't need to say a thing," I said. This guy was a typical asshole. I turned to try to find Katie and the others at the front of the bar, but I couldn't see any familiar faces. I checked my phone and saw we had about fifteen minutes until the last call. Katie was probably outside in the alley, so I approached the back entrance and let myself out.

When the door swung shut, I heard a noise and a soft laugh. I turned around to see the firefighter right behind me. His smile was back, and he stood there staring at me with his hands in the pockets of his jeans. I would've considered this guy incredibly creepy if he weren't so good-looking.

I was easily violating the first rule of Women's Safety 101.

"Can I help you?" I asked slowly and looked around to make sure we weren't the only people in the alley. Groups of people passed us, and none were the group I was looking for.

The firefighter shrugged. "I was going to come with you." He took a few steps toward me and took my hand, leading us to the main road. I didn't even try to get my hand out of his since he didn't give me time to react to the gesture. He stopped right before the road and waited for my direction.

I laughed when he looked at me and raised his eyebrows. I decided to blindly go with the flow.

"Let's head up toward my apartment," I offered. "Hopefully, we can catch up with Katie."

We turned on Court Street and headed toward the railroad tracks. He slowed our pace, and I was forced to follow his lead. "Who is Katie?"

"She's my roommate. I lost her and the people we were with at the bar."

"What is she dressed as?"

"She's my robber." I laughed and looked over at him. "I'm not a very good cop."

"You look pretty good to me."

I rolled my eyes at the cheesy pickup line. Yet somehow, the words coming out of his mouth sounded inviting.

"Where's the rest of your squad?" I teased.

"I had a partner." He shrugged and smiled at me. "But you know how it goes."

I scanned the crowd in front of Jimmy Johns and spotted the bright orange fabric of Katie's costume. I cupped my free hand around my mouth. "Katie!"

Katie bit into her sandwich and eagerly waved in our direction. She closed the space between us and looked the firefighter up and down. "Who's this?"

I stared at him and stifled a grin. "Uhm."

He smiled. "I'm Bryson."

"Bryson," I answered and turned to Katie. I wasn't sure if I would be thanking her for leaving me at the bar or giving her shit for it. "This is Bryson."

Chapter Eighteen

JAXON

November 2015

My head was pounding.

I rolled over and waited for my eyes to adjust. I squinted at the red light coming off of my alarm clock. It was eight in the morning.

I groaned and buried my head back into the pillow. I played a demo reel in my mind of what I could do later since it was too early to start the day.

If I slept for another hour or two, I could down a Gatorade, pick up Pollyeyes breadsticks, and see if Maci was home. She kept bothering me to watch this show with her called *One Tree Hill*, and I figured twenty-four hours was a long enough stretch for us to move past Friday night.

"What time is it?" Heather mumbled next to me.

I felt myself already getting annoyed with her voice. I didn't even remember coming home with her last night.

"You should probably head out," I said into my pillow. "I have shit to do today."

I felt the weight of my bed shift as Heather got up. I was relieved she didn't fight me to stay and hang out for a little while.

I started to drift off again when I heard her voice from the hallway. "I can't find my keys."

I moaned and turned to face her. She shrugged, trying to look innocent. I knew I would have to physically hand this girl her keys to get her to leave.

"Yo," I deadpanned and slid out of bed. I checked to make sure I had on boxers before slinking into the hall.

Heather checked the kitchen counters again while I looked over the living room. I had to do the best I could to look around the girl who was passed out on our couch, but from what I could gather, the keys weren't there.

"Did I leave them in your room?" Heather asked.

"I don't know, Heather, did you?" I snapped. I decided right then and there that this would be the last time Heather stayed over.

"You don't have to be such an ass." She rolled her eyes. "I'm trying to get out of here."

The girl on the couch behind us stirred. She blinked a few times and took in her surroundings.

A door opened down the hall, and slowly our apartment returned to life. It could look rough the morning after a night out.

Connor came strolling into the kitchen. He was dressed for the gym and holding an orange Powerade. He looked like he hadn't had a drop to drink last night. He shot me an amused grin when he saw me. "Rough night? I know Kennedy was out till three, and Jared never came home."

I laughed. "Bryson didn't get in until three?"

Connor took a sip of his drink, and his eyes narrowed. "Paige?"

The girl on the couch slowly stood up and giggled. "I guess I didn't make it to the bed last night, huh?"

"I'll drop you off on my way to the gym." Connor walked over to her and helped her with her stuff. Connor was always ridiculously nice to the girls he brought back. Even though he hadn't slept with Paige, he still offered her a ride home.

"Can you take Heather home too?" I practically begged Connor.

"My keys are *here*," Heather snapped.

"Don't care!" My voice grew louder, and I gestured toward the door. "Get the fuck out."

Another door shut down the hall. Bryson emerged from his room, looking showered and ready to head out. He laughed when he realized the scene that was unfolding in front of him.

"I'll be back for my keys," Heather said, looking from me to Bryson. "I'm not dealing with you two idiots."

"You could just not come back." I shrugged. "Ever."

Connor motioned for Paige to start heading downstairs, nervous for what was about to happen next.

Bryson smirked and opened the fridge, pulling out two water bottles and setting them on the counter. He was nosey. He would stay for this whole thing.

"If you don't want me here, why the hell do you hit me up?" Heather demanded.

I took a deep breath and paced back and forth. "Don't worry. I'll make sure to move you down to number three on my list. You won't ever get a call again asking if you're free to suck some dick."

"You're a piece of shit, Jaxon," Heather spat, her voice trembling when she said my name. She reached around the counter, grabbed an empty beer bottle, and whipped it across the living room. I ducked to the left, and when I looked up, she was gone. Her aim came only inches from my head.

"What the hell, J?" Bryson laughed and had to lean on the counter for support. "That girl is wild."

"Never again." I ran my hands through my hair and groaned, making my way back to my bedroom. I closed my eyes, eager to sleep off the rest of the hangover.

I played back what I remembered from the evening in my head. My clearest memory was getting a picture from Maci of her and Katie. Everything went downhill from there. It took everything I had not to find her last night and kiss her again. The only thing that helped was taking shot after shot of Jack Daniel's.

The next thing I knew, we were off to the bars, and Heather managed to find her way into my bedroom. I couldn't even remember if we slept together.

A soft voice came from my doorway. "Jaxon?"

I knew that voice. I got butterflies at the sound of it.

I looked up from my phone and saw Maci in an oversized Tampa Bay Lightning T-shirt and black leggings. A mini movie played in my head as I stared at Bryson's clothes. It went just like the film I had been featured in two nights ago. Only Bryson's version made it to the end. There was an ache in my chest, and it felt like someone had punched me in the throat.

She spoke a little louder now that the blender in the kitchen drowned out our conversation. "Was that you screaming?" She was nervous to hear my reply.

I didn't know how to answer her. She had never heard me speak like that to anyone before. I had been able to hide this part of myself from our friendship. As soon as I let that side out for someone, it was hard to reel back in.

"Damn." She crossed her arms. "Is that what I would've had to look forward to?" She sounded like she was joking, but I sensed her underlying disappointment.

"Nah." I sat down on the edge of my bed and sighed. "You wouldn't have thrown a beer bottle."

"You were the last person I expected to run into here," she admitted and leaned against my dresser. "I'm not really sure what to say."

I could feel the asshole part of me coming through the cracks in my chest. I *hated* that Maci was standing in front of me in Bryson's shirt. I had just made her come two nights ago. I guess if I wasn't going to sleep with her, she had to find someone else to do it, right?

I shoved that selfish thought to the back of my head. I was man enough to know when I was out of line, and if it were any other girl, I would've said those words out loud. I had no filter when it came to hurting their feelings, but I would crumble if Maci fell apart in front of me. I couldn't imagine hurting her.

It was my decision to stop things, and I didn't want Bryson to know that this was the girl he had just told me to sleep with on Friday. Certain things were better left unsaid for everyone involved.

I made sure my voice was even before I responded. "There isn't anything to say."

"This isn't gonna make things weird, is it?" she asked nervously. "Running into each other like this?"

I could read Maci without her having to say anything, and I felt uneasy at the thought of our friendship changing. I wanted to be around her too much to suddenly not have her in my life at all.

I leaned back onto my bed and put my arms behind my head. "Nothing has to be weird, Mace. We both hooked up with someone last night, and we wouldn't have even known about it if you hadn't picked out Kennedy in the bar."

Her eyes narrowed. "Kennedy?"

"Yeah, Kennedy," I repeated, and when her expression didn't change, I understood why. "Bryson?"

She cocked her head to process the new information. She smacked me playfully, and I smiled sleepily at her, trying my best to convince her that this interaction wasn't weird at all. That it didn't kill me to see her in Bryson's shirt instead of mine.

She squeezed my shoulder. "I'll text you later."

I nodded into my pillow and dragged my comforter up to my chest. She shut my door on her way out, but I still heard Bryson's voice in the kitchen and her giggling at whatever he said.

Chapter Nineteen

MACI

November 2015

"Katie, I was mortified," I exclaimed from our dining room table. "*MORTIFIED.*"

Katie laughed, trying to keep her knife steady while she listened to the recap of my morning run-in with Jaxon. She would look up at me in between chops and start laughing again.

There was never a dull moment in our apartment.

"It's not funny!" I smiled and slumped into my chair. "Out of all fucking people, I had to sleep with one of his friends."

"Please"—she slid the diced onions into the Instant Pot, added some minced garlic, and hit Sauté—"how were you supposed to know that he was talking about Bryson when he mentioned his friend, Kennedy? You guys will laugh about this when you tell the story at your wedding."

I rolled my eyes, and she laughed. Katie was always a hopeless romantic in the end.

"He probably thinks I'm just another slut on campus," I moaned and tried to get the image of Jaxon's face when he saw me in his doorway out of my head.

We had almost slept together on Friday, and I was already recovering from a hookup with his roommate on Sunday morning. Jaxon and I had our fair share of conversations regarding our past. I knew that his body count was slowly inching toward the triple digits, and he knew that I could count my sexual history on one hand. Well, I guess it was two hands now.

Oh my god. And just like that, I was a two-handed woman.

But regardless of the many comments that slipped up in conversation and the playful back and forths we had about hookups, it didn't make the situation any less weird. Talking about it was one thing, but seeing the other person with someone else? That was another. I would have been *devastated* if this was the other way around.

Fortunately for me, his hookup had left using a beer bottle for her dramatic exit right before I left Bryson's room. When I thought of how he spoke to her, it made the hair stand up on my freshly shaved legs. He sounded like someone I didn't even know.

"You need to stop getting in your head. He was kicking a girl out when you found out he lived there. Why is it okay that he got to sleep with somebody else and you couldn't?"

I sat taller in my seat, thankful for Queen Katie and her voice of reason.

Katie watched as I registered the double standard. "Tell me about Bryson."

A nervous laugh escaped me at the sound of his name. Images from last night started to cloud my head as I tried to playback every little detail. Once we got back to our apartment, he quickly persuaded me to come back to his place to chill in the hot tub. We filled two travel mugs with Mike's Hard and walked all the way from my apartment to his.

"You didn't recognize the building?" Katie asked once I was done with the intro. "You've dropped Jaxon off at his place before."

"He took me through the back entrance." I shrugged. "And I was in that bubbly-buzzed phase. He could've walked me into another bar, and I would've just rolled with it."

"I do love a bubbly-buzzed Maci." Katie shook her head and smirked. "And I bet Bryson did too."

I rested my head in my hand and sighed. "It was good, Katie. *He* was good."

I remembered the way his hands felt going up my sides and the way they cupped my face. I remembered how his kiss was soft and gentle at first, almost like he was asking permission, before he laid me on his bed and kissed his way down to my bathing suit bottoms.

"Are you going to see him again?" Katie interrupted my erotic playback.

I didn't know how to answer her question. I felt a ping of disappointment and realized that we hadn't discussed any next steps on our drive to drop me off this morning. Bryson had been nice in our sober morning-after scene, but I knew absolutely nothing about him.

A new feeling I didn't recognize started taking over my headspace. I let it drown out any doubt I would have normally focused on for the remainder of my Sunday. For the first time after hooking up with someone, *I didn't care if we saw each other again.* There was no anxiety about deciphering what had happened the night before. If I didn't see him again, it would suck. But it wouldn't ruin anything for me in the future.

Bryson was gorgeous. Light-brown skin, golden-brown eyes, and a panty-dropping smile all wrapped in a body of tender muscles. I could only *imagine* the lineup of girls who had been in and out of that bedroom before me.

In just a few short hours, he was able to make me feel comfortable enough to sleep with him and even stay the night. Those were two events I never decided on that quickly when I first met someone. Some charming conversation and smooth moves, and I was comfortable just letting it all go. I wasn't sure if that said more about me or how guys had treated me in the past. I also didn't know which one was more pathetic.

"I don't know!" I said excitedly and noted Katie's confused expression. "We didn't talk about it. Katie . . ." I smacked a hand on the table in front of me and gave her a moment to process my mood swing. The words gained momentum as I came to my mind-shattering realization. "This could be my Fun Dip. This could be the hookup that doesn't matter!"

"So Jaxon is out of the running, then?" Katie's voice went up an octave, and she tried not to sound disappointed.

"Jaxon took him*self* out of the running," I stated firmly. I didn't want to show any signs of weakness to Katie. Jaxon had also become a part of her life when we formed a friendship.

I could look into this Fun Dip situation as long as Jaxon remained a part of my life. The possibility of losing Jaxon, unlike the carefree response I had to Bryson, scared the shit out of me.

An entire school week went by without seeing Jaxon or Bryson, and I tried not to look too much into it. I understood that I was just a girl from the bar to Bryson and that I was just an option to hang out for Jaxon, even though Jaxon's explanation hung much heavier on me than Bryson's.

Jaxon hadn't come to Journalism and Publications all week. When I texted him what he missed in class, he responded with a thumbs-up emoji, one of the most pathetic responses of our generation. It was borderline devastating to our friendship, and I knew he was avoiding me.

I missed Jaxon to the point where it hurt to think about him. I missed having him near me and knowing he would be there if I called him. It was nauseating to know that if I called him right now, he would probably send my pathetic ass to voicemail.

I started the third body paragraph for my essay on "Differentiation Among High School ELA" and glanced down at my phone. I tapped the screen in case I may have missed something while I was typing, but it was just as dry as when I looked ten minutes ago.

It was Friday afternoon, and I was done with classes for today. Katie would be home from her last class in about an hour, but I couldn't stay in my own headspace much longer. I sat my laptop on the coffee table and strolled into the kitchen to pour myself a hefty and much-needed glass of Moscato.

I knew my friends in *One Tree Hill* would understand, so I propped my feet up on the coffee table, sipped my wine, and sang out loud with Gavin DeGraw to introduce the cast. One large glass in, and I was cheering on Brooke Davis as she fought for equal rights at Joe's Crab Shack.

"Yes, queen!" I laughed at the screen and pursed my lips at my empty glass. I probably should have eaten a sandwich before attempting to drink away my sorrow.

I padded back into the kitchen to pour the remainder of the bottle into my glass when I heard my phone ding. I held my breath, hoping to see Jaxon's name and the creepy side-eyes emoji on my screen.

Instead, I saw Bryson's.

I lowered myself slowly onto the couch and stared blankly at the TV. Brooke Davis was scribbling her name on the class president sign-up sheet when I picked up my phone and read the message.

Bryson

What are you up to?

I didn't know what to say. It was as if, even though we had already slept together, I was talking to him for the first time.

I took a picture of my wine glass with *One Tree Hill* in the background and hit send. I needed a little more time to draft an actual response with words. I barely sat my phone down before he responded.

Bryson

Drinking already huh? Feel like pouring me a glass?

A laugh escaped me, and I stared at the screen. Was he inviting himself over to day drink with me? It *was* almost four. I decided that the weekend had officially started, and I deserved a little more credit than that.

Maci

Just finished the bottle. Wine goes quick around here!

The empty evidence sat on the corner of the counter, judging me for working through it so quickly. When he didn't text back right away, I propped my feet back up and watched the last fifteen minutes of the episode. When my phone vibrated on the coffee table, I bit my bottom lip and tapped my glass. This time it was a phone call instead of a text.

I cleared my throat before I answered. "Hello?"

"Hey. What are you doing?"

"Still sipping my wine." A goofy grin spread across my face. "What are you doing?"

"Walking," he said and then muttered, "Oh, shit." Sounds of car horns erupted from the other end of the line.

"Are you walking or playing in traffic?"

"I just ran across Wooster," he explained, like it was something he did every day. A bell chimed in the distance, and I pressed the phone harder against my ear to try and hear more of the background noise.

The line went silent for a full minute before I asked, "Bryson, what are you doing?"

I heard a cooler door shut. "Getting beer. You invited me over, remember?"

I glanced around the apartment and wondered if I should tidy things up or at least light a candle. Then I glanced down at my sweatpants and old T-shirt and decided to change into something that showed a little more skin. I leaped up from the couch and ran into my room.

"Can you get some Black Cherry Mike's Hard for Katie and me?" I slipped off my clothes and found a black tank top and my favorite joggers. I tugged on my cleavage just a little bit and replaced my sports bra with a regular bra for some extra curve.

"You won't drink Natty?"

"Not since I was seventeen." I laughed and took one last look in the mirror before returning to the living room. I turned on my wax warmer and slipped a fresh cranberry-orange cube into the warming plate.

Bryson thanked the cashier in the background, and the bell from earlier chimed again.

My eyes narrowed. "Are you walking here?"

"It's nice outside," he said. "I'll be there in ten."

"It's like fifty-five outside," I argued.

"So, nice for shitty Ohio. I'll see you soon."

Just as we ended our conversation, I heard a set of keys from the hall, and Katie rushed into our apartment. She was a frazzled mess, with a giant Bowling Green tote in one arm, her car keys in the opposite hand, and a bookbag that looked like it weighed eighty pounds.

"Thank the *fuck* it is Friday," she exclaimed and made a beeline to her bedroom. She emerged back to the living room in a blue V-neck tee and leggings. "Did you finish off the Moscato? Bitch, I could've picked up a bottle on my way home!"

I laughed and handed her my glass. "Drink up. We are hosting my Fun Dip in about ten minutes, and he is bringing us Mike's."

Her eyes widened, and she gulped half the glass in one breath. "Which one?" she teased and snapped immediately back into her natural self, leaving Frazzled Katie for Monday morning.

"Funny," I deadpanned and headed to our storage shelf underneath the coffee table. My old GameCube from middle school was our hosting go-to when we weren't throwing parties. It had the needed classics like Mario Kart and Mario Party, games where everyone could play and drink.

"So, Bryson, huh?" Katie gestured to the Mario Kart disc I held in my hand. "If it were Jaxon coming over, you wouldn't be worried about how you're going to entertain him." She lifted her eyebrows as she sipped.

I knew that she was teasing, so I laughed and shook my head to ignore the accuracy of her statement. I probably wouldn't have even changed if it were Jaxon coming over. The last time he was in this apartment, I was practically naked, and he requested I put some shorts on. Part of her comment stung just a little bit because we hadn't had a real conversation in almost a week.

"Don't mention Jaxon," I said quickly. "I don't know if Jaxon has said anything to Bryson, and things are already weird between us."

"Can it *be* weird if you haven't seen each other *since* the morning run-in?" Katie walked her empty glass to the sink. "Where is this Fun Dip with the Mike's?"

"I don't know, Katie." The Mario Kart music played repeatedly on the TV screen. I hit mute and prepared the speaker for Katie's Drunk Betch playlist. "But if it helps my situation with Jaxon, I don't want those worlds to collide just yet."

I had yet to learn what the history was between Jaxon and Bryson. I knew they were friends, but the last thing I wanted to do was bring Jaxon up in conversation when Bryson didn't even know I knew him.

As if she read my mind, Katie tapped her nails against the counter and pursed her lips. "Do you think he knows? Do you think Jaxon told him? I don't think Jaxon would do that."

There was a knock on the door, and we both jumped. I gestured with my hands that we needed to drop the conversation ASAP and yelled, "It's open!"

Bryson strolled in with a case of Black Cherry Mike's Hard in one hand and a case of Bud Light in the other. He wore a plain white shirt that popped against his skin and red basketball shorts. He kicked his shoes off and smiled down at me since I was still sitting on the floor. "What's up?"

"You went with Bud Light, huh?" I stood up and flashed a flirty half-smile. "Decided you deserved better?"

"You had me feeling some type of way about them." He walked over to the fridge to deposit the drinks.

"Can you hand me a Mike's?" Katie asked.

Bryson tore open the box and rose slowly from inside the fridge. He bit his bottom lip and pondered his next move. "Kathy?" He pointed and handed Katie her drink.

"Katie, actually. But kudos for getting the letter right." She took the bottle, popped off the top, and smiled. "And how well you found the apartment."

"I remember bits and pieces of last weekend." Bryson shrugged and made himself at home on the couch next to me. "What games do you guys got?"

He smelled like he had just gotten out of the shower. His body heat radiated off him and made me hot underneath my sweatpants. Since it was decent outside, we didn't have the furnace on. I was tempted to open a window to get some fresh air, but his eyes connected with mine, and suddenly I found it hard to move.

"Katie and I were going to beat you in some Drunk Driving," I offered and leaned in closer to him when I stood up to get a drink. He might have his cologne, but I knew for a fact that he thought my Night perfume by Victoria's Secret smelled sexy. He told me right before he kissed me in the hot tub.

"Do you guys care if my friend Jaxon comes over?" Bryson asked his phone screen and then glanced over to me at the fridge. "He says he knows you from a class last year or something. He's chill."

If I had grabbed my drink prior to his question, I would've been cleaning my party foul off the kitchen floor. I wasn't mentally equipped for this merge to happen so soon.

"Yeah, that's fine!" Katie answered for me and started the game. She raised her eyebrows at me and handed Bryson a controller, who was once again focused on his phone. "Let's get a race in before he gets here."

With just one look, Katie reassured me that things would be fine. I buckled up and trusted her instincts. I could tell she wasn't sold on Bryson, but her demeanor shifted as soon as he mentioned Jaxon.

I pushed the butterflies in my stomach aside and focused on the man in front of me. They needed to chill the fuck out and realize that Jaxon told Bryson we knew each other from last year.

That was a lie.

The whole reason we didn't sleep together was so that nothing changed between us. I trusted his instincts and agreed that our friendship wasn't worth the risk. I just hoped that this wasn't the start of him proving me wrong.

Chapter Twenty

JAXON

November 2015

It felt weird going to Maci's place, knowing it was Bryson who extended the invitation. I didn't even know if Maci wanted to see me. Our text thread had been pretty dry this week, and I would be lying if I said I hadn't been avoiding her. But I would also be lying if I said I didn't miss the shit out of her.

I crossed the parking lot behind her apartment building and took a swig of my flask, which at this point in my trek, was only half-full of Jack Daniel's. I needed something to take the edge off while I tried to navigate this new territory.

Since I met Bryson two years ago, we have shared the common goals of hitting up girls, having fun, and keeping it casual. He'd been my best friend since I moved to BG. We knew almost everything about each other. I knew he wanted to be in accounting and work with Wall Street billionaires. He knew I wanted to be in sports management and work for my dad's agency. I knew his parents got divorced when he was young. Both remarried different people and then got divorced again. He knew my birth mom left when I was two, and I hadn't seen her since my last court hearing.

We had a lot of things in common when it came to girls, but never once had one of us slept with someone that the other had a history with. It had been an unspoken bro code between us, and it was just easier if he didn't know the whole story with Maci.

I jogged up the stairs to the apartment and took another swig of my flask. I had to get my shit together. I was well versed with Bryson's pattern, and he wouldn't keep Maci around long. I didn't know why that bugged me so much since this wasn't new information.

I did the exact same thing to the broads I hooked up with, and since I could never pull my usual on Maci, I had to stop things when I did. Neither Bryson nor I knew how to be in a relationship, and neither of us was interested in finding out how. She understood how I was with girls and soon, she would see that Bryson and I were very much alike.

There was a fit of shouting on the other side of the door, followed by Katie's high-pitched laugh and Bryson screaming "No!" to whatever they were doing. I knocked on the door, fully aware of what waited for me on the other side. A few seconds went by before Maci answered.

Even though she was only in a black tank top and joggers, she looked sexy as hell. The way her blue eyes glanced up at me let me know that the Mike's Hard in her hand wasn't her first drink. She offered a shy smile, and my body relaxed instantly. It had been five days since I'd seen her in person, and I couldn't help but smile back.

As badly as I wanted to pull her against my chest, I decided against it. The whole backstory I created about how we met last year would be harder to play out than I thought.

"Hi there," she chirped and hesitated to move toward me.

I grinned. "Hi there."

She looked me up and down one more time before she shifted to the side of the doorway and allowed me to pass her.

Bryson leaned over the back of the couch to smack my hand. "What's up, my man?"

I laughed and placed the beer I brought on the counter. I heard Maci follow me into the kitchen, and I drained the rest of my flask. I had a feeling I was going to need it.

"So." She tossed her empty bottle into the trash. She leaned over the counter, and I knew by her expression that she had been itching to say what she had prepared for me. "We met last year, huh?"

I cocked my head to the side and waited for her to continue.

"Is there anything else about our fake history that I need to know about?" she asked softly, so it was only her and I who heard the conversation. Bryson and Katie were completely invested in the track they were playing on Mario Kart.

"We met last year. And that is pretty much it." I grabbed a beer out of the fridge and cracked it open.

"Are we friends, at least?" She caught the fridge door before it closed and reached in to pull out a jug of cranberry juice, followed by a bottle of vodka from the freezer. She glided past me and I was immediately drawn to the smell of her perfume, taking me back to last weekend in her bedroom. I watched her make a cranberry vodka and take a big sip of her drink.

"Yes, Mace, we are friends," I answered carefully, a little nervous that she might be taking this the wrong way. "I just didn't mention anything about last weekend. Or really anything that has happened since we met."

"So pretty much don't mention anything that's *actually* happened since we met?" she snapped.

"What are you guys doing?" Bryson shouted from the couch over the music. "We are starting another race. Get your drinks!"

Katie slid in next to me and looked from me to Maci. "Everything good?" she asked, feeling out the awkward space between us.

"Great." Maci shrugged and downed the rest of her drink. She stopped by the fridge again on her way back to the couch to get another Mike's.

I watched her lean into Bryson and say something that prompted him to smile. He took another sip of his beer and glanced over in her direction. I'd seen that look come over his face too many times to count. He was riding a good buzz and had every intention of being with Maci at the end of the night.

"*Is* everything good?" Katie mumbled under her breath and looked up at me as she leaned into the fridge. "I didn't realize we were shifting into a vodka evening. I might invite Tyler over after all."

"I'm fine. Tyler again, huh? I might have to have a talk with this guy, you know, make sure he's treating you well?" I plastered on a smile and ignored the punch in my gut when I saw Bryson kiss Maci out of the corner of my eye.

Katie rolled her eyes and smiled. "I'm sure you would be *really* insightful. But I appreciate the concern." She joked at first, but the last part sounded genuine.

With all the time I spent at her place, I knew a lot about what went on in Katie's life. She was hard not to like and easy to get along with. Maci was lucky to have a friend like her.

"Anytime," I said, meaning it wholeheartedly. "Don't be targeting me during this race, okay? Truce?"

Katie laughed, and although I could tell my answer didn't entirely convince her, she gave me a high five and followed me into the living room so we could start the next race.

⁓⁓⁓

I didn't realize how much time had gone by until I was staring at an empty case of beer.

I focused on my phone screen long enough so I could make out the time. It was one thirty in the morning.

"Fuck," I said and stood up, using the couch to get on my feet.

"You good over there?" Maci smiled up from her seat on the couch next to Bryson.

I replied with a nod. My phone buzzed in my pocket, and I looked down to read the message. It was Heather.

"Oh, I'm good." I raised my eyebrows at the invitation that glowed on my screen.

Bryson let out an obnoxious chuckle. He knew by my reaction the exact offer of the text I had just received. Just like I could tell by the way he leaned into Maci and randomly grabbed her hand that he planned on coaxing her into the bedroom soon.

At the thought of Bryson on top of Maci, I tossed my empty beer can into the trash. I needed to leave an hour ago.

I was no good for Maci, and pretty soon, Bryson would show her exactly why I had to say no the other night. Maybe Bryson hadn't shown that side of himself yet. He usually reserved that experience for the second or third encounter, according to his timeline.

"I'm heading out," I said. My thumbs hovered over the phone screen and tried to text Heather back so I could get her location. I refused to bring her back to my place again.

"You're walking all the way home?" Maci asked, breaking away from Bryson's body weight in her lap. There was a hint of concern that lingered in her question.

Bryson sat up and checked his phone once Maci was off the couch. He was probably texting Sandra or Morgan back.

I couldn't remember the name of the leech he was with last night.

I shook my head and slipped my phone back into my pocket. Heather let me know she was home, and I really needed to leave before my drinking got the best of me.

Why the hell was I feeling some type of way about Bryson just being Bryson? I literally did the same shit and followed the same pattern. But I already knew the answer to that question. It was because it wasn't some random broad this time. It was Maci.

"Kennedy, you have a key?" I asked Bryson.

"Yeah, I'm good," Bryson said to his phone screen.

"Do you want to stay on the couch?" Katie offered and started gathering beer bottles from the coffee table. "It's late."

"I'll be okay," I reassured her, and she rolled her eyes.

I left the apartment and heard Maci whisper something to Katie before the door closed. I didn't need to turn around to know that Maci followed me into the hallway. "Jaxon?"

I looked over my shoulder and then turned to face her when I saw her walking toward me. She closed the space between us and pressed her body into mine. I planted my feet to prevent us from falling backward and let my arms pull her into my chest.

Every drunken cell in my body wanted to throw her up against the wall and persuade her to come home with me. The remaining sober part of me won, and I rested my chin in her hair. "What's up, Mace?"

She looked up at me and took a small step back. "I just wanted to say bye. And to tell you that if you ever ignore me for that long again, Jaxon Hayes, I know where you live now, and I'll find you."

I caught myself staring at her mouth and smiled when she finished her threat. "Throwing that last name at me, huh?"

"I wanted to make sure you didn't hate me," she whispered and crossed her arms in front of her chest. She took a few more steps back and leaned against the railing that looked over the main parking lot of the building.

My phone buzzed in my back pocket, and I knew it was Heather. I realized what Maci was saying, and I couldn't leave her feeling like this. I hated that she was going to sleep with Bryson tonight. I hated that she slept with Bryson the night after we almost did. But I didn't want her to think that I wanted to stop being friends.

I walked over to her and gripped the railing, placing one hand on either side of her hips. I leaned forward so my forehead rested on hers. Her perfume flooded my senses, and I took a deep breath to remind myself where I was and who was in the apartment down the hall. Her eyes met mine and I ached to rest my hips in between her legs.

Still, I had to keep my walls up and around the fact that I couldn't give her what I knew she wanted. She wanted me to always be the guy she was friends with, and I couldn't show her who I would become if we slept together. Everything with us would change, and our friendship would disappear into feelings of bitterness and arguments. I didn't know how to do the morning-after. I didn't know how to be the loyal rom-com boyfriend, and honestly, I didn't want that label.

"I don't hate you, Maci . . ." I pursed my lips.

"You don't know my last name, do you?" She shook her head like she was disappointed. "Jesus, Jaxon."

I shrugged, and she rolled her eyes.

"It's Lawson." She smiled. "Continue."

"I feel like I knew that." I shrugged again and prepared my lie. "I wasn't ignoring you. I just got busy this week, that's all."

I forced myself to return the space between us and started my way down the stairs. "I'll text you tomorrow," I shouted up at her.

She waved goodbye and turned to head back to her apartment. She'd sleep with Bryson, and I would sleep with Heather. I ignored the ache in my gut and knew that it couldn't be any other way if I wanted to keep Maci around.

Chapter Twenty-One

MACI

December 2015

There were only a few days left until winter break, and I was never in more need of a vacation.

Finals week had arrived. While everyone else was pretty much done with the semester, I had to stay on campus until Friday since that was my last exam. Bowling Green would be a ghost town by tomorrow.

On the upside, it was officially the season of Christmas, by far my favorite time of year. It was also Katie's, so naturally our apartment looked straight out of a cozy Hallmark movie. The only light in the living room came from the perfectly placed strands that decorated the windows and hung around the kitchen counters. A cute red and green Christmas tree sat in the corner of the room, and our stockings hung off of the TV stand. Katie's snow globe collection was spread out around the living room, and a lit garland ran along the outline of the ceiling.

While Dr. Seuss's *How the Grinch Stole Christmas* played on the TV for background noise, I watched Katie fill up another duffle bag and add it to the corner of the living room. It was slowly becoming a mountain of her belongings.

"Jesus, Katie. You're only going home for a month." I took another sip of my wine, and my phone buzzed in my hand. It was Bryson.

He was right on schedule. Every Wednesday night between eight and nine, Bryson's name would appear on my
screen. It had been a month of seeing Bryson once or twice
during the school week and usually once on the weekends.
We always met up at my place because I was pretty sure if
I ran into Jaxon while I was there to see Bryson, I would
combust on the spot.

Balancing time slots in my apartment became a talent I
never intended to perfect. Wednesday night was Bryson, and
Thursday was Jaxon. Friday or Saturday night was Bryson,
and Jaxon was usually over on Sundays. Throw Katie and
Tyler's schedule in there, and this place was a madhouse with
a revolving door for relationships.

Because Jaxon made it very clear that Bryson was to know
nothing about our past, I had to pretend that I barely knew
him whenever they were in the same place together. That
night of Drunk Driving in my apartment was enough to
show me that I never wanted to act like that around Jaxon
again. It stung to see how easy it was for Jaxon to erase
everything about us.

After my third time hooking up with Bryson, I decided it
was time to put a little more clarity into my Fun Dip situation.
I never knew what he did outside of our time together, but
the way he never let his phone out of his sight was hard to
ignore. If Bryson was going to hook up with other girls,
that was completely and totally fine with me. Even though
I didn't expect him to be exclusive with me, I did expect him
to respect me enough as a friend to be honest about it.

I asked Bryson point blank if he was hooking up with other people and assured him that I didn't care either way. I stripped my question of any judgment and had even practiced on Katie to ensure there wasn't an underlying tone in my voice that read, "Please, God, no. Just be sleeping with me."

In a short and quick response, and to my total surprise, Bryson said he wasn't.

I took another sip of wine and watched Katie shove a fifth hoodie into her duffel. As much as I wanted to believe Bryson, and I wanted to believe him with every bone in my body, I knew in my gut that he wasn't telling the truth. I was equally annoyed and angered about it.

A Fun Dip was supposed to be carefree and easygoing. Convenient and low risk. Yet here I was, trying to make sense of why a guy would lie about something when there was no reason to. It was also a very concerning sign that I got butterflies whenever his name lit up my phone screen. I wouldn't know simplicity if it slapped me right in the face.

Maci

I'm at home, but I am helping Katie pack. Girls night.

I slid my phone onto the coffee table and tried not to look disappointed. Katie had to listen to way too many recaps of my inner dialogues already. I just wanted to turn it off for a little bit.

"Are you seeing Tyler again before you leave tomorrow?" I asked, trying to remember the last time Katie even mentioned Tyler.

Katie shook her head and sighed. "I am done with Tyler."

I caught my next sip of wine just in time before it dripped onto my black tank top. That was the last thing I expected her answer to be.

Katie laughed at my reaction and zipped up her last duffel bag. "I cut it off last night. It was too much work and not worth my time."

Grabbing the bottle of wine from the counter, she made her way over to the couch and took the empty seat beside me. I took another sip and let her continue.

"Truth is, I didn't see us going anywhere. I don't know." She shrugged and twisted the cap off of the bottle to help herself to a full glass of Moscato. "I just don't want to waste time with someone who is at a dead end right now. It got to the point where I wasn't even sure if we were friends, and I didn't like how he made me feel about myself."

I nodded, hearing every word she said and needing no more explanation. I envied how easy it was for Katie to see a situation for what it was.

"I love how strong you are," I admitted and grabbed her hand.

"I don't think it has anything to do with strength." She laughed and squeezed my hand back.

"I just want you to be happy. I can't think of anyone more deserving. And good for you for putting yourself first. We will go prospecting when we get back from break. Find you a more stimulating hookup."

"Yes, girl." She clinked her wine glass against mine, and we both peered down at my lit-up phone screen. Bryson's name was plastered right in the center of it.

"Wednesday night, huh?" Katie smiled into her glass and raised her eyebrows.

I shook my head. "Not tonight. I told him I was busy. I'm surprised he even texted me back since I am not available for his services."

"Damn. You really think he's only talking to you for sex?"

I shrugged, honestly not knowing how to answer her. The cleaner I tried to keep the line drawn between Bryson and me, the more he blurred it. I would get mad at him for something, and he would suddenly show me why I wanted to keep him around. He would give me glimpses of the guy he *could be* without the asshole that seeped into his brain at a constant flowing rate.

"Are you sure you are okay with everything with Tyler? You were seeing him for . . ." I counted the months on my fingers. "Nine months? Almost ten."

"Over and done." Katie gestured toward the table when my screen lit up again. "Are you going to answer that? And better yet, if the answer is no, why not? What happened?"

I smirked and grabbed my phone to read the text.

Bryson

Nbd.

When are you done with finals?

Maci

Not until Friday. I won't be home until that night.

Bryson

Hit me up when you get back.

"My problem is I can't just let it go that he is probably sleeping with other people and lying about it," I admitted.

Katie's reaction just proved how insane I sounded. Her eyebrows knit together, and she glanced up to the ceiling as if the answer was plastered above us next to the cheerfully lit garland.

"Why are you making a hookup complicated?" she finally said, sounding a little aggravated with my confession.

"Honestly?" I took a long sip of my Moscato, draining the glass. I tried to give myself some more time to come up with a good answer and came up blank. "I really don't know. I think I just expected him to see me as a friend, at least? At least care enough about me to be honest?"

Katie got off the couch to retrieve a second bottle of wine from the top of the fridge. She popped the cork, tipped the bottle over to fill my glass to the top, and then filled her own.

"First of all, as brutal as this sounds, he doesn't owe you that. It is okay for a hookup to just be what it is, and sometimes that doesn't make you friends by default." She took another sip. "Second, how do you know he is lying?"

Katie's words sunk in, and I sighed, knowing she was once again spot on with her analysis.

I shrugged. "Just a feeling. He's so sneaky about everything."

Katie sucked her teeth and grinned playfully. "Why don't you just ask Jaxon if he's lying? *He* won't lie to you."

I rested my head on my hand to hide my smirk. Since his last final was the same as mine, I knew that he was still in Bowling Green. I felt a little higher at the sound of his name.

"Can I do that?" I asked suspiciously, and Katie laughed into her glass.

"I don't see why not!" she exclaimed. "Use your resources!"

I nodded, becoming more convinced by the minute that her suggestion wasn't a bad idea.

"Ugh, Tyler just asked if he could come over." Katie rolled her eyes at her phone screen and continued scrolling on whatever app she was on.

I raised my eyebrows at the thought of Tyler begging for Katie to give him one last night. "Are you going to let him?"

"No." Katie shook her head and tossed her phone to the side. "As tempting as some average dick tonight sounds, I am good with going to bed early so I can head out early tomorrow."

We laughed over our last glass of wine and talked about how we would spend our winter break. I would miss Katie during our month apart, but I couldn't wait to hear about her Christmas in Seattle while she visited family and all the shopping she would do in Chicago while she was home for New Year's.

"I'm calling it." Katie sighed. It was just after eleven thirty, and she looked exhausted. She grabbed both of our empty glasses and placed them in the dishwasher. Faith Hill's "Where are you Christmas?" hummed from the TV screen while the credits rolled, providing the perfect ending to our evening.

Until a few seconds later, when we were both scared shitless by the pounding on our front door.

I stayed planted on our couch, not alarmed enough to provide a physical reaction to our unplanned visitor. Katie crept into the living room from the kitchen and stared blankly at the door. We both jumped again when the pounding continued.

"What the fuck?" Katie demanded and took a few steps closer to the door. She scampered back over to the couch when a third round of bangs sounded from the hall.

"Katie!" a familiar voice screamed.

It was Tyler.

"Katie, please answer the door," Tyler slurred. It was clear he graced us with this visit after having too many drinks. I totally wasn't judging. Finals week was a shitshow for everyone's schedule and gave us more free time than we knew what to do with. "Katie, baby, please, I'm sorry. Please answer the door!"

"Are you sure it was just an average dick?" I said slowly, trying to stifle a laugh.

Katie scowled and made a beeline to the kitchen table to retrieve her phone. "Get out of here, Tyler!" She took four long steps to the front door and glared through the peephole. She immediately backed up when he responded with more banging.

"I can't fucking leave!" Tyler yelled. There was a short pause, and he continued his plea. "I'm not leaving until you talk to me!"

"Leave, or I am calling the cops!" she threatened and double-checked the deadbolt.

There was a loud banging, followed by multiple footsteps running down the hallway and a chorus of shouting and laughing. Katie and I stood in the middle of the living room, both of us watching the door. When she didn't speak after a minute or so, I decided to break the silence.

I crossed my arms. "I have to say, that was pretty ballsy for Tyler."

"Ballsy?" Katie exclaimed, looking a little panicked.

I suddenly felt a pang of guilt in my chest. I could tell by the look on Katie's face that she was a little shaken by the whole incident.

"He can't get in here, Katie. There are times *I* can't get in here, and I have a key to the fucking door." I gestured to the door and tried my best to reassure her of our hefty barrier.

She laughed, understanding exactly what I was talking about. Since day one of living in this apartment, we had both been contestants in the game of "Will my key let me in today?". Every time the lock stuck I thanked the lovely landlords of BG for doing a shitty job with their property upkeep.

"Maci, what if he comes back?" Katie asked, and the urgency returned to her voice. "Those were probably his idiot roommates who were with him."

"Then he comes back." I shrugged. "And he and his shitty roommates meet two tired and pissed-off females."

She rapidly shook her head. "He can't come back here, Maci. Tyler and his roommates are *crazy* when they drink." She paced around the living room with her arms crossed in front of her chest.

"Katie—"

"Can you ask Jaxon to come over?" She looked nervous about whatever thoughts were running through her head. "I know it's late, but he'll come if you ask him to."

"You don't think that's overreacting just a little bit?" I said gently, careful not to downplay her concern. I would call the US Army if Katie asked me to.

"Absolutely not!" Katie scowled. "I've watched enough true crime, and I refuse to ignore the early signs. Let me know when he's on his way over."

I cocked my head and watched her walk over to the fridge. She pulled out a Mike's Hard and offered me one.

"You're that confident that he'll come?" I challenged, trying to ease the tension I saw brewing on her forehead.

The corner of her mouth pulled up while she was mid-sip. "I bet you the next bottle of wine."

I rolled my eyes and snatched my drink out of her hand. I spun on my heels so she couldn't see my facial expression while I dialed Jaxon's number. I didn't know why I was nervous. I had called him dozens of times before this. He answered on the third ring.

"What's up, Mace?" He didn't sound tired at all, and I could hear *Call of Duty* in the background.

I pursed my lips. "I have a favor to ask you."

"Of course you do," he said playfully.

Under different circumstances, I would've had something snarky to say back. "Katie's ex just tried getting into our apartment," I said softly.

"Tyler?"

"Yeah, Tyler." I was impressed with his memory. It just emphasized how crappy Bryson's was. "He was pretty drunk, and it sounded like he had a bunch of guys with him."

"Are you guys okay?" His voice grew more urgent. There was a fit of yelling in the background, followed by a stream of fake gunfire. "You locked the door, right? Like you didn't try to go out into the hall?"

"Yeah, we're fine." I looked back at Katie. She tugged on her earring and stared down at the counter. There had to be more to the story she wasn't telling me. "Katie's a little nervous that he will try and come back."

"I'll be there in ten," Jaxon said, bringing my focus back to our conversation.

"But I didn't—"

"You didn't have to ask, Mace, I can just tell." His voice was soft, like he was whispering right next to me. "I'll call you when I'm outside. Don't unlock the door until I call."

I turned to smile reassuringly at Katie. "Okay." I felt safer knowing that Jaxon would be over soon. Once he walked through the door, I knew that his presence alone would shift the entire mood.

As soon as I mentioned that Katie was worried, he wasted no time adjusting his plans. It was one thing for him to be concerned about me, but it was a whole other type of turn-on for him to be worried about my best friend.

It sucked to know that if I had just had the same conversation with Bryson, he wouldn't have even batted an eye at the situation. It sucked even more that I would've done anything to see him care for a fraction of what Jaxon just offered me. At this point, I felt like the only reason I was keeping Bryson around was because Jaxon didn't want to be anything more than friends, but I didn't want to travel down that dark rabbit hole.

Katie cocked her head, and I watched a small wave of relief wash over her. "Red or white?"

"I love that boy." Katie sighed and tossed her empty drink in the trash.

"So do I," I murmured into the tip of my bottle. It was low enough so Katie couldn't hear it, and I could try to ignore the fact that I had admitted it.

Chapter Twenty-Two

JAXON

AS SOON AS I hung up with Maci, I ran into my room to pack an overnight bag. Connor and I were the only ones left in the apartment, and we were playing video games when Maci called.

Connor studied my bag from the couch and paused his game. "You heading out?"

"Maci called me and said some guys just tried to get in their apartment." As soon as the words left my mouth, I waited to see if Connor picked up on the name I had just dropped.

Earlier, when Maci called, he was completely invested in the game, so I knew he wasn't paying attention. Now his attention was on me.

Connor's eyebrows knit together. "Maci. As in, the girl Kennedy has been messing around with, Maci?"

I couldn't tell by his tone if he thought it was weird that she called me or if he was just double-checking that he was thinking of the right girl.

"Yeah," I said casually. I decided to throw in some background to help everything make sense. "We met in class last year, so we were friends before she met Bryson."

Connor was completely unphased by my answer and turned off the PS4. "Let me grab a few things, and I'll come with you."

"You don't have to, man. I'm sure it's nothing."

"You just said some *guys* tried to break into her apartment. I'm coming with you," Connor insisted, making it very clear that it wasn't an argument.

I gestured down the hallway to let him know I would wait for him to get ready.

Connor was the classic good guy. He came from a good family and always took the moral high ground. He had always been fascinated with how Bryson and I operated, and while he didn't always agree with how we did things; at the drop of a hat he would be there for us no matter what. Connor had been roommates with Jared back when we were living in the dorms, and the four of us got along so well that it just made sense to all room together.

Since it was just the two of us left on campus, we locked up the apartment, and I drove us over to Maci and Katie's.

"Do they know who it was?" Connor asked as we turned down Court Street.

"Katie's ex," I explained. "Katie is Maci's roommate. Really cool girl."

"Do you know the guy?"

I shrugged, thinking back to the very few times I interacted with Tyler. "I met him once, I think. Don't really know anything about him. But Katie's a smart girl so if she broke up with him he's probably a dick."

"Hmm," Connor stated and looked straight ahead at the road.

I was relieved that it was Connor with me and not Bryson or Jared. I wouldn't have to pretend anything in front of him when it came to Maci.

I parked the Jeep right next to Maci's Elantra in the rear parking lot. Her back right window was cracked, and I shook my head. She was way too comfortable in her surroundings.

Jaxon

Coming up the stairs.

The door to the apartment opened as soon as we entered the hallway.

"You don't follow directions well," I said as soon as I stepped foot in the living room.

I instinctively looked around as if Tyler had snuck inside and was hiding among the Christmas decorations that flooded the apartment. Connor locked the deadbolt as soon as both of us were inside.

"What do you mean?" Katie demanded. She looked exhausted.

I threw my bag on the couch and smiled softly at her. "I just meant that I told Maci not to open the door until I was standing in front of it. I heard there's a psycho ex running around here or something?" I pulled Katie into a hug. She smacked me playfully on the chest, setting the mood between us back to normal.

"Down the hall is hardly not following directions." Maci leaned against her bedroom doorway and crossed her arms, remaining on the other side of the living room. She looked just as exhausted as Katie did.

"This is my roommate, Connor." I turned to make introductions. "This is Katie and Maci."

"Nice place." Connor smiled at Katie and surveyed the Christmas display. "Definitely more cheerful than ours."

Connor's poker face completely sucked ass. I bit my lip to keep from smiling and turned to focus on the lights that lined the ceiling. I had a hunch when I first met Katie that she was totally Connor's type. Here he was, proving me right.

A shy smile appeared on Katie's face. "We were just about to start another Christmas movie. Any suggestions?"

Connor helped himself to a drink from the fridge as if he was just here last night doing the same routine. I raised my eyebrows at Maci, attempting to get any kind of reaction from her. She mirrored my expression and cocked her head. I loved how we were on the same wavelength.

"I heard *The Nightmare Before Christmas* goes fantastic with Mike's." Connor pulled out two bottles. Katie joined him in the kitchen, and they were immediately sucked into their own bubble.

Maci bumped me with her shoulder, and I opened up my arms so she could wrap her tiny figure around mine. It felt good to have her near me, to feel her relax into my touch.

"Do you guys offer that on tap yet?" I gestured toward the bottles of Mike's on the counter.

"It appears that way." She smiled sleepily into my chest. When she looked up at me, the lights above us appeared in her blue eyes. "Thank you for coming."

"Are you gonna stay awake for this movie?" I grinned at the way she was barely keeping her eyes open.

"Probably not." She released her grip and lowered her voice to a whisper. "But I don't want to leave Katie if she isn't going to be able to sleep."

"I don't think she's going to need us," I whispered back and motioned to where Connor and Katie were setting up the movie.

Connor was holding the remote out in front of him, and Katie was laughing at something he had just said. Neither of them looked our way one time.

"Katie?" Maci piped up, and Katie shot her a look like she forgot she was in the room. "Has Tyler texted you or anything?"

"No," Katie said confidently. "I think I'm good!" Her eyes widened, and she shot us a look that read, "No need to hover, get lost".

"I can chill out here if you want to go to bed," I offered.

The last time I was in that bedroom, we almost had sex. I heard her say my name in a way that I would *kill* to have spoken again. But when she shot me a look of confusion and her eyes flicked from me to the hallway, I knew what was coming.

"Don't be stupid, Jax. You can sleep in my room."

I did my best to swallow around the lump in my throat.

"Come on," she coaxed quietly. "We are totally not needed here."

***

It felt weird being back in Maci's bedroom. Even though I was still coming over to chill throughout the week, I never had a reason to make an appearance here again.

As soon as I shut the door behind me, Maci crawled into bed and wasted no time getting comfortable. She tucked herself snugly under both of the comforters and adjusted her hoodie.

"How do you sleep like that?" I snapped playfully.

"Like what?" Maci asked.

I took a few steps closer and pointed to all of the bedding. "With all of this *nonsense*. I woke up sweating the last time I slept here."

Maci's eyes met mine and I knew she was thinking about the last time I was in this room with her. She blinked a few times as if it would reset her memory and allow us to start over.

She cleared her throat and pointed to her desk. "There's a charger over there if you need it."

I stripped off my shirt and slid in next to her. The more words we exchanged, the more awkward this revisit would be. I kept my basketball shorts on and made sure there was a little bit of space between us. The silence was somehow incredibly loud, and the minimal light that her only window provided amplified the silent exchanges happening between us.

"Is Connor a good guy?" she asked after a few minutes.

I was relieved to hear her voice. I turned my head and found her lying on her side and staring at me. I raised my arm across her pillow, opening the invitation for her to come closer if she wanted to.

"He's a great guy," I admitted.

"He seems like Katie's type."

My eyes narrowed. "Wasn't the guy just trying to break into your apartment, Katie's type?"

"Yeah." A small smirk appeared in the corner of her mouth. "But Tyler was her hookup type."

"What's the difference?" I said, intrigued to hear more. I wanted to keep her talking. I missed this, listening to her explain all of the thoughts she had going on inside her head.

She stared at my chest, and I held my breath. It felt wrong to be this close to her and not touch her. I wondered if this only felt weird because I had never shared a bed with a girl without having sex. I had never actually just *slept* with someone.

That was a fucking lie. I actually *had* done this before. It was back in October and it was in this same bed. That seemed like a lifetime ago.

"Hookup types are guys you don't really care about." She met my gaze, and her half-smile resurfaced. "They are temporary. When a girl meets a guy who is actually her type, she knows. It becomes so obvious that even her best friend can tell."

We both looked toward her bedroom door when Katie's laugh echoed from the living room. When I looked back at Maci, she was biting the inside of her cheek, her eyes locked on her hand that was resting on the bed in front of her. She was in her own head about something.

I brushed my hand against hers to bring her back. "What's up, Mace?"

Her eyes darted back up to mine. She took a deep breath, preparing for what she was about to say next.

"Shoot," I coaxed.

"Is Bryson a good guy?" she whispered.

I rolled over on my back to hide any reaction that might have appeared on my face. I knew this part was coming. This was what I wanted to avoid when I stopped us from having sex that night, Maci asking these questions, but instead of them being about Bryson, they would've been about me.

I rolled back onto my side, my face only a few inches away from hers. "Kennedy is Kennedy." I took another breath and chose my next words carefully. "Bryson is . . . Bryson. Bryson and I are a lot alike, Mace. There's a reason I didn't sleep with you that night."

Maci waited for me to keep going. I wasn't sure if her lack of reaction was a good sign or a bad one.

"Bryson is never going to treat you the way you want him to. He's going to do whatever he wants to do, regardless of what he tells you. He isn't a bad guy, but he is my best friend, and I know him."

She nodded and winced. "So the chances of him sleeping with anyone else right now?"

"Oh, absolutely high," I stated without a hint of doubt.

"Hmm." She inched closer to me, so her head rested in the nook of my arm.

I pulled her tighter against me, letting her know I heard her response but didn't know what else to say. She wrapped her arm around my chest, and I waited until her eyes were closed before I closed mine.

This was the first time that Maci asked me about Bryson. This wouldn't be the last time he lied to her. While I felt a little weird spilling his usual routines, I realized they weren't just his, but mine too. It was easy to give Maci a rundown because I just had to think about the usual shit I pulled on girls I hooked up with.

Her statement from before made a lot of sense. Maci seemed to like Bryson a lot more than she led on, and I could tell she wanted more from him. No matter how she tried to justify this hookup she had going with Bryson, she wasn't the hookup kind of girl. I knew that from the first few conversations I had with her. She would never be okay with who he was.

If we had slept together that night, I wasn't sure if we would have had a different outcome. She wanted honesty. I never had a reason to be honest with women before. Honesty existed in relationships, not in hookups. The only difference between Bryson and I was Bryson didn't care if he was a temporary thing for Maci. He would cut her off tomorrow if he wanted to.

"Goodnight, Jaxon," she mumbled against my side.

"Night, Mace."

For the first time in my life, I didn't want to be temporary. I wanted to keep this girl around. I just didn't know how to do it yet without falling for her and into a territory I knew nothing about.

Chapter Twenty-Three

MACI

December 2015

IT WAS FUCKING HOT. I was thankful that Jaxon was still asleep because I assumed that watching me peel my face off his bare chest wasn't how he wanted to start his day.

Once I was freed from his salty grip, I tore off my comforters and let myself bask in the breeze of my ceiling fan. Jaxon had turned my cozy sanctuary into a heat box overnight. But I didn't dare complain about the view he offered me.

He was on his back, his chest chiseled and completely exposed. A layer of sweat glistened against his tan skin. He had one arm above his head, and the other lay next to him where I was only a few moments ago. He looked completely at peace with whatever he was thinking about. There wasn't a single line on his face. Even in his sleep, he was incredibly good-looking.

I stripped off my sweatshirt and threw it in my closet. I missed the hamper and it smacked into the door, causing Jaxon to jump out of his slumber.

"The fuck?" Jaxon stirred and sat up to see where he was. He rubbed his eyes and turned over onto his side.

"Jaxon?" I prompted and tried not to smile down at him. "It's already nine. You don't have a final or anything this morning, do you?"

"My last final is tomorrow. Same as yours," he mumbled into the pillow with his eyes still closed.

I nodded even though he couldn't see me. I slipped quietly out of the bed and made my way to the kitchen for a much-needed cup of coffee.

While the Keurig was heating up, I peeked around the corner to make sure I didn't wake Connor with my need for caffeine. Only, Connor wasn't on the couch, which meant he must've been in Katie's room.

I pointed to Katie's closed bedroom door and silently screamed in her honor. I didn't want to get too excited, but with the way those two hit it off last night, it was hard not to.

"I see someone didn't sleep on the couch." Jaxon came up from behind me and wrapped his arms around my shoulders. "Morning, Mace."

His weight on my back woke every cell in my body. Who needed caffeine when you had a half-naked Jaxon Hayes to hug you from behind?

Fuck Folgers. I would take this every morning from here on out.

"I thought the same thing," I said, returning back to earth once he released me from his grasp. I watched him stroll into the kitchen, shirtless and in a pair of basketball shorts, searching for a mug. With each cabinet he opened, the look of confusion grew more apparent on his sleepy face.

"Over one more." I pointed, and he chose my Professor of the Dark Arts Harry Potter mug from the next cabinet.

Now the universe was just being cruel. He even made my nerdy coffee cup look sexy. I'd never be able to use that mug again without thinking of him shirtless in my kitchen.

"Mace?" Jaxon stared at me.

I snapped out of my daydream. "What?"

"I asked if you had any sugar."

"You don't need sugar. The creamer in the fridge door tastes just like the Dunkin order you get," I insisted.

He didn't argue. We had ordered the same iced coffee since the first week of classes, and he trusted my judgment.

No sooner than Jaxon slid my mug into the Keurig, Katie and Connor joined us in the living room. There was an awkward moment of silence, but overall it wasn't the worst entrance I'd been a part of.

"Morning." Katie smiled and turned her head so only I could see her expression. It was a clear sign that we needed to talk once we had a moment alone.

Jaxon walked my mug of hot coffee over and handed it to me.

"There's coffee, Connor. And creamer in the fridge," I offered and took a seat at the dining room table.

Katie sat down next to me and rested her head in her hands. I watched Connor shoot an adorable smile in her direction as he pulled two mugs from the cabinet. My heart swooned for my best friend. It was incredible timing that on the same night Katie's stalker ex showed up at our apartment, she was blessed with the buff blond gem that stood in front of me and prepared her coffee.

I turned to face Katie. "Any updates from last night?" I didn't want to drop Tyler's name and spoil the mood.

"No." Katie shook her head. "But that makes me even more nervous. I expected to hear from one of his douchey roommates or something by now. Silence with Tyler is actually worse."

I placed my hand over Katie's and met her gaze. "It's going to be fine. You're going to head home today, and by the time we come back from break, this will totally blow over."

"Yeaaah," Katie dragged out her answer and turned toward Connor. "Connor is actually from Michigan City, and I drive past there on my way home. I offered to give him a ride."

Connor sat down next to Katie. "My last final is tomorrow afternoon."

"You know I hate making that drive by myself." Katie shrugged and took a sip of her coffee. I read right through her innocent facial expression and knew I shouldn't ask any other questions.

"Yeah, it makes sense." I offered a small smile in support.

Jaxon's hands grasped the back of my chair, his toned arms on either side of me. "Do you guys have anything to make breakfast?"

Katie and I exchanged a playful smirk. We knew full well there was nothing here that fit the breakfast category. Going grocery shopping didn't make sense since we were so close to break. We had been living on takeout for the last few days.

Connor looked at the two of us with an amused grin. While I knew he wasn't happy with the current circumstances Katie was in with Tyler, he was enjoying his stay with us.

"We can go shopping for some stuff," I said. "Let me change, and I'll run up to Kroger."

"Let's get dinner stuff too." Katie stood and downed the rest of her coffee.

"Can you make that chicken fried rice with the bacon?" Jaxon asked eagerly.

"That sounds bomb," Connor added.

I looked up at Jaxon. This cozy morning had turned into an all-day affair, and no one was mad about it.

"It's Thursday." He read my mind and shrugged. "I'm usually here anyways."

"I can make that," Katie answered and gestured for me to follow her into the hall.

We left the boys at the table, and I followed Katie into her bedroom. She waited until I was inside before she shut the door behind me.

"Can we have a moment?" I pleaded softly so my voice didn't travel.

"Yes!" She mimicked my reaction and we both laughed hysterically.

"Connor seems really sweet," I swooned. "Did you?"

"No." Katie shook her head but couldn't hide her massive grin. "But we were up all night just talking. He is really sweet. He didn't even try anything."

"Are you okay if they are here all day? I wasn't sure if you wanted some space."

"I'm totally fine with it," she assured me. "Are you fine with it?"

"Yeah." My voice took an unexpectedly high pitch.

Katie pursed her lips. "Did anything happen last night?"

"Nope," I said quickly.

"Because Jaxon's not . . ." She spoke slowly so I could finish my thought at the same time as her. "Fun Dip material?"

"Not Fun Dip material. Right." I nodded.

A playful smirk resurfaced on her face, and she sighed. "Well, I'm going to go rally our new *troops*."

"Katie?" I stopped her halfway to the door. "Why did you ask me to call Jaxon? Why not Sam or someone else we know who is still on campus?"

Katie took a deep breath and exhaled slowly. "Because I knew he would come. I trusted him to be here and knew he would take care of things"—she paused before opening the door to the hall—"and because I knew you wanted to see him."

It was like I told Jaxon last night. When a girl met a guy who was actually her type, she knew. It became so obvious that even her best friend could tell. The only problem with my type was I seemed only to want guys that didn't want me back.

Chapter Twenty-Four

JAXON

December 2015

Even though there were only a few students left on campus because of finals, Kroger was packed.

While Maci and Katie roamed the store to pick out snacks, Connor and I walked up the spice aisle for the fifth time. Katie gave us a very specific list of items to get, and neither of us knew what sesame oil looked like.

"Is it really any different than olive oil?" Connor picked up a bottle and set it back on the shelf.

"I'm going to go with yes, but honestly, I don't fucking know," I snapped, getting more irritated by the second.

I looked up and down the aisle and spotted a woman who looked to be in her mid-thirties. She had a little boy in the seat of her cart, and she wore a matching workout set. She looked like a mom and more importantly, like someone who could help me.

"Excuse me?" I approached her and turned up the charming smile a bit. The color surfaced in her cheeks, letting me know I had her full attention.

"Do you know what sesame oil looks like?" I asked, looking her up and down.

"It's on the same shelf as the soy sauce." She nodded to the section behind me, and a slight grin appeared on her face.

"Thank you," I answered sweetly, waving to the little boy. A genuine smile crossed my face when the little guy waved back.

Connor must've overheard our conversation because he was holding a bottle of sesame oil when I turned around. It was comical to see him with a grocery basket full of items we would never buy for the apartment. He looked so domesticated. "What's next?"

"Rice," I half-read off of the paper. "Balsamic rice."

Connor led us to the next aisle and searched the rows of boxed rice.

"It says bagged," I clarified with a hint of sarcasm. I gestured toward another section where Minute Rice was frowned upon.

Connor surveyed the options and shook his head. "Let me see the paper," he demanded and snatched it from my hands.

My phone vibrated in my back pocket.

Maci

Heading to check out now. Almost done?

Jaxon

Just getting rice.

"Did you find it?" I asked Connor and tucked my phone away.

"Balsamic rice." Connor shook his head like a disappointed parent. "It's *basmati* rice." He held up the list for emphasis and threw the bag of rice into his basket.

"Dude, it is a Thursday morning, and I'm *grocery* shopping with you. And I'm running on an empty stomach. Give me a break."

We started toward the registers and double-checked the list one more time to make sure we didn't forget anything.

"So this is what you do every Thursday, huh?" Connor asked as we rounded into the bread aisle. "Lounge around Katie and Maci's apartment and get food made for you?"

"Apparently, I shop now, too," I joked.

There wasn't an accusing tone in Connor's voice, but I couldn't help but feel like I was being found out. I didn't go out of my way to hide the routine I had going with Maci, but I didn't openly talk about it either.

"And you haven't slept with her? Maci, I mean?" Connor asked with genuine interest and then quickly added, "You haven't slept with Katie, have you?"

I stifled a laugh. I didn't know if I should be offended or impressed by how well Connor knew me and my habits. "No, I haven't slept with either of them. Just friends."

"Just figured I would ask now instead of finding out later," Connor admitted.

"Katie is all yours, man." The slight smile on Connor's face made it clear that he was satisfied with my answer.

We approached the registers and joined the girls in line, where they had a cart full of different snacks and drinks. I scanned their selections, approving the Doritos, pretzel rods, buffalo chicken dip ingredients, and beer. There was also a bottle of Blood Orange SKYY Vodka and a jug of cranberry juice.

Katie rifled through Connor's basket and rolled her eyes directly at me. "No bacon? You specifically asked for bacon in this rice."

"Jesus, Mary, Joseph," Maci mumbled and laughed at Katie's face.

I shoved Maci's shoulder and dragged a hand down my face. I didn't wait for Katie to instruct me to go hunting for another item. I exited the line and made my way to the back of the store toward the meat section.

"Wait! I need a specific kind," Katie yelled and ran up next to me. We made it halfway to our destination before Connor texted me.

Connor

Ramen.

I rolled my eyes and looked up at the ceiling. We were never getting out of this store. "Come find me in the pasta section once you're done. I'm gonna get some ramen," I said and broke away from Katie.

"Ramen?" She turned her nose up and stopped walking.

I stretched my arms out and walked backward to answer her. "Your new boy-toy is requesting ramen."

I loved getting a rise out of Katie almost as much as I loved messing with Maci. She swatted the air in front of her and continued in the opposite direction.

I still had a smile on my face when I found the last case of chicken-flavored Cup O'Noodles. However, it quickly evaporated when I realized who was a few steps away. I recognized the frat boy's haircut and the smug look on his face.

It was Tyler.

I had a decision to make. I wasn't there when last night's event happened, but either way, he didn't look like the good guy in the retelling of the story. Katie wasn't specific about what had happened prior to him coming over. He was alone, and if I approached him, I would catch him off guard. I might also make things worse for Katie if I said something, but I took a few steps forward, and my protective instinct won.

"Tyler, right?" I approached him and kept my tone casual. I didn't want him getting defensive right away.

"Do I know you?" he asked, completely unbothered by my approach. I didn't expect him to remember me.

"We met once. We went out with Katie and Maci a few months ago."

His face fell as soon as Katie's name left my mouth.

"I heard you had some trouble over there last night." I tightened my jaw.

"What I do with Katie is none of your fucking business," Tyler threatened. He kept his voice down, not wanting to draw any attention to our conversation. "If I want to see her, I'll find a way to see her."

His answer was possessive and didn't carry an ounce of emotion. I was all too familiar with guys exactly like Tyler. Heat prickled in my fingertips, and I forced myself not to throw the first punch.

I took another step forward, and he didn't flinch. "Actually, it is my fucking business. Katie's a good friend of mine, and she doesn't want to see you anymore. Stay away from her."

A condescending laugh escaped Tyler, and I tightened my grip on the box I was holding. I could knock this douchebag right on his ass in a second.

"Let me put it this way." I mimicked his reaction and made direct eye contact. "If you come near their place again, I'll break your fucking jaw."

Tyler's face went stoic. He swallowed his reply and didn't move.

"I've thrown down with tons of shithead frat boys just like you. Last time I checked, I'm still pretty good lookin'." I smirked and looked him up and down. "Don't try me, man."

Tyler hesitated for a moment and finally turned around in the opposite direction. He didn't look behind him, and I waited until he left the aisle before I headed toward Katie.

Chapter Twenty-Five

MACI

December 2015

No matter how I positioned myself in the nook of Jaxon's arm, the back of my head throbbed.

Images of flashbacks ran through my mind, and I tried to recall the events that led up to my rocking headache.

Katie's fried rice, cranberry vodkas, Drunk Driving, the Drunk Betch playlist, and Ride the Bus against Jaxon were all core memories of last night. I didn't even remember coming to bed.

I reached for my phone, and when I saw I had five more minutes until my alarm, I laid back down.

Jaxon murmured something and pulled me closer to his chest. I sighed and wrapped my arms around his waist. It was so easy being like this with him.

My stomach ached at the thought of leaving Jaxon for a month. It would do me good to get away from Bowling Green for a little bit, but that didn't make missing him any easier.

Katie would be getting up any minute now to start packing her car. I was happy I packed mine yesterday. It was one less thing I had to do before making the trek back to Columbus.

"Mace," Jaxon mumbled. "What time is it?"

"Almost nine."

"What time is the final?"

I smiled sleepily against his chest. "Ten-thirty."

He relaxed against me, and a light snore drifted from his slightly parted lips. My alarm was going to go off any second.

The familiar beeping sounded next to my pillow, and we both jumped out of our cuddle session. I quickly slid the alert off while Jaxon sat up and rubbed his hands down his face.

"Go back to sleep." I placed a hand on his shoulder and gently coaxed him back onto the bed. "I'll wake you up when it's time to leave."

"I'm up," he said with his eyes still closed.

I rolled over top of him to get off the bed. He moaned at first when my knee went into his side but let out a deep laugh when my feet hit the ground.

He stared at me with sleepy dark-green eyes. "I'm *really* up now." Butterflies erupted behind my navel and fluttered into the lower parts of my chest.

We still had finals to do, goodbyes to give, and half a day ahead of us, but I already missed him.

⁓

After a sappy goodbye with Katie and a bear hug with Connor, I drove Jaxon and I to campus for our Journalism final. We arrived on time and sat in our usual seats. The professor got us started right away, probably just as eager to start winter break as we were.

For the final, we had to write an article analysis separately and create a demo article with our partner. There was no way to prepare for the final before the session, but Jaxon and I moved quickly through it with fifteen minutes left to spare. Once we handed in our article, we were free to go.

"One last Dunkin run?" Jaxon asked as we passed the store on campus.

I checked my phone. It was already noon, and Jaxon had a nine-hour drive back to North Carolina.

"It'll be quick," he reassured me. "I need something before I start driving."

"Are you buying?"

"I suppose," he answered playfully and opened the door so I could walk inside.

"So, what's Christmas like in North Carolina?" I asked once we were in line. "Is it at least warmer there than it is here?"

"It's warmer. But it's pretty low-key. Just my parents and my brother if he can come into town, which last I heard, he is. I spend time with friends and catch up with people. It's nice going home."

"Your brother is older, right?"

"Alex is . . ." He pursed his lips and looked at the ceiling. "Twenty-four? We're three years apart. He works out in California, but depending on who he is dating at the time determines if he comes home or not for holidays. He told me he met someone at a wedding and that she seemed cool. But we'll see."

The guy at the register sighed. "Can I help you?"

Just as Jaxon was about to order, his name was called from further down the counter. "Jaxon? I have it down here."

Jaxon ran a hand through his hair and nodded at the register as if to say, "Thanks anyways."

A petite brunette greeted him on the other side of the counter. She wore a big smile and made the required Dunkin baseball cap look cute. She slid the iced coffee across the counter and set a paper bag in front of him. She paid absolutely no attention to me. It was our Thursday order, prompt and ready on a Friday afternoon.

"Thanks, Reagan." Jaxon tried to turn away before she had the chance to say anything, but she was too quick.

"Heading home for break? Heather said she texted you yesterday, and you told her you left."

I took a long sip of my coffee and pretended to be interested in something outside.

"I was going to, but I decided not to," Jaxon said.

"Oh, okay! Well, if you want to hang out after break, let us know! Heather and I are cool again. No more drama between us." Reagan shot him a look like there was much more to that invitation.

Jaxon nodded and didn't say another word. Instead, he followed me outside and glanced over at me as he sipped his coffee.

I knew he was waiting for my reaction, so I finally caved. "Reagan and Heather are cool again. In case you didn't know."

As much as I didn't want to hear about his conquests with other girls, I craved this topic of conversation. Jaxon and I used to talk about past hookups and relationships all the time. Well, his hookups and my relationships. We hadn't since I slept with Bryson and it felt nice to be on familiar ground again.

"Heather is the girl I kicked out of my apartment that morning." Jaxon shrugged. He knew he didn't need to elaborate on what morning he was talking about. "Reagan is one of Heather's roommates. When Heather found out Reagan slept with me, she got really pissed off. They didn't talk for months."

"Did you continue to talk to them?"

"Oh, absolutely," he answered quickly, and I laughed. "Heather is kind of obsessed with me, so she is easy to keep around for some butt. But Reagan was much more laid back about it, and when it became too much drama, we just stopped talking."

I tried to look past his choices of words, but I couldn't. He sounded just like Bryson.

"Well, it sounds like they're both offering up their services," I joked, ensuring I didn't sound disappointed. He nudged me playfully with his arm and went around the car to the passenger side.

On the short drive back to my apartment, I reflected on the first half of my junior year. So much had happened in just a few short months. I met a guy I couldn't imagine my life without and a guy I could hook up with that fit my Fun Dip criteria. Unfortunately for me, they weren't the same person.

I wanted to be more with Jaxon, but he didn't want to be more than friends with me. Bryson was a great hookup guy, but I struggled with how he made me feel about myself and what I wanted. It truly was a travesty, having two hot guys running around in my headspace at such an exhausting rate.

We pulled up to Jaxon's Jeep, and I got out to hug him goodbye. I refused to part ways with an awkward car hug.

He wrapped his heavy arms around my shoulders, and I slipped mine around his waist. His body heat radiated through his hoodie, and his familiar scent of body wash relaxed my shoulders. I tried to soak in the feeling one last time before I went without it for a month.

He dipped his mouth to my ear and whispered, "I'm gonna miss you, Mace."

His breath was hot on my neck, and a familiar tingle returned underneath my belly button. I squeezed my eyes and reprimanded myself for getting emotional. I cleared my throat to hide the evidence and answered, "I'm going to miss you too."

These past few days were exactly what I needed. All of the extra time with Jaxon solidified that I could do the "just friends" gig if that was what he wanted. Even though things changed a little bit after the Halloween run-in, the foundation was still there. I hated how this goodbye was so hard for me.

"I'll see you in a few weeks." His voice was husky, and he sounded tired.

I released his waist and turned to walk back to the driver's side of my car. The faster I left, the faster I could be alone with my thoughts. Every cell in my body wanted to gravitate back over to him, grab his face, and kiss him like I did back in October. But I wouldn't allow myself to risk it, not after we almost lost everything.

"Mace?"

I stopped halfway into the car, and my eyes met his gaze.

"Let me know when you make it home." He grinned and climbed into his Jeep.

Part Two

Chapter Twenty-Six

MACI

January 2016

Heading back to Bowling Green had become like muscle memory. It was one of those instances when you knew you were driving, but you didn't remember how you ended up somewhere. Before you knew it, you were putting the car in park but couldn't remember pulling into the parking lot.

I wasn't sure if that even made sense. I was too exhausted at the thought of lugging all my belongings back into the apartment to care.

"Are you there already?" Katie asked.

I had spent the last hour of my drive talking with her so I stayed awake. It was Saturday night, and most people wouldn't be back on campus until tomorrow, possibly even Monday, depending on what time their first class was.

My car hummed quietly in the lot of our apartment. "I just pulled in." I sighed and turned off the engine.

"Text me once you get settled. I love you!"

"I love you too, Katie." I grinned and ended the call.

Returning to Bowling Green felt refreshing, like I was returning to a different version of myself. Back in Columbus, I was wrapped up in old friends, old drama, and a life I didn't plan to return to after leaving high school. My mom had practically begged me to stay another night after my brother, Chase, headed back to Pittsburgh with his boyfriend. My dad spent most of the break traveling for work, and I wondered if there were times she got lonely being by herself. I felt bad leaving her alone, but I wanted time to relax before the new semester started on Monday.

Once I got everything inside, I collapsed along with my bedding onto the living room floor. All of the Christmas decorations were still hung, and I relaxed into the warm sensation that flooded around me. It was good to be home.

I basked in the silence for only a minute or two before deciding it was too quiet without Katie. I pulled up our Spotify account on the TV and hit shuffle. "Hello" by Adele drifted through the speakers, and I pulled myself up to start unpacking.

After an hour or so, I rummaged in the fridge until I found the leftover bottle of SKYY Vodka from last month's haul and the tiny bit of stagnated cranberry juice. I shook the bottle of juice and stared as the bubbles settled. It might not be the freshest drink I've ever thrown together, but it would have to do. I had no plans of leaving this apartment tonight.

Once I sank into my usual spot on the couch, I turned on my new binge series. The familiar tune of *Sex and the City* danced from the TV, and I pulled a blanket over my legs. I missed Katie and the company she would typically provide in this setting. But she would be back tomorrow, and we would have plenty of time to catch up.

About halfway through the episode, my phone buzzed on the coffee table.

Bryson

What's up?

Maci

I just got done unpacking. You?

Bryson

Just chillin. Want to hang out?

Maci

Only if you are cool with a Sex and the City binge. I am exhausted.

Bryson

I'll head out soon.

I sighed into my glass. I wasn't expecting to see Bryson so soon after returning, and I could feel the glare of Charlotte York's judgemental stare through the screen.

Usually, I would get out the GameCube, change into a cuter outfit, or check the drink stash before Bryson came over. This time just felt different. I didn't care about the appearance of the apartment or myself, for that matter. It had been a long break, and the space allowed me to put some things into perspective.

I was an option to Bryson, and if he didn't like what I presented, then screw him. There was no way a guy like him didn't hook up with multiple women over winter break. I was still stuck on the fact that when I asked him if he was seeing anyone else, he straight up answered no. For absolutely no reason at all, he lied just to lie.

But still, the sex was good, and Bryson was gorgeous. I couldn't complain about having a filler when the guy I really wanted was completely fine in the friend zone. Jaxon made it very clear over break that he had no problems hooking up back home with girls. He just didn't want to hook up with me.

Two incidents happened over break that I couldn't get out of my head. On a night Jaxon said he wanted to talk, I received a wonderful phone call from a girl with no name saying that Jaxon couldn't come to the phone right now because she was borrowing him for the evening. It might've been innocent had I not heard Jaxon's full-blown drunken slur in the background asking me not to be upset. While I wasn't upset at first, my reaction shifted the more I stewed in the rejection.

The first incident would've been fine if the second one hadn't followed it up. On New Year's Eve, a different girl with no name posted a series of Snapchats to Jaxon's story. It was pretty much a porn catalog for anyone lucky enough to be Jaxon's friend. Unfortunately for me, I was one of Jaxon's top friends, so I got copies sent to my personal account for emphasis.

I guess I thought that if I wasn't aware that Jaxon was having sex with other people, there was still a chance he might change his mind about being more than friends with me. But that thought quickly evaporated when I was reminded that he had a life outside of BG, outside of the little bubble I lived in when he was with me. Maybe all of that happened over break because of the simple fact that I *desperately* needed to move on from the idea of being with Jaxon. Whatever the reason, I was for it.

Damn. Only an hour back in Bowling Green and here I was, questioning all of my self-worth. This stupid college town really had a way of saying, "Did you have a good time getting away from it all? No worries! Welcome back, and here is all the shit wrong about you."

My phone buzzed on my leg.

Bryson

On my way.

I bit my lip and watched Carrie Bradshaw spin her daily drama to her girlfriends over lunch.

Perhaps I needed to reevaluate my options. Even though I found a hookup, it was doing the opposite of what I wanted it to. Half a semester was left, and I had plenty of time to find a new prospect. Maybe the next guy wouldn't cause me to overthink everything I did along the way.

After tonight, I would scrap Bryson and start over. I took another sip of my cocktail and sunk further into the couch, trying not to go deeper into my thoughts than I already was.

***

A knock on the door woke me up from my cat nap about ten minutes later.

"Coming!" I yelled from the couch and shrugged the blanket off my shoulders.

I opened the door, and Bryson stood in front of me, looking even better than the last time I saw him. He was in a hoodie and sweatpants, yet somehow he looked like an advertisement for American Eagle's winter line. His golden-brown eyes looked sleepy, but his smile said he was excited to see me.

"Hey, you." He brushed past me and swung his book bag onto the couch. A wave of his cologne mixed with Black & Mild tagged along with him. He smelled just like I remembered before break.

As soon as the door was shut, he closed the space between us, pressing my body against the wall. He ground his erection into my hips, and if I wasn't awake before I answered the door, I certainly was awake and present now.

I narrowed my gaze. "Hey to you too."

"I'm happy you're back," he murmured against my lips.

I leaned into his kiss, and his lips moved slowly against mine. His hands traveled down to my waist, slipping underneath my shirt and lingering on my stomach. My muscles tightened, unwillingly reacting to the cool and familiar touch of his hands.

"You must've been lonely in that apartment by yourself," I joked. Even though I had just given myself a pep talk prior to his arrival, I couldn't keep a level head when his mouth was traveling against my jawline, his breath warm and heavy behind my earlobe.

He laughed and leaned back to look at me. "You have no idea."

He bent down and grabbed the back of my thighs, lifting me against the wall but spinning us around so we could fall on the couch. I released my grip around his neck so I could pull at his sweatpants. He hovered over me and trailed kisses until he found the sensitive spot on my neck. A moan slipped from my lips, and I followed the V of his hips until my hand was wrapped around his cock. We fell completely into each other, picking up right where we had left off before break. I had missed him on top of me.

"Very lonely." He grinned.

I gazed up at him and clasped the back of his head to draw his mouth back to mine. When he tried to pull away, I tugged his bottom lip between my teeth.

A sexy smirk curled into the corner of his mouth, sending a rush of sparks between my legs. He slipped his shirt over his head and tossed it across the room. Even though it was a sight I had seen so many times, I caught myself staring at him. With just one swift movement, he revealed a six-pack and toned arms I couldn't wait to be wrapped up in. His body was gorgeous.

"Take these off." He pulled at the band of my sweatpants. While I worked to slide them over my feet, he reached behind the side of the couch for his bag.

"And this." He gestured toward my shirt and threw a condom on the coffee table. I giggled as he kissed up my stomach, his lips closing around my nipple. He sucked softly at first, but he quickly became more eager once his fingers brushed my panty line and found their way between my legs. My nails dug into his shoulder blades when he stuck two fingers inside me.

"You're so wet," he growled and grasped the back of my neck with his free hand to pull my mouth to his. He kissed me roughly, matching how his fingers moved against my G-spot. I could feel myself closing around him, begging for him to keep going as I climbed closer and closer to a release. I whimpered against his lips when his thumb teased my clit.

Just as I was about to climax, Bryson threw himself toward the end of the couch and drew my legs apart with his forearms. I stared at him, half of me frustrated at the sudden halt but the other half of me eager for what was coming next. His cocky grin resurfaced, and without breaking eye contact, he lowered his mouth. I watched his tongue stroke my clit, and my head fell back against the couch. I moaned and gripped the armrest behind me. Once he slipped his fingers back inside me and matched the rhythm with his tongue, I couldn't hold out any longer.

"Oh my god," I whispered right before I closed my eyes and clenched my thighs to try to stop them from shaking. My heart thudded heavily against my chest, and my breath came in gasps as I tried to come back down. While I recovered,

I could hear Bryson unwrapping the condom. He sat down on the couch and grabbed at my waist. He never wasted any time with transitions.

"Come here," he ordered and pulled me into his lap. He slowly slid himself inside me, filling me over and over again.

I gripped the back of his head and slammed my hips against his, matching his pace and finding the angle I needed to put me over the edge one more time. His hand returned to my clit, adding to the pressure I had built up inside me.

"Keep doing that," I begged, placing my hands on the cushion behind his head. I slowed down our pace and ground my hips against the movements he was making with his thumb. "Harder."

He let out a slow exhale and smiled up at me. Obeying my command, his eyes never left mine. His hands kept perfect time with his strokes until suddenly I was close to seeing stars. His thighs shook slightly, and I could tell he was close.

"Come for me," he pleaded.

As if those words were all I needed, I began to shake against his chest, sinking my fingernails into his back. I felt his teeth on my shoulder as I cried out, his fingers gripping my backside. A soft groan slipped through his teeth, and his forehead fell against my chest. We sat tangled up in skin and sweat, neither of us attempting to move.

"It's hot," I finally said, sliding onto the cushion beside him. I grabbed the blanket I had used earlier and wrapped it around my naked body. Having sex with someone was one thing, but sitting around together naked was another.

Bryson tossed the condom in the kitchen garbage. On his way back to the couch, he pulled out a purple bag of Skittles from his book bag. He raised his eyebrows and tossed a few of the candies in his mouth. His hungry stare reminded me that I was still naked underneath Katie's Chicago Blackhawks blanket.

The Maci from earlier would have to get over herself. There was no way on God's green earth that I was scrapping this fuckboy hookup.

Chapter Twenty-Seven

JAXON

January 2016

After a late night of drinking, I liked to play this game with myself to see if I could guess where I was before I opened my eyes. Since late-night drinking was something I did more often than I would like to admit, I got pretty good at sifting through my foggy memory to come up with clues for my current location.

I couldn't move my right arm, which meant someone was lying on top of it. The blanket on top of me felt heavy, letting me know I wasn't at home because I would never sleep with this thick of a blanket. It smelled like flowery perfume, and suddenly, images of a matching black and red lingerie set filled up the memory reel from last night.

Blonde hair, brown eyes, and was it a hip tattoo? I was at either Rachel's or Cora's house. Based on how things were going last night, my guess was Rachel.

"Jaxon?" a soft voice murmured from the edge of the bed. It was Cora.

Eh. I had a fifty-fifty shot.

I pulled my arm out from under her side and admired her ass in what was left of her lacy black underwear. I needed to make an exit ASAP without waking another round of, "Where are you going? Do you want to get breakfast or something?"

I slipped into my jeans and located my shirt on the floor in front of the closet. As soon as my hoodie was over my head, I heard the iconic line linger off the pillow Cora was sunken into.

"Where are you going?" she whispered and sat up so she could see me. She ran a hand through her tangled mess of curls. "Do you want to get breakfast or something?"

I shrugged. "Can't. I have to head back to school today." I grabbed my phone from the end of the bed and cracked open the bedroom door to take a peek in the hallway. If I made my exit now, I would avoid running into anyone else in the house.

"You're really just gonna—"

I cut her off by shutting the door. I didn't have time to explain myself more than once. Cora had known me since high school, and if she didn't know how I operated by now, that was her problem. I was pretty sure we had done this run around a year ago, the summer after my freshman year at BG. Same outcome, different day.

According to the location tracker on my phone, my Jeep was parked outside on the street. I had no idea how it got there, but I didn't have time to care. Cora shared a house with three other girls, and I was pretty sure I performed this same vanishing act on two of them. I needed to put miles between me and this location.

Once I was safe in the car, I took out my phone to assess any further damage. I had a text from my brother telling me he was home for the night, a text from Heather asking if I was back at school yet, and a text from Bryson. I tossed my phone on the passenger seat and rested my forehead on the steering wheel. I shouldn't have expected a text from Maci, but I still hoped she would let me know she made it back to campus okay.

Over break, I may have done too well of a job making sure that Maci knew I wanted nothing more than just a friendship. It was the only way to draw a clear line between what she deserved and what I could offer. She had to be reminded of the guy I was outside of our hangouts and the time we spent together, especially after the few days we had before leaving for break.

I replayed the scene repeatedly in my head of us saying goodbye at her apartment. Only in this updated version I kissed her, and I kissed her in a way that let her know I would be thinking about her every single day while I was away from her. In this version, I didn't sleep with anyone else while I was here. In this version, I called when I said I would call, and there weren't any drunken interruptions from other broads or pictures of half-naked girls.

But I didn't know how to be anything more than what I was currently doing to Cora. Maci already had one guy doing that to her. Right now, the only difference between him and me was our names.

A sharp pang came from my gut. I knew Bryson was already back in BG, and I had a good feeling I knew where he was waking up this morning. For Bryson, keeping a girl around for three months was out of character, and it completely sucked that Maci had to be the exception. I had *never* wanted someone this bad that I couldn't have before.

My phone buzzed on the seat. When it buzzed more than once, I looked over at the screen. It was my mom.

"What's up, Ma?" I mumbled. I dragged a hand down my face and leaned against the seat, waiting for the pounding in my head to subside.

"Hey, baby," she chirped. "Rough night?" The sound of pots and pans clanging in the background let me know that she was in the kitchen, and I was on speakerphone.

I smiled and relaxed at the sound of her voice. After a night out, she knew all too well what kind of position I was in by this time in the morning. "Not at all."

She laughed. "What time are you taking off today? You're coming home first, right? I have to be at the luncheon by eleven to help set up the gift baskets."

"I'll be there soon, Ma." I sighed. "I'm going to hang up now because I feel like my head is close to exploding."

"Drive safe." Her voice sounded further away and completely unphased by my hangover. "Alex should still be here when you get back too. Boy is still in bed, so it's safe to say he isn't in a hurry. I love you."

"Love you too." I hung up and started the trek back home.

Since it was a Sunday, there wouldn't be too much traffic on the outskirts of Charlotte. But since my head felt like it was splitting in two, I decided to take the scenic route to avoid any surprises. I loved coming home for breaks and an occasional long weekend visit, but North Carolina was a world away from Bowling Green, Ohio. A month had felt like a year, and I was ready to get a break from city life for a little while.

Since I had rolled into my hometown, it had been the usual pattern of reuniting with friends, locating a party or scene for the evening, going with the flow of where that night would take us, and hanging around someone's house all afternoon until we could repeat the cycle. Most of my friends went to school, but some had taken other avenues after graduation that kept them here all year round. Either way, whenever we got back together, it was as if no time had passed.

After twenty minutes, I rolled up to the gate and punched in our code. I was happy to see that Alex's car was still in the driveway, along with my mom's. As soon as I stepped out of the Jeep, I was greeted by a familiar voice.

"Jaxon Hayes." Bella smiled from the front porch. Her blonde curls were in a messy bun on top of her head, and she was in leggings and a light purple sweater.

"Bella Kingsley." I grinned and scooped her up in my arms.

Bella had been like a sister to me since I met her in elementary school. She quickly became close with Alex when we were growing up, and my mom completely latched onto the idea of having another girl in the house all the time. She came to holidays and family functions and even tagged along on a few of our vacations. There was a week in high school during my freshman year when she stayed with us because of a lousy fight with her mom. Bella was family.

She rested her hands on my chest and stared up at me. "I am so happy I got to see you before we left. My flight got in last night, and I was disappointed that you weren't here when Alex brought us back."

I stared at the freckles that ran along the bridge of her nose. I didn't even know that Bella was going to be in town.

Bella's gaze narrowed, and she slowly shook her head. "Your brother didn't tell you, did he?"

I played back all of the recent conversations Alex and I had. "Imma go with no."

"He's such an idiot. Come inside. Your mom said she has something to give you before you leave."

I followed Bella through the obnoxious double-door entrance that led into the foyer. It smelled like lavender, vanilla, and lemon Pledge. It smelled like home.

"Jax is back," Bella announced and led us into the kitchen, where Mom was putting the finishing touches on some bakery trays, and the familiar sound of Tina Turner played in the background.

"Hey, baby." Mom wiped her hands on her apron and untied it from her waist.

I admired her from behind the breakfast counter. She usually wore her tight dark curls in a ponytail, but she liked to wear them down when she was scheduled for a presentation. She had on red lipstick and some eye makeup that made her green eyes pop even more against her light-brown skin. Even though she didn't give birth to me, I always got comments about how we had the same green eyes. I loved it, and I loved her for being my mom.

However, Evelyn Hayes was not one to be messed with, especially dolled up and sporting one of her pantsuits.

"What's up, bro?" Alex's voice boomed from the foyer as he entered the kitchen. He smiled and shoved my shoulder on his way to the fridge. "You heading out soon?"

I crossed my arms over my chest and leaned against the counter. "I have a few things to pack up first. Someone told me you have something to tell me?" I widened my eyes and stared accusingly between Bella and my brother.

Bella covered her mouth and rolled her eyes in Alex's direction. She was hiding a toothy grin, and my brother bit his lip.

"You guys finally did it, didn't you?" I beamed.

A metal serving spoon clanged into the sink making everyone jump.

"Jaxon Reed!" Mom scolded me from across the counter.

"Date!" I added quickly and gestured toward Alex, who was now standing with his arms wrapped around Bella's shoulders. "They finally decided to date!"

"Mind in the gutter much, Ma?" Alex shook his head, pretending to be disappointed in our mom's quick outburst.

One glance from Mom warned us not to push her any further. Alex and I were a lot taller than her, but that look was just as scary now as it was when I was looking up at her as a kid.

"I swear the Lord could've warned me about having two boys," she muttered.

"Some girl you met in California, huh?" I teased the happy couple standing in front of me and shook my head. When we were growing up, everyone always told them they should date or at least see where it goes. The way they fit together was just unmatched. They looked perfect together. "It's about damn time."

"Alex wanted to tell you in person," Bella swooned.

Bella had a serious boyfriend when she graduated from high school, and when that didn't work out, she got into another relationship with a guy from her graduating class at Brown. Alex had dated around and gone out with tons of girls after high school. After he moved to California, I figured their shot was over and done with. It made me happy to see that I was very far off.

I stuck around to hear the story of how Bella went out to the west coast for her cousin's wedding and messaged Alex to see if he was free and if she could crash at his place. One thing led to another, and they decided to give it a shot.

"Three months!" I exclaimed and grabbed a banana off the counter. I wouldn't make it if I didn't get something in my stomach before this drive back to BG. "You have been dating for three months, and neither of you said a word." I shrugged. "Damn."

Three months put them back in October when Maci and I almost hooked up. It seemed like an eternity ago.

"Happy, happy, yes, yes." Mom waved her hands above the three giant cookie trays in front of her. "I need everyone to grab a tray and place them *gently* into the trunk of the Range Rover."

Once Mom's car was packed to the brim with everything she needed for her event, I kissed her goodbye and wrapped my arms tightly around her. She always cried when I left to go back to school, and it always pained me to see her so upset.

"I'll call you when I get there, okay?" I promised.

"Please be careful. You know how I get when you make that long drive by yourself," she choked, holding back a few tears.

"I know, Ma. I will."

She took a deep breath and continued, "This came for you today." She pulled a letter from her suit jacket, and I immediately recognized the bright red stamp in the bottom left corner.

**MAILED FROM
A STATE
CORRECTIONAL
INSTITUTION**

"I wasn't expecting that." I searched her face to see if there was anything else. The letter felt heavy in my hand, and a knot formed in my stomach. It had been five years since I received one of them.

"It came yesterday morning while you were out. It's up to you what you decide to do with it," Mom explained gently. Usually, my dad delivered any kind of stress-related news to me regarding my birth parents. Reed was better at keeping emotion out of things.

I nodded and ran a hand through my hair, unsure what to say next.

"And call your dad," she commanded, her tone shifting back to normal. "His flight should be taking off soon, and I know he will want to talk to you before he lands."

Just as she began her last sentence, my phone buzzed in my sweatpants pocket. We laughed at the name that lit up the screen. It was Dad.

"I always say that man knows everything!" Mom wiped under her eyes for any evidence of our goodbye.

"I love you." I grinned and backed away so she would make her luncheon on time. I also had a few more things to pack and more goodbyes to give.

I watched her drive away and called Dad back as soon as she cleared the gate of the property. Even though I was saying goodbye to my life in Charlotte for a few months, I had one hell of a life in Bowling Green to return to.

Chapter Twenty-Eight

MACI

January 2016

I really needed to consider using one blanket if I was sharing a bed with someone. Not that it was a common occurrence, but did all men run like space heaters during the night?

It was a little after nine, and Bryson was still asleep. Since he was against the wall, I crept out of bed without waking him up. I needed a shower and a cup of coffee ASAP. I decided the shower took priority since I was covered in sweat and had sex not just once but twice last night.

The noisy plumbing in the shower sprang to life, and I stood under the cascading water for a few moments to bask in the warmth. It ran down my stomach and back, washing away last night's decisions and returning my sense of self back to my limbs. I never felt recovered after sex until after a shower. It was like an emotional reset button.

The familiar scent of my rainwater and lavender body wash filled the bathroom, and I let my mind wander. I was excited to see Katie and eager to hear how the rest of her break with Connor went. It felt good to have Bryson reach out so soon after getting back, and I felt okay with my headspace surrounding him and his bullshit.

Just as I was getting around to Jaxon, I felt a hand on my waist.

"Scoot over." Bryson ushered me toward the front of the tub and climbed in next to me.

"Seriously?" I whined and then laughed when I saw the smile on his face. "You couldn't let me have my shower?"

He ran his gaze up and down my wet body and shrugged. "I figured you could share."

Since my shower lacked a condom dispenser, we completed round three back in my room.

After another post-sex rinse, I relaxed comfortably in the corner of my bed, aimlessly scrolling through Instagram. It was the usual feed after a winter break with tons of vacation photos, exotic location trips, and groups of high school friends reconnecting. Suddenly my page looked incredibly bare, regardless of all the cute pictures I had on my account.

I gasped at my screen when an adorable photo of Katie and Connor in front of Cloud Gate popped up next. Since Bryson hopped back into the shower, I surveyed the empty room around me. "Are we social media official?"

Just as I double-tapped the photo, Bryson's phone went off on my desk. Even though it was on the other side of the room, I could tell it was a text message. It was rare that Bryson was without his phone, but I couldn't let my curiosity get the better of me. I never wanted to be that girl—the crazy obsessive type of woman who, in the end, lost their mind because of the asshole they had second-guessed since the beginning.

So I decided not to be. I drafted a text to Katie to see what time she was arriving back from Chicago in an attempt to distract myself. As soon as I thought I was in the clear, the phone went off again.

"Can you see if that's my roommate and if he needs to be let into the apartment? He forgot his keys when he left," Bryson shouted from the shower. His voice was calm and collected like I would find nothing on his phone even if I wanted to search for it.

At the risk of sounding too creepy, I didn't tell him that Connor wasn't back yet because Katie was still forty-five minutes away. I knew for a fact that Jaxon had his keys, so by process of elimination, it had to be their fourth roommate that started with a J.

I knew way too much about a group of people I didn't even live with.

"Yeah, I can!" I shouted back and walked over to the phone.

I tapped the screen, and a preview of the message appeared under the name Kenzie. Underneath that message was a preview of the second message. Deciding that it was better to draw the line there, I placed the phone back on the desk and backed away before I could shift gears in my decision-making.

The door to the bathroom was slightly cracked. I turned my head to deliver the answer to his question when his phone lit up again. This time, one word appeared clear as day in the message preview.

Kenz

...chlamydia

"Wait, what?" I exclaimed to the same audience I asked about Katie and Connor going social media official.

Once I opened the first message, the rest of the read was a black hole. A tornado could've raged through my apartment, and I would've had no idea.

Kenz

Hey

Kind of awkward and I don't know how to say it

Just letting you know I have chlamydia.

The words became harder to make out the more I read. A fourth text came in, and I realized that the words weren't hard to read, but my hands shook uncontrollably. My chest was on fire, and I felt like one of those cartoon characters with steam blowing out their ears.

Kenz

I am reaching out to the last few people I hooked up with. Sorry.

I marched into the bathroom with the phone still in my hand and a completely unscripted reaction I was prepared to roll out without warning. I burst through the door and dragged the shower curtain open. Bryson stared at me with soap dripping down his chest.

"No roommates need you, but some girl with chlamydia does." I chucked his phone into the tub. I left him under the running water and went straight to the living room to gather his shit.

The more time that passed, the more upset I felt. I could accept Bryson as a liar, but this crossed the line. It was one thing for him to say he wasn't sleeping with anyone else, but it was a whole other lens to look through when he was rinsing off the sex we just had, and I was reading about an STD.

"What the fuck?" Bryson stormed into the living room with a towel around his waist. He wiped his phone off and scrolled through what I assumed was the evidence I had just read.

"Get out," I demanded and pointed to the door. I grabbed his candy and his phone charger and threw them in his book bag.

"What the fuck is your deal?" He backed into my room and returned wearing the clothes from the night before. "Seriously, what is your problem?"

"Did you not read your phone?" I raised my eyebrows. "I get that you are *very* far removed from saying anything truthful. But how the hell are you still acting like there is nothing for me to be mad about?"

"There is nothing to be mad about." His tone read like I was completely out of line, and his face was stoic. It was almost like this conversation was a waste of time for him to even have. I had never seen him like this.

I pointed to the phone in his hand. "I just had sex with you twenty minutes ago. Some girl texts you that she has chlamydia, and I'm not allowed to be upset?"

"We have only used condoms. Chill out," he snapped. He grabbed his bookbag and hoisted it on his shoulder, making a beeline toward the front door.

"Are you *fucking* serious? You tell me you aren't hooking up with anyone else, and in one text message, I find out that not only do you have an STD, but you lied about some stupid bullshit I told you I didn't even care about!"

"Really? This is you not caring?" Bryson spat and gave me a look like he was completely disgusted with what was standing in front of him. "I don't owe you any kind of answer. It's none of your business what I do. I haven't seen that girl in over a year. Probably just some crusty hoe using this as an excuse to reach out."

I couldn't afford to focus on his disgusting language right now. My head was spinning. I wasn't in the wrong, but somehow he was turning this conversation around for it to be my problem.

I rolled my eyes. "Whatever, Bryson."

He slammed the door behind him, and everything was silent. I sat on the arm of the couch with my hand over my mouth. I didn't think feeling anger, embarrassment, and sadness simultaneously was possible. It was a wild cocktail brewing in my stomach. A wave of nausea overcame me, leaving an unsettling cramp in my gut.

Part of me thought he would turn around and knock on my door so he could try and explain. When he didn't return, anger won over the emotional battle in my headspace.

He lied to me. I had every right to be upset.

Did he even have chlamydia? I actually didn't have that official answer. But I just accused him of having it, so why didn't he provide a straightforward answer?

Bryson was a dog, but I had a feeling that anything that stood in the way of him having sex was unacceptable in his book of nonsense.

After a few deep breaths and an attempt to dissect what the fuck just happened, I locked the front door and ran into my room, where I allowed myself to cry for five minutes before I got my shit together and tried to figure out what to do next.

Chapter Twenty-Nine

Jaxon

Januuary 2016

After five minutes of driving around the lot, I finally found a parking spot near our building.

Exactly five minutes after nine, I texted my mom to tell her I had made it back. She responded immediately and said she would call me tomorrow night when I was done with classes.

As soon as I unloaded my Jeep, I would have to find out when my classes actually were. My student portal unlocked months ago for the spring semester, and since I was getting down to my last handful of courses, I made sure I signed up right away. I just hoped that I chose a reasonable hour to start my Monday schedule.

I could hear noise coming from the apartment before I even got inside. I was halfway up the stairs to the second floor when I heard Jared yelling at Connor. They were in their usual positions on the couch, completely invested in a game of Call of Duty. Half a bottle of Tito's was on the coffee table in front of them, along with two shot glasses, and a twenty-four case of Bud Light.

"Already, huh?" I grinned over the bass booming from the surround sound and tossed my bags on the living room floor.

Jared took his shot and leaned forward on the couch to see me. "Do you need any help?"

"Actually, yeah." I gestured toward the door. "My mom sent a bunch of food, and I have a few more bags."

With Connor and Jared's help, we emptied the Jeep in one quick trip. Soon the kitchen counters were littered with snacks, bottles of alcohol, and refills of cleaning supplies. I stared at the haul and shook my head. This would have to wait until tomorrow. All I wanted to do was unpack my bedding and pass out.

Bryson came through the front door a little after ten. He threw his book bag on the recliner without saying a word to any of us. I could tell by his expression and how he paced down the hallway that he was pissed about something. I wasn't sure where he was coming from, but since he had his book bag with him, that meant he had been gone all day.

"What's up, Kennedy?" I leaned over the counter and watched him walk back down the hall. After a minute or so, he finally made eye contact with me and shook his head.

"It's that girl I've been hooking up with, man," he scoffed. "She lost her fucking mind on me today."

This drew Connor's attention. He was officially dating Maci's roommate, Katie, and was also very well aware that I was friends with Maci. He leaned forward and grabbed my attention from the couch behind Bryson. I gave him a quick nod so he knew not to press the issue any further.

Bryson wasn't just hooking up with Maci. He could be talking about a few girls, and Connor seemed to forget that detail.

"Which one?" I adjusted my tone so it came out as a joke.

"That Maci chick! She was pissed because some girl I slept with like a year ago messaged me and told me that she has the C."

"The C?" Jared asked without looking away from his game.

"Chlamydia," I answered quickly. "Dude, do you have chlamydia?"

Bryson's mouth formed a hard line, and the rest of us busted out in a fit of hysterics. My laugh lasted a little longer than theirs because I had the pleasure of picturing the interaction he was pissed about. Maci must've been livid, especially since I had just told her before break that Bryson had no problem lying to her.

"No, you assholes," Bryson snapped before a smile appeared on his face. He couldn't resist being back here with us and bullshitting about our sex lives. He directed his next question toward me. "Do you remember that Kenzie chick from Miami?"

I nodded. "That was like a year ago."

Bryson lifted his arms in emphasis. "No shit!"

"Why did you let the girl you're banging have your phone? Are you nuts?" Jared asked. The game he and Connor were playing was paused now, and everyone was invested in Bryson's story.

I fought to keep my facial expression from shifting. I got used to not having a reaction when Bryson talked about Maci, but hearing Jared talk about her as "the girl you're banging" left a bad taste in my mouth.

Connor picked at a button on his controller, and I could tell he was getting a little uncomfortable with the conversation. The few days before break allowed Connor to get to know Maci. He liked her, and he liked her even more since she was Katie's roommate.

"I was in the shower, and my phone kept going off. I thought it was one of you guys needing to get into the apartment..." He pointed to Jared. "Specifically, you because your dumbass never has your keys. So I asked her to check it for me, and she read Kenzie's messages. She completely lost it."

Jared restarted the game and chuckled. "You're too much."

"Like what the fuck," Bryson moaned and then smirked in my direction. "These leeches, man. I left her place earlier this morning, and I'm still annoyed by it."

I laughed because I would have had the same reaction if I were in his position. "I'm going to bed." I rounded the end cap of the counter and placed a hand on Bryson's shoulder. "Just another day."

He shoved me, and I shrugged at Connor. He shook his head and widened his eyes to let me know he was staying out of it.

I shut my bedroom door behind me and threw myself onto the bed. I didn't even bother to change out of the clothes I spent all day driving in. I was too tired to shower and didn't feel like unpacking anything else tonight.

My schedule this semester wasn't bad at all. I had three classes every day of the week, and nothing started before nine. My earliest class was on Tuesdays and Thursdays, and I was done pretty early on Fridays.

It would be weird not having a class with Maci this semester. I was in the habit of seeing her every week. We hadn't spoken since New Year's, and that was ten days ago. It was the longest we'd ever gone without talking.

I pulled out my phone and brought up our text stream. I decided to take my shot.

Jaxon

Bryson doesn't have chlamydia. She's some girl from last year.

I didn't want to over-explain it or bring up any new topics. This gave me the perfect excuse to extend an olive branch that was directly related to what happened to her recently. The text bubbles appeared and then disappeared on my screen. Two whole minutes went by before she responded.

Maci

Noted.

Chapter Thirty

MACI

January 2016

"I'm going to need you to give me a *very* detailed summary of what happened," Katie demanded from my passenger seat.

Back at the apartment, I allowed Katie one hour of peace to unpack before I exploded into her bedroom with the Bryson chlamydia story. Since we had already planned to go grocery shopping when she returned, all follow-up questions had to wait until we were on our way to Kroger. So far, she was doing a horrendous job of hiding the amused look on her face based on the high-level summary.

I took a deep breath and provided more details about the treacherous tale. "He was in the shower and told me to grab his phone . . ." I paused for dramatic effect, and Katie leaned eagerly in her seat. She was dangerously testing the elasticity of the seatbelt. "Some girl was texting him about having chlamydia, so I naturally assumed he had it. We had just had sex, Katie. I was a *tad* on edge."

"So you just accused him of having chlamydia?"

"Yes, Katie, I accused my hookup of having chlamydia. We established that information. Now, what do I do?"

We rolled to a stop at the red light on Wooster, and I turned to face her. The logical side of Katie had taken over.

"I don't think you can recover from this." She furrowed her brow. "Jaxon told you he doesn't have it and gave you the details Bryson wouldn't. I think you just need to apologize and wait it out. If he reaches back out, that's great. If not . . ." She shrugged and shot me a sympathetic grin.

"I don't think the usual 'I'm sorry' is going to cut it here." I laughed nervously. The light turned green, and I stepped on the gas.

"You bought him Skittles, Mace." Katie gestured toward the backseat, which held a few bags from our Walmart trip.

Returning home from a long break meant a desperately needed grocery haul, even if that meant a shopping trip on a Sunday evening. Our apartment was starting to look like we had been robbed.

"Well, yeah, I know he likes them." I shrugged. "And I don't like your tone. I can hear the judgment."

"So an 'I'm sorry' won't suffice, but a bag of Wild Berry Skittles is supposed to set the tone for forgiveness?" Katie cackled.

I pursed my lips and had to bite the inside of my cheek to keep from laughing. "I don't know, Katie. There is no *manual* on how to apologize for accusing someone of having chlamydia. There is no *reference guide* on how to navigate the shitshow that has become my life. God, Katie, when did this become my life?"

"Halloween, I think it was," Katie murmured to the window.

"Tell me about Connor," I pleaded as we pulled into our parking lot. "Please shine some light back into my perspective on love and relationships. I need to hear about how happy you are."

During the multiple trips it took going up and down the stairs from my car to the apartment to unload groceries, Katie filled me in on everything Connor. By the time we had the fridge stocked and our cabinets looking like people actually lived here, my cheeks hurt from smiling.

"He texted me every day over break. Eventually, he asked if he could come and visit me before we headed back to school. So he drove out to see me, and I showed him Chicago. It was the best time I have ever had with a guy," she gushed, and I could tell she was trying to hold back her excitement at the risk of sounding too cheesy.

So I boiled over for her.

"Katie!" I squealed and jumped onto the couch. "So when did things become official? Who asked who?"

She took a deep breath and smiled. "He asked me a few minutes before we took that picture under Cloud Gate. He was so sweet. He said he understood that we only met a few weeks ago, but he didn't want to go back to school with me thinking that he was interested in anyone else." She shrugged. "I didn't even hesitate, Mace, and you know me when it comes to making a decision like that."

Katie only dove into something serious after weighing the pros and cons. I was shocked that she didn't make Connor draw up a chart right there in the heart of Chicago.

"I also slept with him," Katie added quickly. She turned and was suddenly invested in the drink choices from the fridge door.

"Uhmmm." I widened my eyes and threw one of the couch pillows at her head. She doubled over in laughter and threw it back.

"Bitch!" I exclaimed. "Tell me everything!"

"Let's just say that Connor is easily the sweetest guy I have ever met. But that sweetness no longer exists once he's in the bedroom. I have *never* had a guy talk to me the way he did. If I think about it, I will get goosebumps all over again."

I applauded above my head. It was a perfect answer. I stared at Katie and sighed, unable to hide my toothy grin and the happiness that swelled in my chest at my best friend finding someone that made her happy.

"I was going to head over to Connor's for the night." Katie sighed. "Want me to extend your Skittles peace offering?"

"That would be perfect, actually." I tossed her the bag of candy and leaned back into the couch cushions. "It will save me from having that awkward moment."

"And then whatever happens next is up to him." She threw her crossbody bag over her shoulder and stood at the front door. "Anything you want me to mention to anyone else who may be there?" Her question was laced with hopeful anticipation.

"One issue at a time, Katie." I managed a small smile, and she shook her head. I heard her internal argument from across the room.

The brutally honest Katie told me to shut the fuck up and just call Jaxon. She emphasized that he and I were *just friends* and that he had more to his life outside of Bowling Green, Ohio. She said that even though it sucked to know he was sleeping with other people, I was the one hooking up with one of his best friends.

I argued that I was just doing what he said he wanted. But at the same time, by doing what he wanted, I felt like he was punishing me for it. I added that it also really hurt my feelings when he lied to Bryson about knowing me.

When our silent conversation ended, Katie nodded and slipped into the hallway.

And just like that, I thought about everything that brought me to this point. Just one semester was all it took for me to be completely turned upside down by two guys I didn't even know a few months ago. I was a little nervous about what the second semester would bring.

Chapter Thirty-One

JAXON

WHEN THE NEXT MORNING rolled around, I woke up ready to start the new semester. Because of my schedule, I had time on Mondays in the morning to get a workout in before class. Once I hit the gym, showered, and made it to campus, I stopped by Dunkin Donuts and made my way to East Hall.

Walking outside officially sucked now. Before break, walking around on campus had just been cold. January brought a whole different kind of winter weather to Ohio, and since Bowling Green was in the middle of nowhere and surrounded by absolutely nothing, the wind chill was unreal.

I gripped my hot coffee and shoved my free hand into the pocket of my jacket. It felt a little weird getting anything other than the iced hazelnut coffee I usually got with Maci, but my hands couldn't handle the cold.

East Hall was one of the older buildings on campus. It offered dusty-smelling heat and old brick walls. It was the type of building that gave you allergies even if you didn't have any.

Introduction to Economics was the last class I needed to complete my business minor. Growing up with two parents who were heavily involved with their own businesses and brands, I knew this class would be a massive waste of time for me. I glanced over the syllabus and sunk further into my seat at the back of the room. It was bullshit that you couldn't test out of classes.

The professor was a man who looked to be in his fifties. He wore big glasses, a clean-cut sweater, and some dark jeans. When he spoke to the room, he focused on the giant textbook in front of him. I rolled my eyes and took a long sip of my coffee. Nothing was worse than a morning class with a teacher who was equally as dull as the subject.

About ten minutes into the lecture, I caved and pulled out my phone. When the professor turned to the whiteboard to write notes, I went into my inbox in search of some entertainment.

Bryson

> Why the fuck did I sign up for an 8:30 lecture on Mondays?

I laughed and kept scrolling.

Connor

> The parking lot for Katie's apartment doesn't tow, does it?

> I'm going to crash there tonight.

My smile disappeared, and I stared at Connor's texts. I had thought about Maci the entire drive back from Charlotte. I thought about her before I passed out last night. And I thought about her when I got my coffee this morning. I hated that she wasn't one of the unopened text messages in my inbox. I hated that I didn't know what to say if I sent her a text.

All because I wanted to make sure there were clear lines drawn.

Connor didn't say anything back. He wasn't someone who pried when it came to drama or personal business, but I knew he was curious when it came to Maci and me. I slipped my phone into my book bag for the rest of class. Suddenly I didn't want anything to do with the world outside of this riveting economics lecture.

⁓

It was almost ten-thirty when my class let out. Since this class was full, I waited until the hordes of people gathered at the door made it into the hallway before I attempted my escape.

I drained the rest of my lukewarm coffee and threw the empty cup in the trash. The building was loud with conversation as two more doors opened and released more people into the hallway. I turned to face the closest exit when I saw the familiar dark curls and bright blue book bag.

"Katie?" I lowered the hood of my jacket and waited a moment for her to turn around.

Katie spun around and smiled as soon as she saw me. She took three giant steps, and I pulled her into my chest for a hug.

"Jaxon Hayes." She adjusted the straps on her book bag. It was tight around the zippers and looked like it was about to burst with the number of items she had shoved into the pockets. "It's nice to see you. It's weird that it has taken this long to see you, actually."

I offered a small smile for her honest confession. Katie always told it how it was, and she was always caught up with what was going on with Maci. I would have loved to see her reaction to the chlamydia incident. There were certain scenes you just couldn't make up in your head.

"I'm figuring out how to fix that." I ran a hand over my fresh cut. I was thankful that my barber back home could fit me in before I left.

Katie sighed and crossed her arms over her chest. "You guys will figure it out. Connor is very invested in your story by the way."

"You mean your *boyfriend*?" I teased, and she rolled her eyes. "Of course he is."

"Never would've met him if it wasn't for you coming to the rescue." Katie looked behind her to survey the area before she continued, "By the way, I want to thank you for what you said to Tyler."

I cocked my head and stuck my hands in the pockets of my jacket. My run-in with Tyler happened over a month ago, and I never intended for Katie to hear it.

"I heard you that morning when we were at Kroger." She lowered her voice. "There was never a good time to bring it up. But I wanted to say thank you. Tyler hasn't been a problem since."

"I told you I would have a talk with that guy." I shrugged. The idea of Katie stressing over some asshat like Tyler made my blood boil. "Connor is a great guy. I am happy you guys worked out."

"Talk to Maci," Katie urged, changing the subject back to my problems. "I have to head to my next class, but don't be a stranger. I have all kinds of recipes for us to try on Thursdays or whatever night dinner ends up being."

It was nice to know that Katie was optimistic about me coming around again. I watched her walk away and laughed when she turned around to make sure I heard her. I nodded and headed in the opposite direction toward the student union.

Seeing Katie reminded me how much I missed the life that I had left here before break. When I left for break, I was spending all of my free time with Maci and hating the fact that she was sleeping with Bryson. I had wanted to see Maci in person since I drove onto the exit for Bowling Green. After the fight she had with Bryson yesterday, there was no way they would be back to normal soon. It would be wonderful if that was the final exchange between the two of them, but the last time I checked, Maci had feelings for Bryson. One of them would cave. The more time I waited to reach out, the more I risked her never talking to me again.

As I passed Jamba Juice, I pulled out my phone and scrolled down my messages until I got to our thread.

Jaxon

Do Thursdays still work for you?

She would know what I was talking about without any more detail. I was taking a big chance asking about our old routine as if nothing had happened, but Thursdays had always been our thing. If we were going to move past this, I wanted the friendship we had or nothing at all. The second option left an ache in my gut.

I scanned the menu while I waited for a text back, trying to distract myself from the fact that I was nervous to get a response. I guess there was a first time for everything. I ordered a strawberry banana smoothie and paced back and forth in front of the pickup counter.

"Jaxon?" The brunette on the other side of the counter called out. She smiled and leaned over the counter to hand me my drink. I returned the gesture and quickly turned so she wouldn't engage in a conversation. She looked like she had some sort of compliment on the tip of her tongue, and I didn't have the bandwidth for it.

My phone vibrated in my pocket. It was Maci.

Maci

I'll check with the chef but that should be okay.

I smiled so hard at her response that my cheeks hurt. I sipped my smoothie and took a deep breath. The gigantic weight that had been sitting on my chest for a few weeks slowly disintegrated. I officially had plans to see Maci in a few days.

Now I just had to get through the next few days and hope she didn't change her mind.

Chapter Thirty-Two

MACI

January 2016

My Monday schedule was kind of a joke. But after the first forty-eight hours I had spent back in BG, it was a much-needed break from the mess that was my life. I didn't have a class until noon, and after that class was over I was done for the day.

Tuesdays, however, were a whole different ballgame.

I had three classes back to back, with my last class being a required section for my methods placement next year. Educational Psychology consisted of methodologies and theory mostly, but it did offer opportunities outside of the traditional classroom experience that I was excited about. There were about twenty of us in the course, and the professor made a point to get to know each and every one of us since we would be together for two two-hour sessions every week.

I truly didn't know how I was going to survive over five hours of lectures every Tuesday and Thursday.

Educational Psychology had about fifteen minutes left in the class, and Dr. Knight showed no signs of stopping her general rundown of the course expectations and the semester calendar. I took a long sip of water, wishing it was iced coffee or something with the appropriate amount of caffeine to shake me out of my desire to daydream.

"On Thursday, I will have applications for internships taking place next summer. They come from all different spaces in education, and I encourage all of you to apply for at least two or three of them." Dr. Knight turned to write some page numbers on the whiteboard behind her. "You will need to read the following chapters for Thursday's class. There will be discussions, and you will be required to draw up a sample assignment focusing on one of the methodologies discussed in the chapters."

After she had jotted down the chapters for Thursday, Dr. Knight dismissed the class. My anxiety started to cloud my chest, putting pressure on my temples and making my mouth go dry. It was the second day back in session, and I already felt overwhelmed with the amount of work I received. I knew that everything would ease into place once I got into the routine for the semester, but it didn't make the starting point any easier.

I lingered at the table in the middle of the room while I waited for the traffic to clear out near the exit. It was littered with pamphlets for a few of the internships Dr. Knight just mentioned.

"Take a few!" she urged and fanned the table with her hands like a game show host.

"Any recommendations?" My eyes drifted over names like Phoenix, Manhattan, Santa Barbara, Tampa, Denver, and Atlanta.

"Honestly, it really just depends on what you're looking for. All of them are great. Take a few options to look over!"

"I will. Thank you." I gave her a small smile and slipped a few flyers into my bag.

Once I stepped into the hall, I called Katie to let her know I was on my way back to the apartment. Only when I went to pull up her contact info, I saw that I had an unread text message. It was from Bryson.

I took a deep breath and moved to the side of the hall so people could pass me. I had a few options for how to respond, but I opted for the simple route.

Had my Skittles attempt *actually* worked? I pursed my lips and decided I needed a different perspective. I pushed on the exit door of the education building and started the cold trek to Lot J. I needed to hear my voice of reason.

"What's up?" Katie answered on the first ring.

"Is Connor with you?"

"No, I'm seeing him later. Everything okay?"

I tucked my free arm against my chest to try and shield myself from the incoming whirlwind of snow. "Bryson texted me. He asked what I was doing later."

"Seriously?" Katie gasped, sounding much more energetic than when she first answered. "I am not even sure what to say to that."

"Me either! That's why I am calling you!" I laughed at how ridiculous I felt. "Did I really save this with a bag of Skittles?"

Katie cackled, which made me laugh harder.

"You should ask him to do something outside of the bedroom," Katie suggested. I sensed her hesitation but appreciated the direct response.

"But that's the best place for him," I whined.

The idea of being with Bryson outside of my apartment was just odd. Where would we go? What would we do? It was as if that option was far beyond something I could comprehend. I wasn't even sure if he would agree to do something other than get each other off.

"I think you have a more important question to ask your-self. But since you aren't going to ask it, I'll ask it for you"—Katie prepared her question—"you're seeing Jaxon on Thursday, and hopefully, you guys can click back to what-ever you were before."

"That isn't a question, Katie," I challenged.

"Is Bryson what you want?" Katie demanded.

Another whip of icy wind hit me from all directions. I threw my bag in the passenger seat and shut the door, crank-ing my heat on high and putting Katie on speaker since I was in a private space.

"Maci?" Katie asked.

"I'm here." I slumped in my seat. My silence was throwing us both off.

Of course, I didn't *want* to want Bryson. Was it concerning that I kind of had feelings for my hookup that would never be more? I was ninety percent sure at this point that it was.

If it were up to me, I would choose Jaxon. I would choose Jaxon every time. But unfortunately, it didn't matter what I wanted when it came to deciding between the two of them. Jaxon made it clear that he wouldn't choose me. I had spoken to a handful of women over break who could testify to that conclusion.

"It doesn't really matter what I want, Katie. Jaxon just wants to be friends. Bryson is a hookup, and my actual love life is just riding the bench and waiting for her turn," I added dramatically.

"You know my hopeless romantic self is a sucker for a cheesy personification of love." She sighed, and I felt her eyes roll through the phone. "And we both know that so far in this Fun Dip experiment, you are so not the hookup type."

"The experiment isn't over yet, Katie. Give me some credit!"

"I'll give you credit when you emotionally detach yourself from Bryson," Katie snapped.

"Fine." I put the Elantra in reverse. "I'll see you in a few. I'm leaving campus now."

I hung up with Katie and responded to Bryson while I waited for a train to pass.

Maci

I'm pretty busy this week.

Let's go out Friday.

I threw my phone on the passenger seat and gripped the steering wheel. Maybe Katie was right. I wasn't the hookup type, plain and simple. But if I accepted that about myself, was I wrong for just wanting to have great sex?

The train passed, and I followed the line of cars over the tracks. My apartment building was only a few houses down from the crossing. I turned into the parking lot, and out of the corner of my eye, I saw my screen light up. I put the car in park and reached for my phone.

Bryson

Just the two of us?

Maci

A bunch of us are going out since it's the first weekend back. Tag along?

The conversation bubbles appeared and then disappeared on my screen. While I waited for his response to my second attempt at my question, I cycled through my usual list of party people. I would be able to assemble a crew for this weekend with no problems. Pregaming at our apartment and meeting out at the bars. It would be no different than the time I invited Jaxon to go out with Katie and me.

Katie would be totally open to going out this weekend, and that meant Connor would come too. If I invited Bryson, did that mean Jaxon would be there?

Bryson

> Yeah we can meet up. The guys were going to go out anyway this weekend.

> Friday?

I desperately wanted to ask if Jaxon would be one of those guys on Friday. But instead of being direct with what I wanted to know, I went with a much more casual response. According to Jaxon, we weren't supposed to be close, and if I brought him up, that would be weird.

Maci

> Sounds good! I'll text you Friday to see where you're at.

Bryson

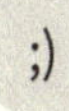

Two things came out of that short conversation.

The first thing was I instantly stressed at hanging out with Bryson and Jaxon in a bar scene. Drunk Maci had proven with both Drunk Bryson and Drunk Jaxon that not all decisions could be thoughtfully made when we got together.

The second thing was I could confirm that the chlamydia argument was finally put to rest between Bryson and me. He had agreed to hang out in a place where people would actually see us together, and everyone knew how effective a winking emoji could be when it came to texting.

It was just an unspoken gesture in my generation.

Chapter Thirty-Three

JAXON

January 2016

This was now the second time I walked up the stairs to Maci's apartment, unsure of how she would greet me when she answered the door. It couldn't be worse than the first time when she answered the door with Bryson on the other side of it, and I was buzzed off a bottle of Jack Daniel's. All of the possible scenarios I played in my head for this reunion already looked better than the first time.

So I wasn't sure why I hesitated to knock. I tapped loudly on the door with my middle knuckle two times and waited. Just as I removed my earbuds, Maci stood in the doorway, wearing a long sleeve shirt and baggy gray sweatpants. As soon as she looked me up and down, that familiar right dimple appeared on the side of her mouth. Even though she looked exhausted, I still found everything about her attractive.

I didn't realize I was smiling until I went to smile back at her.

"What's up, Mace?" I said hoarsely and cleared my throat. The swell in my chest proved how much I missed her over break.

She let out a sigh and her shoulders relaxed. "Hey."

She took two steps toward me to close the space between us. Her tiny arms wrapped around my waist, and I pulled her into me, pressing her hard into my chest and resting my chin on her head. I took in her familiar scent of lavender mixed with the perfume she wore. She smelled like the night we went out.

She went to turn into the living room, and I grabbed her wrist.

"Hey," I said softly.

She met my gaze, and the words caught in my throat.

"If you ever ignore me again, Maci Lawson, I know where you live now, and I'll find you."

She smiled at the familiar line she pulled on me a few months ago. I tugged on her wrist to let her know I wasn't done.

"Don't do that to me again," I whispered.

Her eyes softened, and I wasn't sure if it was the moment of vulnerability or the fact that I could read her without words, but I knew she felt the same way.

"Perfect timing!" Katie's high-pitched voice came from the kitchen. "Once Connor gets out of the shower, we can eat."

I stepped into the living room and closed the front door behind me. I tossed my bag on the side of the couch like I usually did and threw an arm around Katie. She smiled over her Instant Pot, and I glanced around the kitchen. It was as if no time had passed at all.

"The place looks bare without your Christmas decorations," I observed and inched back toward the food. "Whatcha makin'?"

"Baked potato soup," Katie said proudly. "There is French bread and salad too."

"Very classy." I nodded.

The apartment felt like a sauna with all of Katie's cooking happening in the kitchen. I tossed my beanie on the dining table and slipped out of my jacket.

"What's up, J?" Connor emerged from Katie's bedroom with a massive grin on his face.

I watched him walk over to Katie. He slipped an arm around her waist and gave her a kiss on the cheek. She giggled at whatever he whispered in her ear. They looked like a nauseating Hallmark movie couple.

I glanced over my shoulder at Maci. She was sitting in her usual corner of the couch and typing away on her laptop, so I made my way over and took the empty cushion beside her.

"Are you still watching the tree people?" I gestured to the TV, and her eyes were immediately on me.

"We don't disrespect *One Tree Hill* in this house, Jaxon Hayes," she deadpanned, and Katie laughed from the kitchen. "You'll watch it with me one day."

"I doubt that." I leaned closer to her and propped my feet on the coffee table. "Who are these people?"

"These are the *Sex and the City* girls," Maci said proudly and closed her laptop.

She was eager to lay this plot line on me. One of the only times she cut into the middle of doing schoolwork was to educate someone about the show she was watching. That someone was mostly me.

"The curly-haired one is Carrie Bradshaw," she explained and adjusted herself so that her feet were in my lap and her back was against the armrest of the couch. I leaned more into her legs, and we fell into our usual binge-watching position.

"She's a sex columnist in New York City, and those are her three best girlfriends," she continued, excited to tell me about all of the different characters, current storylines, and which episode she was on in the series.

"So this chick just comes to lunch and makes her friends listen to her bullshit every day?" I pointed at the screen, somehow invested in the lunch conversation being had about Carrie giving up smoking for Aidan.

"Damn, Jaxon." Katie appeared on the floor in front of me with a steaming bowl of soup and a small salad. "Disrespecting *One Tree Hill* and *Sex and the City* in one day? You might not be invited back."

"You guys just need better shows," I stated matter-of-factly.

"Says the guy who hasn't taken his eyes off the screen since he sat down," Maci challenged.

Connor joined Katie on the floor at the coffee table. At the sight of two dinners in front of me, I forced myself up and jogged into the kitchen. Maci followed behind me soon after.

"I like your hair short." She smiled when I passed her a bowl.

"It was lookin' a little rough," I admitted. "How is your new schedule?" I wanted to tell her that my schedule wasn't as good now that we didn't have class together, but I didn't.

"Busy. It actually sucked. My classes seemed way easier last semester compared to what I've had so far this week."

"When are you on campus?"

"Mondays and Fridays are pretty low-key, which is nice. Yesterday wasn't bad, but Tuesdays and Thursdays are horrible. Today I had over five hours of lectures to sit through." She rolled her eyes and topped her salad with ranch dressing. She passed me the bottle, and I added it to mine.

"It will get better." I popped a cherry tomato in my mouth and turned toward the living room. "Just like Bryson's chlamydia."

Katie's cackle took over the space, and I bit my lip so I wouldn't react to the expressions happening around me. Connor shook his head at the TV screen and tried not to laugh. Maci's eyes went wide, and her mouth fell open. I held her gaze, knowing full well the risk I had taken when I let that comment fly into the open air. It was a fresh wound, and we had just reunited less than an hour ago. But the Maci I knew before break would've embraced the dig because that would mean we were back to normal.

I watched her expression loosen, and a shocked smile appeared on her face. She smacked me on the shoulder, and I doubled over in hysterics, giving Katie and Connor permission to join in.

"You suck, you know that?" she said softly, so only I could hear. "I may cancel my subscription to your Snapchat porn channel if you keep it up."

My smile disappeared, and it was her turn to burst into hysterics.

"What did we miss?" Katie leaned forward and did her best to look around the counter.

Maci was dialed in on my reaction, and I could feel myself losing against the witty grin plastered on her face. She looked me up and down. "You didn't miss anything."

It was hard not to get turned on when Maci challenged me. She never hesitated to call me out, which was something I wasn't used to unless it was coming from one of the guys. Sure, broads had called me names, screamed in my face, and even threatened to run me over with their car. But when words left Maci's mouth, they held a different meaning.

I was right back in her bedroom that night when I said no. That same night I pretty much gave her up to Bryson. I wasn't sure that if I could go back, I would make a different decision. I wouldn't sleep with her, but I would make damn sure that she didn't run into Bryson. He was the spitting image of the version of myself that I didn't want her to meet. Maybe if she hadn't run into him, this wouldn't be so hard.

I liked her. I cared about her. When I was away from her, I missed her. I hated that she was sleeping with Bryson, and I hated that it could've been me. It could've been me in the sense that we would have the same outcome and eventually fall out and end up hating each other. But I wouldn't have to watch my best friend sleep around with the one girl I couldn't shake and get out of my head.

The one girl I fell for.

I watched her walk back to the living room and settle into her spot on the couch. As she blew on her soup, her right dimple reappeared, and she gestured for me to come and sit next to her. My chest felt like it was unraveling from the inside out. Suddenly, I was wrapped up in words I wanted to say but didn't know how.

I couldn't tell her how I felt. What good would that do? It would be shitty for me to say something and then disappoint her when it didn't work out. I didn't want to date her; I just didn't want her to be with anyone else. The vicious circle of thoughts was mind-numbing. They were selfish, and I was in no position to dangle feelings in front of Maci just to reel them back in.

I sat beside her, and she waited patiently for me to get settled. Once my feet were back on the coffee table, her legs stretched across my lap. I leaned back into our binge-watching position and paused the multiple conversations in my head.

The four of us sat around the coffee table with one of Katie's dinners while Maci's show played in the background. Connor checked out Katie every chance he could, and Katie acted like she didn't notice. Maci's body was next to mine, and I tried to make up my mind about what the hell I was doing.

It was like a break didn't even happen, and it was like we never left.

Chapter Thirty-Four

MACI

JANUARY 2016

IT FELT INCREDIBLY COMFORTING to have Jaxon back in our apartment on a Thursday evening. Having him here made me feel better about all of the stress and anxiety that came with starting new classes and figuring out how the semester was going to work.

There wasn't a day that went by over break when I didn't think about him. All the times I went out with friends to hometown bars and house parties, I wanted to look across the room and see him staring back at me. I wanted him to come up from behind me when guys hit on me or when they got too close to let them know that I was his. All the time I spent away from him made it clear how much I depended on him to show up for me. I needed him in a way that scared me and overwhelmed me with the fear of losing him.

When I was in high school, I had two relationships. One guy lasted about six months, and the other guy lasted a year. When I got to BGSU, I dated Isaac, a sophomore on the football team. All three of them had slept with me and made me experience the ups and downs of emotions that came with relationships. Yet none of them compared to how Jaxon made me feel.

Jaxon handed me his empty bowl of soup since my legs were still in his lap. I set his dish on the coffee table, and his arms rested casually on top of my shins. It was such a natural pose to be in, but somehow with Jaxon, it felt intimate. I ached to have him skim the back of my thighs with his hands and lean over so his body was above mine. Of course, for many reasons, that would never happen. Katie and Connor were right in front of us on the floor, and the body language I just envisioned didn't happen between friends.

"What time does your last class end tomorrow?" Katie asked.

"I should be home by three-thirty." I placed my empty bowl on Jaxon's and snuggled into the corner of the couch.

Even though it was only a little after seven, I felt like going to bed. I was half-tempted to when I saw that Jaxons's eyes were closed. But I wasn't ready for him to leave yet, and tonight we didn't have any excuses for him to stay with me.

Connor shifted into the recliner and pulled Katie into his lap. All four of us looked like we were battling a food coma.

"We need to get some drink stuff for tomorrow before people come over," Katie said sleepily, resting her head on Connor's chest.

I envied how easy it was for her to be with Connor. He had been here a lot this week, and I couldn't name anything I didn't like about him. He was sweet, gorgeous, and treated Katie like she was a queen. I mean, she was, but as her best friend, it was my job to look for red flags she overlooked because of her love blinders. So far, I came up blank.

"That sangria drink you made last time was pretty potent," Jaxon said with his eyes still closed. I wasn't aware that he was listening, and I didn't know if he was coming out tomorrow.

"Are you coming here tomorrow with me before we go out?" Connor asked.

I bit the inside of my cheek and shifted my gaze back to Jaxon. His green eyes popped against his black hoodie, and his sleepy expression tested every impulse in my body. How could someone be that gorgeous just sitting on a couch in sweats?

He was waiting for some sort of answer, and I wasn't sure what to say. Connor's question stemmed from a whole different conversation I had with Bryson earlier this week.

"That's my bad," Katie piped up. "Maci and I were talking about going out this weekend while she was on her way to class, and I told her I would text you about it. I probably got distracted."

I shook my head and played along with Katie's lie, saved once again by her elite quick-thinking skills.

Jaxon shrugged. "It's fine, Katie. I know I come in second now that Connor's here."

"You better know that." Connor smirked. Katie rolled her eyes and giggled when Connor tickled her side. He looked back to Jaxon and continued, "I know the guys are meeting at the bar, but you can come with me to pregame here if you want."

"The guys?" Jaxon looked directly at me now. There was no more batting around the one piece of information no one had mentioned.

"Your roommates are coming out too." I shrugged and kept my voice steady.

If I sounded nervous at the thought of Bryson and Jaxon being at the same place at the same time, I would ruin everything we achieved to get back to normal tonight. He blinked, and his face showed no sign of emotion. He was going to make me say his name.

"Bryson and Jared?" I added.

"That's cool." Jaxon nodded at Connor, and the tone reset in the room. "I'll let you know if I'm coming here tomorrow or not."

⁓⁓⁓

About an hour later, I woke up in the middle of an episode of *Sex and the City* and found the rest of the living room asleep. Katie and Connor were snuggled up in the recliner under a blanket, and Jaxon's temple was resting on my kneecap.

I didn't want to wake him up. He looked so cute and innocent when he slept. Once I woke him up, I knew he would say he had to go. I lightly shook my leg, and his head swayed. He blinked a few times and inhaled sharply when he realized he wasn't home.

"Jax." I smiled and ran my fingers through his short hair. He inhaled again and dragged a hand down his face.

"What time is it, Mace?" he murmured.

"Almost nine."

He rose from the couch and walked into the kitchen for a bottle of water. I watched him drain half of it and survey the kitchen.

"What are you looking for?" I asked.

"Do you still have that ramen?"

I stood up and padded over to him. Doing my best to be quiet, I pulled two Cup O'Noodles out of the box under the sink and offered him one. I popped mine open and poured the freeze-dried vegetables into the garbage can. The way they looked all wrinkled and aged freaked me out.

"Maci!" Jaxon whispered urgently, and his eyes went wide.

I surveyed the area around me and tried not to scream. The last thing I wanted was an unwelcome rodent for Katie and me to be on the lookout for. "What? What is it?"

He peered into the trash can. "You just dumped the delicacies!" His focus returned to me, and I could tell he was appalled at how unbothered I was.

My shoulders relaxed, and I knew the area was safe from critters. "The delicacies?" I tried not to laugh, but a small chuckle escaped me.

He opened his cup and placed it under the Keurig. "It's the best part of the noodles!"

With my mouth hanging open, I stared as he covered the cup and used a fork to weigh down the paper. He crossed his arms in front of his chest and leaned against the counter. I laughed again when he shook his head, looking like a disappointed father.

"Those are not the best part. They look all wrinkled and gross! Plus they've probably been in these cups for like three years."

"But they come alive when you make the broth." He gestured toward his cup.

"Anything that comes alive in anything is something I want no part of," I argued. I placed my cup under the Keurig and watched as it filled up with hot water.

While Katie and Connor continued to sleep, we stood in the kitchen and ate. He told me about his trip home and how nice it was to see his family. I told him about Chase and how I thought he was going to propose to Trey.

"How long have they been together?" he asked.

"Almost three years." I twisted my fork and pulled out a ball of noodles. I popped it in my mouth and swallowed. "He's great, and I know my brother adores him. Plus, he's been bringing up really random topics with me. He asked me the day before he left how I thought sage and navy looked together."

Jaxon smiled and leaned against the counter. "I found out my brother is finally dating this girl we grew up with."

"Alex?"

He nodded. "Her name is Bella. She's like a sister to me, but Alex and her have always had a thing for each other."

"Is she the girl from California?" I grinned.

He looked surprised that I remembered that much of our last conversation before break.

"Yeah." His lips curved into a small smile, and he set his empty soup cup on the counter. "I should probably get going. I have to get up early and finish a stupid discussion board assignment before class."

I tried not to look disappointed when I watched him gather up his things from the living room. He took a few steps toward the door and turned around to face me. He closed the space between us and opened his arms up for me to come closer.

I set my soup down and leaned into him, breathing in the scent of his hoodie.

We broke apart, and I took a deep breath to stop my voice from shaking. "Are you going to come out tomorrow?"

"Probably," he answered like the question wasn't awkward at all for me to ask. "I'm just not sure if I'll come here first or see you at the bars."

I nodded, and he smiled back before he walked out the door. I cleaned up our ramen and kept the kitchen light on in case Connor or Katie woke up. I snagged my phone from the end table, and it buzzed in my hand.

I shook my head at his reminder and followed his instructions.

I didn't know if that comment went too far. I hated the feeling of being worried about if I was pushing past the line of friendship. Everything I said and everything I did felt like it had to be censored. I didn't want him to run off if he caught hints of me wanting more, but he didn't make it simple either. It was like tiptoeing around something that would be so easy, but somehow we made it so hard.

Chapter Thirty-Five

JAXON

January 2016

Bass boomed from the living room, followed by the usual yelling and screaming when we had people over before we went out. I chugged half my beer and pulled out the last paragraph of my first Economics paper. I had waited until the last minute, and it was almost eleven and only a few minutes from being late.

Connor left to go to Maci and Katie's about an hour or two ago. I wasn't lying when I told him I had to finish this assignment, but I still felt a little shitty about it. So now here I was, trying to think around the nonsense happening in my living room and trying not to think of what Maci was doing right now at her place. It wasn't going well.

There was a knock on my door, and Heather strolled in without warning. She had a drink in her hand, and her tits spilled out of her top.

"Nope." I pointed back out in the hall.

"I'm just saying hi." She took a few more steps into my room.

"No, the fuck you're not." I emphasized my extended arm. "Get out. I have shit I need to finish."

Heather rolled her eyes and closed the door behind her. She made my skin crawl just with her presence. No matter how shitty I treated her, she was always right there and ready to take more. It just made her easier to dislike as a person.

I didn't want my mood to be ruined by Heather somehow getting invited over here. Being an asshole tonight was the last thing I wanted to do.

There was a knock on my door, and Bryson walked in with two shot glasses. "How much longer, J?"

When I saw the massive grin on his face, I decided to give up. I typed out a poorly written sentence and submitted the document. I had four minutes left until the cutoff time, and there was nothing else I could do to save this assignment.

I took the shot from Bryson and chased it down with the rest of my beer. Bryson cheered as he walked down the hall. "Last call for shots!"

I shut my door so I could change and get a moment without any other interruptions. I put on a gray Henley and dark jeans. It was cold outside, but I would sweat in the bars if I wore any other layers. One chooses to be hot inside or cold outside this time of year. There was no in-between.

Out in the living room, Jared and a few guys from the football team were playing beer pong. Random groups of people I didn't recognize stood around laughing and talking over the loud music. Bryson was in the kitchen pouring shots with Heather and yelling random shit over the counter.

Reagan stopped me just as I rounded the corner. She hooked her thumbs through the belt loops of her jeans. "What's up, you?"

"Just getting a drink," I said dryly and continued my walk to the kitchen.

Bryson yelled for everyone to grab one more shot before we headed out to the bars. People swarmed to his request, and shots were passed throughout the crowd. He threw a hand on my shoulder and raised his glass. Everyone followed, and there was a moment of silence as we threw it back.

I grabbed a beer from the fridge and pulled my room key out of my pocket. Shot-gunning a beer seemed like a good way to get a buzz going. My idea prompted a few other people to do it too, and soon one beer became three.

After a few minutes of filing out of the apartment, we were on our way.

The walk to the bars was just as shitty as I anticipated it to be. I picked a dumb night not to wear a hat, especially since I just cut my hair.

My phone buzzed in my pocket. It was Connor. I had texted him before we left to see where he was at with Maci and Katie. As soon as we got onto Main, he answered.

Connor

The Attic.

I caught up with Bryson, who was walking with some girl I didn't recognize.

"What's up, man?" I smiled. The girl stopped talking and shot me a grin. "Let's hit The Attic."

"I love The Attic!" the girl beside Bryson screamed and tried to link her arm through his. He shook her off almost instantly and walked a little faster so it was just the two of us.

"That girl is weird." He pulled out his phone, and I averted my eyes when I saw Maci's name on his screen. He typed something back. "The Attic is fine."

There was no line to get in when we approached the bar. After the guy at the door checked our IDs, we went upstairs to the entrance. "Shut Up and Dance With Me" by Walk the Moon boomed through the speakers, and the bar was packed.

I led Bryson, Jared, and some other people from our party to the bar. A few people trickled away to the dance floor and the stripper pole in the corner of the room. It was a wild scene, and it wasn't even midnight yet.

"Jack and Coke!" I yelled to the bartender and handed her my card. She started my tab and returned with my order.

I took a long sip and scanned the room for a familiar face. I looked away immediately when I saw Heather and Reagan on the stripper pole. I didn't want either of them anywhere near me tonight. They screamed when the song changed to "Trap Queen" by Fetty Wap, and the whole bar sang with the opening. Connor's plaid shirt caught my eye as the chorus erupted throughout the place.

I crossed the room and smacked his shoulder. He lit up when he saw me.

"What's up, bro!" Connor's eyes were glossy, and he had some color in his cheeks. It was a rare occasion to see Connor drunk, but it was always hilarious.

"Jaxon!" Katie screamed and pretty much tackled me to the ground. I planted my feet to keep us from falling and hugged her back.

"How come I don't get that greeting?" Connor teased and grinned down at Katie.

"Don't complain about the types of greeting I give *you*," she snapped, and I raised my hands innocently to back out of it.

I lowered my mouth to Katie's ear. "Where's Mace?"

She pointed to the balcony. "Outside, I think. With Sam!"

I nodded and weaved in and out of the crowd to the balcony. It was still cold outside, but heaters hung from the rafters, making it bearable to stand there.

It didn't take me long to find Maci. She was laughing at something Sam said at a small table by the railing. I recognized a few people standing around them from the last time we went out together. She looked hot in a blue crop top, a black leather jacket, and jeans. Her hair was curled again, and I could see her blue eyes from only a few feet away.

Bryson approached her from behind and whispered something in her ear. She laughed and turned to face him with a giant grin on her face. I took a deep breath and approached the table, ready to get the rest of this night over with.

Chapter Thirty-Six

MACI

January 2016

It was happening. The moment I had dreaded since that night of Drunk Driving in my apartment. I had Bryson in my ear as Jaxon approached our table. They were in the same place again, and I felt myself sweating in my leather jacket. I had such high hopes for this outfit, and here I was, melting into it.

"My man." Bryson extended his hand, and Jaxon shook it the way guys do. It seemed silly since they just arrived together, but I would never understand the unspoken language guys had.

"Sup." Jaxon leaned onto the table. He raised his eyebrows at me, and I smirked back. He couldn't greet me or address me like he normally did because Bryson was here. It wouldn't fit with the lie he scripted.

I looked him over and admired how his shirt hugged his chest and arms. His cologne rolled off him as he leaned in to take a drink, and I had to turn away before I drooled on the table in front of me. Bryson suddenly felt heavy on my back.

Last night I was talking over ramen and delicacies with Jaxon. Now I was picturing him naked, while the guy I was hooking up with was literally right behind me.

Bryson lowered his mouth to my ear. "You want another drink?"

I nodded. I needed more than a drink. I needed the whole bar. I watched Bryson walk back inside and disappear into the crowd.

I didn't want an awkward silence to hover over the table, so I skimmed my hand against Jaxon's. "Hey, you."

"You look good." He gestured toward my outfit and turned his body to face mine. Butterflies erupted behind my navel, and I thanked the dark lighting for hiding the color that rose to my cheeks.

"You don't look so bad yourself," I said just before Bryson returned with my beer. Our gaze lingered for a moment before Katie and Connor's arrival brought us back to the group.

"I want a Green Giant drink!" Katie yelled over the music. Sam encouraged her with a high five and looked at me for my reaction.

"I am not freezing my ass off at Tiki bar so you can get a drink, Katie." I shook my head and took a sip of my beer.

She stuck out her bottom lip, and Connor laughed.

"Don't encourage her, Connor!" I giggle-yelled over the table. "You guys go then!"

Jaxon turned to face Katie. "Let's stay here for a little bit. Come do a shot with me."

Katie squealed and followed Jaxon and Connor back inside the bar. My chest loosened a little at the separation. Being around Bryson with Jaxon standing only a few feet away was almost impossible.

I looked back at Bryson, and he moved so he was next to me. He leaned in, and the familiar smell of Black & Mild mixed with his cologne swept over me.

"You wanna take a shot?" He gestured toward the doorway and grinned. His golden-brown eyes were glossy, and I knew he was feeling good. His smile was contagious, and I couldn't resist the charm that seemed to effortlessly seep out of him.

I nodded, and he grabbed my hand to stop me from heading inside.

To my total surprise, he cupped my chin and pulled me in for a kiss. I almost buckled right there in the middle of the balcony crowd. We were in public, and his tongue weaved against mine. People walked by us like it was another Friday night, not paying us the slightest bit of attention. Even though that was exactly what was happening, I felt like every pair of eyes was locked on us.

Bryson pulled away, and his mouth spread into a drunken smile.

"You're probably gonna regret that later," I warned.

He shrugged. "Let's hope not."

We broke away at the pool tables, completely forgetting the shot he offered. He went toward a group of people I didn't recognize, and I joined Katie, Jaxon, Connor, and Jared at the bar. They had just taken a Green Tea shot when I approached the counter.

"Maci!" Katie screamed and threw her arms around my neck. I was literally gone from her for two seconds. Clearly, other shots had been taken before the one I witnessed.

Connor handed me something pink, and I knocked it back. It tasted like strawberry.

"That was amazing!" I yelled and hugged Katie around the waist. I steadied her and leaned our body weight against the bar.

"Wanna take a hit?" Jared asked Connor and Jaxon. He made a smoking gesture with his hand and motioned toward the back entrance of the bar.

Katie nodded at Connor to let him know it was okay, and Jaxon made eye contact with me. I ached to run my hands down his chest, feel his sculpted abs against my fingers and press my body against his. I knew it was the booze, but I wanted to go back to a few months ago. When Jaxon was the only guy I thought about, and Bryson wasn't an option.

Jaxon's dimple dug into his cheek, and he reached over to squeeze my hand. Warmth shot through my arm, and I offered him a small smile. The guys crossed the bar and were soon out of eyesight.

"God," Katie whined and removed her hands from my shoulders. She stood taller and shook her curls right before she side-eyed me. I could tell she was getting her second wind.

"What's up?" I laughed and raised my hand to get the attention of the bartender. I ordered two cranberry vodkas, and she returned a few seconds later.

"Nothing." She sighed and grabbed her cup. She took a sip and locked her eyes back on mine. I could tell that Logical Katie was still hanging on. "Can I have an honest drunk moment with you?"

"Oh boy." I took a long sip of my drink.

As I prepared for her admission, I watched her face shift into a look of worry. Her body tensed, and she averted her gaze down to the countertop.

"Katie, what's—" I was side checked by a guy in a pale green button-down.

"Katie," Tyler demanded and wrapped his hand around her wrist.

My protective instincts took over, and I shoved into the side of him. "What the fuck, asshole!" I screamed over the music, gaining the attention of a few people that surrounded us.

Tyler shoved his elbow into my shoulder, and I gripped the back of his shirt to keep from falling. He knocked me so hard that I stared in the complete opposite direction.

I scanned the room for a familiar face. Out of the corner of my eye, I saw Bryson by the pool tables, making out with a girl in a bright red tank top. My stomach sank, but I spun back around to address the issue at hand.

"Tyler, please get off me." Katie grabbed at his hand and winced when he tightened his grip.

"You think you can just ignore me? I need to talk to you," he growled.

I jumped and wrapped my arms around his neck, using my body weight to pull him away from Katie. I tightened my arms, and his hands flew to my forearms at his restricted airflow. We had officially caused a scene to the point where people backed away from us.

"Maci!" Katie screamed when Tyler spun around so he faced me. His elbow hit my mouth, and I tasted blood. I didn't recognize him in this state. His eyes were bloodshot, and there was a fire ignited in them. He looked furious.

"Back up!" he screamed in my face.

I braced myself as he pulled back his arm, but nothing came. I felt the pain of my hip hit the counter, and when I opened my eyes, Jaxon and Connor were at the bar.

Jaxon's arm shielded me from Tyler, and he lunged into his chest. They fell to the floor, and my breath caught in my throat. Jaxon's hands hit Tyler's face over and over again until a few guys from the crowd ran in to pull him off.

"I told you I would break your jaw, you fucking prick!" Jaxon yelled and wiped his mouth with the back of his hand.

"Get the fuck out!" the bartender yelled over the counter.

"Let's go, J!" Connor's voice stood out from the crowd, and I watched him pull Katie to the front entrance.

Tyler was motionless on the ground when I pulled on Jaxon's arm. I needed to get him out of here before the cops showed up. He let me drag him a few feet, and the crowd parted for us. He laced his fingers with mine and led us down the stairs and to the street.

The sound of sirens wailed from the other side of the building. We went through the parking lot and came out on Court Street.

Jaxon dropped my hand and ran his fingers through his hair. Neither of us said anything until we were in front of Brathaus.

I stopped walking. "Jaxon?"

He spun around and stared at me. His mouth parted, and his eyes zeroed in on my mouth. He took two giant steps and placed his hands on both sides of my face. "Are you okay?" His voice was still laced with anger from the scene we had just left.

"Yeah, I'm fine," I reassured him and removed his hands. "Are you okay?"

He pressed his forehead to mine and closed his eyes. His breaths came quick and grew even shakier the more he tried to calm down. I swallowed and tried to ignore how close his mouth was to mine. Suddenly, a moment that was frightening and uncertain felt so safe and natural.

"Fucking prick." He turned and looked up at the sky.

A gust of wind barreled down the street, and I crossed my arms in front of my chest. I watched Jaxon pace back and forth on the sidewalk with his hands locked behind his head.

When I saw Jaxon kicking Heather out the morning after I slept with Bryson, I always thought that would be the most

Jaxon ever made me feel uneasy about him. Seeing him in that light made me nervous about being around him, afraid of the moment that I might be on the receiving end of it. That was nothing compared to what I had just witnessed. It was like he had blinders on, and Tyler's face was the only target.

I had never seen him so angry. He looked like someone I didn't even recognize. I stared at the blood on his hands and shirt. I replayed the moment when I thought Tyler would hit me, and tears sprung to my eyes.

Images of Bryson lip locked with some girl in the corner worsened the kick in my gut. I could've been laid out on the bar floor, and Bryson wouldn't have even known. I had just made out with him, and he carelessly moved on within fifteen minutes.

Why was it so hard for him to care about me?

"Hey," Jaxon said and wrapped his arms around my shoulders. I wiped my tears on his shirt and sank into his embrace. He tightened his grip and rested his temple on my head. "It's okay," he whispered in my ear, and I nodded into his chest. I didn't want him to see me upset since this incident had nothing to do with me.

Connor's voice echoed down the road. "Jaxon!"

Katie started crying at the sight of us. I ran to her for a hug, and she sobbed into my shoulder.

Out of the corner of my eye, I saw Bryson emerge from the back entrance of The Attic. Heat rose from my stomach and engulfed my chest. I needed to be angry at something, and he just volunteered himself.

"Can you take her home, please?" I asked Connor, and he nodded.

"Where are you going?" Katie asked.

"I'll meet you there," I reassured her. "Give me a few minutes."

"I'll wait for her." I heard Jaxon say as I crossed Court Street.

I moved quickly to where Bryson was standing with a few guys I didn't recognize.

"Asshole," I yelled as soon as I was close enough for him to hear me.

His smile grew at the sight of me, and that pissed me off even more. I wanted to knock that drunken smile right off his face.

I shoved his chest, and he planted his feet to avoid falling over. The guys he was with took a few steps back to give us space. Bryson's eyes darkened, and his smile quickly evaporated.

"Did you even see what happened in there?" I sneered, and his mouth formed a hard line. "No, you didn't. You couldn't have seen anything because you had your tongue shoved into some other girl's mouth."

He shifted his gaze, and I could tell he was pissed with this conversation.

"What the fuck is your problem?" he spat. "Your friend gets into some shit with some frat guy, and you're pissed at me?"

"I'm pissed because you're a fucking asshole. You make out with me, do the same routine on some other girl, and now you're all smiley and shit expecting me to be excited to see you? Look at my lip, Bryson! That could've been a lot worse in there."

"And it's none of my business, though!" he exclaimed, his voice reaching the same level of frustration as mine. "You get mad about dumb shit! I'm not your fucking babysitter, and I'm not your boyfriend. I don't know why you do this."

I stared at him, and he stared back. He showed no emotion on his face and wore the same expression he had after our fight last weekend.

"I'm fucking done, Bryson." I shook my head and turned to walk away.

"Hold up." He grabbed my hand and pulled so I faced him. "Why are you doing this?"

I shrugged. "Because for the first time, it's easy for me to." The words left my mouth so effortlessly that they shocked me. I attempted to walk away again, but he pulled me back.

"I'm sorry," Bryson lied and shook his head. He was annoyed and ready to be done with this conversation. "I'm sorry," he repeated, sounding more sincere. "Are you okay?"

I took a deep breath and tugged one final time before he let go. I left him standing there outside the bar. I kept a steady pace and crossed back over Court Street with a lump in my throat and a punch in my gut.

Chapter Thirty-Seven

JAXON

I WATCHED MACI WALK across Court Street from inside Brathaus. I had no idea what she and Bryson were screaming about, but it was too damn cold for me to stand on the road and wait for her.

I finished the rest of my Legal Joint and walked out the door just as she stepped onto the sidewalk. She didn't speak. She just turned and started the walk back to her apartment. I walked silently beside her and glanced over every now and then to make sure she was okay while I got into my own head.

I was angry all over again. But this time, it had nothing to do with Tyler or what had just happened with Katie. This all stemmed from Maci and Bryson. I was tired of seeing her with him. I was tired of hearing the comments he made about her and tired of Maci accepting the shitty way he treated her. I just watched them have a screaming match outside of the bar like they had some sort of extensive history to argue about. They didn't, but they had very different expectations for what they were and where it was going.

Maci wanted him to care about her, and Bryson was *never* going to be the guy she wanted him to be. I was angry with her because Maci knew all that, and she put up with it anyways.

The walk from Brathaus was short. I followed Maci up the stairs of her building, and she gestured for me to go in first when we got to the apartment. Connor sat on the living room couch.

"She's in the shower," Connor mumbled and ran his hands over his face. Walking into that scene from outside had made both of us sober up real quick. He continued and directed his attention to Maci. "I couldn't get her to calm down, so I told her to wash off and take a moment before she filled me in on what happened."

Maci nodded and squeezed Connor's arm when she passed. She opened the bathroom door just wide enough for her to slip inside.

"What the fuck, man," Connor groaned.

"Just another Friday," I said and took a seat at the dining table.

A laugh escaped Connor's chest, and he helped himself to a beer in the fridge. The apartment looked like a tornado had gone through it, and I forgot that people had been here only a few hours ago.

"Want one?" He extended a bottle in my direction, and I took it.

I twisted off the cap and took a sip. I didn't even know what I was doing here, but I had a feeling Connor wanted me to stay. He saw me in his girlfriend's apartment and thought it was a regular thing. He liked being able to share this part of his life with me. The other guys wouldn't be about it.

"I have some extra clothes if you want to shower," Connor offered and nodded at my hands.

I pulled the shirt I wore away from my chest and assessed the damage. I hadn't noticed my appearance until now. My hands hurt, but nothing looked broken. I flexed my fingers a few times and shrugged. The sight of Tyler lying on the floor was worth every punch I threw. After I saw the look on Katie's face and Maci's lip, he was lucky I didn't kill him.

Connor took a seat across from me. "Are you good, J?"

"Yeah." I nodded. "I'm good."

"It all happened so fast," he admitted. "I owe you, man. Thank you."

I shook my head. "I didn't think twice about it."

We sat in silence for a few minutes and drank our beers. I wasn't sure when it happened, but sometime over the course of my friendship with Maci, I developed a genuine friendship with Katie too. I never looked at her as someone I would hook up with, even before her meeting Connor. But I cared enough about her to throw a few punches on her behalf.

"Fuck." I sighed. "I left my credit card at the bar."

"I'll go get your card." Connor stood up and pulled his phone out of his pocket. "If you go back there, someone will remember you."

"You don't have to do it now. It's been a rough night, man. Sit back down," I said.

Connor tapped his thumbs furiously against his phone screen. He looked anxious just standing there. "I wanna go now before the cops leave. I want to make sure they know who it was that started the fight. My dad knows some of the law enforcement here and will make sure Tyler pays for what he did." He was determined to walk out of this apartment no matter what I said to him, so I nodded and watched him leave.

Just as the front door closed, Katie appeared in the living room in Connor's Michigan hoodie and a pair of sweatpants. I offered a small smile, and she took the seat across from me that Connor had just left. I heard Maci turn on the shower, giving Katie and me a moment to ourselves.

I reached my hand across the table and ran my thumb over her fingers. It was weird to see Katie like this. She seemed like the type of girl that didn't put up with anyone's shit. Tyler must have done something to really shake her.

"Katie?" I asked softly.

Her light-brown eyes met mine. She looked alert and exhausted at the same time.

"You probably don't want to talk about it, but I'm going to ask anyway since it's just us." I took a deep breath before I continued, "What happened with Tyler? What did he do that made you stop seeing him?"

Katie bit her lip and stared down at her fingers. We sat in silence for a few minutes before she gave me an answer.

"About a week after Halloween, I was hanging out with Tyler at his place. He and his roommates ended up throwing an 'impromptu party,'" Katie quoted in disgust. She paused, and I took a sip of beer to let her know I wasn't rushing her recap.

"He got drunk," she emphasized. "*Very* drunk." She stopped her story again and inhaled sharply through her nose. "That was the first night he grabbed me to the point where he left bruises on my arm."

I gripped my beer bottle to keep my face from shifting. I had been right about Tyler from the start.

"At first, I didn't think anything of it." She shrugged. "Then, two nights later, it happened again. Only this time, he got angry. He scared me so much that I left after we slept together."

It wasn't easy to listen to, but I remained silent. I was sure this was the first time Katie had told this story out loud.

Tears formed in the corners of her eyes, and she wiped them away. "I know the signs." She sniffed. "I know I should've ended it after the first time it happened. I almost didn't even leave after the second time it happened. I told myself that he didn't mean it and that he was just drunk."

I leaned forward, and her eyes rose to meet mine. "He's not going to come near you again," I promised.

She nodded, and this time she allowed her tears to fall. I squeezed her hand, and she squeezed it back.

A few months ago, I would've been annoyed having to deal with tears. But there wasn't a single part of me that didn't want to be sitting across the table from Katie. Everything about this felt different.

"People like Tyler don't choose to be better," I said softly. "I had someone important in my life choose alcohol and drugs over me a long time ago. Not saying that Tyler does drugs, but it's the same concept."

"I'm sorry," Katie empathized and didn't push for more information.

"You deserve someone like Connor." I changed the subject. "He's one of the best guys I know."

She shook her head slowly and crossed her arms over her chest. A warmth returned to her eyes, and she stared at me. "Who do you deserve?" she asked in a soft-spoken voice.

I cocked my head and sighed. I smiled at her straightforward question and was happy to see some of the Katie I recognized. We both knew what she was really asking me, but I had no idea how to answer her.

I knew what I wanted, but what I *deserved*? That part threw me off. I knew what Maci deserved. She deserved a guy that would treat her well, be loyal to her, and sit through all of her obnoxious chick flick shows. I didn't know how to do relationships.

"I'm rooting for you," Katie said with a small smile.

As soon as I opened my mouth to respond, Maci appeared in the living room in shorts and a long sleeve shirt. Even though her face was stripped of makeup and her hair was a wet and tangled mess, I found everything about her attractive.

"Where did Connor go?" she asked and approached the table.

"To get my card." I leaned back in my chair and threw my empty bottle in the trash. "I left it at The Attic."

"Shit"—she rolled her eyes—"mine is there too. I'll have to get it tomorrow or later today, I guess, since it's already almost two."

It was hard to believe we were still on the same day. I dragged my hands over my face and stood up. "I'm gonna get going."

Katie eyed me suspiciously. "You don't wanna just stay?" She sounded surprised to hear me say that I was leaving.

I shook my head. "Not this time."

Katie rose up from the table and threw her arms around my neck. "Thank you," she whispered.

"Anytime." I gave her a quick squeeze before she released her grip.

"I'll walk you out," Maci offered, and I followed her into the hall. Once the front door was closed, she turned to face me. "You really don't want to just stay?"

Tonight was filled with many things neither of us planned to be a part of. Katie's run-in with Tyler, my knockout with Tyler, Maci's argument with Bryson, and having to cut the night short were all on that list. I expected Bryson to interact with Maci, and I expected them to be with each other for part of the night. What I didn't expect was my reaction to something I had already been aware of for three months.

Since Maci met Bryson, I had been dealing with it in the best ways I knew. I didn't want to deal with it anymore. I felt pissed off that she couldn't see what was happening right in front of her. She was waiting for Bryson to want to be more, and he was just trying to keep an option open.

"I just need some space, Mace," I admitted, my tone sounding sharper than I intended it to.

"You need space." She crossed her arms. She searched my face for a hint of context and shook her head. "What's up, Jaxon?"

"Tonight was a lot," I snapped and felt myself reeling into the jackass headspace. She felt the shift and took a step toward me.

"Yeah, it was. I'm sorry all of that happened, but for what it's worth, and I'm sorry if this sounds shitty"—her eyes met mine—"I'm glad you were there."

I shrugged. "I'm always there, Mace."

The skin around her eyes softened, and I knew she was getting into her head. I just didn't know what else to say.

"Yeah." She turned to head back inside. "Good night, Jaxon."

Chapter Thirty-Eight

MACI

January 2016

As soon as I shut the door, I made a beeline for the bathroom. I turned the shower on as high as it would go and turned the sink on using both the hot and cold water knobs. I steadied myself against the sink, and I sobbed uncontrollably.

My whole body shook, and I lowered myself onto the toilet seat. I covered my face with both hands and let my chin fall. I had allowed myself to cry earlier in the shower once Katie was out of the bathroom. I cried over how shitty I felt because of Bryson. I cried because I saw Tyler's fist coming toward my face every time I closed my eyes. I cried because of how terrified Katie looked back at the bar and how she crumbled into Connor.

But this new round of tears had everything to do with the man who had just left. Tonight was a nightmare, but he was there when I needed him. He was there when Katie needed him. It didn't take much for me to know if something was off with Jaxon. Another sob escaped my chest, and I reflected on how much had changed between us since we met at Myles Dairy Queen.

Two months was all it took for me to fall for him, and two months was all it took for us to mess it up. One weekend changed everything we had. Winter break forced us out of the bubble we created, and now here we were, five months later, stuck between where we wanted to be and what was easy. We were like some fucked up timeline we just couldn't get right.

I closed my eyes and took three deep breaths. I stood up, wiped my eyes, and turned the hot water off so I could splash cold water on my face. When I looked up, my reflection in the mirror was unforgiving. I desperately needed sleep.

I turned off the shower and emerged from the bathroom. The lights in the apartment were all off except for the kitchen light. Katie and I always left that on in case one of us got up during the night.

My bedroom felt cold that night. Even though I was exhausted, I couldn't get comfortable or get my mind to slow down. It was like I got a third wind as soon as my head hit the pillow. I pulled one of my spare blankets out from underneath the bed and shook it out over top of me.

I checked my phone one last time before I put it on the charger. I had no idea what time I fell asleep.

⁓⁓

The morning after a night out was always slow-moving. My eyes struggled to open as I felt the exhaustion, stress, and nausea from last night slowly seep into my body. I rolled over and clutched my extra pillow, breathing in the clean scent of laundry detergent and traces of my shampoo. For whatever reason, that actually made me feel worse.

I checked my phone for the time and saw it was almost one-thirty in the afternoon. I couldn't remember the last time I slept this much of the day away. I listened for any signs of life out in the living room, and nothing came. Maybe Katie and Connor were still in bed too.

My bladder eventually shoved me from my room. I stood up, and a wave of last night's cranberry and vodka hit my stomach. Steered by the stress of last night, it made its way to the base of my throat, and I ran to the bathroom. I shut the door behind me and heaved my head into the toilet. There was a light knock on the door as soon as I turned to sit against the base of the sink.

"Maci?" Katie said from the hall. "Are you okay?"

I cleared my throat and stood up. "Yeah, I'll be out in a minute."

I quickly brushed my teeth and gargled some mouthwash. When I walked into the kitchen, Katie and Connor were sitting at the dining room table.

"Good morning." Connor attempted to be his usual, cheerful self, but none of us knew what the appropriate tone was for this morning.

"Morning." I shot him a half-smile and squeezed Katie's shoulder on my way to the fridge.

Both had steaming cups of coffee in front of them, but I opted for a Dr. Pepper and a granola bar this afternoon. All of us were getting a late start to our day.

"Hey," Katie said as soon as I sat down. I was glad that she looked well-rested despite how our evening turned out. "I know we were supposed to go out with Sam and Owen to Toledo tonight, but I'm just not up for that scene. Are you okay if I stay in?"

I cracked open my pop and took a bite of my granola bar. "Are you kidding? Do you mind if I third wheel?"

"Do I get to pick at least one of the movies?" Connor asked, realizing he just became outnumbered.

"I don't care what you put on that screen." I shook my head and took another sip of pop. I wasn't sure how Dr. Pepper managed to cure me whenever I was nauseous, but it had become a staple in my BGSU lifestyle. "As long as I get to lay around all day and do absolutely nothing, I'm down."

"Text me what you want from the store," Katie offered. "Connor and I are going to run to Target for some snacks."

"The one in Perrysburg?" My eyebrows knit together. There were several stores within a one-mile radius that they could go to. Perrysburg was at least twenty minutes away.

"I just want to browse." She shrugged her shoulders and rose from the table.

Sometimes a woman just needed to browse the nearest Target. No further explanation was necessary.

About an hour later, I was curled up on the couch in an empty apartment. My hair was thrown into a messy bun, and I scrolled aimlessly through Pinterest on my phone. I didn't want any glimpses of the outside world today. I just wanted to curl up and become a part of the couch.

I wanted to text Jaxon, but based on his plea for space last night, I decided against it. If he needed space to figure out whatever he needed to figure out, so be it. I wouldn't stand in his way.

My phone buzzed in my hand as soon as I added a Chicken Gnocchi soup recipe to the Pinterest board Katie and I shared. I stared blankly at the screen and rose up off the couch when I saw Bryson's name. This had to be some sort of mistake. This guy had no reason to talk to me, let alone call me.

I hesitated at first and finally answered the call. "Hello?"

"Hey," Bryson said.

I waited for him to say more, but nothing came. "Do you need something?" I said slowly and kept my voice level. I didn't feel like being pissed today.

"Yeah, I need you to accept my apology."

I sat up straight. "Excuse me?"

"I'm sorry you got so upset last night."

"You realize how backward that sounds, right? You can't apologize for how I reacted to something you did. You're basically just saying that you're sorry without actually saying you're sorry," I explained.

"But I am saying sorry." I heard him smile on the other end of the line.

"That doesn't count!" I exclaimed.

"Give me a break. I was drunk, and some shit happened that upset you. I'm sorry you reacted the way that you did, but I didn't do anything wrong."

I shook my head. "You really are an asshole."

"I'm just being honest."

"That's a first," I snapped and sank back into the couch.

"Whoo," he howled and laughed into the phone. I pictured his facial expression, and I giggled. "You're wild."

"And you're something else. I have scrolling to get back to." I sighed. "I'll talk to you later."

"So we're good then?" he asked.

I took a deep breath and closed my eyes. I had absolutely no reason at all to give him another chance, regardless of whether we were a thing or not. Bryson didn't give a shit about me or what we were, or how we ended up. He cared that I still picked up the phone.

The thought of not speaking to Jaxon left me feeling empty inside. Maybe that was the reason this whole conversation with Bryson seemed so nonchalant. I was suddenly very unbothered by what I witnessed at the bar.

The only person that truly mattered said he needed space from me. Suddenly, having some convenience back in my life seemed like a decent choice.

"We'll see," I answered, and I heard his hearty laugh right before I hung up.

Chapter Thirty-Nine

JAXON

February 2016

Two and a half weeks went by since that night at The Attic. During those two weeks, Maci and I exchanged a total of four text messages and three memes. There was no Thursday dinner or meeting up for coffee. It was like everything about our routine was on pause. Even though I requested the space, being in it sucked ass.

It was officially February, and I was already looking forward to spring break. The third week of classes brought more cold weather, more exams, and more essays. The semester continued to drag, and I was quickly running out of steam.

Bryson and I sat in the student union with sushi and smoothies from Jamba Juice. We both had an hour to kill before our next class and some work to submit before that class started. The procrastination made an early appearance this semester, and I have been paying for it so far.

Bryson was zoned in on his laptop, typing away on some paper he had for his Investment Analysis course. I stared at the blinking cursor on my half-finished economics essay. It annoyed me how much bandwidth this class took up when I felt I didn't need it. My grade didn't necessarily scream overqualified, but it was hard to apply myself to a subject I felt I could teach. The more I stared, the heavier my eyes got.

"I'll be right back," I murmured and stood up.

Bryson nodded without taking his eyes off the screen. He slipped in his headphones and continued typing.

Since it was early afternoon, the student union was packed. Everyone was between classes, either getting a late lunch, a coffee, or escaping the cold.

I stopped walking and changed directions. Suddenly, a coffee didn't sound half-bad. The line for Starbucks wrapped around the counter and then some. I joined the crowd and pulled out my phone to pass the time.

As soon as Instagram loaded, a photo of Connor and Katie appeared on my feed. They were outside, and it was snowing. They both wore winter hats, and Katie laughed while Connor kissed her on the cheek. I shook my head and double-tapped on the picture. It seemed like forever since the last time I saw Katie. Part of me expected her to reach out and ask why I wasn't coming around.

I knew that Maci was still seeing Bryson. I wish I could say I was surprised. They seemed to be in the exact same place before they had their screaming match outside of The Attic.

I sighed and stuck my phone in the pocket of my North Face. I needed a distraction and to drop the topic of Maci for a little while. If she wanted to deal with Bryson, that was her choice. I was too comfortable with our friendship and needed to take advantage of the space I had asked for.

"Excuse me?" I tapped lightly on the shoulder of the girl in front of me.

From the back, I saw an army green jacket, straight dark-blonde hair that rested on her hood, and a gray beanie. When she turned around, I noticed her hazel-colored eyes and the freckles that ran over the bridge of her nose. She was cute, and her grin told me she was interested in what I had to say.

I grinned. "What are you getting?"

"What am I getting?" she repeated, and her smile grew. The line moved up, and we got a little closer to the register. "A peppermint mocha with almond milk." She sounded a little unsure when she answered, "Why?"

I shrugged. "Every time I get up there, I just choose something because I don't really know coffee," I lied. "I wanted something good."

"And you trust my judgment?" Her eyes narrowed, and she turned to face me.

"You seem very well put together."

She held my gaze, and her mouth parted slightly. "I'm Layla."

"Jaxon." I held out my hand, and she shook it.

"What are you doing after this, Jaxon?"

I knew exactly where this was going. "I have class in about a half hour, but after that, I'm free."

"Can I get your number?"

"Absolutely." I smiled, and she offered her phone.

The line moved quicker than I thought it would. It gave me just enough time to chat with Layla but not too much time where I felt the conversation was forced. I bought her coffee, and we parted ways once we left the line. I still had to grab my things from the table and head to the education building.

Layla messaged me as soon as I found a spot in the lecture hall.

Layla

Do you like burgers?

Jaxon

I do like burgers.

I sipped my drink and did a double take at the cup. It was different from my usual hazelnut coffee order, but it tasted amazing. I stared down at the conversation bubbles dancing on the screen. She hadn't even included her name in the first text message. Most girls were quick to make sure I knew who it was.

Layla

Let's go to Beckett's after your class. They have $5 burgers on Wednesdays.

Jaxon

Sounds good :)

The professor for the class entered the hall and set his materials down at the desk. I slipped my phone into my jacket pocket and opened my laptop. It was still on my economics essay from earlier, so I typed out a few sentences until class started.

After three Google Documents of notes, two discussion boards, and a pop quiz, I was done for the day. I hated coming into the education building for class, but it was one of the only buildings on campus with lecture halls big enough for specific sections. There were always cohorts of excited soon-to-be teachers and colorful posters hung on every corner. It was the exact opposite of the corporate style I was used to.

I walked across the first-floor lobby and stopped as soon as I hit the stairs. I noticed her right away. I wasn't sure if it was because I secretly looked for her or because I wanted to see her.

Maci stood next to her friend Sam. They were both looking at some papers she held in front of them.

I wanted to walk over to her and say something, but I didn't have anything else to say. It had only been two and a half weeks since I saw her, but it felt like an entire season had passed. I just needed some more distance to get my mind back on track with what I was comfortable with. I hadn't slept with anyone since break, and it was out of character for me to go a few weeks without having sex.

I tossed my empty coffee cup in the trash and shifted my direction so I could leave unnoticed through the back entrance of the building. I pushed through the doors and pulled out my phone.

Jaxon

Ready when you are!

Layla

Perfect timing. Just got out of the shower. Give me 15 minutes!

Jaxon

Sounds good. Mind snagging me from campus on your way there? :)

I slipped back into the student union to get out of the cold. There was no way I was walking all the way to Beckett's from campus, and I didn't feel like taking the shuttle back to Falcon's Pointe to get my Jeep.

Layla

I'll park in front of the union. Text you when I leave!

Chapter Forty

MACI

February 2016

"Please tell me you at least applied to these three!" Sam exclaimed and stole two more pamphlets from my pile. He poured over the words Manhattan, Santa Barbara, and Tampa. "Talk about a fun location! Could you imagine living it up in Manhattan?"

I swiped back the handouts and laughed at his supportive excitement.

On Tuesday, my Educational Psychology class heard back from the internship coordinators for applications we sent in a few weeks ago. I successfully heard back from four regarding my status. It didn't mean I was accepted, but I passed the requirements and was in the running for four internships for the summer of 2017.

It was a long shot, but I still felt excited at the opportunity.

I shrugged. "I won't have any updates until next spring, so I have some time to make my pros and cons charts."

We walked out the front exit of the education building and started the trek to Lot J. Sam also parked in that lot.

"How is Katie doing?" he asked, throwing his fur-lined hood over his head.

"She is okay," I answered honestly.

It hadn't taken long for everyone on campus to hear about Tyler's incident at The Attic. Tyler was in a fraternity, so news traveled fast once people caught wind of who was involved in the fight. There were a ton of bystanders that night who knew Tyler from his involvement around campus. Everyone the cops talked to had spoken on Jaxon's behalf, explaining how Tyler was drunk with his hands on Katie and threatened to hit me if Jaxon hadn't gotten in the way. Last I heard, Jaxon wasn't even contacted by the police.

Tyler was banned from The Attic, removed from his fraternity, and faced suspension from Bowling Green State University. He wasn't even allowed to attend classes or step on campus. This all went into effect Monday afternoon, shortly after everything even happened.

Connor's dad used to work with the chief of police in Bowling Green and pushed the entire investigation. While Connor had the best intentions when he chose to call his dad and push for support, I wasn't sure if Katie saw things that way. She didn't want to file charges or take further steps when making Tyler pay. She just wanted everything to be over.

Tyler faced the consequences he had been given so far because Connor's dad encouraged the university to act against violence. Whenever a university was threatened because of a student's activity, they worked quickly to remove that student's association with the school.

"Has anyone even heard from Tyler?" Sam asked.

I shook my head. "I don't think so." The last I heard, Tyler had to spend a few days in the hospital, thanks to the damage Jaxon had dealt.

"Damn." Sam sighed. "I hope this doesn't sound insensitive, but I am *dying* for a fun night out. Do you think Katie will be up for a low-key evening?"

We stopped in front of my Elantra, and I turned to face him. Sam unlocked his Camry from the opposite row and waited for my answer.

"Describe *low-key* for me, please." I knew full well that Sam didn't even know the definition of low-key.

He pursed his lips and looked up at the sky. "What about Nate and Wally's? Fishbowl races, maybe some shots at Brathaus, and then we can hit Jimmy Johns and go home?"

I stared at him and thought about his proposal.

"Low-key," he repeated.

I laughed and threw my bookbag into the passenger seat of my car. "I will run it by her and see. Are you free both Friday and Saturday?"

"Saturday works better, but I can make Friday work if needed!" Sam started walking to his car and turned around to wave goodbye.

I returned the wave and slipped inside the Elantra to crank the heat.

When I returned to the apartment, I was surprised I didn't walk in to see the happy couple cuddled up on the couch. It was empty and eerily quiet.

I locked the door behind me and surveyed the place one more time.

"Katie?" I yelled into the silence.

No one responded.

I shrugged and went into my room to change and unpack my bookbag. I had totally different classes tomorrow, so I prepared my books for Thursday's routine and charged my laptop so it was ready in the morning.

My stomach growled. It was almost four, and I hadn't eaten since my bagel for breakfast. I stared at the fridge and frowned at the options. My phone buzzed in the pocket of my sweatpants. I immediately checked to see if it was Katie, and I was surprised when it wasn't.

It was early for our usual Wednesday conversation starter. Bryson continued his routine of hitting me up on Wednesdays after his attempted apology a few weeks ago. The familiar knot in my stomach formed at the sight of his name on my screen. I hated how much I enjoyed his attention. Even I knew how pathetic it was to continue to see him after what happened at The Attic.

I tossed my phone on the counter and grabbed a Dr. Pepper. I took a long sip and stared at the conversation bubbles on my screen. I'm sure I would think back to this time in my life and shake my head, but right now, Bryson eased the ache in my chest carved out by everything that had happened recently.

Jaxon and I were at a standstill, and I wasn't even sure where that left our friendship. Katie had gone through something very real and traumatic, and she was still dealing with that. She also had Connor, who had rightfully taken up most of her time.

I was lonely. Bryson might not have cared about me, but his company and penis did the job.

After a large order of Pollyeyes and two rounds of sex, Bryson was typing away in my room on his laptop. Katie and Connor returned from dinner and a movie shortly after Bryson arrived, and thankfully we had already shifted to my bed by the time they came back.

My bedroom door was open, and so was Katie's. I could hear the intro of *Gilmore Girls* from across the hall and texted Connor.

Maci

How is she doing? Gilmore Girls again??

Connor

HOW MANY SEASONS ARE THERE

I chuckled at his response and shook my head. He had no idea what he was in for. *Gilmore Girls* was at the top of the list for Katie's comfort show, but given the circumstances, it was also a reason for me to worry about how she was really doing.

"How's it going over there?" I asked Bryson and looked up from my screen.

He was shirtless and leaned back in my desk chair. He stretched his arms out, and the muscles in his back flexed. "I'm almost done. Just gotta write a conclusion."

"What for?" I walked over to the desk and peered over his shoulder.

"It's a business proposal for one of my classes," he explained.

It was the first time Bryson actually sounded serious about something other than fucking, women, or a combination of both. It was kind of hot.

I nodded and turned to walk back to my scrolling position on the bed. He grabbed my hand and continued to stare at the screen.

"Give me a kiss," he prompted and turned so I could place my mouth on his. He smiled against my kiss and tugged on my bottom lip.

"Finish your paper," I ordered playfully and retreated to the other side of the room.

It was nice being with him and spending time together doing something normal like homework. Things had shifted a little bit since the incident at The Attic. Somehow conversation came a little easier, and he was more flirty when we were alone. I didn't filter as much when I talked to him, either. I determined that must be what happened when you already decided that you hated someone for who they were but not for what they could do for you in bed.

I laughed and filed that one away for an inspirational quote to lay on Katie. It was up there with my Fun Dip line from the costume store that day Jaxon fixed my car.

And just like that, I was back in the headspace that revolved around Jaxon. I scrolled through our text thread and stared at the most recent exchange of messages. It was weird to see them labeled under a date that was so long ago. It wouldn't be hard just to shoot him a text, but his request for space stopped me. It sucked feeling ignored, and it hurt that we got here because of what he wanted.

I thought back to his exact words from that night.

It's for the best. Now nothing has to change. If we had gone through with it, you would hate me in the morning.

I wanted to shout bullshit from the roof of my apartment building and plaster it across the sky so he could see it from

Falcon's Pointe or wherever he was right now. He lied, and *everything* had changed.

"Done!" Bryson exclaimed and spun around in the chair. "Feel like hot tubbin'?"

"Hot tubbin'?" I repeated. He was referring to the hot tub back at Falcon's Pointe.

"Yeah," he said, throwing his hoodie over his bare chest. "Grab your suit."

"Okay," I stammered and did as I was told. I packed a bag and poked my head into Katie's bedroom to let her know I was leaving.

Bryson leaned in behind me and directed his attention to Connor. Katie scowled at the sight of him halfway into her room. I bit my lip from laughing and felt relieved to see a glimpse of Sassy Katie. It had been a while since anyone saw her.

"You have a key?" Bryson asked.

"Yeah, I'm good, man," Connor mumbled.

"So it's just Jared who is an idiot." Bryson grinned, and Connor laughed. Bryson turned his face toward me. "You ready?"

"Yeah," I answered half-heartedly and followed him downstairs to the parking lot.

Chapter Forty-One

JAXON

February 2016

Burgers at Beckett's went exactly how I anticipated it too.

Layla and I stayed there for a little while, and each ordered two drinks. I asked her about her major and what year she was at BG. She asked me where I was from, and when I told her North Carolina, that spun the usual conversation about my family. I gave her the general rundown of how both of my parents owned businesses, and I left out everything else.

When she reached for the check and offered to buy my drinks, I asked her if she wanted to come back to my place to watch a movie or something. We both knew what I meant by that. From there, she drove us back to Falcon's Pointe, and no sooner than my bedroom door was shut she made a move on me.

Now we were an hour later in the aftermath.

"Seriously, Jaxon, where did you throw it?" Layla laughed. She sat on the edge of my bed and covered her tits with her arm while she searched the floor.

I fanned my arm toward the closet and rolled over on my side. "Somewhere in that direction."

She shoved my shoulder playfully. I watched her scan the floor, and she took a few steps in the direction I pointed to.

"Why are you worried about your boobs?" I chuckled. "I literally just saw you completely naked a few seconds ago."

"It's not the same." She giggled nervously and turned around so she could strap on her sparkly red bra. She faced me once it was secured and walked around the bed to get her shirt.

I reached for her wrist and felt the familiar pull in my groin. My cock got hard under the blankets, and I pulled her back down next to me. I placed my hand on her face and kissed her softly. Girls always fell for the soft kiss shit.

"I *really* have to go," she whined against my lips. "I have a paper due by eleven tonight."

I kissed her again and let my head fall against my pillow. "You owe me another round."

"Do I now?" she challenged playfully and stood up so she could pull on her jeans.

I got dressed in some sweatpants and a hoodie and watched her slip her sweater over her head.

I shrugged and ran a hand through my hair. "Yeah, you do."

"And exactly when would this next round be?" Layla bit her bottom lip. She was hot and the kind of girl that didn't have to try. The sex was good, and we connected well in bed. She wasn't awkward or weird. Her dark-blonde hair was still in loose curls even after our hookup, and her hazel eyes were bright against the makeup she wore. I stared at the freckles that danced across her nose.

"Whenever you want," I answered, and we made eye contact.

She closed the space between us and placed her mouth on mine. It was the sign I needed to know that I could add her to my hookup list. Some compliments, joking around, and those soft kisses really went a long way.

It felt good to be in this familiar routine. Since I returned from break and reunited with Maci, I hadn't slept with any girls or even tried to take them back to my place. Being here with Layla felt good. Not knowing what would happen next or if I would see this girl again felt natural.

"I'll walk you out," I offered. I opened my bedroom door and led us out into the hallway. There were no signs of life, and the apartment was awkwardly quiet.

"Your place is nice for living with all dudes." She surveyed the area and stopped as soon as we closed in on the front door. "Most guy apartments I have been in are disgusting."

"You've seen a lot of guy's apartments, huh?" I kept my tone light so she knew I was joking. I wasn't at that level with her where I could make comments like that and actually mean them.

She gasped and smacked me in the chest. "So what if I have! A bit sexist, are we?"

Her answer threw me off a bit, and my instinct took over. I knew I might lose her as a prospect.

"Just stating the facts," I said more seriously this time. "I just met you today, and now here we are."

Her mouth fell open, and she read my expression to see if I was being serious. I shrugged to try and lighten the mood. If I pissed her off just by explaining how our evening went, I didn't want this girl coming here again anyways.

She searched her purse for her keys. "I'm not sure what to say to that."

I stood there while she waited for me to say something back. When I didn't move closer to her, she continued her thought. "Maybe we will run into each other on the weekend sometime and have that other round."

I smirked at her and took a step forward. "I'll see you around then."

Layla gave me one last kiss, and as soon as she slid her hands onto my hips, the front door opened. Her mouth immediately broke from mine, and she spun around to face the doorway.

Bryson strolled in with Maci right behind him. Both of them were in swimsuits with towels wrapped around their waists. Maci's eyes landed on mine as soon as she assessed what was in front of her. She didn't show any emotion, but I knew from the look in her eyes that she wasn't expecting to see me.

Bryson smiled. "Sup, man."

Maci followed him down the hall to his bedroom. She completely ignored me the entire way there.

As soon as Bryson's door shut, Layla spun back to me. "I think my roommate has slept with yours."

I signaled for her to leave by opening the front door. "Probably."

Suddenly, I didn't care if I saw Layla again. Once she was gone, I grabbed the keys to my Jeep. I didn't know where I was going, but I didn't feel like being at the apartment.

Chapter Forty-Two

MACI

February 2016

He was kissing someone. He was saying goodbye to one of his hookups.

Ever since I met Jaxon, I have seen a few versions of him. Jaxon who kicked girls out in the morning. Jaxon who kicked the shit out of frat guys. Jaxon who was empathetic and gave advice. Jaxon who cared about his friends. Jaxon who got drunk and sent sex photos.

But seeing Jaxon with his lips against some beautiful blonde babe was not the version I wanted to see.

I drove home shortly after my hot tub hangout with Bryson. Jaxon's door was closed when I left, so I wasn't sure if he had stayed or not after bidding his goodbyes to Blondie. It felt weird to be in that apartment with Bryson while Jaxon was there. I knew that was the risk I ran when I agreed to the hot tub, and part of me wondered if that was the only reason I agreed to it.

It pained me to think he was thriving in this whole *I need space* request he laid on me a few weeks ago. I missed him, and there was nothing I could do about it right now.

I'm not sure which one of us was entitled to start our next conversation based on what happened Wednesday night, but it was already Friday morning, and my messages came up empty.

I sipped my hazelnut iced coffee and climbed up the stairs of our apartment building. My last class of the day was canceled, and I decided to use my extra hour and a half of freedom to do absolutely nothing.

When I walked in, Katie was at the dining room table typing away at something on her computer.

"Hey," she said without looking up.

"Happy Friday," I mumbled and threw myself on the couch.

February in Bowling Green was just depressing. It was cold all the time. It looked miserable outside, and going out suddenly sounded like a chore. I was running out of time to ask Katie about a low-key evening at Sam's request.

"We need something fun, Katie." When she didn't answer, I raised my head to look at her.

"I have five minutes left in this quiz," she answered quickly.

I laid my head back down and closed my eyes. At the risk of falling asleep, I decided to cipher through all of the stressful tabs I currently had opened in my head.

I was completely swamped with schoolwork. Every day, more reading was assigned, and every other day, I had some sort of assessment. Since I was getting an English minor, most of my assessments were papers and essays. I didn't mind the writing, but it took a lot more of my time than a quick quiz or test would.

Educational Psychology was getting better. Dr. Knight was a challenging professor, but she had a ton of experience in the field and knew what she was doing.

While my course load was hard this semester, I was learning a lot. My grades were good, and I hadn't skipped a class yet. I really couldn't complain.

Bryson's tab always threatened to cause a malfunction. Half the time, it was closed. The other half, he was in my bed or on my couch, depending on if Katie was home. He continued sleeping with other girls, and I pretended to believe him when he said he wasn't. I had even caught him at The Attic making out with someone else, and he still pushed his story. He was truly unbelievable.

Tyler's case was still pending. Connor's dad had done his part to get him kicked out of BGSU. Tyler ended up moving back home to southern Ohio, and the rumor was he would attend Ohio University in the fall. It was disgusting how he could just mosey on down to the next school and be an asshole there, but unless Katie pushed for domestic charges, there was nothing anyone could do.

But regardless of how it turned out, it comforted me to know that Katie wouldn't have to see him around campus. She had to feel better knowing he was far away and out of sight. I still got sick to my stomach at the image of Tyler's hand heading straight for my face. I didn't mind him being so far away, either.

"Done!" Katie exclaimed and smacked her laptop shut. "Thank the fuck it is Friday."

I sat up and watched her walk over to the fridge. She pulled out a bag of salad, and her eyes met mine when she noticed me staring at her.

"Where is Connor?" I asked.

"I'm not sure." She shrugged. "Last time I talked to him was this morning before his class."

I tried not to look completely shocked at the fact that she didn't have a concrete answer for her boyfriend's whereabouts.

"God." She dropped her fork into her bowl. "Are we really that pathetic where it's weird if I don't know where my boyfriend is?"

I giggled and didn't judge her fresh relationship. "It's still the honeymoon phase. You guys just hit a month! You're supposed to still be obsessed with each other."

She shook her head and came to sit in the recliner in the living room. It was nice having just Katie and me in our space again.

"Get back to your fun topic." She shoved a forkful of salad into her mouth. "I know you want to."

I wasted no time and decided to deliver the request. "Sam wants us to go out tonight. He asked me to see you if you think you're ready for a low-key evening."

"Does Sam *do* low-key?"

I shrugged. "He laid out a pretty chill route for us to take."

Katie pondered and chewed more of her salad. I checked my text thread with Jaxon for the twentieth time today, so she didn't feel rushed in her thought process. I pursed my lips and dropped my phone on my lap.

"What's that you're doing?" she demanded with a sly smile.

"What?"

"You're pouting."

I shook my head. "Don't change the subject. What do you think about tonight? No pressure. We can have a movie marathon if you don't have plans with Connor. If you do have plans, I will entertain Sam."

"We may be running out of movie options here, Mace." Katie sulked and stared down at her hands. There had been non-stop movie marathons since that night at The Attic. "It would be nice to go out."

I raised my eyebrows. "Really?"

"Yeah," she answered like she was trying to convince her-self. "I know Connor has been wanting to go out with the guys. Maybe I can suggest that to him, and then we can go out with our group. Get some space?"

"Are you sure?" I wanted to double-check before I got all excited and jumped into our usual going-out routine.

We would need to get drink supplies and plan outfits. My stomach had butterflies just thinking about it. I really liked Connor, and I loved him for Katie, but going out with just Katie felt like old times.

"I'm sure," Katie confirmed. "I think it will be good for me. It will be good for us." She gestured toward my phone to let me know more questions were in my future.

"I'll let Sam know," I added quickly so she couldn't change the subject.

"We can go to the store to get stuff after I finish this." She held up her bowl and pulled out her phone. She glanced up from her screen, and I froze. "And we can also catch up on whatever scene you keep replaying in your head. I know something's up."

"There's always something up, Katie," I mumbled.

Katie sighed and went into the kitchen. "Jaxon or Bryson?" I smirked at her, and she widened her eyes.

"What?" she exclaimed. "Am I wrong?"

"No." I chuckled sadly.

She eyed me while she walked into her bedroom to grab her purse. Her eyes were still on mine when she returned.

"Jaxon," I said.

"Shocker," she mouthed.

Since it was still early in the day, Kroger wasn't crowded. We had about an hour before locals started wandering in for weekly grocery shopping and more students ended their classes.

Katie and I weaved in and out of aisles, picking up snacks that looked appealing. We took our time and wandered aimlessly. I plopped two cartons of cranberry juice into our cart and sighed.

"Am I allowed to comment now?" Katie scanned a bottle of pineapple juice and added it to the cart.

I had just told her about my run-in with Jaxon at his apartment and his interrupted lip lock with Blondie. "I suppose."

We rounded the corner and entered the soda aisle. I grabbed a case of Dr. Pepper and slid it underneath the cart. With the amount of alcohol I planned on drinking this weekend, it was a much-needed addition.

"You and Jaxon have been dancing around each other since you tried to hook up. He's got a thing for you, Mace, and you absolutely adore him. I also adore him. He's a great guy. You will continue to be in this weird state you guys have created until one of you does something about it," Katie rambled like she had this speech prepared months ago.

We stopped walking and stood right in the middle of the wine aisle. I turned to face Katie, and she continued, "I know you don't want to try anything because you're afraid of messing it up. You are scared to lose him as a friend, and I get that. But can you honestly tell me that things have been the same between you guys since break? Since November even?"

"He literally said that he *couldn't* sleep with me, Katie." I shook my head and grinned. "And that was much more than a *comment*."

"Because he cared about you as a friend," she argued. "Doesn't that mean anything?"

"Of course, it does, Katie," I stammered.

I started walking again so I could try and focus on something other than this conversation. Katie held up a bottle of sangria, and I nodded in approval. She placed it in the cart and waited for me to continue.

"Jaxon doesn't do relationships," I emphasized, unable to process going through another routine like the one I had with Bryson. "He's had plenty of chances to make a move on me, and he hasn't. I'm going along with what's in front of me because I just want him in my life, even if that means we never go past friends."

We approached the self-checkout and unloaded our haul.

"So your solution then is to just be miserable until it eventually wedges you guys so far apart that you can't fix it," Katie said bluntly.

I blinked and let her words sink in. "He told me I would've hated him in the morning, and he said that nothing would change," I replied softly. I bagged up the last few items and stuck them in the seat of the cart. "It's not my fault he lied."

A look of sympathy washed over Katie's face. She threw her arm around my shoulders and gave me a soft squeeze. "I know I keep saying this, but you guys will work it out."

I looked over at her and smiled. "Is that Hopeless Romantic Katie, I hear?"

"Bitch just won't give up." She shrugged.

We both laughed and loaded up the car with our pregaming supplies. It was clear that we both needed tonight, just for very different reasons.

Chapter Forty-Three

JAXON

February 2016

For a Sunday morning after a night out, the apartment was quiet.

I felt relieved that no one was next to me in my bed. My head throbbed, and I didn't feel like dealing with the morning-after. However, the empty condom wrapper on my floor hinted that someone had been here. I just had no idea who.

Bryson's voice came from the other side of the door, followed by the laughter of a broad I didn't recognize. It wasn't Maci, and my shoulders relaxed. I instantly threw my hands in the air and dragged them down my face. It was infuriating that I even cared.

Once I heard the front door shut, I dragged myself out of bed and put on some sweatpants. I did a quick peek in the hall to see if anyone else was up and moving and made my way into the kitchen. I did a double-take when I saw Connor making bacon and eggs at the stove.

"Why are you here, man?" I blinked a few times and sat at one of the bar stools.

"I live here," he answered casually.

"You know what I mean. You usually live at Katie's on the weekends. I'm surprised you didn't head over to her place last night."

Connor shrugged. "We decided to do a weekend out on our own. I think she just wanted some girl time. She hasn't been out since that night at The Attic." He looked up at me from the burner. We hadn't spoken about that night since he gave me my card the day after it happened.

"Well, that's good she's going out again, I guess?" I tried. It was nice to hear that Katie was doing okay. After I learned what happened with Tyler, I was glad the fucker got kicked off of campus.

Connor nodded and went back to scrambling his eggs. It smelled amazing.

"Can you make me some?" I begged and laid my head down on the counter.

"Rough night?"

"Honestly, I'm not sure." I gestured to the bottle of Advil behind him on the counter.

He reached for it and handed it to me.

"Can you pass me a Gatorade?" I asked.

"Dude!" he exclaimed. "Anything else you need?"

I sighed. I popped three pills and took a long sip of Gatorade.

This was the third Sunday I wasn't hanging out with Maci. It was the third Sunday I wasn't waking up and looking forward to lounging around her apartment while Katie made dinner in the crockpot. We would cycle through shows, and I would spend the day napping and working on assignments that were due on Monday.

I had slept around. I had my space. I wasn't sure how much longer I wanted to keep this up.

Connor set a full plate of food in front of me. "Can I ask for some advice?"

"Shoot." I bit into a piece of bacon.

"Katie and I have been together for a little over a month, so by spring break, it will be two months . . ." he began.

I stared at him, dumbfounded by the fact that a question regarding relationships was being directed toward me.

"Is it too weird to ask her to do something like a trip for spring break?"

"Kennedy and I bring randoms with us all the time on trips." I shrugged. "I'm sure it's totally fine to bring your own girlfriend."

Connor nodded and stuck a forkful of scrambled eggs in his mouth. He still looked unsure about whatever he was contemplating.

"Listen, man, I've never once been close to relationship territory, but if you feel weird about it, then maybe don't mention a trip?" I tried.

"My family owns a really nice condo up in Port Clinton. It's not far from here, and it would be big enough for a bunch of people to go," Connor said.

I chewed on my bacon and waited for him to keep going.

"Would you go?" He looked up from his plate with an innocent stare.

I grinned. "Are you inviting me on your spring break trip, Connor?"

"I planned on inviting the other guys too, but you have a different scenario than they do."

My mouth turned to a straight line, and Connor shook his head. He asked me because if Katie said she wanted to go, she would invite Maci.

"I think it's Bryson you might want to clear that up with. Not me," I argued.

"I'm not worried about Bryson," Connor said. "I'm bringing it up to you because you and Maci are *actually* friends."

I took another sip of Gatorade and didn't say anything. I wasn't sure what to say about what he was suggesting. Bryson was the one who was hooking up with Maci. Connor needed to clear this idea with him, not me. Maci and I could be in the same place and not cause any drama.

"Can I give you some advice you didn't ask for?" Connor rested his elbows on the counter. He could see the wheels spinning in my head.

"Aren't you going to anyway?" I deadpanned.

"I know you aren't in a *relationship*." He paused to gauge my reaction. When I didn't have one, he continued, "But if you care, man, sometimes it's just easier to apologize. And if you and Maci don't do apologies, then be the one to reach out first."

Connor had good intentions, but when he compared my friendship with Maci to a relationship, the bacon I just ate churned in my stomach. I didn't want to have to worry about this shit.

"I'm gonna run over to Katie's, and I'll probably stay there tonight," Connor said.

I nodded just as my phone buzzed in my pocket. We both knew the subject was dropped. After Connor left, I washed the dishes in the sink and headed back to my room. My phone buzzed again, and I pulled it out to see who it was.

Reagan

> Sorry to head out so early. I had to work this morning.

> Last night was fun ;)

Sirens wailed around in my head. I fell onto my bed and dragged my hands over my face. I was at the point where

I had too much space, so much space that I was starting to recycle through girls I had slept with before.

I jumped into the text thread I had with Maci. I could already see Connor's smug smile as I quickly typed out a sentence just to delete it.

How the fuck did I start this up again? I told her I wanted space.

The only time I saw her after that was when she walked into my apartment with the guy she was fucking while I was ushering the girl I just fucked out. Neither of us really had anything to apologize for, so that just left me with Connor's advice of saying something first. Some suggestions before he left would've been nice.

My phone alerted me that it was in low battery mode. I must not have plugged it in last night to charge.

"Did that bitch take my charger?" I mumbled under my breath and searched my end table.

Now Reagan had something to reach out to me about. She and Heather must've been cut from the same crazy cloth.

I dug out my spare cord from the top drawer of my dresser and froze. My hand brushed over the rough edges of the envelope, and the stamp of red ink stood out against everything else.

The letter my mom gave me was still unopened, the same as the day she handed it to me before I left Charlotte. I pulled it out and examined the familiar postage.

**MAILED FROM
A STATE
CORRECTIONAL
INSTITUTION**

Time moved slowly as I continued to stare at it as if my eyes would burn a hole through the envelope and the words would be read to me. I sat down on my bed and swallowed. At first, I hesitated. But eventually, I slid a finger underneath the sealed flap and tore open the letter. I unfolded the paper inside and held it in my hands.

For the next half hour, I read a letter from my birth father, John Krane.

Chapter Forty-Four

MACI

February 2016

I STARED AT THE blinking cursor on my laptop screen. There was only one class left in my schedule before I could head home, and somehow I managed to put off an article for Educational Psychology until the last minute. I had an hour break before that class started, but I had no idea how to begin the assignment.

I rubbed my temples and itched my forehead with my beanie. Even though I was sitting inside the student union, I was still freezing. I drained the rest of my iced coffee and crossed my legs. I'm sure my cold choice of caffeine didn't help me either.

In a way, I still felt like I was recovering from this past weekend. Katie and I followed Sam around downtown BG for both Friday and Saturday nights. I found it a little strange that Katie chose to go out without Connor on both weekend nights, but I decided that it wasn't that much of a red flag that I needed to ask her about it. I wasn't sure how much the Tyler stuff was being pushed into her relationship since Connor's dad got Tyler off campus. I assumed that was the source of the space between them.

But still, I enjoyed my time with Katie this weekend and the rest of our usual gang. It felt good to have a little taste of the past before Katie and I met the guys from Apartment 4G at Falcon's Pointe.

My phone buzzed next to my laptop, and my playlist was interrupted by my ringtone. I winced as the loud tune flowed into my headphones, and I hit the green answer button. "Chase?"

"Hey." Chase sighed, and I heard a car door slam. Ever since my brother deemed text messaging as the elite form of communication, he never called me.

"Is everything okay?" I said slowly.

"Not really." His voice was shaky, and I heard another car door shut.

"What is it?" I demanded urgently. "Chase, what's the matter?"

"I cheated on Trey"—he took a breath so he could finish his sentence—"and he just broke up with me."

My mouth fell open, and I didn't know how to respond. I knew that Chase wasn't calling me for a lecture. He called me because he knew I would hold off on giving him one.

I inhaled through my nose to calm my initial reaction. "Are you okay? Where are you now?"

I heard the sound of another car door and the ding of Chase's dashboard. He must've been leaving their condo.

"I'm not sure what I am, honestly." He began to ramble, "But please don't say the obvious. I just packed up my car, and I guess I'm headed to Columbus. But I don't want to go back to Mom and Dad's house—"

"Come stay with me for a little while," I offered. "I'm sure Katie won't care. You can take some time and process in a judgment-free zone."

"Judgment free for how long?" Chase joked, but the sadness still laced his words.

"As long as you need." I grinned, meaning every word. "Text me once you hit Ohio. I should be out of class and back at my place when you get close."

"Okay." He sighed, and his voice returned to normal. Having some sort of plan in place helped him calm down. "I'll text you in a little bit. Thanks, Mace."

"Take your time, and I love you. See you soon." I hung up the phone, and Adele returned through my headphones.

As I listened to the words of the iconic anthem "Hello," I processed the last few minutes and texted Katie that we would have a house guest for a few days. She was as shocked as I was to hear of the breakup, but she assured me that having Chase stay with us wouldn't be a problem.

I brought my attention back to my laptop and revisited my blank document. I now had forty minutes to knock this essay out, and I only had half of my sources. It was only Thursday, and I desperately needed it to be the weekend. Really I just needed someone to finish this paper for me.

In the record time of twenty minutes, I was able to crank out two paragraphs using the sources that I had. At this point, I felt like settling for a crap grade. I hadn't received anything lower than a B since the beginning of the course, so it wouldn't be detrimental to my average. Maybe Dr. Knight would start the class with one of her case study videos, and I would have time to add more. I decided to take that chance.

Even underneath all of my layers, the hairs on my arms stood up once I caught a whiff of his cologne. Soon, the familiar black North Face jacket entered my peripheral.

Jaxon took the seat across from me and placed his hands clasped in front of him on the table. I slowly removed a headphone from my ear and had to double-check that my mouth wasn't hanging open.

"Hi." His dimple crept into the side of his mouth. A Carolina Panthers beanie covered his dark hair, and he had some stubble on his face. I had only seen him with facial hair once or twice before. I was definitely a fan.

"Hi." I let out a shaky breath and paused Adele.

If I wasn't still reeling from the phone call with Chase, I might've broken down right there in front of him. Sure, I was mad at him for giving us a break while he figured out his need for space, but not a day passed when I didn't miss him. It was actually concerning how scared I was of losing him. At this point, this man could start the next World War, and I wouldn't paint him any differently.

"I'm sorry, Mace," he said. I could tell he was nervous by the way his eyes flicked from me to the table. "We haven't had to do apologies before, but I'm sorry that I've been M.I.A."

I shrugged and closed my laptop. "You were getting your space."

"Yeah." He grinned and let out a chuckle. "I was hoping to be done with that."

I pretended to ponder his apology. It couldn't really be this easy to move on from another setback, could it? Even after spending some time apart, having him in front of me made it seem like no time had passed. He was one of my best friends. Maybe it was supposed to feel this simple.

"Can I come to dinner tonight?" he asked. He was hopeful that I would say yes. I imagined he missed Katie's cooking.

"How did you know I would be here?" I changed the subject.

His eyes narrowed. "We have very persuasive roommates."

I returned the gesture. "I should've known. Katie doesn't surprise me, but Connor, too, now?"

He shrugged and leaned back in his chair. "I know Katie misses me. It's been a while."

"She does talk about you nonstop." I played into his joke, and he smiled.

I sighed at the sight of him back in front of me and immediately caved. I wasn't sure why I even pretended like there would be another answer. "I guess you can come to dinner."

He opened his mouth to speak, but I cut him off.

"Oh, shit," I gasped. "My brother is going to be there."

"Am I not approved to meet your brother?" he asked suspiciously.

"No," I deadpanned and quickly shook my head as soon as I realized what I had just said. "Of course you are. But Chase is coming here because his boyfriend just broke up with him."

"That sucks." Jaxon looked at me empathetically. "Did he say why?"

I reminded myself that the conversation I had with Chase before Jaxon sat in front of me actually happened. "He cheated on Trey," I said to the table.

It felt weird to say it out loud without knowing the whole story. When I looked up, Jaxon was staring at me. His green eyes popped against his black hat, and his lips looked fuller now that they were surrounded by facial hair. I felt the familiar tug behind my belly button and demanded that my libido take a backseat to this conversation.

"Shit." He sighed. "Maybe they will work it out. You said they've been together for like, what, three years?"

I nodded. I wasn't sure how Jaxon would respond to relationship drama, considering he had never been in one. But as far as support went, his suggestion was on the right track.

"I've gotta head to class," I admitted. I shoved my laptop into my book bag and gathered up my belongings.

He stood with me, and I immediately closed the space between us. He wrapped his arms around my shoulders and squeezed. I breathed in his scent, and he tightened his grip.

"Jaxon, I can't breathe." I laughed, and he let me go.

"I'll swing by around five," he said.

"Five," I repeated.

We parted ways, and even though the breakup news with Chase was heavy, reuniting with Jaxon made me ten times lighter.

While it always seemed simple to get things back on track, we never ceased to find things that would derail us all over again. I just hoped that this mend would last longer than the last one.

Chase got into Ohio from Pittsburgh right on schedule. He had about a half-hour or so until he arrived in Bowling Green, and I wasn't sure who was more anxious about his arrival.

Katie worked furiously in the kitchen on some buffalo chicken crescent roll she found on Pinterest while I tried to distract myself with homework. Jaxon and Connor lounged in the living room on their phones and pretended to watch Katie's current binge show *Gossip Girl*.

I was happy to report that Katie was finally out of the *Gilmore Girls* kick, which meant that she was feeling better about the Tyler incident. I stared at the glory of Blake Lively as Serena and tried to think of my next sentence. I was interrupted by the peanut gallery.

"This could be the worst show yet," Jaxon said without looking up from his phone. "The only reason it's decent is because Blake Lively is in it."

"Typical," Katie shouted from the kitchen, and I laughed to agree with her.

"Leighton Meester is hot too," Connor added. His elbow rested on the arm of the recliner, and he was completely invested in the show.

"Who is Leighton Meester?" Jaxon asked.

"Blair," Connor answered quickly.

"Who the fuck is Blair?" Jaxon exclaimed, and we all laughed. It was nice having him here again, and I knew Connor also enjoyed having him back.

Katie joined us in the living room and took her usual seat next to Connor in the recliner. He put his arm around her, and she relaxed into him. "It will be ready in about fifteen minutes," she announced.

I rested my head on the back of the couch and glanced away from my computer to give my eyes a break. Dr. Knight assigned another article essay, and her requirements were killing me.

"Take a break," Jaxon murmured next to me.

His voice vibrated against my body, and I got goosebumps. He was leaning up against my side, and his legs were extended onto the coffee table. I kept waiting for him to say he was too hot since he still had his beanie and hoodie on, but I had a feeling he was too comfortable to care.

"I have to get this done," I said sleepily and flicked the pom-pom of his hat.

"You don't have that class until Tuesday," he urged. He glanced up at me, and my eyes met his. I tried to stop myself from smiling but it was involuntary at this point. My body had no control when I was with him, and I desperately needed it to chill the fuck out.

I immediately switched gears when there was a knock at the door. Katie and I exchanged a glance as soon as another round of knocks followed.

Katie's eyes narrowed. "Did he fly here?"

I stuck out my bottom lip and placed my laptop on the end table. Jaxon shifted so I could get up, and everyone watched me walk over to the door.

I peered in the peephole, and Chase's wide smile greeted me when I opened the door. "What's up, sis?"

I laughed and ushered him inside. "What's up, Sheesh?"

Chapter Forty-Five

JAXON

February 2016

There had been a few times back home when I ran into a brother of a girl I hooked up with. It always happened in a club, and the conversations always ended with them calling me an asshole or them trying to hit me. I considered both endings to be fair because I was indeed an asshole to their sister.

Katie immediately got up to greet Chase, and his smile widened. He hugged her the same way he hugged Maci.

"Chase, this is Connor, Katie's boyfriend." Maci gestured toward the recliner.

"What's up, man?" Chase took a few steps toward him so they could shake hands. "You being good to my girl?"

"Always." Connor nodded, and Katie giggled.

Maci motioned to me from behind Chase, and I sat up so I could extend my hand to her brother.

"My name's Jaxon, man," I offered. "Nice to meet you."

Without hesitating, Chase shook my hand and smirked. "Nice to meet you."

I'd have to ask Maci what that was about later. I knew I only cared because he was Maci's brother, but the thought of Chase not liking me bugged me.

"I'll check on the food," Katie said, disappearing into the kitchen.

"Do you have anything to drink?" Chase slipped off his jacket. He hung it on one of the hooks near the door and followed Maci to the fridge.

As soon as I saw his Pittsburgh Penguins shirt, I thought of Bryson and that morning I ran into Maci in his Tampa Bay Lightning shirt. I tried to ignore that replay and focused on the show in front of me.

Serena and Blair were complaining about an outfit, and a guy with a bow tie offered to help. The shows in this apartment killed me.

"Oh, *that* kind of drink." I heard Maci say from the kitchen.

"Beer?" Connor spun around so quickly in the recliner that he almost slipped off the side.

I chuckled and peered in the direction of the kitchen. The cranberry juice and vodka were already on the table.

"Eat some of this first." Katie shoved a plate into Chase's chest. She glared at Connor and insisted that he do the same.

Maci unscrewed the cap of the vodka and poured it into two glasses. She hovered over the third glass and looked at Katie. "Are you having one?"

Katie sighed and took a bite of the crescent roll and buffalo chicken dip concoction she had on her plate. "I suppose."

Maci smiled and caught me staring at her as she poured into Katie's glass. She liked having her brother here, and I liked seeing her so carefree and happy. Somehow, it made her even sexier.

I got up from the couch, and before I made a plate of food, I grabbed a beer from the fridge. I wasn't expecting to drink tonight, but I was okay with the mood shift. I was getting way too invested in the rich kid show on TV.

"Babe, this is amazing," Connor said with his mouthful.

Everyone nodded in support of his comment.

"Thanks." Katie beamed and took a sip of her cocktail.

"So, what's it like here on a Thursday night?" Chase asked Maci. Half of his drink was already gone, and I had a feeling he would be requesting a second soon.

"This." Maci giggled. "Katie cooks, I do homework, and Connor and Jaxon come over to get free food."

"I work for that food." Connor shrugged, and Katie slapped him on the shoulder.

I nudged Maci's arm. "I used to buy you breakfast."

She smirked. "*Used to*. Key words there, my friend." She shoved the last bite of food from her plate into her mouth and got up to go into the kitchen.

I turned on the couch to face her while she walked away. Her ass looked fantastic, and I had already lost my train of thought when she turned around and noticed me staring at her for the second time tonight.

"I owe you . . ." I counted back in my head. "Three morning coffees then."

She frowned when she realized I was accurate in my tally. It was a huge shift from last semester.

"Fine." She shrugged and returned to the couch next to me. "It's a date, Jaxon Hayes."

"There's that full name again." I rolled my eyes and got up to get another beer. I noticed Chase's empty glass. "You want another one, man?"

"Absolutely," he said without hesitation.

Connor held up his empty can. "Me too."

"Another one?" Katie asked Connor after I handed him a beer. She sounded surprised.

I watched them go back and forth in the playful bickering way they always did. I shook my head and backed into the kitchen to make Chase another drink.

Maci's lips brushed against my ear. "Not too strong, okay?"

The hair on my neck stood up as her warm breath flew across my skin. I glanced down at her, and she smiled just as she took a sip of her drink.

"You look like you're up to no good," I said slyly and turned my body so I faced her.

She studied my face for a moment, and I watched her eyes linger on my chest. They made their way back up to mine, and I swallowed. The last time she looked at me like that was when we were standing on a street corner, and she was taking me back to the bedroom down the hall.

"Not tonight." Her lips formed a small half-smile. "If I drink too much, my therapy session might come out too early."

I glanced into the living room and back at her. "Chase?" I whispered.

She nodded and took another drink. She set the empty glass on the table and reached behind her to grab a beer from the fridge.

"So Bud Light is the safer choice, huh?" I teased.

She watched me pour Chase's drink, and I caught her smiling. If the reel in her head matched mine, we were both in her bedroom picking up where we left off . . . when she was on top of me.

"What's up, Mace?" I grinned down at her. I half-hoped she would say something to let me know she felt the mood shift between us

"I missed you," she admitted.

Katie's party playlist started playing in the background, and we both looked toward the living room.

I had admitted to Maci a few different versions of *I missed you* before, but it felt different hearing it the other way around. When we returned to campus after break, the first time we saw each other, I asked her not to ignore me again. Now that my mind was taking a trip down the route of our exchanges, I actually told Maci I would miss her before break too.

Maci lightly squeezed my bicep and snagged her brother's drink off the table. I hadn't noticed I was holding my breath until she returned to the couch.

We both knew we didn't like to be away from each other for long periods of time. I had no idea why I thought getting some space would help me get my mind off her. Every time we were back in the same room, I felt like I was seeing her for the first time all over again. My breath would catch in my chest, and I ached to do things that felt natural to me. I wanted to touch her and kiss her and make her feel good. But I knew the guy that woke up the next morning would go into survival mode and completely crash everything that happened the night before. The thought of sleeping with Maci didn't scare me off, but how I would treat her afterward definitely did.

Chase's voice boomed from the living room so he could be heard over the music. "Ten out of ten, Jaxon." He raised his glass for emphasis, and I acknowledged him.

After a few rounds of Drunk Driving, I was buzzed and felt my second wind creeping into my system. Maci had just beaten Chase for the fifth time in a row, and every time they finished a race, her smile grew bigger, and her eyes grew glossier from the alcohol. Chase was now four drinks in, and since I was his designated cocktail mixer, I knew he would have to crash soon. He was a big guy, but he only had one plate of food when he got here a couple of hours ago, and he drank at least two-thirds of the vodka.

Katie and Connor were riding the same level, both laughing uncontrollably and stealing kisses when they thought no one was looking.

"I'm gonna step outside." Chase stood up and surveyed the room. "I managed to snag some bud before heading up. Anyone else wanna join?"

Connor and I exchanged a look and followed Chase out of the apartment.

"Well damn, okay then!" Katie laughed just as the front door shut.

Connor led us around the corner to a balcony that peered out over the parking lot. It was secluded from the main hallway, and a few chairs had been left there by previous owners.

I leaned against the railing, and Chase did the same. There was a soft breeze, and even though it was freezing, it felt nice to be outside. Maci and Katie's apartment was usually kept warm, but after a few drinks, it started to feel like a sauna.

Connor took a seat in one of the empty chairs and offered his lighter to Chase. Chase handed him a rolled joint and turned around to face the parking lot.

"I would do anything to come back here right now," Chase said and leaned back to grab the joint from Connor. He took a long hit and passed it to me.

"You went to BG?" I exhaled, and smoke drifted in the opposite direction.

"I went to Cincinnati, actually," Chase explained. "It's where I met Trey."

We continued to pass the joint between the three of us. Connor and I exchanged a look at the mention of Chase's very recent breakup. I wasn't expecting him to be so open with the conversation, especially since it was like pulling teeth to get Maci to open up about certain things.

"I just meant I'd do anything to be back here in this chapter," Chase said. "Everything was so simple in college. Anything could happen at any time."

"Did you and Trey date in college?" Connor asked.

"Yeah." Chase chuckled, and he looked like he was playing back a memory in his head. "We met my junior year, and by the beginning of our last year, we were together."

"Hmm." Connor stared at me like he had something else to say.

I warned him with one look not to say anything more about what I already knew he was thinking. He sucked at remaining neutral when it came to Maci and me. Drunk Connor could be a loose cannon if he was feeling confident enough, and I wasn't sure what Chase knew about our history.

"Do you still wanna be with him?" I asked.

Chase didn't look surprised at my question. I couldn't tell if he looked sad or if everything from the evening was hitting him all at once. He stared out into the parking lot for a moment before turning his head to answer me. "I dunno. I'm not even sure if he would pick up the phone if I called him." He lightened up and changed the subject. "But enough sob talk. How did you meet my sister?"

Connor smiled smugly in the chair behind Chase.

"I gave her my ice cream at Dairy Queen." A laugh escaped my chest at the memory.

"She said you had a class together too, right?" Chase asked.

"Journalism." I nodded

That day seemed so long ago, back when she was just a ghost emoji on my phone. Somehow a few text messages transformed into a coffee and dinner routine that led us up to this point.

"I didn't know you guys met before your class," Connor said. He sounded disappointed that there was information he didn't know. "I was at Dairy Queen that day. Was Katie with her?"

"Yeah." I smiled and turned to face Connor. "I saw Katie that day and totally thought she was your type."

"And you met Katie through Maci?" Chase asked Connor. He had relaxed a lot since the change in subject.

"Actually, I met her because I came over here with Jaxon," Connor explained.

Chase nodded like he knew where the conversation was headed. "Tyler. He was kicked off campus, though, right?"

"Yup," Connor confirmed proudly.

Chase turned his gaze and pointed toward me. "And you beat his ass."

I shrugged. "Something like that."

Chase didn't even try to hide the giant smile that was plastered on his face. He seemed to approve of my decision to lose my shit on Tyler.

"Why did she call you, Sheesh?" I asked, putting the attention back on him. When Chase got here, it was the first name Maci called him. She had never mentioned that nickname before.

He laughed and shook his head a few times. "When she was little, and my parents tried to get her to say my name, it always came out as Sheesh instead of Chase."

I stared out into the parking lot and pictured Maci running around as a little kid. A few months ago, I never imagined myself having a conversation with the brother of some girl I had just met at the beginning of the year.

Who the fuck was I kidding? I never expected to fall for the girl I saved as a ghost emoji either.

Chapter Forty-Six

MACI

February 2016

It had been two solid days of Chase moping around our living room. I could deal with some sad songs here and there. Anyone with taste would never turn down a chance to belt "Wrecking Ball" by Miley Cyrus or "Thinkin' About You" by Frank Ocean, but I drew the line at sappy country songs. That shit was just depressing.

"Mace?" Katie peeked her head into my room and widened her eyes.

I stared at her sympathetically as Brooks and Dunn's "Neon Moon" blared through the speakers.

She took a few steps toward me so she could lower her voice to a whisper. "I am all about supporting Chase's recovery, but could we please tone down the music choice? I am happy in my relationship, and the mood here has been so depressing that I wake up questioning myself."

I rubbed my temples and laughed at Katie's comment. There was so much truth to her statement. "I'll talk to him today," I offered.

"Perhaps you could chat with him sometime before Connor and I get home from dinner tonight?" Katie asked hopefully. She had been gushing about some surprise dinner Connor had planned for them for Valentine's Day. She even had me excited to learn the details.

"Yes," I promised. "You and Connor will not be having romantic Valentine's Day sex to any of this negative energy." I fanned my hand in the direction of the living room.

"I appreciate your support," Katie stated, turning on her heels to leave.

Once she was gone from my room, I reached for my phone and dialed Jaxon's number. He picked up on the fourth ring.

"Did you call to wish me a happy Valentine's Day?" I could tell he was smiling on the other end of the line.

I shut my door and tried to cancel out some of the depressing lyrics happening in the other room. "Not exactly. Are you free for a drive?"

"Damn. You can't even wish me that after I mention it?"

"Jaxon, I don't have time to recognize a holiday I know for a fact you've never celebrated," I snapped.

"What are you talking about? Many girls I've talked to have wished me a happy Valentine's Day before. Sometimes I even get gifts."

"Charming," I stated. His laugh came through the phone, and it felt good to be back in this place with him again—even if that place was me longing for more.

"Are you up for a drive?" I asked again.

"Where to?"

"Honestly, I don't care. I need out of this apartment for a little while," I said as the violin intro of Rascal Flatt's "What Hurts the Most" pierced my ear drums. "Can you be here in five?"

"Minutes?" Jaxon laughed. "Yes, I will roll right through campus for you, Mace."

"Perfect," I beamed. "See you soon."

It wasn't hard to bypass Chase in the living room. I shot him a quick wave and a promise to be back soon. He just nodded and sunk deeper into the couch. I had never seen him like this. He was usually active, confident, and alert. This version of him was such an unattractive sight.

Jaxon's Jeep rolled into the parking lot a few minutes after I made it downstairs. It was a rare day in February when the sun made an appearance, so I was comfortable in jeans and a hoodie. I exhaled loudly at the sight of Jaxon behind the wheel of his Jeep, wearing mirrored aviators and a backward snapback. He was just too hot to look at sometimes.

Just as I expected, I was hit with a wave of his cologne when I climbed into the passenger seat.

"What's up, Mace?" He smiled behind his aviators and waited until I shut the door so he could peel out of the lot.

I sighed and leaned back in my seat. "Thanks for coming."

Once we hit Main Street, Jaxon made a right. He kept stealing glances in my direction while I steadied my eyes on the road in front of us.

"Are you gonna fill me in on what you're stewing about over there?" he finally asked and rested his right hand on the gearshift.

"I am not stewing," I argued. "Long story short, Chase is starting to drive our apartment a little nuts."

"He's only been there for a few days. Didn't you tell him he could come here 'judgment free'?" he mimicked my quote.

"There is still no judgment!" I exclaimed. "But it has been a nonstop show of sappy country songs and cocktails, and I'm not sure how much more I can take before I end up exploding on him anyways!"

Jaxon moved his sunglasses so they rested on the top of his hat. "Do you think you only feel this way because you disagree with what he did?"

My mouth formed a straight line, and I stared at him. "What do you mean?"

"*I mean* . . ." he said slowly and looked at me for permission to keep going. "If he would've just broken up with Trey, like mutually, would you be this impatient with how he is handling it?"

I stared back at the road and pondered Jaxon's point.

My gut response was no. I knew my lack of patience stemmed from Chase putting himself in this situation. Of course, I didn't know the whole story yet because he hadn't filled me in, but until I heard his side, I had nothing else to go on. At first glance, Chase was sulking in a situation he chose to be in when he chose to cheat. In my head, it was really that simple.

"No," I admitted. "I wouldn't be this impatient. But isn't it my job to make him see something from a different perspective?"

"You mean *your* perspective," Jaxon corrected. He tightened his lips to hold back his smile.

My mouth curved into a grin. "No. I just want him to see that if he expects something to change from this, he has to decide to do something about it. Sitting around and listening to Rascal Flatts and George Strait is not going to make things better with Trey."

"I don't know either of those people," Jaxon muttered. "But I do know that it's okay to take some time and figure out what you want."

"But he wants to be with Trey."

"That's what he said when you asked him?" Jaxon pushed but kept his tone casual. I knew there was something else he wanted to say.

"He wouldn't be so upset unless he still wanted to be with Trey," I explained.

"Well, when *I* asked him if he wanted to be with Trey"—he raised his eyebrows and shot me a quick glance before stopping at a red light—"he said he didn't know."

My eyes narrowed and he bit his bottom lip. "When did *you* ask him about Trey?"

The light turned green, and he averted his attention back to the road. "When we were smokin' at your place," he said like it was something he did every Thursday with my brother.

I sat up a little taller and thought back to that night. They *were* out on the balcony for a while. I mean, it was long enough for Katie and me to duet "Promiscuous Girl" and "Last Night" right before doing a few races of Drunk Driving.

"What else did you talk about while you were *smokin'* on the balcony?" I demanded.

Jaxon shrugged. "Nunya."

"Okay," I mocked him, and he laughed.

We rolled to another red light, and his hand slid back over the gearshift.

"Why do you put your hand there?" I gestured between us.

He followed my gaze and understood my question. "I used to drive stick all the time," he explained. "It's a habit."

"Is this Jeep a stick?" I asked.

Ever since he fixed my Hyundai a few months back, I found it incredibly attractive when he talked about cars. Normally I didn't give a shit about cars, trucks, or any kind of model of anything as long as it worked and got me to where I needed to go. But hearing Jaxon talk about it was a total turn-on.

"No, Mace," he answered like it was cute for me to even ask.

I prepared myself to continue the Chase conversation. "So what? I'm just supposed to figure out what he wants and nurture whatever answer he gives me?"

"Mace, I have no experience with the type of conversation you are about to have with your brother. When it comes to relationships, I get the basic background information, and that's it," Jaxon stressed.

If I weren't so conflicted, I would've had some snarky comeback about Blondie or one of his hookup girls to poke some fun at him. But all I kept thinking about was the story Chase hadn't told me yet. I wasn't sure how I would react once I heard everything.

"I just don't know"—I took a deep breath—"I just don't know if I can sit there and listen to him justify how he could cheat on Trey. It's not like it was some guy he was hooking up with for three weeks, Jaxon. He was with him for three years. I love Trey."

"Just hear him out, Mace," Jaxon urged. "Maybe there was something going on that led them to this point. Your brother is a guy, and we do stupid shit."

"But he's supposed to be one of the good guys," I mumbled pathetically, and Jaxon placed his hand on my thigh. Heat trickled up my leg, and I felt a dip in my stomach.

"It'll all work out," he reassured me and gave my leg a quick squeeze. He placed his hand back on the gearshift, and my entire body had to recover from his touch.

I stared out my window at the passing buildings. There were dozens of small businesses I hadn't seen before. We had been driving for so long down Main we must've gone a few towns over.

"Where are we going?" I asked and glanced over at him.

"I"—Jaxon looked both ways before he hooked a left—"am taking you for some food."

"Why?" I said, trying not to sound too shocked at his response.

"Because it's almost four, and I haven't eaten since noon." He laughed. "And we are at least fifteen minutes away from your apartment right now. We can stop and get some wings or something."

I shook my head at his typical guy way of thinking, and he stared at me like I had just asked him a question he didn't know the answer to. "Jaxon, we can't just walk into a restaurant. You need a reservation at most places on Valentine's Day."

"Fuck." His mouth fell open as he realized what I had just said. "I totally forgot what today was."

"You *literally* just asked if I was calling to wish you a happy Valentine's Day like a half hour ago," I snapped.

His tongue grazed his bottom lip, and he shot me a half-smile. "Am I keeping you from any plans if we get some food?"

"Nope," I deadpanned and pulled out my phone to make sure Chase hadn't tried to contact me. He was probably too deep in the couch to even notice that I was still gone.

"Then this will make up for the coffee I owe you," Jaxon said.

We pulled into a plaza that had a local sports bar on the end of the strip. There were quite a few cars parked outside, but not enough to indicate that it was crowded and we wouldn't get seated.

Jaxon turned off the engine and shifted to face me. "Ready?"

I stared him up and down and took a moment to fully appreciate this day's turn. I never thought I would ever do anything on Valentine's Day with Jaxon, but if I kept reminding myself that this was just another outing between friends, it would be fine.

I was notorious for overthinking things like this. I wasn't going to allow this to be one of those times.

"Ready." I nodded and followed him inside.

Chapter Forty-Seven

JAXON

February 2016

It was almost six thirty when I dropped Maci off at her place. We had been at the bar longer than expected, but my impromptu decision to get some food turned into something we both needed. Ever since that night at The Attic, we hadn't done anything just the two of us. Being with Maci was easy. It was nice to hang out and just act like we used to be before everything got complicated.

As soon as I pulled out of her parking lot, I dialed my mom's number to have our annual "V-Day Chat" as she liked to put it. My parents always went to dinner around seven on the lovey-dovey holiday, so I had some time before she had to leave to meet my dad wherever he made reservations.

"Hey, baby," she exclaimed as soon as she picked up the phone. It felt good to hear her voice.

"Happy Valentine's Day, Ma." I smiled and turned down my music. "You all ready for your date with Dad?"

She sighed. "I have some finishing touches, of course, but it never helps that your father doesn't tell me where we are going. A woman needs to have this information."

"Well, whatever you're wearing, I already know you look beautiful."

"So what are you up to? Are you coming from some-where?" She changed the subject and then quickly rescinded her question. "Don't tell me if I really don't want to know the answer to that question."

"I just dropped off a friend at her apartment." I was careful to leave out any leading information, but she caught on quickly.

"*Her* apartment?" she piped up.

"Just a friend, Ma," I emphasized and turned into my parking lot.

"Uh-huh," she stated, and I laughed at her obvious disappointment. My mom knew me all too well. Growing up, she always tried to keep an open household and maintain respectable boundaries. She loved knowing what was going on in my life but always appreciated filters when they were necessary.

Even though she knew how I was with women and how I felt about being in a relationship, she hadn't lost hope that one day I would call her to say I went on a date or that I was bringing someone home to meet her. At least she had Alex for that, especially now that he was with Bella.

I turned off my Jeep and sunk into my seat. "How are things? How are you and Dad?"

"You know he's busy, baby. We both are. But we're doing good. Alex and Bella flew back to California shortly after you left. Have you talked to your brother?"

"I haven't. It's a shitty excuse, but I've had a lot going on. I'll call him tomorrow. I'm sure he's busy with Bella tonight."

A lump formed in my throat, and I took a deep breath. It only took a few seconds for her to know what was going through my head. It had been eating at me for days, and I hadn't taken the time to fully reflect on the letter I received from John Krane.

"You read it, didn't you," she said sadly. I knew she didn't mean to sound sad about it, but talking about John Krane wasn't easy for either of us.

I swallowed and looked up at the ceiling of the Jeep. "Yeah."

"Well, you know I'm here if you want to talk about it. It's been a while since he last sent you something. It took everything I had in me to give it to you when it came."

"Revisiting anything that has to do with him or Karina just always puts my life in perspective, you know?" I admitted. The weight on my chest shifted as the words came out of my mouth. "After I read it, it made me think about a fight I had with a friend. Maybe it wasn't a fight, but it made me reach out to her when I wasn't sure if I should."

"Things will happen like that, baby. As painful as reminders can be, sometimes it takes us having to revisit them for us to see what we already have," she said in a soothing voice.

My shoulders relaxed. "I miss you, Ma," I whispered.

"I miss you too, baby," she choked out, and I immediately felt bad.

I knew being away from Alex and me was hard for her. Usually, our phone conversations were light and fun, and I made sure to save the heavy stuff for when I saw her in person. Sometimes shit just slipped through the cracks when I didn't know what else to do with it.

"Now, don't get all worked up before your hot date, Ma," I teased and laughed a little for emphasis. I didn't want her to picture me sulking outside my apartment in my Jeep, even though that was exactly what I was doing.

"Oh." She sniffed, and a chuckle escaped through the phone. "I'm not worked up. Just miss my boys, that's all. But I do have to—"

"Catch your *limo*?" I emphasized. Dad always ordered her a limo to the house so she could meet him for their date. He worked a lot running his business but never failed to show her how much he still loved her.

"Make sure you get your V-Day gift, and don't let those boys eat it all," she said sternly.

I got out of the Jeep and crossed the parking lot. "Well, it was either Jared or Bryson who brought whatever it is in because Connor is out with Katie. So the odds could go either way."

"Oh, that sweet boy! I forgot he was dating that girl—"

"Go catch your limo!" I cut her off, and we both laughed.

She took a deep breath, and I felt her smile on the other end of the line. "Happy Valentine's Day, J. I love you."

"I love you too, Ma."

We hung up just as I reached the door of the apartment. When I walked inside, I was greeted with the familiar scene of Jared playing Call of Duty. A giant bouquet of chocolate-covered strawberries sat right in the middle of the bar counter. It took up almost half of the space.

"Jesus, Ma," I murmured and double-checked the card. Sure enough, it was an Evelyn Hayes original, complete with gift wrap and all. I swatted the bright pink ribbon that kept the cellophane wrapped around the bouquet and shook my head.

"Now that you're home, can we have some of that?" Jared asked.

I grinned. "Go for it, man."

As soon as I rounded the corner of the counter, Bryson emerged from his bedroom, followed by some broad I didn't recognize. I shook my head and stifled a laugh at Bryson's usual "I'm ready for this girl to get the fuck out" face. He had wide eyes, and his mouth made a straight line. Jared looked up long enough to witness the scene and laughed.

Bryson's guest stopped right in front of me and pointed at my chest. Her eyes narrowed, and she pursed her lips. "I think you slept with my roommate."

"Probably." I rocked on my heels and casually went around her. There was a knock on the door, and Jared, Bryson, and I all exchanged a look. It was clear that none of us were expecting someone.

"My ride's here." Bryson's hookup walked to the door, and when she opened it, my blood immediately boiled.

Heather stood on the other side of the door. We made eye contact, and I was positive I snarled at her. Bryson patted my shoulder and rounded into the kitchen for a drink—but I knew he wanted a front-row seat to the madness that quickly unfolded in front of me.

"Jaxon?' Heather said casually, like she had no idea I lived here. She took a few steps into the apartment, and I pointed back into the hallway.

"Nope," I deadpanned and emphasized my extended arm.

Jared cackled from behind me, and Bryson hid his amusement by pretending to take sips of his water. I hated both of them right now.

"Get out," I exclaimed when Heather looked at me like I spoke French. She rolled her eyes and turned to head downstairs. The other girl followed her and slammed the door behind them.

I ran my hands over my face, and the laughter around me grew. Eventually, I gave in and rested my elbows next to the giant bouquet of fruit that still sat untouched on the counter. "Ugh," I groaned and laughed at the same time.

"Honestly, bro," Bryson said, "I had no idea they were roommates."

I shook my head. "We need like a ten-mile radius of caution tape around that fucking house."

Bryson and I now officially slept with every girl at that address. I didn't know the one I just saw, but Heather and Reagan ran close to the crazy train, so I imagined she had to be equally nuts to make it on the lease.

Bryson stared at me. "Well, to add to that shit." He widened his eyes like he did when he had to tell me something he knew I wouldn't like.

"What did you do?" I asked.

"Technically, Connor started everything when he invited us to Port Clinton," he countered.

"What did you do?" I repeated a little more seriously.

"It turns out Heather's dad owns a few condo complexes in Port Clinton . . ." Bryson allowed me to process his words while Jared laughed more behind me. "And she and her roommates will be there at the same time we will be."

I chuckled. "You're both idiots." My eyes flicked between Jared and Bryson. When Bryson's wide eyes were replaced with a cocky grin, I knew he was telling the truth. I threw my arms in the air, and my voice grew louder. "Why the fuck would you invite the gang of girls that together we both have slept with?"

Bryson mimicked my body language and cocked his head. "Too many people are going for us to fit in Connor's place. I remembered that Heather had some property out there, and she was the first person who came to mind. It was one of the many things she babbled about while you tuned her out."

"The first person?" I repeated. "And there were no other options? Man, we all tune Heather out, don't act like you don't."

"No one was trying to pay for a place," Jared added. "Now more people can go. It'll be fun."

Bryson smiled and headed toward his bedroom. "It's all good, man."

Jared hopped off the couch and unwrapped the gift my mom had sent. He bit into a strawberry with an amused look on his face.

"I'm going down for a workout," I said. I had only been home for ten minutes, and I already felt like I needed a breather. I ran into my room to change, and when I came out, Bryson and Jared each had a fresh strawberry in their hand. They stared at me, and we all broke into the same grin.

"Unbelievable." I shut the front door behind me.

Chapter Forty-Eight

MACI

February 2016

I could hear David Nail's "Let it Rain" as soon as I made it to the second floor of the apartment building. I cringed as I unlocked my door and wasn't surprised to find Chase sitting on the couch.

"Chase!" I yelled over the music. He looked over the couch and sat up when he saw me. He shot me a small smile and turned down the sappy lyrics.

I plopped down on the couch next to him and stared at him innocently. "You have been doing this for two whole days now. Can we finally talk about it?"

Chase sat his tumbler down and ran his hands over his face. "Can I take a shower first?"

I gestured toward the bathroom. "By all means."

As soon as the water went on in the bathroom, I scurried around the living room to tidy up. I cleared all of the empty take-out boxes and beer cans and filled up an entire trash bag. It was obnoxious how much shit had been left lying around. Katie and I were both very clean people, and it was painful to see our shared living space taken over by someone in Chase's state. I dusted the coffee table and sprayed the couch with Febreze before I sank into the fresh-smelling cushions. It looked like a brand-new room.

I replayed Jaxon's advice in my head one more time to prepare my dialogue. Hanging out with him at the bar was exactly what I needed before this moment. He made me feel calm and put together even when my world was falling apart. Being with him was easy, and even though he had only dropped me off a few minutes ago, I already missed being around him. I took a deep breath and kept myself focused on the task at hand.

When Chase emerged from the bathroom, he was in basketball shorts, a Henley, and his hair was styled with gel. He looked like a version of himself that I recognized.

"Nice to see you again," I said gently and sat up a little when he took the seat next to me. I brought my legs to my chest, and he placed a hand on my kneecap.

"I'm sorry I've been such a buzzkill. I know you and Katie have your own stuff going on, and you don't need to be involved in my shit. I'll be outta here tonight," he assured me and rested his feet on the coffee table.

"Chase, I'm not kicking you out," I said sternly, and a puzzled look crossed over his face. "I'm trying to understand what is going on."

His hand dropped from my knee, and he rested his hands in his lap. I imagined it was hard trying to start a story in which you were the bad guy. My heart sank as I watched the skin around his eyes turn soft. I knew he was hurting.

"What happened with Trey?" I pressed.

"I was at one of my work events," Chase began, and I sat back to listen. "Trey and I have been rocky for a while, Mace. It's like we both became adults and once we left college, we had to get serious about boring shit like bills and where each of us would be for work. I would look at myself in the mirror and try to see glimpses of who I used to be when we were together in college, and I couldn't see it."

He dragged a hand down his face. My eyebrows knit together as I processed his words. My shoulders fell, and I pictured Chase in his beautiful three-story condo with Trey, both avoiding each other because they were unhappy. It was the total opposite of what they presented when they had an audience.

"A few months ago, I realized that the spark we had when things were exciting just wasn't there. When we graduated, when we bought the condo, when we redid the kitchen . . . those were all things that allowed us to grow and move together. We had things to look forward to, ya know?" He shifted his gaze to me and continued, "But now that we both have jobs we love and our own things going on, I just feel like we are moving in different directions. We don't do the little shit anymore. I'm not sure if either of us is really happy with what we chose."

I nodded to show I understood what he was saying but didn't want him to pause his story. He took a deep breath and kept going.

"I had a conference for work in Cleveland last weekend. Those events can get a little crazy. Since my job is to sell and promote liquor, it's always easier to involve it in conversations I have with potential vendors."

I swallowed and could already picture the scene that Chase was standing in. Katie and I accompanied Chase to a conference over spring break last year. We met him for a weekend in Cincinnati and had a blast. It was a perfect place to meet new connections, but there were times when it could definitely get out of hand. You had a bunch of people away from their everyday lives in a big city and staying in a fancy hotel paid for by their job. It didn't take much persuading for some people to step outside their normalcy.

"It just happened," Chase stated matter-of-factly. We both knew he didn't need to provide the details because, at the end of the day, it didn't matter how it happened. "It happened, and I told him as soon as I saw him when I got back."

I expected to feel angry at Chase when he got to the end of his story. I had filled my head with tons of possibilities that made Chase look like an asshole. But the man who sat in front of me didn't come off that way. My heart sank further into my chest, and I felt the burn behind my eyes.

"Do you still love him?" I whispered and wiped the corners of my eyes.

His eyes slowly met mine, and he shook his head. "I don't know," he admitted. He looked tired and void of any emotion. It was like everything he had was spent over the last few days on this couch.

"It's okay to take time and figure out what you want." Jaxon's words flowed from my mouth, and I surprised myself with how different my reaction was.

"I don't know how much time I have." Chase dragged a hand down his face. "I know Trey, and he won't wait for me. I'm not even sure if I still have a chance of fixing things."

"You haven't talked to him?"

"No." Chase sighed and stood up. He paced around the living room and placed his hands behind his head.

"You haven't reached out to him at all?" I asked a little more urgently.

"No, Mace," he said sternly.

That rattled me a bit. Chase got here on Thursday, and it was already Sunday. In that span of time, he hadn't even *attempted* to reach out to Trey and apologize or start the process of talking things through. He got to sit there and sulk because he had the full picture of what happened and how he saw things in their relationship over the last year. Whether they were unhappy or not, Trey deserved better than that, and he deserved to have some sort of closure.

I exhaled sharply through my nose and stared at my brother. "You've been sitting here moping about something, and you don't even know if it's over?" My voice started to climb, and suddenly, the calm and collected coat I wore into the conversation slipped off.

I could already picture Jaxon shaking his head. "Chase, if you don't want to be with Trey, then that's fine. But you cannot sit here and wallow in sad country music and a bottle of vodka if you haven't even tried to fix it!"

"I don't know what I'm fixing!" He raised his voice to meet mine. It was laced with hurt from the breakup and confusion about what to do next. "I want to at least talk about what happened, but I know Trey. He isn't going to make it easy."

"You don't get to decide that though, what is easy and what isn't easy. You made a choice, Chase . . . and this is the aftermath of that choice."

He lifted his eyes to meet mine, and we both stared at each other.

"Trey is sitting around waiting to see if you're going to fight for him and what you guys had," I explained softly.

Chase crossed his arms and leaned against the wall. "I don't know what to say to him," he admitted.

"You tell him the truth," I suggested softly.

Our eyes met again, and I offered him a sad smile. He returned the gesture and sat back on the couch.

"Whatever you decide, I support you." I placed my hand on his kneecap. "But don't just throw away a conversation you really want to have just because you think it's easier."

Chase nodded and shoved me playfully. He then caught my shoulder and pulled me in for a hug. "Thank you for the pep talk," he murmured.

I smiled into his shoulder. "Anytime, Sheesh."

The following morning, Chase was on his way back to Pittsburgh.

Chapter Forty-Nine

JAXON

February 2016

I SENT ANOTHER ROUND of obnoxious honking from the wheel of my Jeep. Bryson said he would be ready in ten minutes—seventeen minutes ago.

A girl wrapped in a long cardigan and matching hat shot a look of disgust my way. Her arms were crossed, and she looked miserable having to walk outside in the cold. I cocked my head in her direction, and a shy smile crossed her face. Bryson emerged from the building exit, and her eyes widened. Her eyes flicked from me to him before she darted inside and shut the door behind her.

Bryson smiled on his way to the car and laughed when he opened the passenger side door. "What did you do to that girl?"

I shrugged. "I looked at her."

Bryson shook his head with a grin still plastered on his face. "You're a cocky asshole."

I checked my rearview mirror. "Okay, kettle."

It was only a five-minute drive to Wings Over, one of the greatest places to ever exist in Bowling Green. It was a small franchise that opened up last year, and the town went crazy for it. Back home, Charlotte didn't have anything that compared to the wings here. Bryson and I got their food at least once a week.

A few groups of people were ahead of us when we entered the shop. It was a little after four, so most people were done with classes for the day. It was also Wednesday, and I knew Bryson and I couldn't be the only ones who needed a little motivation to finish the week. I had some extra push since I had dinner to look forward to at Maci's on Thursdays, but until last week, I hadn't had that for a while either.

"J." Bryson bumped my arm, and I snapped out of my daydream. "Didn't you bang that bitch?"

I peered at the line in front of us and searched the crowd.

"Blonde with the hat," Bryson added when he saw me struggling.

I sucked in a breath and nodded. My mouth formed a hard line, and I stared at Layla, who stood a few groups up from us. I thought back to how Maci walked in with Bryson that night and the look on her face when she saw me with Layla.

"Worth tapping again?" Bryson smirked at his phone screen and glanced up to see my reaction.

I shrugged and shot him an amused grin. "We'll see."

"Next in line!" the cashier yelled, and the entire line shifted up a few steps.

Bryson let out a frustrated sigh and shoved his phone into his pocket. I watched his mouth form a hard line, and his eyes narrowed on the person in front of us.

"What's up?" I chuckled. His face went from stoic to aggravated to confused in seconds.

He shook his head and dragged a hand down his face. "I usually hook up with that girl from your class on Wednesday, and today she's giving me a hard time about it."

"What do you mean a hard time?" I turned to face him, genuinely interested in how Maci could be screwing with him. It was too good to be true to think she was losing interest in him.

"Usually, I just text her, and she invites me over. But today, she's going back and forth with me about how she might not have time." He shook his head like he was trying to process the situation. "But then she suddenly has time if I bring her food."

I laughed, and Bryson looked annoyed it wasn't me in the situation. I didn't waste time delving into the irony of that.

"Just bring her some food," I suggested, gesturing toward the menu. "All girls love Mustang Ranch." I had ordered Wings Over with Maci before and knew it was her favorite.

We got to the front of the line and were called to order. I saw Layla out of the corner of my eye. She was staring at me from a nearby table, waiting for her food to be done. She leaned in to whisper something to her friend, and they both looked over in my direction. There was no way she didn't recognize me—we had just slept together last week.

As soon as I completed my order, Bryson started his. I grinned when he asked for an order of boneless Mustang Ranch, and he shoved me in the back. We both laughed, and the cashier was anything but amused with our hold-up of the line.

"Anything else?" The cashier printed off our receipt before either of us could answer. Bryson shook his head and took the paper.

We took a few steps to the right and joined the smaller crowd waiting for their food. I pulled out my phone to look busy so that Layla wouldn't come over. My plan immediately failed, and I watched her cross the lobby to where Bryson and I were standing.

"Jaxon," she stated, forcing me to make eye contact with her.

I grinned politely and pointed at her. My eyes narrowed, and I cocked my head—giving off the impression that I had no idea what her name was. It was a classic move Bryson and I made.

She smiled and shook her head. "Don't act like you don't remember me, you jackass."

I cracked at her confidence and nodded. "Layla."

She crossed her arms. "How have you been?"

"Good," I said. "Busy." I hoped that by being short, she would get the hint that I didn't want to have this conversation.

"I never heard from you," she said sternly. There was a hint of playfulness in her tone, but I'd had so many conversations with so many broads that I honestly wasn't sure if that meant anything anymore.

"Like I said, I've been busy." I shrugged. I could hear Bryson's chuckle from behind me.

"Order number forty!" a team member yelled from behind the counter.

Layla rolled her eyes and brushed past me, putting an end to our awkward reunion.

"I thought you said she was normal?" Bryson asked once she was out of earshot.

"She was." I shrugged and turned to face him. "Just not sure if I want to hit it again yet."

A few minutes went by, and we talked about next season's football predictions and this semester's class schedule.

"Order number forty-four!"

Bryson crossed the lobby and picked up the bag of food from the counter. He pulled out his phone as we headed to the parking lot and glanced in my direction. "Do you mind dropping me off at Maci's place on your way back? She lives down the street."

I swallowed and had to clear my throat so my answer came out in a steady voice. "Yeah, man, not a problem." I held the door open for him and unlocked my Jeep.

I darted back inside and leaned across the table that Layla and her friends were sitting at. "Are you free tonight?" I asked right in front of the whole table.

Her eyes grew wide, and her fork froze halfway to her mouth. She looked me up and down, and I raised my eyebrows to encourage her to be quick with her answer.

She smiled. "I can swing by in like a half-hour?"

"Great," I deadpanned. I pushed off the table and turned back toward the door. The cold February air hit my face, and I felt myself spiraling. It was like living in a scene that played on repeat, but I didn't want to be in it.

Why did this happen every single fucking time? Maci and I would get good again, and then somehow, her ongoing hookup with Bryson would get brought into the picture. If he wasn't doing something to piss her off, then he was doing something that offset her expectations of him—and when they picked back up, it got to me every time.

A pit formed in my stomach as I pulled into Maci's parking lot. Bryson removed my box of wings from the bag of food and cocked his head. "Thanks for the ride."

When I got back to my place, I threw my wings in the fridge. I no longer felt like eating, and when Layla showed up, I did what I was best at. I bagged her and told her I had shit to do so that she would go.

I took a quick shower, threw on some basketball shorts, and fell onto my bed. As soon as my head hit the pillow, my phone vibrated.

Maci

> **Port Clinton?!**

I did a double-take at the screen. Connor must've finally popped the question to Katie, which meant Maci was now invited to join the trip. I knew this text message was coming, and part of me enjoyed that she was texting me while Bryson was at her place.

The idea of Maci, Bryson, and the rest of our world being locked away in two condos for a few days seemed like a recipe for disaster. Enough happened on its own, with an entire campus as a buffer.

Jaxon

I rolled over and closed my eyes. I didn't have the bandwidth to think about a trip that was two and a half weeks away. Instead, I went to bed pretending that my best friend wasn't sleeping with the only girl I couldn't stop thinking about, no matter how hard I tried to forget her.

Chapter Fifty

MACI

March 2016

"Katie, I'm not sure you understand the urgency of this situation," I emphasized from the kitchen table. I was making a packing list for Port Clinton—a trip we were leaving for tomorrow.

Spring break had finally arrived, and while most students were heading home on this lovely Friday evening, we had to pack. My column of check marks only had two completed items, and I felt myself getting anxious.

"Could you *please* stop pretending that you are nervous about the packing list, and can we chat about what is *really* throwing you off?" Katie snapped back. Her duffle was open on the couch, and she was tossing articles of clothing into the living room from her bedroom. Her hill of options was slowly turning into a mountain.

I pursed my lips and slid the notebook away from me. "I'm not sure what you mean."

"Maci." Katie laughed and emerged from her bedroom. "I literally walked through the door twenty minutes ago. I know you've been stressing about this trip, but we both know it isn't about the fucking packing list."

I innocently widened my eyes and pushed her to continue. I knew full well what she was referring to. Jaxon and Bryson were going to be on the same trip as me, and I had no idea how I would handle it. Things were going great with Jaxon, but things were also going okay with Bryson.

"We have gone through this." Katie sat down across from me at the table. "Connor's condo has five bedrooms, and one of them belongs to just you."

I nodded and released a breath I didn't realize I was holding.

"It's going to be fine," she emphasized, smacking my hands playfully. "Bryson has his own room, so it shouldn't be a problem."

As she walked back toward her room, I shifted my body to follow her. "Should I be bothered by that?"

"Bothered by what?" Katie popped her head back out into the hallway.

I laughed at the expression on her face and continued, "We've been hooking up since November. I shouldn't be bothered that he hasn't made *any* comments about this trip? Like sharing a room or hooking up while we are there—"

"Here's the thing." Katie made herself visible again in the living room. Her tone told me that I was about to receive word from Blunt Katie. "He's a Fun Dip, Mace," she enunciated, "and while he's the only guy *you* are dipping on, there are probably plenty of other girls he is dipping *in*."

"Clever, Katie. Thank you for that extended metaphor."

"We've gone over this." She laughed. "Yeah, it's shitty that he lies to you, and you have every right to get upset about that. But when it comes to how you guys interact with each other, you both are very free to do whatever you want."

I nodded and shot up out of my seat. "I'm going to start packing."

"Hold on!"

I peered around the corner and met Katie's prying eyes.

"That is only half of the nonsense I know is rolling around in your head." She fell on the couch next to her overflowing duffel and ran a hand through her ponytail. "What about Jaxon? What are your concerns for him?"

"Nothing," I answered honestly and shrugged. "Other than Bryson being there, I really don't worry about Jaxon. Same story, same ending."

"Good," Katie stated.

"Anything *you're* worried about?" I padded over to the recliner and rested my head in my hands. "We may as well do a double-sided status check here."

Katie smiled at my statement. "I have nothing to worry about."

I shook my head and knew that I was kidding myself if Katie had any concerns at all about this trip. Her boyfriend of two months had just asked her on a spring break getaway to his family's condo. What sorts of problems could arise out of that?

She tossed a hoodie into her bag and rested her hands on her lap. "Actually, there is one thing."

I shifted back into the recliner and listened to Katie's sudden need for advice. I stared and waited for her to make eye contact, but her eyes never left the bracelets on her wrist.

"Katie?" I prompted.

She shifted her gaze to me, and the words left her mouth quickly. "Is it possible to be in love with someone after only knowing them for a few months?"

Startled by her admission, I took a moment to digest what she was asking me. She and Connor met in December, and it was just now March. It was a short timeline, and she was worried that it was too soon to feel the way that she did about Connor.

I met Jaxon back in August. Two months into our friendship, I knew I cared about him more than a friend. I knew that I was scared to lose him the moment after we tried to hook up.

In short, my answer to Katie was simple—it was possible to be in love with someone after only knowing them for a few months because I had been falling in love with my best friend since I met him.

"In the words of *Sex and the City*," I said calmly. Katie stared at me with hopeful eyes, and I smiled reassuringly. "Abso-fucking-lutely."

Katie raised her eyebrows. "So I'm not crazy?"

"Nope," I snapped and stood up. "You are not crazy."

She relaxed and threw herself back into packing. I followed her lead and decided to focus on my own empty duffel that sat unbothered in the middle of my bed.

"However"—I peeked into the living room, and Katie paused her packing—"you did just get advice from someone who has a Fun Dip and a guy she can't have. Do with that what you will."

"Is it too late to uninvite you to this trip!" she yelled from her spot on the couch.

I tossed a pile of clothes I had already pulled from my laundry into my duffel and scanned my room for last-minute items. "Abso-fucking-lutely," I murmured.

Chapter Fifty-One

JAXON

March 2016

When Saturday morning rolled around, it was the first taste of spring weather Bowling Green had all season. It was sixty-five degrees—according to my phone—and the sun shining through my blinds made my room warmer than usual.

I blinked a few times to adjust to the light and checked the time. My alarm was set to go off in a few minutes. I could hear movement in the living room already. Since everyone was leaving from our apartment, I assumed that people had arrived early. There wasn't anything else to do but pack the cars and wait to leave.

I rolled out of bed and took a quick shower so I could get down to the parking lot. I set my duffel and my bookbag on the bed and double-checked that I had everything I needed.

When I emerged from my room, a small crowd of people was standing around our living room. I recognized most of them—people from parties we threw and a few guys from the football team. There were two girls I didn't recognize that Jared was talking to. I cocked my head in his direction, and he returned the gesture.

A familiar voice came from behind the counter. "Hey, Jax."

My eyes landed on Heather, and I adjusted the grip on my bags. I continued walking toward the front door and jogged down the stairs. It was too early to deal with Heather, especially since I hadn't had a drop of coffee.

I unlocked my Jeep, and the trunk popped open. A few bags fell out at the release of the door, and I shook my head. I should've known that Bryson wouldn't take the time to pack the trunk correctly.

"Fuckin' Kennedy," I said to no one in particular.

Minutes later, Bryson, Jared, and the rest of the apartment came walking down the stairs just as Connor pulled into the lot with Maci and Katie.

"Did you lock up the place?" I asked Bryson.

He nodded and sipped his Monster. "I'm gonna ride with Brad and Aaliyah. Are you good?"

I looked toward Brad's car and saw the exact reason why Bryson wanted to ride in that vehicle. Aaliyah was Heather and Reagan's roommate. He hooked up with her a few weeks ago, and she had invited one of her friends from home to come on the trip. Aaliyah's friend was right up Bryson's alley—someone who would be gone from campus after break and a notch on his belt he wouldn't have to see again.

"I'm good," I assured him, and he shot me a grin.

Connor appeared and looked over the trunk situation. "Hey." He shook his head and knew it had Bryson written all over it. "Katie and I only have two bags between the two of us."

"There's plenty of space back there," I said. I started the engine and cranked up the heat so it was warm when we were ready to go. The last thing I wanted to hear for the first fifteen minutes of the drive was Katie complaining about how "chilly" it was in the backseat.

Connor scanned the crowd in the parking lot and looked back at me. "Who else is riding with us?"

I rolled my eyes and knew where he was going with this. I watched Katie and Maci laughing as they unloaded the trunk of Connor's car.

Connor gestured toward Heather, Reagan, and some people I didn't know. "Maybe ask Maci to ride with us?" he offered innocently and walked around to the backseat.

Just as he left my side, Heather came strutting across the parking lot. My mind went into panic mode, and I jogged over to where Maci and Katie were. There was no fucking way I would last for an hour in a car with Heather. I would probably toss her ass out of it as soon as we hit the highway.

I grabbed one of Maci's bags. "You're riding with us."

She glanced up at me, startled by my sudden arrival. Out of the corner of my eye, I saw Heather turn back around toward the other cars.

"Good morning to you, too," Maci said sarcastically, and Katie laughed. It was safe to admit that she hadn't had any coffee yet either. Katie bumped Maci's shoulder, and they both looked to where Heather and the other girls were standing.

Maci nodded slowly and understood my request. "Rough night?" she teased.

"No," I mocked her tone.

"Baby, can you start loading up Jaxon's car?" Connor asked from the open trunk of the Jeep. He sounded eager, and I could tell he was ready to leave. Katie nodded, and he started walking toward the other cars.

"So that's Heather," Maci said casually once it was just the two of us. "Oh, and Reagan?" Her voice jumped two octaves at the discovery, and her mouth fell open. She was completely amused, and I had to fight against the smile that dug into my cheeks.

"Yes," I said calmly, and her grin widened.

"Can we stop for coffee?" she asked, pulling the last bag out of Connor's car. She slammed the trunk shut and turned to face me.

"Yeah, but not right away. Connor might lose the last of his patience if we stop before we even leave Bowling Green."

We both looked over to where Connor was talking to Bryson and Jared. His face was serious, and our other two roommates wore their usual go-with-the-flow expressions. He looked exhausted when he walked back over to where we were standing.

"I gave them the address and gate code of the plaza. Heather said her place is right across the lot, so they're on their own." Connor pulled off his hat and ran a hand through his hair. He placed it back on his head and took a deep breath. "Ready?"

"Shotgun," Maci said and hiked the strap of her duffle onto her shoulder. She brushed past me and made a beeline to the passenger side door.

I was surprised to see her in athletic shorts and a hoodie since it was still kind of chilly out, but I didn't complain about the view. Those were the same pair of shorts she threw on after we almost hooked up.

When I slid into the driver's seat, Maci was already scrolling through a playlist on her phone. She plugged it into my USB port, and a fluffy green blanket draped over her legs. Katie was sprawled out in the back seat with her feet in Connor's lap. She looked like she was ready for a nap.

Maci slipped her phone into the cup holder and turned down the volume on the stereo. She wasn't awake enough yet for a full-on jam session. "Power Trip" by J. Cole came on, and I glanced behind me to make sure the parking lot was clear.

"They're going to follow us," Connor said with his eyes already closed.

Maci crossed her arms over her chest and shot me a sleepy smile. I reached over and squeezed her bicep, and a soft laugh fell from her lips. I loved the view of her in my passenger seat.

I steered out of the parking lot and led us toward Highway 80. We drove for about fifteen minutes before Jared realized he had forgotten his ID back at the apartment.

"Are you shitting me, man?" Connor moaned into his phone and shot me a look in my rearview.

I laughed and shook my head.

"But you have the address," Connor pressed, and a moment of silence followed. "Yeah, we can. I think the girls want coffee anyway."

Connor gestured toward the right side of the road and signaled for me to get off the highway. I threw on my turn signal and got off at the next exit.

Maci sat up in her seat. "Turn right. There's a Dunkin at one of the gas stations."

I followed her directions and turned into a gas station that had seen better days. My gut reaction was to get back on the highway and look for another coffee place. Many people were hanging around the entrance of a building that didn't even look big enough to house a Dunkin.

I pulled up to the last pump available and jerked my head toward Maci when she unbuckled her seat belt.

Katie surveyed the scene. "You're gonna get coffee from here?"

Maci turned around to face her. "If it looks off, there are always the Starbucks cans of coffee by the energy drinks."

An older gentleman in a Cleveland Browns beanie walked past the hood of my Jeep and peered casually inside the cabin. I stared at him until he was past the next set of pumps.

"We'll go somewhere else," I said, gripping the gearshift.

Maci put her hand on mine, and I glanced over at her.

"We are already here," she assured me. "It'll be two seconds."

I slid the gearshift back in park, and she hopped out of the passenger seat. She threw her blanket back inside and stuck her hands in her sweatshirt pocket. I watched her look both ways before crossing toward the building.

I scanned the scene as she crossed because I knew she wasn't paying attention. Two guys smoking cigarettes turned their heads to watch her enter the building. Another two guys that stood in front of piles of firewood for sale did the same thing.

I turned off the engine and stepped out onto the pavement. "Hey, Mace!" I yelled across the parking lot.

She spun around and looked surprised to hear me say her name.

"Get me a Gatorade." I smiled.

She returned the gesture right before entering the store. I knew she probably rolled her eyes as soon as she turned around, but if it let everyone know she wasn't by herself, an eye roll was worth it.

Even though I didn't need a ton of gas to reach a full tank, I didn't want to get back in the car until Maci got back. I slid my debit card into the machine so I could top it off.

I stared out at the wide-open field that was next to the parking lot. Trees lined the outskirts, and the sun was just peeking over the top of the green wall. Being in such a country state was weird when Charlotte was so busy and city-like. At least where I grew up, it was congested with businesses and buildings that stretched to the sky. Out here, it felt like I was worlds away.

The lever clicked on the handle to tell me the gas had stopped. I tucked it back into the pump and looked back to the entrance of the building. Maci still hadn't returned, and it made me nervous that she was in there alone.

I opened my car door and peered inside. "I'm gonna run in and see what's taking so long."

Katie looked up from her phone and peered over my shoulder. "Jaxon, she's right there."

I turned around and watched Maci cross the parking lot. My shoulders relaxed, and I hadn't realized I was holding my breath until she was right in front of me. This girl had walked a few feet away just to go into a store, and I was imagining all the things that could go wrong. While it was a sketchy gas station, nothing was out of character for the area. I was just in my own head.

Is this what catching fuckin' feelings does to you?

Maci slowed as she approached the Jeep and studied my expression. "You good?"

"Yeah." I swallowed and offered her a smile. "Just making sure you're okay."

"How thoughtful of you." She laughed and climbed into the passenger seat. She sifted through her bag of drinks and placed my Gatorade on the driver's seat.

"They just got back on the highway," Connor announced.

"Finally," Katie murmured, and Maci laughed.

Before anyone else could devise a reason to prolong our stop, I pulled out of the parking lot and merged back onto the highway.

"You look like you need a coffee," Maci interrupted my train of thought and slid a drink into my cup holder. "It's

Mocha, so it's a little different from what we normally get from Dunkin. But you'll like it."

I popped the tab, and my mouth curved into a half-smile. "You say that like you know me or something."

"You know I do," she snapped playfully, sipping her drink.

I chuckled and didn't bother to argue.

Chapter Fifty-Two

MACI

March 2016

Around the halfway mark, we lost the happy couple to a mid-morning nap.

Katie and Connor were still watching movies in her bedroom when I got up to go to the bathroom around three last night. Even though Connor stressed the importance of being on time this morning for our group departure, he sure didn't mind keeping Katie up way past her usual bedtime.

"Late night for them?" Jaxon murmured and glanced up in his rearview.

I laughed and brought my legs up to my chest. Jaxon leaned forward and turned up the heat on my side of the car when he saw me shift under my blanket.

I side-eyed him suspiciously. "I know you're warm already."

"Nah," he answered playfully, keeping his eyes on the road.

I studied him and leaned back against the headrest. I loved when he wore his hat backward, and I especially loved his new Miami Heat one. I was always drawn to the color black, and Jaxon had a pretty neutral wardrobe. With the exception of some Carolina and BGSU clothes, he wore a lot of black, white, gray, and red—and of course, it looked good on him.

"Have you heard any updates from Chase?" he asked.

"Yes and no." I sighed. Since Chase returned to Pittsburgh to try and fix things with Trey, the status changed every other day. "I'm better off tracking the weather."

"Tracking the weather?" he repeated, amused by the statement.

"Yes." I giggled.

"So, they are off and on then?"

"One day, they're working it out, and the next day Chase is on his way home again." I shrugged and played with the tab on my canned coffee. "I just thought that it's supposed to be easier once we grow up, ya know? Like you shouldn't still have to be dealing with that stuff."

"I think certain parts of your life become easier," Jaxon said. "But there are always going to be hard parts, Mace. Getting older doesn't stop bullshit from happening."

"What do you want to do when you grow up?" I asked.

He did a double take to ensure I was being serious with my question, and a small smile curved into his dimple. "You know I'm in sports management. I wanna be an agent."

"I know, but what do you want to *do*? You can't just sit in your house when you're an agent. Where do you want to go?"

"I wanna run my dad's business out in California for a year or two. Then I'd like to open up an office and manage my own branch out on the east coast." He shrugged. "Be closer to my mom. I know it's hard for her with all the traveling my dad does for work, and my brother is out in Cali a lot too."

"That was a quick answer," I teased. "You've thought about that a lot?"

"All the time," he admitted. "My dad has a huge book of business—one of the biggest agencies out there. I know he won't just hand it to me, but I want to learn everything from him. Who to talk to, how to network, what makes a good deal . . . everything."

"He sounds like an amazing dad," I noted.

Jaxon's expression went soft and he glanced over at me quickly to keep his eyes on the road. "The best."

Hearing Jaxon talk about his family was always refreshing. I only knew the life he had at school—with classes, friends, girls, and the little bit of routine that we shared. Whenever he talked about his hometown and how he grew up, I tried to squeeze a few other questions in there. I craved to know everything about him whenever he chose to share it.

"What about your mom?" I sipped my canned coffee, and a huge grin spread across his face.

He completely lit up the moment he talked about her. "My mom is actually pretty badass. She would kill me for using that language to describe her, but she's like a superwoman. She runs her own event planning business and even takes on some of the catering herself because she loves being in the kitchen. She's given me everything—along with my dad."

"How long have they been married?"

"They got married when Alex was two . . . so twenty-three years. But they dated before that, so they like to joke that it's been a little longer. They actually met in high school and reconnected after college."

I nodded, impressed by anyone who could be together for that long and still be happy.

"What are you thinking about?" Jaxon observed when I didn't say anything else.

A smile broke my focused expression when he called me out. He always seemed to know when I was getting into my head before I could. "I think that it's awesome that your parents are still happy after being together that long. Sometimes I wonder about mine."

"Your mom sounded cool when you called her after I fixed your car," he mentioned.

"You remember a phone conversation I had with my mom from back in October?" I emphasized.

He shrugged like it would be insane if he didn't remember. "At least your end of the conversation. I remember a lot about that day. I sometimes hear that T-shirt song too."

"Thomas Rhett." I nudged him playfully. "See, you're just dying to be a country boy."

"Nope." He shot me a sexy grin. He flicked on his turn signal, and we glided onto an exit ramp.

Connor shot up from his napping position against the back door as the Jeep slowed down. His sudden movement made Katie bolt up, and she glanced around at her location. It was like their half-hour snooze made them both forget where they were.

"How far are we?" Connor stretched and pulled Katie's legs into his lap.

"We have about ten more minutes. We're in Port Clinton," Jaxon said, peering into the backseat. "You guys better rally up because we're starting the party as soon as we get there."

My stomach growled, and I drained the rest of my coffee. "I can't even think of alcohol until I get some food."

"Oh, we'll have food too," Jaxon confirmed. He slowed at a red light, and our surroundings became less open and crowded with businesses and restaurants. Condo complexes and apartments started to pop up the closer we got to the water.

I cracked the window, and a gust of fresh lake air wafted into the cabin. Katie groaned and pulled her blanket over her head.

I laughed at her gut reaction and turned around in my seat. "Connor, where can we stop for groceries?" I didn't see any chain brand stores popping up as we continued down the road.

"There is a market at the next light. Jared just texted me and said they want to stop somewhere and eat, but I'd rather make food at the place."

"Let's do that," Katie said and sat up. She drank the rest of her coffee, and I cheered into the rearview, applauding her for her effort.

Jaxon and Connor laughed as we pulled into a lot for Sal's Food Market. It was a family-owned store—comparable in size to the Kroger we had back in Bowling Green. The four of us roamed the aisles, everyone throwing in items that fit the long weekend agenda.

About forty-five minutes later, we had a cart full of essentials and an obnoxious amount of alcohol that would last us way longer than the four days we would be here. Back on campus, we were spoiled with options if we ran out of drinks. There were plenty of stores open late and gas stations within walking distance, but out here we were limited. No one wanted to take that chance.

"As soon as we unload everything, I am making my Blood Orange Sangria," Katie announced to the car once everyone was in.

"Oh no," Jaxon and I said at the same time.

We looked at each other and laughed, recalling the drink that Katie served the first night Jaxon ever went out with us.

Katie's mouth fell open, and she leaned forward like she was going to scold our behavior.

"Did I miss something?" Connor asked. He looked offended at the inside joke the three of us shared.

"You missed the best drink ever," Katie defended her bartending skills and fell back in her seat.

I spent the last few minutes of our journey in my head, recalling everything her deadly drink prompted. Blood Orange Sangria was how Jaxon and I both started our evening together, but the way we ended it was much messier.

It was insane how much had happened since October. I had never craved someone the way I wanted Jaxon. I didn't think it was possible to want him more today than I did back then. Everything that filled the gaps of time between when we met and where we were now just pushed me closer to him. He had become one of the most important people in my life.

I watched Jaxon type in Connor's gate code, and we pulled inside the complex. Beautiful navy and white condos lined the coast on all sides of the peninsula. There were breaks every three or four condos so people could access the beach from the parking lot, which had been tastefully landscaped with white roses and trimmed hedges. Our gang was about to look very out of place in such an upscale-looking neighborhood.

Connor instructed Jaxon to go all the way to the end of the strip. His family owned the last condo on the right-hand side, which was easily the biggest property in that row.

"Home sweet home," Connor said and climbed out of the back seat.

Jaxon turned off the engine, and the rest of us emerged from the Jeep. I heard Jaxon let out an exaggerated stretch on the other side of the car. Katie jogged excitedly to the trunk, and Connor popped it open. We all grabbed armfuls of grocery bags and started the process of unloading.

We weaved through the short path from the parking lot to the front door of Connor's condo. He unlocked the door, and it was clear it had just recently been cleaned. We were hit with a wave of lemon, clean linen, and coconut. It was an interesting combo, but as soon as I laid eyes on the view of the lake directly at the back of the living room, it all made sense.

Once down the hallway that extended from the front door, we entered the kitchen and dining area, which fed into a gigantic living space. A huge L-shaped couch, a loveseat, and an oversized recliner all faced a flat-screen TV mounted above a fireplace. It was cozy and breathtaking at the same time.

"Baby, this is gorgeous!" Katie exclaimed and set her armful of bags on the counter. A huge smile spread across her face, and Connor stared at her like he was noticing her for the first time. He hoped to get this exact reaction from her, and he certainly didn't disappoint.

"Yeah, when you said you had a place up here, I wasn't really sure what to expect," Jaxon added. He walked across the living room and peered out the back sliding door to have a full view of the lake.

"There are two bedrooms down the hall toward the front door, but Katie and I will be in the one on the left since it's the master suite," Connor said. "There is a bedroom over there next to the fireplace and two bedrooms downstairs. It does get warmer down there, but there is a game room and a den down there too."

"Jared's ass can go downstairs." Jaxon turned away from the window to face the rest of us. His eyes briefly met mine, and a breath caught in my throat. He gestured toward the door next to the fireplace. "I'll take the room over there."

My chest loosened as the first part of the trip I was nervous about unraveled. I felt immediately relieved that Jaxon chose his room first and even better that Bryson wasn't here yet. It just made for a smooth transition.

"Does the bedroom down the hall have a bathroom?" I asked Connor.

"All of the bedrooms on this floor have a bathroom," Connor said, hoisting his duffle onto his shoulder. He grabbed Katie's hand, and they walked toward their bedroom.

"Perfect." I sighed and picked up my bag.

"Pssst," Jaxon whispered.

I stopped halfway down the hall and stared at him.

His eyes narrowed. "Does Katie cook breakfast on trips?"

A stream of giggles and shouting came from the master bedroom. We both peered in the direction of the noise and then back at each other.

"I think we may be on our own for breakfast," I admitted sadly, and his lips formed a small pout. "Unpack and we will throw something together. How hard can it be?"

He pulled his hat from his head and ran a hand through his hair. The last time I saw him was Thursday, and he must've gone to the barber sometime after that. His hair was just short enough to where it didn't curl. I liked when his hair had loose waves, but there was something about how a fresh cut looked on him.

He disappeared into his room, and I went down the hall to mine. I placed my duffle on the bed and lay next to it. My room was pretty big, with a king bed in the center of the space. There was a dresser I planned to take advantage of and a small closet next to the bathroom door.

As I unpacked my belongings, I bit the inside of my cheek and smiled when I heard more sounds from Katie and Connor's room. Their door was shut, but we all knew there would be many doors shut this weekend. It was the first time since winter break that any of us had freedom outside our regular school schedules.

It was also the first time Jaxon and I spent any time together outside of BG, and I had a feeling it would be harder than I thought. Being under the same roof as him and sleeping down the hall just felt unnatural. Even if we weren't together, Jaxon stayed in my room whenever he spent the night. Of course, he would need his own room if he planned on sleeping with Heather, Reagan, or any other girls he may have already hooked up with on this trip.

I palmed my forehead and sighed to give my nerves a chance to calm down before I unnecessarily started them up. I had plenty of time left on the trip to get worked up about things. Especially since the guy I was hooking up with could enter the condo at any moment, and the one I really wanted was only a few doors down the hall.

Chapter Fifty-Three

JAXON

MARCH 2016

AFTER SIFTING THROUGH THE bags of groceries we got from the market, I decided that sausage, bacon, and eggs were good to start with. Breakfast was actually something I knew how to make since I made it with my mom every Sunday growing up.

"Did you hear me?" Alex's voice came through the phone.

I hadn't spoken to him since I left Charlotte, and he called during his morning jog to catch up. I took advantage of the time since Maci was still in her room.

"Kind of," I lied. I pulled out a bag of shredded cheese and searched the cabinets for any seasonings.

"I talked to Mom, and she said that John wrote to you. What did he say?" Alex asked.

His question threw me off, and I stared blankly at the frying pan I had just placed on the stove. Unlike Evelyn and Reed, who eased into conversations about John and Karina, Alex was much more upfront about things. He was a typical older brother in that way. While he never came off rude or imposing, he surprised me every time.

"I swear that woman could lead a gossip train," I murmured.

"You know Mom doesn't like to bring that stuff up to Dad if he's away working. She confided in me a little bit last weekend, and I think she's a little worried about you that's all."

"Confided in you?" I smiled. "What are you, a therapist now?"

"Shut up, asshole. I gave you some time to bring it up, and you didn't. Now, this is me reaching out."

I took a deep breath and peered down the hall to make sure no one was coming. "He wants me to come and see him." The words left my mouth, and I felt my chest tighten. The last time I thought about the letter was when I talked to Mom on Valentine's Day.

"What!" Alex exclaimed. "He hasn't written to you in like five years. What did you say back?"

"It isn't a text message, Alex." I smirked. "I haven't been able to say anything back."

He paused for a moment. I placed a giant green bowl on the counter and leaned on my elbows next to it. I knew he had more questions.

"*Are* you going to say anything back?" he asked.

"I don't know," I whispered quickly.

"Well, why does he want to see you?"

Heat rushed to my face, and my heart began to pound against my chest. All I told our mom was that I had read the letter. I hadn't told anyone about the contents yet.

"He didn't say," I admitted. "He sounded different in this one, though, compared to the other two he sent."

"Is he up for parole?"

"He can't be. This is his second offense. And he said in this letter that he still has a few more years."

Alex sighed. "Damn."

I heard a door shut down the hall, and soon, Maci rounded the kitchen corner. When she noticed I was on the phone, she leaned into the fridge and pulled out a jug of orange juice. She grabbed a bottle of champagne off the counter and jogged into the living room. I watched curiously as she held the bottle as far away from her face as she possibly could. She peeled away at the foil and winced as she got closer to the cork.

"I'll call you later, man. I'm about to make some food," I said into the phone.

Maci unscrewed one side of the clip on the bottle and jumped back when it didn't do anything. I shook my head and laughed at her ability to make something so simple look so cute.

"Where are you at?" Alex prompted in a lighter tone than before.

"I'm up in Port Clinton. I'm on spring break this week."

"That's right. Mom told me that. Call her sometime this week to let her know when you'll be back in town."

"Are you able to fly back for a little bit?" I asked.

"I'll be home for a long weekend. Bella couldn't take off Monday and Tuesday, so we will land Wednesday night."

I nodded just as Maci made eye contact with me. Her eyes were wide, and her mouth formed a tight line.

I held up my finger to let her know I was almost done. "Text me before you fly out. I'll be back in BG Tuesday night, and then I'm driving home Wednesday morning."

"Sounds good, J. See ya." Alex hung up, and I set my phone on the counter.

"What are you doing?" I prompted playfully. I walked over to where Maci was standing with the bottle still extended from her chest.

"I can never pop it." She laughed nervously and thrust the bottle into my hands.

I unscrewed the clip in one swift motion, and the cork shot into the couch. Some champagne spilled on the hardwood in front of us, and she ran into the kitchen to grab a towel.

"See? Nothing to it." She wiped up the spill with her foot and grinned at me.

"Yeah," I answered sarcastically.

She took the champagne and bounced back into the kitchen. "Do you want one?"

I nodded, and she grabbed another glass from the cabinet.

I rubbed my hands together and stood in front of the stove. "Ready to make some food?"

Maci spun around to face me and sipped her drink. She smacked her lips a few times to test the taste and gave a satisfied nod. Her hoodie cut off right at her shorts, and I caught a sliver of her stomach when she crossed her arms over her chest. I fought the urge to reach under the thick material and run my hands up her stomach.

Maci grinned. "I thought I would just watch you cook." She pulled out her phone and scrolled with her thumb. "Want to Want Me" by Jason Derulo played from a speaker above the fireplace, and she closed the space between us to assess the items on the counter.

I pulled the carton of eggs to the side and cracked all twelve of them into the bowl. I took a handful of shredded cheese, garlic powder, salt, and pepper and whisked it together. "Did we get milk or half and half?"

She narrowed her eyes at me, and I almost spit out my mimosa.

"You've never put milk in your eggs?" I exclaimed.

"Who puts milk in their eggs?" She turned around and handed me a carton of milk from the fridge.

I unscrewed the cap and poured it until it looked like a good ratio. "People who don't want dry ass eggs."

It was her turn to laugh, and she hovered over the sink so her drink wouldn't spill on the counter.

"I'm going to start on the bacon and sausage. Can you cook the eggs?" I eyed her suspiciously.

I grabbed another pan and laid out a few strips of bacon along with some sausage links. I watched Maci light the burner for her pan, and before I could stop her, she poured the bowl of eggs into an ungreased frying pan.

My hands instinctively shot to my head, and my mouth fell open. "Maci," I grunted slowly.

With a spatula already in her hand, she looked at me with a puzzled look on her face. I quickly grabbed another pan and sprayed it down with cooking spray. I bumped her out of the way with my hip and poured the eggs into the freshly sprayed skillet. She snagged the dirty one from my hand and placed it in the sink. I could tell she was trying not to laugh.

"Have you never made eggs before?" I exclaimed.

She wore the same expression she had when I asked her about the last time she got an oil change. "I'm a tad inexperienced," she admitted.

"Oh boy." My voice went up a few octaves. I took the spatula from her hands and started the folding process for her. "You've gotta be quick with eggs," I explained and handed her the spatula so she could try again.

She broke them up into smaller pieces and glanced over at me to make sure she was doing it right. I nodded slowly and smiled down at my own pan.

The song changed to a country song I didn't know, and her body instantly swayed to the beat. She grabbed a plate from the cabinet and sat it on the counter.

I stared at her, completely turned on by how adorable she looked dancing next to me in the kitchen. I licked the center of my bottom lip and smiled when she turned to me and belted out the next set of lines. She spun around and sang about calling someone baby and running her fingers through her hair. Her eyes fell on mine, and she pointed at me with a giant smile.

As her body language matched the song lyrics, my lips parted slightly at the swing of her hips and her hands in her hair. She continued to sing as she returned her attention to the stove. I watched her empty the eggs onto the plate, and she flicked off the burner.

I had no idea how we got to this point. I had no idea how I went from having Maci on top of me five months ago in her bedroom to not being able to touch her right now.

I wanted to grab her hips, pull her against my chest, and kiss her. I'd hoist her up on the counter, and I wouldn't care if the food burned on the stove or the eggs got cold. She would be the only thing I needed to start the day.

The front door opened at the end of the hall, and the noise snapped me out of my daydream. I clicked off the burner in front of me, and the familiar voices of Bryson and Jared entered the kitchen.

"What's up, guys!" Jared exclaimed and threw his bag on the recliner. "Whatcha makin'?"

Connor emerged from the hall, and Katie followed closely behind him. "Didn't you guys just eat?"

I smirked when I saw her in Connor's shirt, and she stuck her tongue out at me.

Bryson rounded the counter to the breakfast bar and leaned forward in front of Maci. He smiled at her, and she shook her head, unable to stop herself from smiling back.

I swallowed at the sight of them so close to each other and focused my attention on Jared. "Everything is done."

"Where are we stayin'?" Bryson asked Connor.

Maci averted her attention to Katie, and the two of them got to work making more mimosas. I knew she was avoiding eye contact with Bryson.

"There are two bedrooms downstairs for you guys." Connor pointed to the basement door. "There's a game room and a bathroom down there too."

"Sweet," Jared said, hoisting his bag back onto his shoulder.

As Jared ran downstairs, Bryson motioned for me to follow him. I recognized that look in his eye, and he planned to start drinking right this second. I grinned and shook my head.

"Hey, Maci, can you make me one?" Bryson smiled in her direction.

She smirked, and they exchanged a glance.

I followed Bryson downstairs, knowing full well that I would need an endless supply of drinks if I was going to watch him flirt with Maci all weekend.

Chapter Fifty-Four

MACI

March 2016

Katie and I poured what was left of our second bottle of Moscato into our empty glasses and clinked them together as Rihanna's "What's My Name" played through the speaker. We had set up camp in the living room and taken over the counter space with snacks and empty Bud Light Rita cans.

The condo across the street decided to host a game night. While Katie and I were all for the group activities this weekend, we craved a little girl time before merging into a new social circle. Neither of us knew any of the girls invited on this trip, and my only experience with Heather and Reagan involved Jaxon.

I didn't care to witness history repeat itself this weekend. It already threw me off to have Bryson here, but Jaxon's past hookups too? It was crazy how many bodies had been shared between the two condos.

Katie sang along to the song's chorus, and I took another long sip of my wine. We both had a great buzz going and agreed it was necessary to go across the parking lot.

"So you don't know anything about any of the girls over there?" Katie asked as if she had just read my mind.

I emptied my glass and shrugged. "Let's see . . . I know Reagan works at Dunkin, and *she's* slept with Jaxon multiple times. I know her roommate, Heather, likes to *stalk* Jaxon, and she's also slept with him multiple times. They both of-fered to sleep with Jaxon at the *same* time."

I laughed at the look on Katie's face, but unfortunately, I had even more insight for her. I drummed my fingers on the counter and cocked my head to the side. "Heather was the girl Jaxon kicked out the morning after I slept with Bryson," I said slowly.

"No!" Katie exclaimed and covered her face with the sleeve of her hoodie.

I buried my face in mine, and we both laughed harder than we should have, thanks to the empty evidence that littered the counter.

Katie shook her head. "I just can't picture him being a jackass like that." It always pained her to see Jaxon in any kind of negative lighting.

"Believe it," I murmured into my empty glass and pouted when nothing came out.

"We need to go over there." Katie laughed at my expression and set her empty glass on the counter. "Are you putting on sweatpants?"

I giggled. "It's probably going to be ninety degrees over there with all of those people."

"Right," Katie agreed. She disconnected her phone from the speaker and double-checked that everything was turned off before we headed out the door and across the parking lot.

The closer we got to Heather's condo, the louder the bass sounded from the property. We jogged the last half of the journey because of how much the temperature had dropped since this morning. When we arrived on the doorstep, I knocked on the door and twisted the handle. It was unlocked, and we were hit with loud music, heat, and a lingering smell of cherry once we stepped inside.

During my initial sweep of the place, I didn't recognize anyone other than Jared. Heather's condo was easily double the size of Connor's, but it lacked charm and crowd control. At least three dozen people were here, and we had only come with twelve bodies. It was possible that I missed a few people at the head count, but I couldn't have been off by that much.

Katie nudged my shoulder, and she led us through the living room. We weaved through groups of people and stopped when we entered the kitchen. Dispensers of pink and orange drinks were on the counter, and colorful stacks of cups sat next to them. Katie and I exchanged a glance and shrugged before filling a cup with Pink Drink and continuing on our mission to find a familiar face.

"I don't see them being upstairs," Katie shouted over the music. "Maybe they are downstairs?"

"Or outside!" I offered.

Not wanting to separate from each other in a crowd of people we didn't know, we decided to try outside since the balcony door was off the kitchen. The same chilly air we just walked through suddenly felt refreshing after being inside.

Another twenty or so people were outside on the wooden deck that stretched a little past the shoreline and hung over the lake. Aside from the light thumping of the music, the waves crashing along the rocks below were actually very peaceful.

I peered down the line of Adirondack chairs and saw Connor's face illuminated in the flames of a small tabletop fire. "There." I pointed. I felt my shoulders relax when Connor smiled in our direction and waved us over.

"Hey, baby," Connor swooned once we got closer. He held his hand out for Katie and gave her a long kiss before pulling her into his lap.

I slid into an empty chair beside them and inched closer to the fire. The little heat it gave off felt good against my bare legs, and I knew if I continued to drink whatever was in this Pink Drink, I would feel warmer any minute.

Connor peered inside Katie's cup. "What do you have in there?"

"Pink Drink." Katie shrugged, and I giggled at her matter-of-fact answer.

"You're lucky I watched Jared and Bryson make those, or else I would toss them over the railing," Connor threatened in the most caring tone possible. He shifted into Dad Mode at least twice a day, sometimes more if it concerned Katie's well-being.

I felt an arm wrap around my shoulder, and I turned to find Bryson squeezing into my chair. He gestured toward my cup and grinned. "Whatcha got?"

"Pink Drink," I copied Katie, and she laughed in the background. I lost it once a snort escaped her, and I leaned my forehead against Bryson's shoulder. I poked him in the chest. "You made it very, *very* strong."

In the last minute or so, all of the alcohol in my body decided to show up at once. I went from buzzed to drunk.

"I do what I can." He looked me up and down. The light from the fire danced in his golden-brown eyes, and I was brought back to the night we met outside Brathaus.

We were interrupted when Brad came over and knocked Bryson in the shoulder. "Kennedy, we're up in pong!"

"I'll be back, okay?" Bryson adjusted, and I fell lightly against the back of the chair.

I nodded and watched him head back into the house. There was a loud gaggle of screaming from the kitchen as soon as he stepped inside.

I laughed into my drink and stared at the fire in front of me. It felt nice not to care about what Bryson did this weekend. It had taken me a long time, but I was getting better at separating him from the guy I wanted to be friends with and the guy I used him for.

I widened my eyes at this new voice in my head. This version of Maci was welcome to pop in anytime. Apparently, she just needed some Pink Drink to show up.

"Hey." Connor nudged my leg.

I paused mid-sip and turned to face him.

"Jaxon was looking for you earlier. I explained to him at least five times that you and Katie were coming later. He's hammered."

I peered over at the hot tub where Jaxon had an arm draped over Reagan. Another girl I didn't recognize was sitting extremely close to him on the other side, but he paid no attention. I lingered over the sight of him shirtless but drew my gaze back to Connor. I had traumatic flashbacks of the Snapchat incident and decided not to witness anything firsthand.

"He looks a little busy," I joked. I shook my now-empty cup and extended my hand to Katie. "I'm going inside for a refill. Do you want more?"

Katie shook her head. "I may switch to beer. Do you want me to go with you?"

I assured her I was fine and made my way back inside. As soon as I slid the door shut and stepped foot into the kitchen, Bryson's arm was around my waist.

"I was just coming back outside," he slurred, his eyes shiny from whatever game he just played.

A girl came over and leaned against his shoulder no sooner than he finished his sentence. She glanced at me and averted her gaze back to Bryson. "Bryson, I thought we were playing pool?" she whined.

Bryson shifted so he could smile at me. "Do you wanna play pool?"

I had seen that look one too many times to know that he was already debating on what bed he was sleeping in tonight.

When his lips landed on mine, I should've turned around and walked back outside to Connor and Katie. Pink Drink Maci was still in the lead in terms of making decisions, but warmth flooded my stomach when his hand glided past my hoodie and brushed the curve of my hip.

"Yeah." I smiled against his lips. "I can play pool."

Chapter Fifty-Five

JAXON

March 2016

Katie's cackle sounded completely different when I was hungover at nine in the morning. My head throbbed, and I felt the back of my eyes pulsing against my skull. There was no way I was moving anytime soon. I didn't even want to open my eyes.

I heard some people moving around. It sounded like someone was coming down the hall and getting closer to my room. I debated turning over on my side, but when I went to turn, my back moved against something firm.

I was on the living room couch. The last thing I remembered from last night was getting into the hot tub after I asked Connor what time Katie and Maci were heading over. Everything went downhill from there.

A door slammed shut, and I heard someone slide into a bar stool. It sounded like the basement door from where I was in the living room.

"Did you?" I heard Katie ask.

"Nothing happened! He couldn't find his room last night," Maci answered her. She sounded amused and annoyed at the same time.

Since I knew Jared wouldn't go into her bedroom, it had to be Bryson they were talking about.

"So he stumbled into yours?" Katie prompted.

"Actually, he stumbled into mine *after* stumbling out of someone else's."

"Eww," Katie spat. She almost got a laugh out of me as she openly despised Bryson.

"Yeah," Maci said. Even laying on the couch with my eyes closed, I knew that Maci's mouth was in a hard line. She was trying not to smile.

"Did you say something to him about it?" Katie asked.

Maci sighed. "Of course I did. And he completely lied about it. I literally watched him go into a room with a girl last night."

"Eww," Katie repeated.

It was one thing to imagine what a typical girl conversation between Maci and Katie was like, but getting a front-row seat to it was a whole different experience. They were usually so in sync, and it was refreshing to get Katie's raw reaction to Bryson.

"Real class act, isn't he?" Maci muttered.

"And yet you are still hooking up with him," Katie teased.

"Katie!" Maci screeched and laughed at the same time.

The noise made me shoot up, and I immediately put my hand on my forehead. My brain felt like it was knocking against my skull. I mumbled loudly and whined into the back of the couch.

"Oh, I didn't see you over there." Katie peered over the countertop. "Couldn't make it to your room last night?"

I glanced over at the two of them in the kitchen, and they both wore the same amused and confused look on their faces.

"Apparently not," I admitted, trying to sit up a little taller.

"You got a little . . ." Maci tapped her neck with her fingers, and I mimicked her body language. "Down . . ." She pointed her finger and cocked her head. "Left . . . there it is!"

Her face lit up with a massive grin, and Katie chuckled. I drew my fingers back, and they were tinted with red lipstick. I had no idea who the mark was from.

"Would you like a mimosa now? Is it too early, or are you trying to roll over last night's sprint into today?" Katie asked sarcastically.

I shot them both a look of disgust, and Maci pulled her mouth into a hard line. She looked like she was going to explode at any moment. Both of them were enjoying this way too much.

"I'm actually feeling pretty damn good," Maci murmured, turning her attention back to Katie.

"Me too," Katie piped up. "I think it was the Pink Drink."

They both burst into hysterics, and that was the last thing I remembered before I passed out against the couch pillow.

About five hours later, I started to feel human again. The recovery consisted of a long nap in my actual room, a bowl of soup from Katie, and a Sprite from Connor. I felt like their teenage son who had partied too hard on the first night of vacation.

"It's not from a can," Katie added proudly when she set a second bowl of soup on my end table.

I sat up and dragged both hands down my face. Once she left the room and shut my door, I decided to force another helping of food down and scrolled on my phone for any evidence of what happened last night. It was actually a good sign that my inbox was empty, and there were no photos or Instagram posts. It allowed me to assume that nothing had happened and that I had nothing to fix or deal with tonight.

A shower was the last piece of the recovery puzzle. I scrubbed at my neck to make sure there were no more marks and did some manscaping so I felt a little more put together. I leaned my forehead against the wet tile and let the warm water run down my back. Already, I felt one hundred times better.

I ran my fingers through my hair so it wouldn't dry flat and slipped on some gray sweatpants. My body felt like it was running a temperature, which was my cue to guzzle as much water as possible.

Too hot to put a shirt on, I wandered into the living room and was surprised to see everyone but Bryson and Connor in front of the TV. I made a beeline for the fridge and cracked open my first bottle of water.

"He lives," Jared announced from the couch.

Katie and Maci averted their attention over to me and grinned. Each of them held a glass of wine in their hands, which made me notice that Jared was holding a beer. I peered over at the time on the stove and saw it was already almost six.

"Connor went on a beer run with Kennedy," Jared said.

"We're heading out around seven-thirty to a club," Katie added and sat up in her seat. "Will you be joining us?"

"Yes, I'll be joining you," I replied in a snarky tone, and Katie shot me a playful smirk. I returned the gesture and reached for more ibuprofen.

"How are you feeling?" Maci rose from the couch and came into the kitchen for a refill.

I guzzled the rest of my water and reached into the fridge for another one. "I've been worse," I admitted.

Nothing would beat the spring vacation trip Bryson and I went on last year. I woke up in some broad's apartment next to two girls, and neither one of them lived there. I spent all day battling a hangover in our condo and didn't feel normal again until the following morning.

No sooner than I tossed my third water bottle in the trash, Connor and Bryson returned with two bottles of Jack, two cases of Bud Light, and three bottles of Moscato. My stomach churned at the sight of the brown liquor, but Bryson's smirk made it clear that I wasn't getting off easy tonight.

The girls quickly took over the main bathroom off the kitchen. All of the plugs were in use, and the counter was littered with a bunch of girly shit I didn't know the names of. Music took over the sound system, and pretty soon pregaming was in full swing. I managed to chug another three bottles of water before Jared shoved a beer in my face.

"Power hour." Jared smiled and tossed me a can.

I cracked it open and joined Connor and Bryson in the living room. We were all seated around the coffee table, where Jared was ready for us to take turns playing Ride the Bus.

Fits of laughter exploded from the bathroom every now and then where Maci and Katie spent the last hour getting ready. Around seven-fifteen, the group started to get antsy about leaving, so much so that Bryson and Connor ran across the parking lot to ensure the other group was ready to go.

"Come on, ladies!" Jared shouted. He poured four shots of Jack and scooted them to the edge of the counter. "What the hell is taking them so long?"

"It's girl shit, man." I shrugged and looked back to the bathroom.

Jared wandered over to the closed door and tapped it with his knuckles.

"We're coming!" Maci yelled from inside the bathroom, and Jared jumped away from the door.

A few moments later, Katie stepped into the hallway. She wore tight black pants, a bright-red long-sleeve top that showed her stomach, and black high-heeled boots. Her hair was in a high ponytail, and she had put stuff on her eyes to make them darker. She also wore red lipstick.

Connor would either lose his fucking mind or tell her to get back into their bedroom to change.

"Damn, girl"—Jared gestured his hand toward her outfit and grinned—"you clean up nice!"

Katie smiled and patted his shoulder. "Thanks, Jared."

In the few days of us being here, Jared had grown on Katie. Once she got it through her head that he wasn't actually hitting on her when he spoke to her, she liked having him around.

"Maci's almost ready," Katie said to her phone screen. "When did they go across the street? I can get an Uber here in like ten minutes."

"They should be back soon," I said, handing Katie her shot. A look of pure disgust washed over her face, and I laughed.

Then, her expression immediately shifted, and she smiled over my shoulder. "Yes! Definitely the mauve lipstick. Red would've been too much."

I turned to see what she was talking about. I swallowed to keep my mouth from dropping and did my best to keep myself together.

Maci wore a navy long-sleeve dress that hugged every curve on her body. The material in the front had a deep V-cut that stopped right above her ribcage, and a dangly necklace hung between her chest. She wore dark pink lipstick, and her dark lashes made her blue eyes pop from across the room.

She caught me staring and took a few steps toward me. "Does it look okay?"

A whiff of her perfume invaded my space, and I took a deep breath to steady myself. I wanted to feel the fabric of her dress in my hands as I tugged it up her thighs. I would make sure she didn't question how good she looked tonight. I'd make her say my name like she did the night I fucked everything up.

"You look amazing," I admitted, careful not to let my voice waver.

We locked eyes, and she smiled shyly at my compliment. There were so many other words I could've used, but the reason I hesitated walked right through the door as Katie handed Maci her shot.

Bryson looked Maci up and down, and a satisfied grin spread across his face. I raised my shot glass as we all cheered for another night on vacation.

Chapter Fifty-Six

MACI

March 2016

It took three Ubers to get both condos to Razzle's.

After everyone divided and piled in, we drove the twenty-minute journey to a lakeside club on the water. Connor had explained that it was the only bar in the area that presented any kind of scene like Bowling Green. There was karaoke, a dance floor, a DJ, and a heated open deck so people could extend outside.

When we pulled up, I felt relieved that I didn't over-plan my outfit. Since Katie and I couldn't get a female's perspective on the place before coming, we were forced to make a judgment call.

Katie convinced me that we were always better off arriving overdressed instead of underdressed. I would never wear this dress out to a BG bar. It was an impulse buy for a holiday party at a club in downtown Columbus.

I was wedged between Bryson and Katie in the backseat. Bryson wasted no time climbing into the van behind me when he saw my outfit. I tried not to notice that Jaxon chose to ride with people from the other condo.

Bryson's hand rested on my upper thigh. I turned to face him as we pulled up to the entrance of the club. "Ready?" he asked.

My mouth involuntarily lifted into a half-smile, and he gave my leg a squeeze. Heat shot up the inside of my thigh and spread into my groin.

The door to the van slid open, and Connor led our group to the entrance. The cold Lake Erie air hit my bare legs, and as the chill settled over the group, we all made a beeline to the double doors. The bouncer checked all our IDs, and soon we were thrown into a mix of bass and flashing lights.

Razzle's was a lot bigger than I thought it would be. A massive dance floor sat in the middle of the space, and two giant bars sat on either side of the crowds of people that moved to the music. A huge stage area sat at the back of the room where a DJ booth was set up, along with a few microphone stands. Two guys performed an impressive version of LL Cool J's "Mama Said Knock You Out," and the lights overhead moved with the beat. The DJ stirred up another hit as soon as their song ended, and the original track played through the room.

"They alternate," Connor explained. "They do a performance, and then they play a track. It keeps the music flowing."

"Let's get a drink!" Katie yelled over the noise.

She grabbed my hand and led us to the bar, where we ordered two cranberry vodkas, and Connor ordered a Jack and Coke. Connor handed his card to the bartender and slid our drinks to us as they appeared at the bar.

Jared appeared next to me and playfully slung his arm around my shoulder. "Are you ordering shots, man?"

I rolled my eyes at Katie, and we laughed. While Jared talked a big game, he was totally harmless. As much as he acted like he didn't care, he seemed to enjoy the company Katie and I provided.

"No shots yet." Connor grinned and took a sip of his drink. He winced and turned to face the dance floor. "Let's get a table."

Rows of tables lined one side of the bar, and we snagged two right next to each other toward the back. I placed my drink on the table in front of me and casually scanned the room for Jaxon. He was at the bar we just came from with Heather, Reagan, and one of the girls from the hot tub. He had just said something that made them all laugh, and when the girl from the hot tub stroked his arm, I had to look away.

"Hey." Katie nudged me.

She forced me to look at her, and I took a minute to reset my tone to a more cheerful one. "What's up?"

I felt an arm slip around my waist, and I turned to see Bryson look me up and down. "Let's go dance," he interrupted and tugged at my hand.

I looked at Katie, and she grabbed Connor's hand. He assessed what was happening and knew he didn't have a choice. We found a spot on the dance floor just as "Hips Don't Lie" by Shakira blasted through the room.

Bryson was just as smooth on the dance floor as he was in the bedroom. He moved effortlessly against me and let his hands wander up and down the sides of my dress. He grinned when I mouthed the words to the song and spun me around so I could grind on him. He grabbed my hands and let his forearms rest on my hips, and it wasn't long before I could feel his arousal on my back.

The tip of his nose grazed the sensitive skin behind my ear, and my breath caught in my throat. "You look so fuckin' hot tonight," he whispered.

I turned back to face him just as the song ended. He tugged on my hand when I tried to return to the table for my drink.

"Come back to my room tonight," he said over the beat of the music. He leaned in so his lips were only inches away from mine.

"We'll see," I teased. My fingers slipped out of his, and I felt him staring as I walked back to the table. It was hard to fight the smile on my face when there was something about Bryson that could make me feel so high.

When I reunited with the group, Jaxon was standing next to Katie, and it looked like everyone was still sipping their first drink.

"We need to liven this table up," I yelled as I squeezed in next to Katie.

Her eyes widened, and her mouth spread into a devious smile. "Karaoke?"

Connor laughed. "I dare you guys."

Jaxon glanced down at us and waited for me to respond. His eyes lifted toward the stage, and he shot me a playful grin.

"Promiscuous?" I averted my eyes from his and brought my attention back to Katie. She grabbed my hand, and the table cheered as she led me through the crowd of people between us and the stage. The DJ greeted us, and Katie put in our selection. We barely had any prep time before we were handed two microphones and ushered on stage.

The song started through the speakers, and Katie and I fell into our routine effortlessly. We had rehearsed this song dozens of times in our apartment this year alone, and we had flawlessly mastered the alternating lyrics and even had gestures to go with certain lines. While I mouthed the words to Timbaland's part, Katie took care of Nelly Furtado's.

About a verse into the song, our table had made its way to the front of the stage. Connor hollered as Katie shot him a wink. She didn't break character, and together we broke into the chorus.

Keeping step to the beat, we both sashayed next to each other toward the crowd. When we reached the edge of the stage, we played into the banter of the song. I caught a glimpse of Jaxon out of the corner of my eye and decided to go for it. I mouthed a verse of lyrics in his direction, and he grinned. He shook his head and clapped his hands as I moved my body to the beat. I turned just in time to react to Katie's next line, and the chorus started again.

Together we finished out the crowd favorite, and the final beats of the song died into the next track. The crowd burst into applause, and I covered my mouth with my hands. Katie threw her arm around my shoulders, and we laughed our way off the stage. Both of us were in awe of what had just happened, and I couldn't believe we had just shared our iconic routine with an entire audience of people.

Connor whisked Katie off to the side, and they fell into a complete lip lock. I wasn't sure if he was marking his territory as a room full of liquor-infused guys who had just witnessed Katie be a total bombshell on stage or if he was actually congratulating her performance.

Jaxon met me at the bottom of the steps. "You two have definitely rehearsed that before. That was pretty damn good."

I looked him up and down, and butterflies rose into my ribcage. He looked completely edible—even in a plain black V-neck and dark jeans. His shirt hugged his chest and the definition in his arms. I watched at least six girls turn their heads as he passed.

I shrugged. "What do you think Katie and I do when no one else is at the apartment? This performance was a long time coming."

His teeth dragged across his bottom lip, and he looked toward the ceiling. "That doesn't surprise me," he teased.

"Sorry" by Justin Bieber began to play, and my hips moved instinctively to the beat. Jaxon noticed the shift in my body language and extended his hand out in front of him. He raised his eyebrows, and a dimple appeared on his cheek. My eyes locked on his, and my lips parted slightly. Our hands met, and he lightly pulled me onto the dance floor.

My heart hammered in my chest as his body inched closer to mine. The giant smile on his face let me know that this was an innocent attempt to see me up close and personal in this dress. I smirked and turned my back to his chest so he could get a different view.

When he grabbed my hands, I wasn't sure if I could curve my body into his or if that would be too much. This proximity had been off-limits since Halloween weekend, and I wasn't sure how to handle it.

As soon as I relaxed into our rhythm, I got a different view of my own. It was a scene I witnessed only a few months back. Bryson's lips were locked onto a tall blonde right in front of the bar. I watched him take a breath and whisper something into her ear that made her giggle.

I thought of last night when he stumbled into my bedroom only after he slept with someone else. I thought of the time at The Attic when Tyler almost hit me, and he didn't even know what happened. I thought of all the times he lied to me and sneaked around a topic he didn't even need to hide behind.

I tried to take a deep breath, and it got caught in my chest. Every time I took a step closer in the direction of being done with Bryson, he found a way to make me feel shittier than the time before. I had wasted so much time waiting for him to change into a decent guy, all while losing sight of what I wanted at the beginning of the year. A hookup with no attachments, and here I was chained to the fucking floor.

I spun around to face Jaxon and leaned in so he could hear me over the music. "I need to get some air."

I crossed the dance floor and made a beeline for the exit. I threw my body into the door and was immediately hit with the cold winter air of Lake Erie. Groups of people passed me on the sidewalk as I paced back and forth.

"What's up?" a guy asked as he looked me up and down.

I rolled my eyes, and he shot me a cocky smile before he dipped inside.

"Mace." I knew his voice before I even looked up at him. It was like a warm blanket being draped over me, and I was sure I could pick it out of any crowd.

Jaxon stared at me with dark-green eyes, and my shoulders relaxed.

"Sorry." I swallowed. "I just needed some air."

Jaxon let out an exasperated laugh and ran his hand through his short hair. He crossed his arms and leaned against the brick exterior of the building. He shook his head and glanced down the street, almost like he was annoyed with something.

"What's the matter?" I took a few steps toward him and stopped when he looked back at me.

"You just don't pay attention," he snapped.

I felt myself getting angry all over again. I didn't understand where this attitude was coming from. "What are you talking about?"

He lifted his body from the wall and closed the space between us. "You don't pay attention to anything going on around you. You can't just run out here looking *like that* by yourself." He looked up and down the sidewalk for emphasis as more groups of people passed us.

I rolled my eyes. "I'm fine."

"You're comfortable," he stated. He took a deep breath, and I could see his patience waning as the conversation continued. "It seems I can't help this pattern I have for looking out for you."

I wasn't sure why his reaction to follow me irritated me even more. I had to reel in my instinct to snap at him and reminded myself that this anger had nothing to do with Jaxon.

We stared at each other for what felt like an eternity. I felt the heat in my ribcage subside, and it was replaced with the urge to fall into his chest and have him take me back to the condo. As I relished in my final straw with Bryson, I was reminded of how far Jaxon and I drifted apart after we decided to try and hook up.

"Why do you sound so upset?" I asked softly.

"I'm not." The skin around his eyes went soft. "I just wished you paid more attention to things, that's all."

As I opened my mouth to respond, the doors behind us burst open and a rowdy group of people spilled onto the sidewalk. When my focus drifted back to Jaxon, he was staring at me.

"I'm sorry." I glanced down at the pavement and felt both embarrassed and stupid. "Of course I'm lucky to have you looking out for me. I'm annoyed about something else, and I shouldn't have snapped at you like that."

"Kennedy?" he deadpanned.

My eyes shot up, and my stomach sank at his expression. His features were no longer soft, and his mouth formed a hard line.

Jaxon averted his attention toward the entrance and met Bryson's hand with his. They shook the way guys do before Jaxon slipped past him to head back inside.

"Everything okay?" Bryson asked. He quickly glanced behind him and held up a finger to Brad and two girls waiting outside a taxi. I followed his gaze and felt my face twist into a scowl.

"What's up?" He read my expression and returned the gesture. "I'll see you when I get back to the condo."

An exasperated laugh escaped my chest, and I shook my head. "Don't bother."

"Don't bother?" He looked confused at my reaction, and rage bubbled up in my chest. I had so much of it that I thought I was going to implode on the sidewalk. But this time, it was spewing in different directions.

One spew was directed right at Bryson, and it grew more prominent the longer the disgusted look on his face festered into my memory. A small spew shot into whatever direction Jaxon stalked off in. I had no idea what suddenly caused his mood to shift when he was fine only moments ago on the dance floor. But the last of my rage was aimed right at myself.

"What's your problem?" he prompted when I said nothing back. "I can still see you later tonight."

"I'm tired, Bryson." I swallowed around the lump forming in my throat. Jaxon had followed me out here, and Bryson was only having this conversation with me because he saw me on the way out. "Please don't come to my room when you get back from"—I gestured toward the car—"wherever you are going."

I turned to walk back into the club, and he grabbed my forearm.

"Why do you act like this?" he asked.

"I'm done being treated like an option," I admitted. A weight I didn't know was there lifted from my chest. "I should've never started this with you."

He sighed and dropped my hand. "Whatever, Maci." Before he turned to leave, I caught a glimpse of his face. He didn't look upset or annoyed—or even disappointed. He just looked done.

And for the first time since I met him, we were finally on the same page.

Chapter Fifty-Seven

JAXON

WE REMAINED AT RAZZLE's for another hour before people wanted to head back to the condo and chill in the hot tub at Heather's. I couldn't say I was upset that the night ended a little early regarding the club scene.

After I watched Maci and Bryson have another argument right before he left in a car full of people, I started to feel last night's choices creeping up on me again. The thought of unwinding in a hot tub sounded perfect.

Since Brad was the only person I recognized in the group of people that left with Bryson, we still needed three Ubers to get everyone home. As they arrived, I purposely chose a different car from Maci. I needed some space to clear my head as I tried to convince the asshole side of me to stay put for the rest of the night. I felt him creep out the moment Maci got mad that I tried to look out for her.

Unlike the guy she got upset about, I paid attention to where she went and what she did. The fact that she took her frustrations out on me was beginning to piss me off. If I lost my shit on her, I wasn't sure if I could recover. I would say things I didn't mean and do my best to make her feel bad. That was just what I did and how I handled situations like this.

Everyone else's bedroom doors were closed when I stepped inside Connor's condo with Jared. I wasted no time changing and grabbed a towel from my bathroom closet.

Jared waited for me in the living room and looked up from his phone when he saw I was ready. "Connor's Uber had to reroute because of an accident. He said to go on over, and they'll catch up." He slipped his phone into his pocket. "I invited this girl that I met at the club. She had a few cute friends too."

"Nice, man." I chuckled.

Jared meant it as a suggestion for me, but somehow it felt like a blow to my chest. It didn't matter what those girls looked like or what they tried to offer me as a good time. None of them were Maci.

We walked across the parking lot and let ourselves into Heather's condo. I was relieved when the living room was empty and everyone else was already outside. I didn't feel like talking to Heather, Reagan, or any other people they might've invited over.

There was a fully stocked bar and a few coolers of drinks on the deck. Jared and I each helped ourselves to a beer and threw our stuff on one of the chairs. I stripped off my hoodie and shuddered as the cold air hit my chest. My brisk walk quickly turned into a jog as I spotted the last free corner of the hot tub.

I slid into the bubbling water and placed my bottle on the piece of plywood that ran around the edge of the tub. Reagan hurried to the free seat beside me, and I sipped my beer so I didn't have to say anything to her.

Heather's hot tub was the size of a small swimming pool and could hold at least fifteen people. The lights on the tub matched the music on the surround sound, and when I looked around, there were no new faces. I recognized everyone in the group that traveled with us from Bowling Green.

My shoulders relaxed, and I sank further into my seat. I tried to pull my focus to the music playing in the background, but my thoughts tugged me in multiple directions—all of them involving Maci. I felt like I was overflowing with a mixture of anger, annoyance, and anxiety. It was a shitty combination.

I wasn't sure why another altercation between Bryson and Maci threatened to push me over the edge. It was just another step in the direction I knew they were going, but how many more steps would there be?

It had been five months of watching my best friend sleep with the one girl I had set aside because I didn't want to risk losing her. Since the night we tried to hook up, things hadn't been the same. I had been trying to justify that I had made the right decision by saying no—but the more time that passed, the more I regretted everything that happened. She hooked up with a guy who did exactly everything I told her I would.

Bryson was everything I admitted I would be if we followed through—that was the part that pissed me off the most.

"Did you?" Reagan's voice rang in my right ear.

I turned to face her and realized she had just repeated herself.

"Did I do what?" I asked.

She wore a devious smile. "Did you think about what I mentioned a few months ago about Heather and me?" She sipped her drink and cocked her head while I processed.

I lightly shook my head and caught a glimpse of Heather sitting on the other side of the hot tub. Fortunately, she was too wrapped up in a conversation with one of Brad's roommates when I noticed her. I didn't want her to try and make her way over here when Reagan was already too close in proximity.

"Hasn't crossed my mind." I sighed and bumped her shoulder. She rolled her eyes and laughed.

While I didn't necessarily want attention from Reagan, she wasn't unbearable in the way Heather was. She was a pretty cool girl, but at the end of the day I only knew her because of one thing—we used to hook up, and I kept her in my back pocket for an easy lay.

Yet here she was, reminding me about an offer that included her and another girl, and I couldn't give two shits. It was infuriating that my mind was wrapped around someone I couldn't have because of a decision I had made. This was why I didn't get tangled up in friendships with girls I wanted to sleep with. All it did was complicate everything.

Just as I felt myself climbing into an aggravated headspace all over again, Connor, Katie, and Maci filed out onto the deck. The girls walked in front of Connor with their arms linked, laughing about something he had said. Katie looked over her shoulder and smiled sweetly at him as he shook his head. They looked effortlessly happy to be exactly where they were. It was so natural for them to be together.

The scene reminded me of our time in Maci and Katie's apartment—the weekend I stayed with them because of Tyler, and all of the visits in between. The endless hours of movies and the TV shows Maci wanted to binge—so much of this school year had been invested in a friendship I cared about more than I wanted to admit. But it turned stagnant when we tried to make it more than what it could be.

Out of the corner of my eye, I watched Maci strip off her shirt and reveal a bright blue swim top. My mouth parted slightly, and I turned my focus back to the rest of the hot tub.

It was painful enough to see her in a sexy-ass dress and not be able to touch her the way I wanted to, but seeing her in a bikini was another kind of torture.

Unfortunately for me, she didn't care about the kind of thoughts I had running through my head. She slid into the water across from me, completely unaware of her effect on me without even trying. She smiled when she saw me and scooted a little more toward Jared so Katie could slide in next to her.

As much as I tried to ignore her, I couldn't help but offer a small smile back. She picked up on my mood immediately. She cocked her head and attempted to read my expression. I shook my head to tell her it was nothing and took another sip of my beer.

Katie eyed the silent exchange between us, which triggered another explosion inside me. I felt surrounded by the pressure that I couldn't escape. All the thoughts built up in my headspace were overwhelmed with trying to keep it together since August, and I wasn't sure how long I could last.

Suddenly, a hand smacked the back of my shoulder. Bryson stood behind me while a few people I recognized from outside Razzle's took up chairs near the firepit.

"Do we still have that bottle of Jack in the freezer?" Bryson asked.

I nodded as Jared motioned for Bryson to walk around to him.

At the sight of Bryson's arrival, Maci started a conversation with Katie and the two of them burst into hysterics. Even though Bryson was standing right behind her so he could get to Jared, she paid him no attention. I wasn't sure what their argument was about outside of Razzle's, but it was hard not to pick up the tension that brewed between them.

"Kennedy, bring out some of those solo cups, too," Jared instructed Bryson. They bumped fists, and Bryson walked back toward the condo. Right before he stepped inside, a leech that was sitting by the fire got up to chase after him. He held the door open for her, and together they disappeared inside.

Maci rolled her eyes and shook her head. She tried to change her expression before anyone noticed, but Jared shifted his attention in her direction.

"What's up?" Jared asked her. He knew that Maci was hooking up with Bryson, but he was very out of the loop when it came to the actual relationship they carried.

"Not a thing," she lied and took a sip of her drink. Her response drew a few people's attention, and everyone returned to their original conversation.

Reagan tried to catch my eye, but I stared past her to the other end of the hot tub, where suddenly, being next to Heather didn't sound half bad.

Bryson returned with the bottle of Jack and a stack of solo cups. He worked with Jared to pour and pass out shots.

"Don't get any of that in the hot tub!" Heather shouted from her seat.

We all held our cups high above the water and looked in her direction.

"I was just about to toast your ass, and you're gonna yell at me?" Bryson smiled at her, and she instantly calmed down.

"I could always bring the offer up to Bryson," Reagan murmured and made direct eye contact with me.

Maci caught the sound of Bryson's name and glanced over at our conversation.

"Good luck with that," I challenged and chuckled at the thought.

Bryson would never fuck around with two girls who were obsessed with me—especially all of the crazy scenes he witnessed firsthand with Heather. If it wasn't simple, Bryson wasn't for it.

My eyes instinctively drifted to Maci, and she raised her eyebrows at the sight of me being so close to Reagan.

"To the host of our gathering this evening." Bryson raised his cup, and the rest of us followed suit. He shot me a cocky grin, then averted his attention back to Heather. "It's a treat knowing you, Heather."

While Heather took his toast to heart, I knew Bryson was really thanking me for sleeping with her. Without my connection, we couldn't have secured a second condo for the trip. We clinked our cups together right before everyone else downed their double shot of Jack. I slid my empty cup into Bryson's, and he went around the tub to collect the rest.

"There's Annie and those girls I mentioned," Jared said quickly, kicking me under the water.

Reagan shot me a look, and I turned to see Annie and her friends undressing at a few of the empty chairs. Bryson patted my shoulder as he passed and nodded in Annie's direction. She smiled at him, and her friends giggled. The redhead stared right past Bryson and made eye contact with me.

I waited for some sort of reaction to surface from a hot girl staring at me from across the deck, but nothing came.

Bryson rounded the corner of the tub and stopped when he got behind Maci. He purposely reached across her chest and whispered something in her ear. She rolled her eyes and whispered something back, which caused him to shoot her a dirty look. He shook his head and walked over to where the girls from Razzle's were sitting by the fire.

I drained the rest of my beer and took a deep breath. Annie, her cute redhead friend, and another girl that was with them all took the empty seats next to Jared.

"This is Annie," Jared said, and she waved awkwardly to the group.

"This is Jenna and Kim." Annie pointed to her friends, and they repeated her gesture.

Jenna shot me a shy smile. If I were in my normal head-space, I would've made it incredibly clear to Jenna that she could sleep with me tonight if she wanted to. She had a pretty face and a cute figure, and she was someone I could hook up with and know I wouldn't have to see again. I was right on the cusp of saying something to her even though I was surrounded by past experiences and a girl I struggled to ignore.

"Fuck, I should've asked you guys for refills." Jared sighed. He rose out of the hot tub and launched himself over the side. "Fuck, it's cold!" he yelled and ran over to the coolers.

"Not so fast!" Heather tried to yell before he came splashing down into his seat. A wave of water flew over the side, and everyone laughed.

"How many did you grab?" Maci asked, and her mouth dropped when she realized he had no bottles left.

Jared shrugged and widened his eyes. "I had to accommo-date my guests." He cocked his head to the left, and Maci bit her lip. She quickly caught onto the fact that Jared was trying to get laid tonight by one of the girls sitting next to him, and she was no cockblocker.

"I get it," Maci said through her teeth and grinned at the newcomers.

Katie laughed at her friendly gesture and sank into Con-nor's chest. Jared had grown on both of them in such a short time, and it was kind of fun to watch them cheer him on. I knew Jared ate up every bit of attention that they showed him.

"I'm not getting out." Connor laughed when Katie glanced up at him with puppy dog eyes. "It's freezing, and I'm not empty yet."

"But I am." Maci pouted and shook her empty bottle for emphasis.

"You better make it quick." Katie chuckled and teased Maci by taking another sip of her drink. "Maybe you won't freeze your tits off."

That comment got a few laughs from Jared's new friends and even Reagan.

I shook my head and looked past Maci's smirk to watch Bryson work his magic on one of the girls he walked in with.

"Jax," Maci sang sweetly and looked at me. I drew my focus back to her to let her know I was listening. She shook her empty bottle and nodded toward my drink. "Are you getting up soon?"

Everyone around us laughed at the shared thought of no one wanting to get out of the water. She smiled at me and waited for my answer.

"She said your name kind of sweet there, *Jax*," Jared teased, prompting more laughs from our side of the tub.

I knew I would probably regret my comment when I looked back on this moment. I took a deep breath and stared back at Maci. Her smile shifted when she read my reaction, and I knew the guy I had tried so hard to hide from her had won. It hurt a little to see her wear an expression I had caused so many girls I didn't give a shit about to wear, but it had become so second nature to me that I couldn't hold back.

I set my beer bottle on the side of the tub. "Believe me. She's said my name sweeter than that."

I lifted myself out of the hot tub and grabbed my hoodie and towel, completely ignoring the icy air as it hit my bare chest. The few people sitting by me in the hot tub were silent, but I didn't stay to see their reactions. It wasn't hard to put what I just said together, especially when you took my reputation and how Maci and I acted around each other.

I headed back through Heather's condo and made a beeline across the parking lot. I didn't want to see the look on Maci's face. I didn't care what anyone else thought. My heart beat rapidly in my chest, and I slammed the front door of the condo shut behind me.

The asshole part of me was out, and once he left there was no reeling him back in. Maci wasn't going to be an exception for what happened next. There was no way around it. I was done.

Chapter Fifty-Eight

MACI

March 2016

I slammed the door behind me as soon as I entered the condo. "What the *fuck* was that about, Jaxon!"

He shrugged. "Nothing I said was a lie."

"But did you have to say it like that in front of *everyone*?" I exclaimed. I almost didn't recognize who I was talking to.

"You mean Bryson," he stated, locking eyes with me for the first time since I entered the room.

I searched for any emotion that might be hiding behind his gaze, but I came up empty.

"Where do you think he went after the bar tonight, Maci?"

"I have my guesses," I admitted.

Jaxon removed his towel from around his waist and ran it through his hair. I knew I'd have to be the one to speak again if we were going to finish whatever this was.

"Why do you care, Jaxon? You know me and Bryson aren't together."

"Then why do you argue like you are?" he snapped, throwing his towel on the couch. "He treats you exactly how he sees you at that moment. I know because I do the same thing with girls I keep around for one thing."

The words left his mouth so easily, almost like they were rehearsed. I realized that this wasn't the first time Jaxon had played through this conversation—but this was the first time I was actually invited to it.

He shook his head. "I told you from the beginning." He took a few steps toward me, and his voice got more intense. "He's *never* going to treat you the way you want him to. He will never give you what you expect from a relationship with him."

I felt the anger rising in my throat. Jaxon wasn't allowed to stand there and preach to me about what I wanted from anyone. The night we almost slept together, I had been crystal clear about what I wanted. He read the signs and ended everything before it could even start.

"I never asked him for a relationship!" I yelled. It was my turn to take a few steps forward and approach him. "The things I fight with Bryson about have *nothing* to do with being together. Do I hate that he sleeps with other girls? It isn't my favorite, but I told him I didn't care about that from the beginning. I care that he respects me enough as a friend to tell me the truth. I get tired of the way he lies about shit and dances around the truth."

Jaxon stared at me with his arms crossed against his bare chest.

"That must be something else you both have in common," I snapped and turned to leave.

"Then why do you deal with it?"

When I turned back around, he was standing in front of me. His voice was softer now, but didn't lack the urgency. "Look me in my face and tell me you don't feel anything for him."

His question caught me off guard. Bryson had excited me since I met him that night on the street. I couldn't deny how he made me feel when I was with him and things were *good*. I held onto glimpses of the guy I wanted Bryson to be for me in those small moments when he made me feel like I mattered to him. It was so easy for me to push aside all of the shitty parts.

But I couldn't ignore the dip in my stomach that I'd felt since the night I met Bryson—back when I was searching the streets of bars just to catch a glimpse of Jaxon's face. Bryson wasn't Jaxon, and no guy ever would be.

I shook my head and sent a few tears rolling down my cheeks. There was a cocktail of anger and helplessness brewing in my bones. It had always been Jaxon I wanted, but it was Bryson who had been there to make *me* feel wanted. Bryson should've never been an option.

"You can't." Jaxon's mutter was barely audible even though he was standing inches away from me. He ran a hand through his hair and paced back to the center of the living room. The muscles in his back tensed, and he rested his hands behind his head.

I exhaled, taking advantage of the space and blinked up at the ceiling. There were two directions this conversation could take. I remembered how he looked at me that night we almost hooked up. I could still hear his words clear as day and the longing in his voice.

Maci, I can't do this.

I stared at him from across the room. His back was still turned to me.

"I need you to say it," I admitted, trying not to sound desperate. I needed to hear him tell me why he was so interested in my choices with Bryson. I needed him to say everything he had wanted to since the night he said no.

"Say what." He shrugged, using a tone he reserved for his morning-after girls.

"Don't you *dare* do that to me." I took a few angry steps forward but made sure the dining room table stayed between us.

"Do what?" he snapped, throwing his arms up in the air like he didn't know what I was talking about. He suddenly looked like he could give two shits about this conversation.

I couldn't hold it in anymore.

"The fuck you know, Jaxon!" I screamed and pointed angrily across the table. "You're the one who said no!"

His eyebrows knit together, and his lips made a hard line.

When he didn't say anything, I yelled, "That night we almost hooked up was the worst mistake I've ever made." The tears built up again, and I swallowed to keep my voice from shaking. "Making up how we met and spitting some fake story to Bryson—you acted like you didn't even know me, and that hurt like hell. You wrote everything we had out of your life as soon as I did the same shit you did the next day! You went and had sex with Heather, but you get a pass?"

"That's not true." He shook his head and balled his hands into fists. "I stopped it because I actually care about you. I know how I am, Maci. Haven't you spent enough time with Bryson to realize how it would've gone?"

"Because this is much better." I gestured to the space between us and met his gaze. "I didn't realize you and *Kennedy* were one in the same person. That you can't make different choices."

His green eyes were soft, and if I was going to say this to him and put everything out in the open, I had to say it now. "I needed you as a friend, and that's what you said we'd be if we didn't sleep together that night. I trusted you, and you've been punishing me for it, and it's bullshit."

"You couldn't have cared that much. You moved on pretty damn quick." Jaxon grasped the top of the dining room chair across from me. His voice was firm, but I could hear the hurt behind it. "I slept with Heather just like I did any other random night. I needed something to distract me from how I was feeling. I so badly wanted to find you and finish what I had stopped."

Jaxon stared down at the table, but when he lifted his head and his eyes met mine—I felt weak at the knees. "But because I didn't, you found the one person I never wanted to be with you. If I knew by saying no, that you would end up with the shit version of me anyway . . . I would've done exactly what you wanted that night."

I shook my head to get back into my dominant headspace. "You can't be mad at me for doing what you chose for us. You can't be upset with me for moving on after you told me nothing could happen. You weren't just some guy to me that night Jaxon . . . I cared about you. Even if it was just as a friend or whatever we were at the time. But I would've rather had sex with you and had a reason to hate you instead of what we've been doing the past few months."

Tomorrow, I would probably regret the next set of words that came out of my mouth. I took a deep breath and continued before I lost the stamina to say it. "I love you, Jaxon."

I peered up to meet his gaze, frozen by the admission neither one of us expected to hear me say.

He let out a sound that was almost like a laugh. "Don't give me that bullshit. You wanted a fling, and you ran into the very guy to give it to you the next night. Love me?" He pushed off the chair and wore a condescending smile. "Did you love me when you were fucking Bryson?"

I clenched my teeth to keep my jaw from dropping. The pull in my chest begged me to retreat from the man I no longer recognized. It was as if he no longer cared that he hurt me, and I wasn't sure if we would ever recover from this conversation.

He cocked his head, waiting for my response—his gaze now stoic and his face relaxed.

I had to get out of here. I refused to break down in front of him and demolish everything we had built since the first day we met. I crossed my arms to stop my hands from shaking and started toward the front door.

"Mace." Jaxon's voice was hoarse and more serious than before.

I didn't turn around. All I wanted to do was walk outside and hit the restart button.

"Fuck, Maci, stop!" Jaxon snapped.

My hand gripped the handle, and I tried to swallow the lump in my throat. It caught me off guard to hear Jaxon this angry. The only sound in the entire place was his footsteps as he crossed the kitchen floor.

"I'm sorry," he said, getting closer.

I turned my head to see him standing about a foot away from me.

"I shouldn't have said that, and I'm sorry I snapped at you," he offered softly. He took a few steps toward me like he was testing the waters.

I examined his face, liberated that the Jaxon I knew was back on the same planet as me. My body relaxed, and I faced him just as he closed the gap between us. He leaned his forehead against mine—a gesture he had done so many times before. But this time felt different, almost like he couldn't accept the consequences of me walking away.

Heat radiated off of his bare chest and onto mine when he rested his forearms above my head. I was trapped, both of us half-naked and caught in the tension that had been brewing since I followed him here.

"What was that thing you said back there?" He smirked, and a small dimple appeared in his left cheek.

"I don't know what you're talking about," I teased, refusing to give in to the smile that so badly wanted to make an appearance. "I said so many things."

He stared into my eyes and repeated the plea I gave him only a few moments ago, "I need you to say it."

A pulse began in my upper thighs and made its way between my legs. Having him close like this ignited a fire in my stomach. My body ached to be against him, eager to give in to everything I had been withholding from it for five months.

"Bryson is my best friend," Jaxon murmured. He skimmed his nose against mine, barely making contact at all.

My breath caught in my throat. I could put my mouth on his if I leaned into him just an inch or two.

The internal battle happening in my head was infuriating. The words hung on my lips, begging to release me from any doubts that formed in my mind. The man standing in front of me had held a special place in my heart since I sat next to him in class last semester.

Jaxon needed to hear me say the only phrase that, in his mind, would excuse him from going behind Bryson's back.

"I love you," I admitted, meaning every syllable as it drifted so effortlessly from the deepest parts of my chest.

He held my gaze for a moment and processed my confession. He grinned, licked the center of his bottom lip, and gently placed his mouth on mine. I put my hands on his chest and leaned into his kiss, exploring his mouth with my tongue.

Warmth spread throughout my whole body as he cupped my face and trailed his fingers across my hip. I melted into his touch, fitting myself perfectly into the curve of his body.

Jaxon gave me a comfort I never felt with Bryson. I didn't want it to stop—I wanted to feel him everywhere and give him permission to do everything that should have happened so much sooner than this moment.

He fisted his hand into the hair at the base of my neck, becoming more urgent with his mouth and quickening our pace. Just as I attempted to explore parts south of his waistband, he broke away to look at me.

"Are you sure you want to do this?" A worried expression washed over his face. "I can walk away right now if you're unsure, but if I get you into that bedroom I don't think I'll be able to stop myself. I don't know how to do the morning-after, Mace. I don't want to hurt you—"

I gently placed my hand on his mouth before he could go any further. I had never seen him look so nervous and found it incredibly adorable. "We don't have to have it all figured out right now," I reassured him. "I just know I want to be yours tonight."

Before I could utter another word, he kissed me again. I giggled against his lips when he grabbed the backs of my thighs and lifted me against the wall. I held onto his shoulders and trailed my fingers down his flexed biceps. I kissed his jawline and down his neck—stopping when his grip on my legs tightened and a small moan escaped his mouth.

I hovered over the sensitive area right where the base of his neck met his shoulder. "Oh, yeah?" I teased and gave him another soft kiss.

His groan melted into a laugh, and he moved us toward his bedroom. Hearing him react to my touch sent a rush of heat in between my legs. I didn't think I could want him any more than I did the last time I was tempted like this. I was terribly mistaken.

He kicked the bedroom door shut behind us and sat on the edge of the bed so I could straddle him. I skimmed my hands down his chest and teased the waistband of his basketball shorts.

"You and these hands." He smiled a sexy grin and shook his head. He grabbed my wrists and placed my hands on his chest. He held them there while he leaned forward to trail soft kisses down my neck. I would never get used to having his mouth on my body.

He tightened his grip when I tried to free a hand, and I laughed. He moved both of my wrists to his left hand so he could shift the top of my bathing suit. His lips moved across my chest, and his free hand gripped the top of my thigh.

"Don't even think about it." He stared at me between kisses, and I had to catch my breath. He took my nipple into his mouth and teased it with his tongue, nibbling softly as he worked his thumb into the muscle of my groin. I moaned and leaned my forehead against his shoulder. He continued this rhythm, sending desire into places I didn't even know existed.

"Fuck," I moaned as he sucked on my nipple.

He stopped and pulled away so he could look at me. His gaze locked on mine, and he licked the center of his top lip, wearing an expression I'd only seen once before. He cupped my face and traced his thumb across my cheek.

His cocky grin resurfaced. "I plan to," he assured me.

Chapter Fifty-Nine

JAXON

March 2016

I wanted her—and tonight she wanted to be *mine*.

Originally, I thought the sexiest words out of Maci's mouth would be my name—moaning my name while I made her lose control of her body. But then I heard her say she wanted to be mine.

I heard her say she loved me—a phrase that had haunted me since I started sleeping around with women. I dreaded the moment when a woman told me she loved me, and I would have to tell her thank you.

But there wasn't any fear when I heard it from Maci. I didn't react at all, and she hadn't expected me to. After the words left her lips, there was no pressure to reciprocate or discuss how I felt. It was a moment of raw and honest emotion that somehow pushed me closer to her.

I slipped my hand around her neck and untied the strap of her bathing suit. She shrugged off the thin material, and it fell in between us. My eyes dropped to her bare chest, and I unhooked the only strap that kept it against her body.

She glanced up at me through dark lashes and searched my face. The last time we were in this situation, she still had her bra on. I had touched her but wasn't rewarded with seeing her like this.

"You're beautiful," I whispered and tucked her hair behind her ears.

She smiled shyly, and I cupped her face with my hands. I kissed her gently, letting her know I had no intention of rushing this.

Her hands slid down my chest and the sides of my ribs. Feeling her touch against my skin made me realize how much I took the first time we did this for granted. I could've kissed her for as long as she let me.

I grabbed her hips and inched us back to the middle of the bed. She hugged my neck and giggled when my hands slid into the ties of her bathing suit bottoms. I released them from both sides, and she was completely naked on top of me.

She kissed down my neck, paying close attention to the spot she had discovered a few moments ago. A laugh escaped my chest, and she leaned back before she pushed me onto the bed. She continued to trail down my chest to my abdomen and stopped at the waistline of my shorts. Her hands slipped underneath them, and she tugged—prompting me to lift my hips so she could drag them down my thighs.

I watched her lips part around the tip of my cock, and I had to lean back against the mattress. If I watched her suck me, I would lose what little control I had left. I dragged my hands through my hair and closed my eyes as her mouth moved up and down, her tongue swirling underneath the head and wetting the shaft. If she didn't stop, I would come.

"Come here," I prompted and gently pulled her hand.

She crawled over me, and I brought her mouth back to mine. I slid my hand down her stomach and slipped two fingers inside her. Her arms shook on either side of me, and a soft moan landed on my lips. Her hips fell into my touch, and I teased her most sensitive spot. I made slow circles with my thumb on her clit and mirrored the motion with my index finger. She gripped the pillow behind my head and leaned back to adjust the angle.

We made eye contact, and her mouth parted slightly. She grazed her teeth across her bottom lip as she came undone over top of me. Her thighs tightened around my body, and she groaned as her head fell against my shoulder.

I moved so I was sitting with her in my lap. She stroked her clit against my erection, riding out her orgasm as she dragged her nails lightly down my sides. I caught her mouth with mine and used my hands to guide her as we moved against each other. Her wet pussy glided along my cock, and I ached to be inside her.

"I want you," she whispered against my lips.

My mouth curved into a grin, and she kissed me slowly. She started to rock against me again, her body in rhythm with her tongue's gentle strokes.

But we were playing with fire, and I didn't want her to do something she would regret.

"There's a condom in my bag," I said between kisses.

She tucked her hair behind her ears and gripped my shoulders. I leaned over so she could pluck the unopened Trojan box out of my duffle.

I leaned back against the headboard and adjusted her on my lap. She wrapped her arms around my neck and ran her fingers through my hair. My forehead rested against hers, and in one slow movement, I eased myself inside her. I groaned against her lips, and she captured my mouth with hers.

We moved slowly, enjoying how our bodies felt pressed against one another. Relishing in what had been building since we first met and making up for all the time we lost. My hands roamed freely around her body—free to touch and appreciate because in this moment she was *mine*.

She began to speed up, moving her hips against me. She moaned and dug her nails into my neck, pushing me dangerously close to the edge. I wasn't ready to get there yet, and if she had kept going at this pace, I wouldn't last much longer.

"Mace, look at me." I brought my hand to her face.

She slowed, and her eyes met mine. I dragged my thumb across her mouth and pulled at her bottom lip. Her right dimple appeared, and her lips formed a naughty grin.

I grinned back and released her lip from under my thumb. "Slow down, baby."

She watched me slide two fingers into my mouth before I rested them on her clit. My free hand wrapped around her lower back, and I prompted her to move again. I quickened my pace with my fingers, forcing her to hold onto my shoulders to stay balanced. She gasped, and I knew she would come if I kept her going at this pace. It was slow enough to enjoy her unraveling in front of me, but I wasn't close to the finish line. I could spend all night inside her.

Her breaths grew sharper, and she leaned her forehead against mine. I kept our pace slow but pumped my hips harder, hitting the spot inside her that would make her come undone. I wanted to feel her release around me, make me wet with how much I turned her on—just like I did the first time I touched her.

"Jaxon," she whimpered, and my whole world went still.

I gripped her hips and rolled us so I was on top of her. I kissed up her neck with my fingers still on her clit, coaxing her body to build again as I thrust inside her. She gripped the pillow behind her and cried out. My name slipped from her lips again as her walls tightened around me, and I felt myself getting close.

I quickened my pace until I couldn't hold out any longer. I shifted my body weight off her and buried my face in her neck. My heart hammered against my chest as I breathed in her scent, inhaling slowly to catch my breath before I lifted onto my forearms and stared down at her.

Maci smiled sleepily, reaching up to trail her fingers through my hair. I bent down to touch my lips to hers, and she pulled me against her. I kissed up her jawline and tugged her earlobe with my teeth. She giggled and pulled the blankets up to her chest. I loved that sound, and I loved her lying naked next to me.

I rolled out of bed and walked into the bathroom to throw away the condom. I kept my eyes on her and slipped on a pair of basketball shorts. She was minutes away from falling asleep, her eyes getting heavier with each moment that passed. I bent down and kissed her forehead. Then I kissed her nose and landed on her mouth.

"Do you want anything from the kitchen?" I murmured, and she shook her head.

Before opening the door, I tossed her one of my shirts and a pair of basketball shorts. I shut it behind me and glanced around the condo to ensure I was clear.

After I grabbed a Gatorade from the fridge, I sat at the breakfast bar and replayed everything that just happened on repeat in my head. I had just slept with one of my best friends—with a girl I cared about more than anything. I waited for the panicked reaction to take over, for the regret to consume me and eat me from the inside out. But nothing came.

I had wanted every part of what just happened with Maci. I wanted to pull her against me and have her on top of me—while I touched her and pushed her to feel things that only I could make her feel. My name on her lips was a sound I would never get tired of hearing. The sweet moans that felt warm on my neck and chest made me hard again just thinking about them.

I drank half the bottle of Gatorade and stilled when I heard someone coming from the front door. I wasn't prepared to face Bryson yet, and the thought of having to see him right now twisted my stomach. I had no idea what I would say to him.

Katie cleared her throat as she rounded the corner of the hall and my shoulders relaxed. She was in her pajamas and looked ready for bed. She must've come back from the hot tub with Connor after Maci and I had our fight.

I swallowed and studied her expression. Even though the door had been closed, Maci was loud. I smiled and thought of the noises she had made while I was inside her.

Katie smiled back and slowly leaned against the counter. She blinked a few times and cocked her head.

"What's up, Katie?" I took another long sip, and her smile grew bigger. Whether she heard us or not, she knew. I swore these girls were in sync.

"Absolutely nothing." She giggled and pulled out a bottle of water from the fridge. "Need another?"

I read right through her innocent stare. It was hard not to smile back at her when I extended my hand for another drink.

She passed me a Gatorade and glanced over her shoulder on her way back to the bedroom. "Night, Jaxon."

"Goodnight," I sang sweetly to mimic her tone and headed back to my room. I was exhausted.

All I wanted to do was pass out next to the beautiful girl in my bed, wrap my arms around her, and replay the night over and over again in my head.

I still had a few more hours before I had to figure out the morning-after.

Chapter Sixty

MACI

March 2016

I woke up in Jaxon's shirt—wrapped in his arms and nestled in the nook of his neck. I didn't want to open my eyes and face the day ahead of us. I didn't want to be anywhere else but here.

Last night was perfect. *He* was perfect. Before last night, when I pictured us sleeping together, I always lacked the real version to compare it to. All I had to work with was everything up until the point when he stopped the final act from happening.

The way he took his time and explored my body sent goosebumps down my legs. Every tender touch of his lips and his hands remained on my skin. When I thought of how he called me baby . . . I was ready to ride him all over again. He made me feel like I was his, and the thought of that ending made my stomach sink.

But it's what I signed up for. He had made it clear that he didn't know how to do the morning-after routine. There were no expectations, and nothing was guaranteed. As long as I didn't lose him as a friend, I couldn't be upset with the outcome he decided on. Last night meant everything to me, but I wasn't sure where his head was now that there was no going back.

I kissed the base of his neck and brushed my hand along his waistline. He stirred and tucked his hand under my shirt, his fingers grazing my back in a circular motion. My skin was on fire under his touch, sending a pull in my groin that made my stomach dip. He swept across the area that sat right above my panty line, and my hips jerked toward him. I giggled into his chest, and he shifted so his sleepy gaze met mine.

"Good morning, Mace," he murmured, his voice husky from just waking up. He pulled up on my shirt, and his hand traveled over the basketball shorts I borrowed.

"Good morning," I murmured back, and I felt his erection against my stomach.

His hand cupped my ass and skimmed over the soft fabric. "I like this."

"Like what?" I prompted.

"You . . . in my clothes . . . waking up in my bed." He emphasized each statement and planted a soft kiss on my lips.

"Jax." I laughed against his lips. "I have to brush my teeth." I fell asleep immediately after hooking up last night and cringed at the idea of morning breath.

"I don't give a shit about that." He shook his head like I was weird for bringing it up.

All of my instincts told me to get up and do it anyway. The idea of Jaxon getting turned off by something so silly was mortifying. It was intimidating to know his history with women and suddenly become one of them. There were so many things I had to think about now that we took this step. Before, they didn't matter because I didn't think I had a chance with him. Now that we crossed that line, I suddenly worried about how smooth my legs felt, knowing I already had morning stubble.

He slid his hand into the waistband of my shorts. His index finger slid over my pussy, and he studied my face as he made slow circles with his thumb against my clit. He pushed two fingers inside me and massaged the muscle that ached for more of him.

"Is this okay?" he cautioned and continued to tease me.

"Yeah." I exhaled and tried not to get lost in my headspace. I wasn't sure where we went from here, and I didn't know what came after last night. But if this was his version of doing the morning-after, then I was all for it.

The sound of Katie's cackling came from the living room. I stared at the door that separated us from the rest of the world and dreaded the moment we had to open it.

"I'll never ask you to be quiet." Jaxon kept his voice down, and I heard the condom wrapper open. He shifted so he hovered over me, his fingers still at work. "I don't care who hears us. But you have to decide what kind of scene you want us to walk out to."

I stared into his deep-green eyes and tried to distract myself from the pleasure building in my core. "You sound pretty confident that I'm going to be noisy."

"Just using experience." He cocked his head and quickened his pace. I gripped the sheets on either side of my hips. His lips parted slightly, and his tongue grazed the center of his bottom lip.

"Oh my—" I started to whimper before he placed his mouth on mine. I moved my hands to the back of his neck and pressed against him to smother any of the remaining sounds I had left. My nails dug into his skin, and he tugged on my bottom lip with his teeth as he slid himself inside me.

"I won't save you again," he threatened with a cocky grin. He began to move, filling me slowly and pulling out just the same.

I relished the intimacy of getting to feel him over and over again in a sweet rhythm. I never wanted to lose this.

"We'll see if I need it." I gestured toward his hips, and he sped up his thrusts.

He slid his fingers into mine and pulled my arms over my head. He transferred my wrists to one hand, allowing his free hand to drift down to my chest. I was completely pinned and unable to move.

He cupped my breast through his shirt and brought my nipple to his mouth. I watched him suck softly on the tender bud and arched my back to let him know I wanted more—I wanted him deeper.

He lifted my leg against his side and sank into me. His hand tightened against both my wrists, and my head fell back into the pillow. I bit my bottom lip to keep from crying out, and a shaky breath escaped my chest when he repeated the motion.

He leaned back to get a full view of me slowly losing control underneath him. Color rose to my cheeks as he teased me with deep strokes. When his eyes locked on mine, I felt an overwhelming sense of emotion that stemmed from my adoration for this man and how incredible he made me feel when he was inside me.

"Jaxon." I exhaled slowly and tried my best to keep quiet. I felt myself teetering on the edge of release.

"Mace," he teased and quickened his strokes.

"Jaxon, I'm gonna come," I murmured.

He grinned. "I know, baby."

His eyes grew dark, and I knew he was enjoying this. He licked the pad of his thumb and caressed my throbbing clit, his gaze never leaving mine.

"Jaxon, kiss me," I begged. "Jax—" I began to moan before he silenced me with another round of kisses.

My moan turned to whimpers against his lips. My hips shook under the weight of his body, and my orgasm erupted through every cell in my being. I took sharp breaths through my nose as I groaned into his mouth.

A soft and satisfied sound left the back of his throat. He released my wrists and I ran my hands over his broad shoulders. His skin was smooth, and a layer of sweat rested on his upper back. He was gorgeous and sexy and everything in between.

"You win," I panted, and he chuckled against my chest.

"Yeah, I fuckin' did." He smiled and looked like he was ready to go back to sleep. He rolled slightly to the side so he could dispose of the condom.

I ran my fingers through his hair and along his jawline. The skin around his eyes softened, and I cupped his chin to bring his lips to mine. Just one slow sweet kiss was all it took to send butterflies to my stomach. He kissed down my neck and rested his head back on my chest. I stroked his back and dragged my fingers aimlessly around the curves of his muscles. I closed my eyes and smiled sleepily when I heard the soft sounds of his snoring.

More laughter erupted from the living room as I felt my body getting heavy with the second round of exhaustion. We slept for two more hours before leaving the perfect little bubble we created in this bedroom—away from everyone else, everything else, and the decisions we'd have to make afterward.

Chapter Sixty-One

JAXON

March 2016

While Maci showered, I decided it was time for one of us to leave this bedroom. I checked that she had enough towels before I went into the living room to find Connor and Katie snuggled up on the couch. *Jurassic Park* played on the TV, and neither of them acknowledged me until they heard the bedroom door shut.

Katie smiled and sipped her coffee. "Good morning."

"Nice night?" Connor teased.

I grinned and shook my head. "You two are ridiculous."

I dragged my hands down my face and checked to see if there was coffee. It was already noon, but my pounding headache told me I lacked in the caffeine department. The coffee pot was almost empty. I poured myself a cup and searched the fridge for creamer. "Did anyone else come back here last night?"

"Jared came back with that girl he invited from the bar." Connor shrugged. "Everyone else must've stayed at the other condo."

I relaxed my shoulders and leaned my back against the counter. I still had time before I had to talk to Bryson. The last thing I wanted was for him to hit on Maci or try and get with her while we were still here. I didn't know how to explain everything, but I couldn't ignore it now that I had slept with her.

Maci emerged from the bedroom with a towel wrapped around her body and another on her head.

"Are we still doing brunch today?" Katie asked from the couch. She slid out from underneath Connor's arm and went into the kitchen to rinse her mug. She playfully bumped my hip with hers, and I shifted out of her way.

"Yeah, that sounds perfect," Maci said and eyed me as she walked from my bedroom to hers. A few minutes later, she came out in jeans and a hoodie. Her hair was still wet, but it was brushed out and pulled to one side.

"Give me five minutes." Katie jogged down the hall, and Connor got up to follow her, leaving Maci and me alone in the kitchen.

Maci crossed her arms in front of her chest and leaned against the wall. I took in the sight of her and wished we had spent a few more minutes in my bedroom. Now that I had her, I wanted her even more than I had before.

She bit the inside of her cheek, and I knew she was getting into her head.

"What's up, Mace?" I prompted softly.

Her eyes widened and she shook her head. "Nothing, I'm good."

"You're lying." I smiled and took a few steps toward her.

She glanced down at my bare chest before meeting my gaze. "I'm fine."

I cupped her chin and pressed my lips gently against hers. When I pulled away, her right dimple dug into her cheek.

"Don't get into your head about this, okay?" I whispered in case Connor or Katie came back down the hall. "We'll talk later."

"Ready?" Katie yelled from the front door and peered in our direction.

Connor came back down the hall pulling on a fresh T-shirt. From the flustered expression on Katie's face, it was no surprise that Connor wore a massive grin. They loved to mess around in any of the spare moments they had before they left each other.

I watched Maci walk out the door with Katie behind her. It felt a little weird to be away from her after we spent last night and this morning together. I shook my head, and when I turned around, Connor stared at me with an innocent look on his face.

"I'm trying really hard not to be nosey," Connor admitted.

"Yes, I slept with Maci last night," I stated. "No, I have no idea what that means. No, I haven't talked to Bryson, and I have no idea what comes next. Did I leave anything out?"

"Doesn't having no idea what that means and having no idea what comes next mean the same thing?"

I pondered his question before I answered. "I guess that just emphasizes how much I don't know." I shrugged and fell onto the living room couch.

"I was gonna go over to the other condo to chill. Jared went over there earlier this morning, and I'm assuming Kennedy is there too. Wanna come?"

"Let me change, and I'll be ready." I forced myself up and ran into the bedroom. I took a quick shower before putting on clean sweatpants and a shirt. I grabbed a hoodie just in case and sprayed a few pumps of cologne.

Connor was waiting for me by the front door when I returned to the living room. We walked across the parking lot to the second condo and knocked on the door. Heather answered and instantly lit up when she noticed I was standing behind Connor.

I followed Connor inside and brushed past Heather without giving her any acknowledgment. I could only deal with one issue at a time today—that issue being the conversation I had to have with Bryson.

Jared was sitting on the couch with Brad playing *Call of Duty*. Aaliyah and one of the girls from last night were at the dining room table, scrolling through their phones. Heather joined them when she realized I had no intention of speaking to her.

Bryson emerged from one of the bedrooms and slapped hands with Jared as he rounded the couch. "What's up?" he asked when he noticed Connor and I were there.

"Not much, man." Connor took the empty seat in the recliner. "Good night?"

Bryson grinned. "Not too bad."

Reagan entered the living room and did a double take when she noticed new arrivals. "Hey, Jax." She smiled and padded into the kitchen.

My stomach sank as another girl I hooked up with went into the dining area. Being around so many past experiences after I had just slept with Maci was a little unsettling.

I walked past the group of girls and kept my eyes forward. I needed some air and made a beeline for the deck. I looked out at the view of the lake and watched the waves crash into the rocks below. It was a nice view as I tried to get out of my head.

It was chilly being so close to the water. I slipped on my hoodie and took one of the seats at the end of the deck. My eyes drifted closed, and I focused on the sounds of the waves. I pictured Maci at brunch with Katie and wondered how that conversation was going. It had only been half an hour, and I already couldn't wait to see her again.

The door to the deck slid open, and I prayed that it wasn't Heather or Reagan coming out to take advantage of the fact that I was alone.

Bryson appeared holding an energy drink and a lighter. He shut the door behind him and took the empty chair next to me. He set his drink down on the side table that separated us and popped the tab.

"Did you stay with Maci last night?" he asked casually.

While I appreciated him taking the pressure off of me by starting the conversation, he completely caught me off guard. Now I had little time to think through what I was going to say.

"She left right after you last night and you didn't come back," he added like it was something anyone would notice.

"Yeah." I swallowed, and a grin spread across his face. He knew there was more—that was the whole reason he asked me the way he did. When he took a sip of his drink and his grin reappeared, I decided to continue. "I slept with her."

"Damn." He smirked playfully and shook his head. "Well, we went two years without bagging the same leech. It had to happen eventually."

He was completely unbothered by the confession, and I wasn't sure why I thought he would react any differently. I took a deep breath and prepared to tell the story from the beginning, but he beat me to the next line.

"What's up, man? Something's off."

"Last night wasn't the first time I hooked up with Maci," I admitted.

He took another sip of his drink. "You've slept with her before?"

"No, I almost did. But I stopped it before it went that far."

An amused look spread across his face, and he waited for me to continue.

"Maci was the girl you told me to sleep with that night you guys went to Columbus," I said.

"Halloween weekend?" Bryson raised his eyebrows, and I watched him think through the timeline. "Shit . . ." His eyes widened, and I laughed. "Literally the next day?" He stood up so he could pace. Bryson never sat still when he thought through something. "That's why you asked me about Stephanie."

I nodded, and my shoulders relaxed. "I didn't know how to bring this up, man. The timing was weird."

"You like her," he said. It came out sounding like a question he hesitated to ask. "And you just watched me hook up with her?"

"I didn't expect you to keep her around for five months, dog!" I said sarcastically and tilted my head.

Bryson howled with laughter. "But why didn't you say anything?" he asked, his voice going up three notches.

"I didn't know how to bring it up. There really wasn't anything to say after I saw that you slept with her. There was no reason to mention it. And then the longer you hooked up with her, the harder it was to bring up," I explained.

He lost it again, and I couldn't help but laugh at his reaction.

"Well, you won't get any comments from me, man," he said once we stopped laughing. "You've got a thing for her, right?"

"I don't even fucking know," I admitted.

This was territory both of us said we would never enter. I liked Maci a lot, but I didn't know where to go from here or what this meant for us. Usually by now, I was ushering a girl out of my room or driving away from hers with no intention of calling.

"Well like I said, I'm good with it." He shrugged. "Just one last comment and then I'm done. You won't hear anything else from me when it comes to her." He sat back down, and I stared at him. "That ass though, right?"

I pushed his shoulder and shook my head. An involuntary laugh escaped my chest. I expected no other way of ending this topic.

"There was a reason it was five months," he teased and stood up so he was out of my reach. "Good for you, man. That's all I'm gonna say."

He lit a Black & Mild and offered me a hit. I took it, and we spent the next hour bullshitting about things like nothing had changed.

Clearing things up with Bryson was something I dreaded doing for a while, but that was nothing compared to what I had to do next.

I had to figure out what I was doing with Maci.

Chapter Sixty-Two

MACI

March 2016

The drive to Joe B's Diner was quiet but hung thick with a conversation that Katie and I both knew we had to have. As soon as we got into the Uber, Katie prompted me to wait until we sat in our booth to start my story. She wanted no interruptions and complete freedom to have natural reactions.

So there we were—officially seated in our booth with menus still flat on the table. I glanced over the drink selection casually and tried to ignore the daggers Katie delivered from the other side of the table.

"Why didn't we just take Jaxon's Jeep instead of getting an Uber?" she asked when she noticed I wasn't budging. She picked up her menu, scanned the options, and tapped on her choice.

"Jaxon doesn't let people drive his Jeep." I shrugged. "And we never mentioned that before when we made these plans."

"Yeah," Katie piped up. "You're right. But that was before, maybe if there was something that happened recently . . ."

"Alright," I snapped and smiled at her. I slid my menu to the side and crossed my arms on the table in front of me. "Where would you like me to start?"

"From the beginning, bitch!" she demanded playfully.

Over the next fifteen minutes, I spared no details when I told Katie the story about the fight Jaxon and I had back at the condo, and how it led up to me spending the night and most of the morning in his bed. She asked no questions, completely invested with eager eyes and a satisfied grin.

I paused when the waitress came over to take our order and again when she brought us two mugs and our coffee carafe. I poured us both a cup and added two sugars and two creamers to my mug. I shook my last packet of sugar and sighed into the booth.

"Katie, I told him I loved him," I admitted softly.

Katie blinked and jerked away from her coffee mid-sip. She set the mug down on the table, and her eyebrows knit together. "Okay." She swallowed. "Wow . . . damn, you said I love you to Jaxon before I could say it to Connor?"

I palmed my forehead. "Oh my god," I whined.

"Oh my god," she repeated in an amused tone.

"Oh my, *wait*—" I pointed at her. "Did you tell Connor that you loved him?"

Katie shifted uncomfortably in her seat. "Well, no, not yet. I'm still figuring out how to say that part. But table that conversation," she said quickly, and a sly smile appeared on her face. "I *need* to hear more about this." She pursed her lips and picked up her coffee mug. "I actually already knew you guys slept together. I ran into Jaxon last night."

"Oh god. Was he crying at the breakfast counter?" I mumbled. The thought of Jaxon regretting everything that happened left an unsettling pit in my stomach.

"Stop that right now," she snapped. "I've told you since day one that boy has a thing for you."

I took a deep breath. "Yes, and does this *thing* mean I get to watch him sleep around for the rest of the year? Or is it a *thing* that we ride out until the semester is over? Either way, I can't be mad. He's told me since the beginning that he doesn't do the morning-after"—I shook my head—"ugh, I knew this would happen. I would sleep with him, and then I'd sit here with you and overanalyze everything."

"Correction, we are not overanalyzing. We are dissecting, and there is a difference," Katie added and pounded her fist on the table for emphasis.

We both laughed and took another pause when the waitress brought our food. I was starving when we first arrived, but talking about everything that happened out in the open made me a little nervous to eat. Katie's French toast and bacon smelled phenomenal. My eggs, bacon, and chocolate chip pancake were suddenly questionable.

I picked up the carafe and refilled my mug. After another sip of coffee, I took a bite of bacon and chewed as I prepared to reenter the conversation.

"Well, in the spirit of dissecting, he did say one thing this morning that stuck with me," I said.

"I doubt that he only said *one* thing that stuck with you, but go on. Let's entertain it," Katie joked.

I smiled as I replayed it in my head first. "He said he would never tell me not to make noise. Which sounds like he is saying that . . ."

"There will be a next time for you to make some noise." Katie nodded and finished the statement for me. Another satisfied grin spread across her face.

I had to cover my mouth so my recent bite of bacon didn't hit her on the forehead.

Katie shook her head approvingly. "Please tell me it was amazing. I feel like he has to be good."

"It was *very* good." I sighed. "It's like he knows what my body wants before I do. It's so different with him. It's different from any other guy I've been with."

"So are you going to talk to him about it?" Katie pushed a piece of bacon around her plate and eyed me suspiciously. "Or are you guys going to continue communicating through silence?"

I went to smack her playfully over the table, and she braced herself. She pursed her lips because we both knew she had a point, and she sipped her coffee in victory.

"I'm stuck." I shook my head and rested it in my hand. "I went into it knowing I couldn't expect anything, so the last thing I want to be is that girl who admitted she loved him and then demanded where we stood. He doesn't do relationships, and I feel like throwing that all in his face might be the death of him."

Katie nodded as she processed my honest admission. "But you aren't just any girl—you are *that girl* to him, Mace."

The skin around her eyes was soft as she spoke, and I felt my shoulders relax a little bit. I didn't realize how tense I was until a huge weight shifted in my chest. Of course I wanted to be special to Jaxon, but ever since I met him, I was positive that no such girl existed.

"You don't know that. He hasn't come out and said any-thing." I shrugged and sat back up in my seat. "And until I hear it from him, I don't think I have a choice but to assume this is a temporary thing." A small lump formed in my throat at the thought of ending things so quickly after they had just started. "I'll just have to let him know if it gets too hard. He told me this morning that we'll talk about it later, but I know him, and he will need prompting."

Katie shrugged. "Just make sure the only prompting you do with your mouth is *actually* contributing to the solution."

"Katie!" I exclaimed.

Katie raised her hands defensively and giggled. "I'm just saying I know how it can be having to talk about things neither of you really want to hash out! Connor and I get sidetracked all the time."

"You don't say," I murmured into my plate. My stomach settled now that we were shifting the focus onto Katie and her relationship. I took a hefty bite of my pancake and chewed. "So talk to me about why you can't say I love you. People just spew it out in that condo."

"I'm afraid to say it first," Katie answered quickly without a hint of shame. "Everything with us has moved quickly since we met. What if we mess it up?"

"Katie, please. You two are like a Hallmark movie."

"But what if that's the problem? What if things are too great? I feel like I'm so happy with him that something terrible is just bound to happen. And it will be much easier when we break up if I never told him I loved him."

"Katie." I swallowed another bite of pancake and placed my hand over hers. "Your ex-hookup attacked you in a bar, and the guy I'm in love with beat the shit out of him." Her eyes met mine, and she broke into a grin. "I think you're good for a while."

We laughed at a memory that seemed so far away. While nothing was funny about the encounter that night, I hoped that clarified what she left with Tyler and where she headed with Connor.

Chapter Sixty-Three

JAXON

March 2016

It was our last night in Port Clinton.

Everyone agreed that since we were heading back early in the morning, we deserved a night off from partying. No part of me wanted to go out to a club or spend another night in Heather's hot tub—but I didn't want to spend our last night sitting in the condo either.

Unless I was locked in my bedroom with Maci all night. We still hadn't talked about last night or this morning, and I knew it was only a matter of time before one of us caved and brought it up.

Since it wasn't supposed to be ridiculously cold outside, Connor suggested a fire down at one of the public beaches. The guys were easy to persuade when I mentioned all the beer we still had to drink. It would be a chill way to end our trip.

Around three, Connor came out onto the deck to tell me he was heading back over to his place. I nodded and he hesitated to see if I was coming with him. When I didn't get up from my chair, he slipped back inside and shut the door behind him.

"I'm probably gonna head over there and shower," Bryson said. He put out his Black & Mild and stood up.

I dragged my hands down my face and looked back out at the water. "I'll meet you over there in a few."

Once Bryson was inside, I stood up and walked over the railing. I leaned over and crossed my hands out in front of me. I wanted to go over to the other condo with a clear head, and I knew a good way to escape for a minute or two. I pulled out my phone and clicked on my mom's contact photo. She answered on the second ring.

"Hey, baby." I could tell by her voice that she was smiling.

"Hey, Ma." I grinned and gripped the railing with my free hand. "What are you up to?"

"What am I up to?" she countered. "I'm on my way to a conference in downtown Charlotte. What are *you* doing calling me on your break?"

I swallowed and bit the inside of my cheek.

"Jaxon Reed, what did you do?" she asked accusingly, and I laughed involuntarily at her tone.

"I didn't do anything!" I argued, and it was her turn to laugh. "I wanted to let you know I'll be home tomorrow night."

"And you're sure there isn't another reason you called to talk to me?" she prompted again, and I felt myself slipping.

I wasn't sure how she did it, but she always knew when something was up. She had that superpower even when Alex and I were kids. It sucked then, and it sucked now.

She continued when I didn't say anything. "You know I love hearing from you—"

"Ma, I don't wanna mess up," I blurted out

"Mess up what?" she replied softly. "Did you already mess it up?"

"Not yet," I said.

"Then you won't mess it up," she stated matter-of-factly.

"My track record agrees with me," I admitted with a hint of shame in my voice.

Mom picked up on it immediately. "So I'll ask you again, baby. What did you do?"

I swallowed and ran a G-rated version of the story through my head.

She chuckled. "Are you censoring for me?"

"Of course I am," I reassured her, and she laughed again. I took a deep breath and turned my head quickly toward the door to make sure I was still alone on the deck. When the coast was clear, I turned my attention back to the water and continued, "I slept with someone I actually might like, and now I don't know what to do."

"I'm trying *very* hard to ignore that you're making this sound like this is the first time you're sleeping with someone you actually like."

I did my best not to laugh. Sometimes her tone was too much for me to take. "I care about this girl—like a lot. We've been friends for a while, and before her, I didn't care if I messed anything up afterward," I explained.

"Well, what do you want to happen?" she prompted.

I shrugged. "I'm not sure."

"Well, what does she want?"

"I'm not sure," I repeated and recognized how lame my issue sounded.

"Jaxon, how are you supposed to know what to do next if you don't know what either of you wants?" she asked in the same tone she used when she questioned how I could forget something on her shopping list.

I turned around so my back was against the railing, and I folded my arms. "I don't want to label anything. This all happened last night, and I just feel like it's too early to figure out what happens next. This is why I don't do the morning-after."

"Well surprise, J. It's the morning-after, and you're sitting here trying to figure it out. So something inside you wants to make this right. You just have to figure out what right looks like for you." I heard a car door slam on the other end of the line. "I just pulled up to the conference center. I love you, baby. Don't be a jackass, and we'll talk more when you get here tomorrow night."

"Go kill it, Ma." I smiled, and I knew she was smiling back.

The hardest part about having a boss-ass businesswoman like Evelyn for a mom was that she always told me the harsh truth about things. I knew she wasn't fond of the lifestyle I had with women. She always told me that as long as I was clear about what I wanted, there wasn't anything she could think badly about. I never made promises. I left everything open because I didn't want to tie myself to someone I couldn't be upfront and honest with.

I couldn't leave everything open with Maci because everything about this was different. I cared about her, and right before I slept with her . . . she told me that she loved me. I never thought I would be in a place where either of those items didn't send me running just because it was the easier option. For the first time, neither of those areas of concern scared me.

I wanted to see where things went with Maci. She spent five months hooking up with Bryson, and he was in a completely different mindset than I was. I didn't see why she couldn't do the same thing with someone who actually cared about her. I wouldn't lie to Maci, I wouldn't sleep around on her, and I wanted to be with her even when I had other options available.

I'd have to work on the phrasing—because it sounded terrible in my head. But so far, it was all I had.

Chapter Sixty-Four

MACI

March 2016

As soon as we got back from brunch, Katie recruited Connor for her much-needed nap. Even though we were doing a low-key bonfire on the beach, it would still be a late night. I forgot that not everyone slept in until noon this morning, and that this was usually the time Katie napped if she was going to.

I changed out of my jeans and opted for some joggers before I made myself at home on the puffy L-shaped couch. I claimed the chaise part of the sofa because it was closest to the fireplace and clicked on the fire. Red and orange flames danced in front of me, and I sank deeper into the corner of my seat. I drew my legs to my chest and scrolled through the TV guide until I was satisfied. One of the stations was playing *Legally Blonde*, followed by *Mean Girls*. I was in for a fantastic afternoon.

I was confused to feel the material of the couch when I reached behind me for a blanket. There was one there this morning, and I didn't feel like hunting it down among the bedrooms. Katie's Chicago Blackhawks blanket was still in my room, so I hopped up and jogged down the hall.

No sooner than I rounded the corner of my bed, I heard the front door of the condo slam shut. I froze, and butterflies erupted in my stomach as footsteps went down the hall and toward the kitchen.

Jaxon was back from the other condo, and while I was excited to see him again, I was also terrified at what came next. As of right now, I slept with my best friend and everything was good. However, once we decided to throw logic at the situation, everything could change just as quickly.

I wrapped the blanket in my arms and took a deep breath. The sooner we got this over with, the easier it would be to move on to whatever came next. Jaxon was still my friend—the guy I could depend on for pretty much anything. That part of our relationship didn't have to change.

I walked the short length of the hallway and stopped in my tracks when I noticed it wasn't Jaxon who had come through the front door—it was Bryson.

He peered into the open fridge and glanced up at me when he noticed I was standing there. His teeth rested on his bottom lip, and he drew his body back so he could lean against the kitchen counter. His arms crossed in front of his chest, and his dimples dug into his cheeks. He was trying hard not to smile at me.

I took a few steps toward him and cocked my head. Bryson's expression seemed genuine, but it was very out of character. I examined his face and processed all of the possible options that could have happened while Katie and I were at brunch. I knew as soon as I saw his cocky grin.

"He told you," I stated.

"Oh, he told me." Bryson jerked his back up from the counter and turned to face me head-on. It was refreshing to hear the playfulness in his voice. All of the times we had messed around and fucked around, I had never seen this side of him.

"Like from the beginning, he told you?" I asked cautiously, still reading into his reactions. "Orrrrrr . . ."

"Like from Halloween, he told me," Bryson added and opened the fridge again.

I pursed my lips and didn't know what to say next. Before I could open my mouth and make another attempt at the conversation, Bryson beat me to it.

"Out of all people, you had to run into me that night, huh?" His smile returned, and the weight in my chest subsided.

"You served your purpose," I said softly. I lost it when Bryson's eyes widened, and his head shot out of the fridge.

"I served my purpose," he emphasized and shook his head. He chuckled, and when his golden-brown eyes met mine, I was brought back to the beginning—when neither of us knew we would be having this conversation.

I burst into hysterics and had to turn away from him. There wasn't any negative energy that hung in the air between us or any awkward spaces we needed to fill. It was the most natural I had felt with him since the night I met him at Brathaus. Yesterday I never would've joked with him about this. We would've had a completely different conversation about where he went after the club or if there were any other lies he told while we were here.

Bryson and I had been on our way out for a while, and when we walked away last night outside of Razzle's, we both knew it.

He grabbed a beer from the fridge and twisted off the cap. Before the fridge door could close, I held it open to reach in and help myself to a drink.

"Hey," I said and extended the bottle in front of me.

Bryson stared and waited for me to continue.

"It was fun while it lasted," I offered.

He clinked his drink against mine, and we both took a sip. He smacked his lips and brushed past me. "It's gonna be weird with you not asking what I'm up to all the time." He glanced behind him and walked toward the door to the basement.

"Well, at least now you can lie to me about what you're up to and I won't give a shit," I shot back, and he chuckled.

I slid back into my seat on the chaise and extended my legs toward the fire. I heard the basement door shut, and I relaxed on the couch. A conversation that could've quickly gone south actually ended on a good note. I wasn't sure if this made Bryson and me *actual* friends, but it felt like a step in the right direction.

I sipped my beer and watched Elle Woods create her admissions video for Harvard. Seeing her chihuahua, Bruiser, prance around the screen reminded me of Clooney, Chase and Trey's dog back in Pittsburgh.

I leaned over for my phone and shot him a quick check-in text.

Maci

Any updates?

Chase

Nada. Still in the doghouse but at least I'm in my house.

Maci

Damn. Did you at least talk about things?

Chase

Yeah. I'm not sure what it means but I know I want to be with him.

I felt a swell in my chest as I reread his last text. Chase loved Trey, and imagining him with anyone else was hard.

My brother wasn't perfect, but I liked to believe he wasn't an idiot.

Maci

Well that's a step!

Chase

You should come to Pitt for a few days during your break.

Maci

YES

The front door of the condo opened again. I leaned forward a little to glance down the hallway, and a giddy grin spread across my face when I saw Jaxon.

His mouth curved into a half-smile when he saw me on the couch. He gestured toward my drink and opened the fridge. "Need another?"

I nodded. He plopped down next to me and rested his arm above my head. He opened his mouth to speak as I was hit with a wave of word vomit.

"I don't want to talk about it now," I said quickly.

Jaxon's shoulders dropped. "Fine by me. We don't have to talk at all." He placed his beer on the coffee table and pulled me in for a kiss. I wasn't sure how much time went by as his mouth moved with mine. He took my drink and placed it next to his so I could rest my hands on his chest. He was warm, and when his body weight started to shift on top of me, Katie's blanket seemed like a pathetic option for the chill.

I loved how he smelled and the familiar touch of his hands and lips as they trailed along my skin. I loved how his eyes grew darker when he was turned on and how his smile dug into his dimples when something made him laugh.

Everything about Jaxon consumed me. I wasn't looking to fall for anyone when we met, but I had no idea he would end up being exactly what I was looking for.

A door opened down the hall and pulled me from my internal dialogue. We sprang apart and laughed at our reaction to being caught—like a couple of teenagers who didn't want to be seen by mom and dad.

"Still leaving at five?" Connor asked sleepily from the kitchen.

"Yeah," Jaxon answered for both of us and glanced in my direction. He sipped his beer and a cocky grin spread across his lips.

The idea of only being able to touch him like I wanted to behind closed doors was excruciating. I had never been so turned on just sitting a cushion away from someone. He looked me up and down right before he went into the kitchen, and my breath caught in my throat.

It was going to be a long night.

Chapter Sixty-Five

Jaxon

March 2016

The public beach was about twenty minutes away from the condo. When we pulled up, the parking lot had a few cars, but the beach was completely unoccupied. Around this time of year, all the beaches in North Carolina were filled with tourists and college kids on spring break. It was also much warmer down there compared to what it was like near Lake Erie.

No one walked to the beach empty-handed since all four cars had been stuffed with coolers, chairs, blankets, snacks, and game tables. Maci walked in front of me with her hands full of grocery bags. I admired how her ass looked in her leggings and instinctively pressed my lips into a thin line. The makeout session I had with her on the couch a few hours ago wasn't going to be enough to get me through the rest of the night. I knew she wanted me just as badly, which made restraining myself even harder.

Connor led us away from the entrance of the beach to an empty fire pit. "Some of the food trucks sell firewood," Connor explained. "If a few people come with me, we only have to make one trip."

"Set up camp, ladies." Jared gestured toward Maci and Katie. The girls exchanged a look, and they both laughed at Jared's instructions.

"I'll get pong set up," Reagan offered and put her chair next to the fire pit. "Jaxon and Bryson, you guys wanna play Heather and me?"

My instincts told me to look at Maci, but I couldn't bring myself to move. It never bothered Maci before to be around girls I slept with in the past, but so much had changed since yesterday. Normally I wouldn't care how girls chose to react, but Maci wasn't just a random I hooked up with. Since we hadn't talked about it, I wasn't sure what the right reaction was.

I froze and turned to Bryson so I wouldn't have to answer.

"Yeah, we'll play," Bryson said. He gestured for me to come with him, and a small group of us followed Connor back up to the parking lot. "That's how it's gonna be now, huh?" Bryson teased, so only I could hear him.

I shrugged, and an exasperated laugh left my chest.

"Don't worry. If they ask you for that threesome again, I'll offer myself as a sacrifice."

"Good luck with that, bro." I laughed, and he burst into hysterics. "That's a lot of crazy wrapped up in two leeches."

We were still laughing when we returned with armfuls of firewood. The girls had set up the chairs and blankets around the fire pit, and all of the snacks were laid out on one of the tables with the coolers stored underneath it. Two other tables were on the other side of the firepit so they could be used for games. It looked like an official party spot from the beaches back home.

"Jared weren't you an Eagle Scout or some shit." I set my wood down next to the pit and moved so others could do the same. "Get this started."

A few of the guys laughed, and Jared scowled at me. "You bet your ass I was."

As soon as the fire was lit, Maci, Katie, and a few other girls grabbed drinks from the coolers and found a seat in the circle. Heather and Reagan stood at the end of one of the tables and waved me to join them. Bryson smacked the back of my shoulder on his way to the game, and I laughed.

I looked over to where Maci was sitting and caught her staring at me. My mouth parted slightly, and she looked me up and down. I watched her gaze linger on my waistline, and she shot me a naughty grin. I almost got hard off of that look alone. She turned her attention back to Katie, and I forced myself to keep walking.

Music started to play from behind me as I made my way over to beer pong. The noise from over near the firepit was replaced with the sound of waves as they crashed against the sand.

"Boys against girls." Heather bounced up and down and shot a ball toward our set of cups.

Bryson and I exchanged a handshake, and I dipped my pong ball in the water before I took a shot. Since I made it, we shot first.

We went back and forth for a while. The girls kept up with the shots that Bryson and I delivered, but after two rounds of getting the balls back, we took the lead. We had played for so long together it wasn't surprising when we ended up running the table for the next three games. Bryson grew louder with every game we won, and by the end of game four, he was feeling pretty good. I drank at half his speed since I drove and desperately needed water.

"I need a break," I announced and stretched my arms over my head.

Bryson nodded and drained his drink. Switching gears almost immediately, he caught Aaliyah as she started back up to the fire.

Reagan wrapped her arms around my waist and hugged herself against my chest. "Let's go do a shot," she suggested innocently and stared up at me.

I laughed. "Let me get a water first." I removed her grip from around my body and took a step away for some space. I wasn't in the mood for her to get handsy.

As soon as I left Reagan's side, Brad and his roommate came over to the table to take my place. I headed toward the coolers and searched around the fire until I spotted Maci. She smiled sweetly at something Jared had said and looked past him to where Heather and Reagen were playing pong. She was looking for me.

I grabbed a bottle of water and walked behind the circle of chairs until I reached hers. "Hey, pretty girl," I whispered in her ear, and she jumped.

She giggled and lowered her voice so only I could hear her. "I like that."

I took the empty chair beside her and chugged half my water bottle. I needed about three more of them before I could have another beer, especially if I was going to play pong with Bryson.

"Is your car unlocked?" Maci asked.

"No, why?" I finished the rest of the bottle and tossed it in the trash.

"Can I have your keys?" She stood up and held out her hand. "I was gonna get Katie's blanket out of the backseat."

I looked over at the path that led up to the parking lot. I couldn't see anything past the other side of the fire, and there was no way I was letting her walk up there by herself. "It's dark up there. I'll walk with you."

She didn't argue with me, and I was grateful for her cooperation. I wasn't ready to explain why she shouldn't go into a dark parking lot in the middle of nowhere by herself. She waited for me to get up, and we walked in silence.

The way her chair was positioned, I was positive she witnessed Reagan with her arms around me. Maci had never questioned me about girls I had been with—unless it was to swap stories or just talk about things we experienced. However, this was before we slept together, and I knew how girls changed in their thinking once that happened.

While I wasn't making out in the corner of a bar like Bryson did, I still didn't know how to gauge her reaction. Even though it was innocent in my mind, it could've looked different in hers. I didn't want to view Maci as just another girl I hooked up with, but I felt like I didn't have a choice. I had witnessed too much between her and Bryson.

We reached the Jeep, and I leaned against the driver's side door. "Does being around Heather and Reagan bother you?"

She was surprised by my question and crossed her arms in front of her chest. "Are you gonna ask me this every time I'm around a girl you've slept with?" she answered playfully.

"No," I said with a hint of caution.

"Okay then, no, it doesn't bug me. You're friends with them, right?"

"Eh." I shrugged and looked up at the sky.

Her eyes narrowed and her mouth formed a hard line. "What is '*eh*'?"

"Just . . . I don't know." I shrugged again and repeated my answer, "Eh."

"Okay," she spoke slowly, like she was talking to a small child. She took a few steps toward me. "Do you still fuck around with *ehs*?"

Her tone was light, but her question was pretty straightforward. Even though it was unexpected, I was glad she got to the point.

"There it is." I smiled and pushed off the side of the Jeep.

She leaned her back against the car door and smirked at me. I knew there was more she wasn't saying, and I needed to prompt it out of her. I placed my hands above her head and forced her to look at me. Her eyes met mine, and she waited for me to continue.

"I don't plan on fuckin' around with anyone else but you," I admitted, not only to her but to myself. It was the first thought I had put into words regarding how I felt about her and what we were doing.

"Can you promise to let me know if that changes?" she asked in a small voice. She sounded nervous, and the skin around her eyes grew soft.

"Is this us talking about what happened last night?"

She cleared her throat, and she sounded more like herself. "I think this is part of it."

Her expression shifted again, and my heart sank a little. I hated to see her try and act like she wasn't nervous in front of me. I wasn't Bryson, and she knew that. But that didn't excuse me from all the times I tried to tell her that we were the same.

"Yes." I offered her a small smile. "I can promise to let you know if that changes."

"Why does everything about this feel so complicated?"

I straightened up and stuck my hands in the pockets of my jeans. "Because neither of us has said what we want."

She shook her head. "I don't think either of us knows yet."

"You don't know yet?"

"I thought I did." She shrugged and looked down at the ground. "I know what I said last night, and that doesn't change. But I don't want to rush into something that neither of us is sure about."

I didn't like where this was going. I didn't want this to be something Maci regretted, and the thought of not being with her again made my stomach turn.

"Let's just see what this is then," I suggested casually. "We've got a few months of school left—let's worry about it when we have to."

She pushed off the car. "So nothing has to change? The only difference is I get to sleep with you now."

I recognized the playfulness in her voice, and I grinned. "That sounds right."

She stretched up on her toes and planted a small kiss on the corner of my mouth. I went to pull her in for more, but she spun around and walked around to the trunk.

"Now pop your trunk and let me get that blanket," she shouted and leaned around the car when I wasn't right behind her.

"Do you want my hat?" I asked when I noticed her bouncing up and down to keep warm.

"Which one?"

I reached into the trunk and pulled out my Carolina Panthers beanie. She lit up instantly and snatched the hat from my hands. She placed it on her head, and I stared at her. I wasn't sure what it was about this girl wearing my clothes, but suddenly the thought of not getting another moment alone with her for a while seemed unbearable.

"Hold on a second." I slammed the trunk shut and dragged her by the hand to the side of the Jeep that faced away from the beach.

I pressed her against the passenger side door, and my mouth collided with hers. She placed her hands on my chest to get her bearings and leaned into my kiss. I fisted one hand at the base of her hair and slid my other under her hoodie. Her skin was warm against my fingers, and she shivered at my touch. Her lips moved quickly against mine, and I could feel my erection against my jeans.

I rested my forearms above her head and leaned my forehead to hers so I could come up for air. She drew in a few shaky breaths and kept her hands on my chest.

She peered up at me through dark lashes. "Can I stay in your room tonight?"

"Yeah, baby," I murmured. I skimmed my thumb against her cheek, and she relaxed into my touch.

She shook her head, and her dimple dug into her right cheek. "Don't do that."

"Do what?"

"Call me baby and expect me not to want you." It came out sounding like a warning instead of a suggestion.

I held her face in my hands and locked eyes with her. Both of us were searching the other to see if there was a reason not to do this, to plunge any deeper into something that neither of us saw an end to. I wanted to be with Maci again, and right now, I didn't want her to be with anyone else.

"Get in the car," I demanded.

She didn't question my direction. I opened the door so she could slide into the back of the Jeep, and I followed in behind her. I pulled the lever on the side of the seat and it jolted into the trunk, giving us the space we needed so she could lie down.

"Come here," I ordered.

She took my hand, and I positioned her so she was lying on the seat in front of me. I kept my body weight off of her as I kissed up her neck. She ran her hands through my hair and drew me closer, my erection hard against her hip. I positioned myself in between her legs and teased her through her leggings. I wanted her to know how much I wanted her, how much I had been thinking about her since she left my bed this morning.

When she tried to bring my mouth back to hers, I responded with a cocky grin. She watched me crawl back down near her feet. I pulled at the waistband of her leggings, and she lifted her hips. I tossed them to the side, and her mouth parted. Her eyes never left mine as I got off the seat and kneeled in front of her.

I placed my mouth around her clit and sucked softly. Her mouth fell open, and another shaky breath left her chest. My tongue moved in slow circles as I stuck two fingers inside her. She fell back against the seat and dragged her nails lightly against my scalp. She started to move her hips, and I buried my face deeper. She groaned, and I grabbed her thighs to hold her against me. I wanted to taste her when she came.

I sat up and slid my fingers back inside her. Her hips shot up from the seat, and her hands gripped the headrest.

I tried to memorize the look on her face as I teased her. "Tell me how that feels, Mace."

"Jaxon," she whimpered, and her hips shot up again. She opened her eyes, and I quickened my pace against her G-spot. I read her body and knew she was close.

"Come on, baby," I coaxed, and my mouth curved into a half-smile.

She cried out and arched her back. I felt her warmth against my hand and returned my mouth to her pussy. I dug my fingers into her thighs and finished her off with quick movements from my tongue. She pushed against my head, and I let her have a break. I would've made her come all over again in a different setting. I loved being the one to make her feel good, and knowing I turned Maci on brought me to a whole new level of want and need.

I leaned around the passenger seat while she caught her breath and tugged open the glove box for a condom. She pulled my mouth to hers, and I pushed myself inside her. Her nails dug into the back of my neck, and she sucked the sensitive spot at the base of my throat. I groaned into her shoulder and slowed the pace of my hips. I wanted to savor this for as long as I could.

She cupped my face with her hands and forced me to look at her. A shaky breath escaped my chest as I took in the sight of her below me.

Everything about Maci turned me on. The way her hips fit perfectly in my hands and how her lips parted as I slid in and out of her with gentle strokes. The freckles that trickled down her stomach and her bright blue eyes. Her smile could convince me to do anything she wanted. There was nothing about her I was ready to be without, and all I wanted to do was make her feel good.

I kissed her softly and slowly to match our bodies' sweet rhythm. I never imagined going slow in the backseat of my car, in a place reserved for quickies and one-night stands. But being with Maci felt different, and I wanted to be with her for as long as possible.

"You feel so good," she whispered in between kisses.

I smiled. "You're gonna make me come, baby. Keep talking to me."

"I warned you about calling me that," she challenged and kissed down my jawline. She grabbed the back of my neck and put her mouth against my ear. "I want you to go harder."

I leaned into the seat and pumped my hips, giving in to her request and feeling her walls tighten around me. Her breath was hot on my skin, and just as I couldn't hold out any longer, she moaned and pulled my mouth to hers. Her kiss was eager at first, but as we both came down, I felt her mood shift. Her fingers trailed through my hair and down my neck and her tongue moved gently against mine. My heart hammered against my chest, and I rested my forehead against hers.

Once I recovered, I rolled onto my side to keep my weight off her. She turned her head to look at me and stroked my cheek with her hand. I kissed her fingers and sat up so we could both get dressed.

We climbed out of the Jeep, and I slid my hand into hers. I planted a kiss on her head and led us back down toward the beach. As soon as we came within eyesight of our group, she dropped my hand and we went our separate ways. It was as if nothing had happened between us back in the parking lot.

While she joined Katie back by the fire, I went to the cooler for another water bottle.

"Where is my blanket?" I heard Katie ask Maci.

I froze and glanced over at Maci to see her expression.

"I must've forgotten it." Maci bit the inside of her cheek, and Katie read right through her lie.

"Forgot it." Katie nodded and averted her gaze casually toward me so she didn't draw attention to herself. "That's what we're doing now."

I turned away and burst into hysterics just as Bryson was coming back from the beer pong tables.

"My man." He shot me a drunken smile and held onto my shoulder. "You ready for another round?"

"Yeah." I laughed and grabbed a beer. "I'm down."

Chapter Sixty-Six

MACI

March 2016

It was quiet in the car the entire ride back to Bowling Green. Everyone was exhausted from a long weekend of drinking, partying, and staying up late.

Katie and Connor lounged in the backseat while I rested my head in my hand against the car door. I stared out the window and felt Jaxon's hand graze my upper thigh. When I turned to look at him, he offered me a sleepy smile and returned his focus back to the road.

For our last night together, Jaxon had kept me up with his constant need to show me how much he would miss me over the rest of the break. I got hot all over again just thinking about how he used his tongue and his hands.

My stomach sank just as fast when I remembered I would be without him for a couple of days.

It was a slow start getting everyone out of the condo, but at exactly ten-thirty, we rolled into the lot of Falcon's Pointe. Jaxon was able to park right outside the door since the lot was empty. Everyone had already traveled home for break, and an eerie silence hung over a building usually buzzing with activity.

Katie jolted awake at the sound of the gear shift. She stretched out her arms, and Connor sat up.

"Ughhhh, I don't wanna make this drive," Connor whined through a yawn.

"I feel that," Jaxon moaned and dragged his hands down his face. He turned his head to face me and pouted.

I shot him an empathetic grin and felt his pain. I wasn't looking forward to the two-hour drive I had back home. I couldn't imagine having to drive nine hours after the last few days we just had.

Brad's car pulled up next to us. We all got out at the same time and began the process of unloading. It didn't take long since most of the stuff from Jaxon's car just had to go into Connor's.

Jared was the first to take off. He pulled his duffle from Brad's trunk and went around to give his goodbyes.

"Do you have a key?" Bryson teased.

Jared laughed. "Yeah, man. I'm good." He rounded the group to Jaxon, and they shook hands the way guys do.

I laughed when he pulled me in for a hug. "Be careful driving," I said.

He winked at me and did a final wave before he ducked into his car.

"Bitch probably still doesn't have a key," Bryson murmured, and we all laughed. He pulled his keys from the pocket of his sweatpants and headed toward the door to the apartment building.

"We're gonna head out." Connor threw his arm around Katie's shoulder. "You ready, Maci?"

"I'll drive her over there," Jaxon offered before I could open my mouth to speak.

"Hmm," Katie piped up, and a satisfied grin spread across her face.

I widened my eyes and did a quick look around the parking lot.

"It's just us." She laughed and extended her arms out for a hug. She whispered reassuringly, "Your secret is still safe."

I tightened my grip around her middle. "See you soon?" I asked once we parted.

She nodded. "See you soon."

I gave Connor a quick hug and waved them both goodbye. Just as they pulled out of the lot, Bryson returned with a few bags and a fresh pair of clothes. I recognized the scent of his body wash and immediately felt weird that I knew that.

Out of the corner of my eye, I watched a silent exchange happen between Jaxon and Bryson. They both laughed.

"Be careful, man." Bryson held out his fist, and Jaxon pounded it. Bryson took a few steps in my direction, and my dimple dug into my cheek when his fist was still extended. He raised his eyebrows, and I laughed at his attempt to make this any less weird than it had to be. I accepted his gesture and pounded my fist against his.

It was probably the strangest way I've ever ended a chapter with a guy, but considering everything that happened between us, I would chalk it up as a win.

～✦～

"It isn't weird at all for you?" I asked when we were back in the car.

Jaxon shrugged and kept his eyes on the road. "There's nothing weird about it, Mace. You guys slept together, and it happened. Sex is sex."

I wasn't sure if I liked how that last part sounded, but I understood the point he was trying to get across. I knew the way Jaxon thought about sex was very different compared to how I did. He saw it as a disposable action, and I took it as some sort of unspoken commitment.

I thought back to the beginning of the year when Katie and I spoke about finding me a Fun Dip. It was hard to believe how much had changed since then.

My parking lot was as empty as Jaxon's. Katie and Connor's cars were gone, and my Elantra sat alone in the usual spot. He pulled up next to it and turned off his engine.

"Do you want me to help you load your car?" His voice was soft, and his hand grazed my thigh again.

"I should be okay." I swallowed. I held my breath and felt the back of my eyes get heavy. I was afraid if I looked at him, I would cry.

"Are you sure?" He got out of the car, and I followed his lead. He rounded the hood and stopped when he noticed my expression. "What's up?"

I shook my head and cleared my throat. "Nothing. Just don't wanna make this drive." I giggled for emphasis. He eyed me cautiously, and I added, "I only have one bag upstairs since it's only for a few days."

"Give me your keys, and I'll warm up your car."

I tossed him the keys, and we parted ways. I ran upstairs and found the apartment exactly how Katie and I had left it. Part of me wanted to say screw the rest of the break and just hang out here on my own until Sunday. Then I remembered that Chase invited me to Pittsburgh, and suddenly, getting away for a little bit didn't seem so bad.

When I got back down to the lot, Jaxon was leaning against the hood of his Jeep. He was texting on his phone and didn't look up until I was a few feet in front of him. He dropped his phone into the pocket of his sweatpants and took my duffle from me.

"This is all you're bringing?" He led me to the Elantra and tossed my bag in the trunk.

"That and laundry from this weekend," I said.

I crossed my arms and waited for the part I dreaded most to come next. I didn't know why I allowed myself to get this way. I was going to see him again in just a few days. If this was how it felt to leave him for such a short amount of time, I had no idea how I was going to cope over summer break.

He pulled me into his arms, and I pressed my cheek against his chest. I breathed in the cologne from his hoodie and tried to file it away for later.

He dipped his mouth to my ear and whispered, "I'm gonna miss you, Mace."

We were in this exact spot only a few months ago, sharing a very similar moment. But back then, I wasn't sure about us. Back then, I drove away even though it killed me not to kiss him after spending a few days together.

To keep myself from losing it completely, I drew back from his chest and cupped his chin with my hand. I kissed him softly at first but then parted my lips so his tongue could weave against mine. He kissed me back and kept his arms wrapped loosely around my waist. His thumbs brushed against my hip bones, and I pressed harder into him so I could savor the way our mouths moved together.

He cupped the back of my head, and I pulled away to look at him. His eyes were tired, and I knew he wanted to get on the road so he could get home. He kissed my forehead. "I'll see you in a few days."

I waited until Jaxon was in his Jeep before I pulled out of the parking lot. A tear escaped down my cheek, and I shook my head at the mess I had gotten myself into. I would never be able to cut this off come May, and I was kidding myself if

I thought for even a second that Jaxon would want an actual relationship. I made a left turn and watched as he made a right in my rearview.

My heart beat rapidly against my chest, and I knew that I was done for. I was dangerously invested in my feelings for Jaxon, regardless of how it was going to end.

Chapter Sixty-Seven

JAXON

March 2016

"Seriously, Ma, you didn't have to do this." I laughed.

She placed a two-tier cake in front of me with a huge smile plastered on her face. It was frosted with white icing and had confetti sprinkles around the top. A ring of candles was placed around the edges. She leaned over me and began to light them.

"We always celebrate your birthday early," Dad added from the other end of the table.

We were all outside on the back patio. We had just finished dinner, and Mom wasted no time getting into dessert. It felt nice to have everyone home for a little bit again. Dad was able to fly in from Cali with Alex and Bella last minute, and I knew my mom was gushing with excitement at the scene of a full table. It was dark out with a little bit of a breeze, but seeing the patio and yard lit up with all of Mom's light fixtures made it feel like summer.

The final candle on my cake was lit, and Alex's voice boomed from across the table. "Happy birthday to you!" he sang loudly, and everyone else joined in.

I covered my mouth with my hand and stared awkwardly at all of them. Bella giggled at my reaction and continued to sing loudly along with Alex. My mom placed her hand on my shoulder and gave it a light squeeze.

When the song ended, I leaned forward and blew out the candles. Their applause made me chuckle, and Mom immediately went to work cutting everyone a slice.

"What did you wish for?" Bella sipped her wine.

"I can't tell you that," I teased and drained the rest of the wine from my own glass.

She rolled her eyes and handed me the bottle so I could get some more.

"What do you want to accomplish this year, son?" Dad pulled his chair back from the table and walked to the bar cart. He refilled his glass with whiskey and a single ice cube.

"I just want to enjoy my last year in school." I grinned mischievously.

He shot me a look of approval. "As you should."

"Don't encourage him, Reed." Mom smacked him playfully on the shoulder. She placed a piece of cake in front of him, and he kissed her hand before she could walk away. It was a simple gesture, but it immediately made me think of Maci.

"J?" Alex pulled my attention away from our parents. When I turned to face him, he was standing up. "Walk with me for a second."

I looked at Bella, and we both watched him walk in the direction of Mom's rose garden. Bella shrugged and grabbed the bottle of wine back from my placemat. "More wine?" she offered the table, and my mom held out her glass.

I followed Alex to the seven-foot hedges surrounding Evelyn's precious rose garden. Once inside, there was a small fountain in the center and multiple garden fixtures she had collected over the years. A wooden bench that was dedicated to her mother sat against the front of the fountain. Alex stood beside it and lit a cigar.

"What's up, man?" I asked.

He offered me the cigar, and I took it from him. He dug into the pocket of his jeans and pulled out a small blue Tiffany box.

"Dude," I exclaimed but kept my voice down.

He opened the box, and a diamond ring sat in the center of it. He grinned and watched me marvel at the piece of jewelry. A lump formed in my throat, and my mouth fell open.

He smiled proudly. "I'm gonna ask Bella to marry me toward the end of June."

"Do Mom and Dad know?"

"Nah. I wanted you to be the one who knew before anyone else."

My cheeks started to hurt from smiling. "Why June?"

"Her birthday is the twenty-ninth, and we'll be here for it. I wanted to reach out to her parents one last time to see if they want to be there, but you know Mom's always been a mom to her. She'll want a parent there."

I nodded and passed him back the cigar. "Congrats, bro. You know Bella is already like family. It'll be nice to make it official."

He placed the box back in his pocket. "And you'll be my best man, right?"

"You seem pretty confident she's gonna say yes." I smirked.

"As long as I don't fuck up in the next few months, I don't see why she wouldn't." He laughed like that thought hadn't even crossed his mind. There was no way in hell Bella would ever say no. She would've married Alex if he had asked her back when they were eighteen—and even then she was dating someone else.

"I'm gonna try to talk her into having it in December at the Welsh Estate." Alex blew a puff of smoke toward the fountain.

"You've really thought about this, haven't you?"

"I have been since I met up with her out in Cali," he admitted.

"Wait, this December?" I gasped and did a quick rundown of the timeline in my head. "If you propose in June, that's only six months away!"

"So what," Alex argued. "I don't need more time. I want to marry her before the end of the year."

I considered his reasoning and nodded to let him know I understood his point.

"You'll get a plus one, but don't bring home some trashy broad from BG," he joked as we started back up to the house.

For a brief moment, I caught myself wanting to bring up Maci in the conversation. I wanted to let Alex know that if it worked out for December, I already knew who would be coming with me to his wedding.

If I saw Maci with me at the wedding in December, that would mean I'd have to find a way for it to work with us over the summer. There was a tiny pull in my chest at the thought of being away from her for three months. I couldn't even pretend like I was considering anyone else.

I wasn't sure how to be anything other than a one-night-stand kind of guy. I had worked through so many girls that I had no idea what number I was even on. I didn't even know if I could be loyal to just one person for an extended period of time. But I knew if there was one girl I would try it for, it was the one I had thought about every single day since she sat next to me in class.

"I promise no trashy broads," I said and held up my arms for emphasis. "I've got just the girl in mind."

Chapter Sixty-Eight

MACI

March 2016

"I may actually kill you if we continue with this conversation," Katie warned me from her seat at the kitchen table. She had a magnifying mirror rested in front of her, and her assortment of makeup was displayed around the table.

"Why?" I snapped over Katie's Drunk Betch playlist and adjusted my emerald-green crop top in the hallway mirror. I paired it with ripped black skinny jeans and black Vans.

We got pretty lucky with the weather for St. Patrick's Day. It was a whopping sixty-two degrees out, but it was clear that spring was just around the corner. The sun shining through our living room window gave me hope that the weather would hold out for the rest of the day.

"Because Maci! When we left Port Clinton, everything was fine. You two couldn't get enough of each other, and now you're asking him for some space?" Katie widened her eyes so she could do her lower liner.

I knew this conversation was coming. Ever since we got back from break on Sunday night, Jaxon had only been here one time and it was in the middle of the afternoon. Our plans to go out for St. Patrick's Day cut into our usual Thursday dinner routine, and I also hadn't slept with him since we got back either—which was a whole other area of torture that my body wasn't on board with.

While my heart begged me to distance myself in case everything went south, my body ached to feel his hands and his touch in places I couldn't even imagine another man being. It was an exhausting battle to sort through.

The whole time I was managing my own emotional war, Jaxon didn't make it any easier by not pushing me. He read all of my signs and didn't question why we weren't picking up where we left off after Port Clinton—either that, or he was getting some from other places.

I shook that thought immediately from my head and focused so I wouldn't mess up my new mauve lipstick. It was a shade Katie told me I needed to own after our night out at Razzle's, and she wasn't wrong. It looked fabulous with everything.

"I didn't ask him for space, Katie. I told him I was going out with the girls for St. Patty's Day. There's a difference," I defended.

"Well, even though I'm *also* going out with the girls, I still plan on meeting up with Connor later at the bars." She turned in her chair so she could face me. "Will *you* be meeting up with Jaxon tonight at the bars?"

"I don't know," I admitted lamely to my reflection.

Katie rolled her eyes and dabbed her red lipstick with a napkin.

I sighed and rolled my eyes back even though she couldn't see me. "Connor's your boyfriend, Katie," I argued. "Jaxon's not my boyfriend."

She let out a hearty laugh, and I could tell she was annoyed with my justification.

"You can't argue with me on that!" I exclaimed. My mouth lifted into an involuntary grin because I knew exactly what her face looked like. "We both agreed to see where it goes, and I don't want to push him any more than I should jump into it."

"What?" Katie spun around to face me and her eyes narrowed.

I replayed the sentence in my head and failed to understand my own wording. I decided to simplify it slowly for both of us.

"I don't want to push him into something he doesn't want," I confessed sadly and shook my head. "Yeah, I wanna be with him. But I also have to consider the other outcome. If we mess this up, there's no going back. I won't lose him as a friend, Katie. He's too important to me."

Katie processed my second attempt at an explanation and went back to her eyeshadow. We paused our conversation for a moment and sang along to the lyrics of "Make Me Proud" by Drake.

"Well, promise me this, then." Katie's tone was much more serious than before.

I put down my mascara and gave her my full attention.

"You'll keep communicating with him, and if it gets too hard for you—you *will* end it. I watched you try and be the hookup type with Bryson, and it fucking sucked. Don't let that become you and Jaxon."

I sighed and stared down at the mud-colored carpet. "Ironically enough, I think my relationship with Bryson is the best it's ever been."

"Because it's no longer you that he's sleeping around on," Katie grunted. It was clear she still wasn't a fan of Bryson.

"And the pisser is he's actually a decent guy to get along with now that I'm no longer sleeping with him," I noted. It was hard not to see a glimmer of humor in the situation.

Katie grinned. "Stop it."

I had to pause my mascara again so I could laugh. "What are you thinking about?"

"I'm thinking about how you, of all people, found the most anti-relationship guys to fuck around with—two incredibly attractive guys that happen to be roommates slash best friends."

"What do you mean, *me of all people?*" I demanded playfully.

"You wanted a hookup at the beginning of the year, remember? You found two guys who fit the role perfectly, and what has that done for you?"

I shrugged. "I'm just not a Fun Dip kind of girl."

"Morgan did say you can't have Fun Dip with a person you actually care about losing," Katie quoted me. I delivered that same line after I invited Jaxon out with us for the very first time.

"Morgan didn't say that I did!" I exclaimed.

"My point exactly!" Katie yelled, and I doubled over in hysterics.

"Shut up and finish your eyes!" I snapped back. "We told Sam we'd meet him at 149 in five minutes."

"Done." Katie tossed her makeup brush on the table in front of her and grabbed her gray leather jacket from the hook by the door. "Let's do a shot to St. Patty's Day 2016. I think we both need it."

"Why do you need it?" I grabbed the bottle of Fireball off the counter and poured two shots. I handed her hers, and she held up her finger.

She took a deep breath and held my gaze for a moment. "I told Connor I loved him last night at dinner, and he said it back."

"You bitch." I laughed. "You almost let me leave without that information!"

We clinked our glasses, downed the cinnamon liquor, and walked out the door.

When we got to 149, the bar was packed. Next to opening weekend and Halloween, St. Patrick's Day was an iconic holiday at BG. It pulled crowds from surrounding schools like Tiffin University, the University of Toledo, and the University of Findlay. It made things difficult for our group when we were used to the regular weekend traffic.

We spent almost an hour at 149 and decided to pop over to Tubby's for some Green Beer. We grabbed a table in the corner of the bar to claim some sort of ground while Sam and Owen ordered shots for everyone.

"God, I hope it isn't—" Katie began, and a tray arrived before she could finish her thought.

"Tequila!" Owen shouted and passed around the plastic shot glasses.

Katie and I groaned and shared a look of disappointment. Neither of us took tequila well. It was a potion designed for anger, drama, and disaster.

"What the fuck." Katie shrugged hopelessly. "Cheers to St. Patty's Day 2016."

My mouth hung open, and I watched her drain the cup of clear liquid. She puckered her lips and stared at me while her eyes glossed over.

"I hate you both!" I yelled at Sam and Owen right before I took my shot. It burned going down my throat, and I felt it make a home in my stomach. A shiver ran up my spine, and I stuck out my tongue so I wouldn't gag.

"You had your fun!" Katie declared to Sam. "Now I wanna see my boy toy." A sneaky grin spread across her face, and I wondered if it was the shot or the fact that Katie had finally said I love you.

Owen leaned his elbows on the table and put his face closer to Katie. "Where is your hunky boy toy?"

Katie's thumbs went to work on her phone screen, and we all waited in anticipation for our next destination. "He's at The Attic."

Sam's fists both shot into the air, and he cheered for his love of The Attic. The crowd behind him had no idea what he was so happy about, but they joined in on the cheering. The sound spread throughout the bar, and our table burst into hysterics. There was always so much love in a college bar after a few hours of drinking. The energy was contagious.

There was a short line to get into The Attic, but it went quickly since the bar decided only to let students with Bowling Green IDs get in. It was refreshing to be greeted by a normal-sized crowd. "Mr. Brightside" by The Killers boomed through the bar, and the dance floor lost it at the famous throwback.

Katie spotted Connor over by the pool tables and pointed him out so the rest of us could make our way over there. She ran into his arms, and he lifted her so her mouth could meet his. It made my chest swell with emotion to see her so happy with a guy like Connor. He was everything she needed in a boyfriend and everything I wanted my best friend to have.

I leaned against the bar and offered to buy Sam and Owen their drinks since they got the last shot. We ordered three Long Islands, and after my first sip, I felt the tequila working its magic. I was officially buzzed, and it came at the perfect time since Bryson took the empty spot next to me at the counter.

"Looking for Jaxon?" Bryson offered with a set of glossy eyes.

I laughed when I saw an expression I had witnessed so many times. He batted his long dark lashes and waited for me to respond.

"He doesn't know I'm here," I shouted over the music.

"He knows you're here," he yelled. "He saw you walk in."

My eyebrows knit together, and I quickly scanned the crowd around us.

Bryson grinned at the shift in my body language. "He's outside."

I rolled my eyes and took a long sip of my drink. I watched as Katie and Connor headed outside to the balcony. I turned to follow them, but Bryson gripped the sleeve of my jacket.

"Hey," he said, doing his best not to slur. My eyes met his, and he took a deep breath. "I'm only saying this because I'm drunk, and I'm only gonna say it once."

"Oh god," I deadpanned and stifled another laugh.

He licked the center of his bottom lip and continued, "And I'm only saying this because you're gonna be around for a little while"—he cocked his head and winced—"at least, I think you are."

"Get on with it, Bryson," I snapped, and he laughed.

He took another deep breath, and his eyes landed on mine for a second time. "I'm sorry if you felt I was an asshole to you."

I shook my head and gaped at the sincerity of his tone. "Another award-winning apology from you. It's such a shame I don't have to worry about those anymore."

"It is an apology!" he exclaimed, and a massive grin spread across his face.

He completely messed up the wording, but I understood where he was trying to come from. I rolled my eyes and did it in a way where he knew I accepted his olive branch. I had a feeling our relationship was headed down an interesting road, especially since Jaxon talked about them rooming together next year too.

The pit in my stomach sank as I thought about next year. It completely plummeted out of my body when I saw Jaxon standing at one of the tables outside with Heather draped over his shoulder, and his face leaned in close to a girl I didn't even recognize.

I was beginning to hate this bar.

Chapter Sixty-Nine

Jaxon

March 2016

I DIDN'T HAVE TO look up to know she had found me out on the balcony. The girl next to me at the table was halfway through her story when I saw Maci out of the corner of my eye. I wanted to look up and let her know that I saw her, but I wanted to tease her just a little bit more before I approached her about the bullshit she put me through this week.

Ever since we got back from break, she had completely shifted her mood toward me. I knew exactly what she was doing. When we got back from Port Clinton, she had freaked herself out on the car ride home and probably talked herself out of seeing me again. My friendship was more important to her than trying to see where things went with me, and she thought it would be easier to break this off if a wall was built between us.

I didn't see it that way—I didn't give up that easily when I wanted something.

"So, yeah, I can like show you back at my place if you want?" The girl beside me grazed my forearm with her fingertips, and I glanced up at her.

"Dibs, Becca." Heather placed her hand on my shoulder, and I immediately shook it off.

"Yeah," I deadpanned. "Absolutely not."

"Jaxon—" Heather started to say something, and I turned so I could leave the table. Her tone indicated that she was under the impression that I would be leaving here with her tonight. That girl could win an Oscar for the stories she made up in her head.

When I looked back to where Maci was standing the last time I noticed her, she was gone. I didn't want to make it obvious that I was looking for her, so when I spotted Connor and Katie at a table with Jared and some broads I didn't recognize, I joined them.

"Hey!" Katie lit up when she saw me. I pulled her in for a side hug, and one of the girls Jared was standing with turned her attention toward me.

"I'm Lindsey." She extended her hand, wasting no time making introductions. She had long curly brown hair and bright-green eyes that popped against her light-brown skin.

"Jaxon." I smiled down at her and shook her hand.

Katie's eyes widened, and Connor turned so he wouldn't have to witness anything that happened next.

As I stifled a laugh from their immediate reaction, I noticed Maci's black leather jacket a few tables away. Since she was facing some douchebag in a dark-green V-neck, she didn't know that I was staring at her.

"Do you want to take a shot?" Lindsey offered sweetly and squeezed my wrist to bring my attention back to her.

I watched Maci throw her head back with laughter, and the douchebag took a few steps closer to her when she wasn't looking.

"Yeah." An exasperated laugh escaped my chest as I watched Douchebag's hand graze Maci's hip line. He waved his hand like he had just picked lint off her jeans, and she ran her fingers through her hair.

Katie followed my gaze to where Maci stood across the balcony. She turned back to the table and reached for Lindsey's hand. "I'll go to the bar with you."

Lindsey smiled and took Katie up on her offer. The two of them headed back inside, and Connor caught himself up on the scene.

He turned to face me and gestured toward Maci. "Do you know that guy?"

"Nope." I chuckled and took a sip of my Jack and Coke.

"Are you gonna say anything to her?"

I smiled confidently. "Not yet."

Connor looked confused by my responses, and I didn't blame him. But he shrugged his shoulders, and I threw my arm around Lindsey when she and Katie returned with shots.

"Jaxon!" Reagan ran up to the table and drew attention from everyone around us. She wore a lit-up shamrock headband that could've stopped traffic and a silver sequin top that barely covered her tits.

Without looking in her direction, I noticed Maci turned around at her table. I picked up my shot and held it up to cheers. Lindsey downed her shot and placed her hands on my chest. Reagan smirked at the sight of another girl with her hands on me and moved so she was across the table from me.

"You said you aren't gonna say anything to her?" Connor interrupted innocently. Katie giggled and wrapped her arms around his waist.

"Not yet, no," I repeated.

Katie rolled her eyes. She was on the same wavelength as me, and I could tell she knew what I was doing. If she thought I was seriously considering hooking up with any of these girls, she and Connor wouldn't still be standing at the table.

"Well, she's leaving with that guy," Connor said, unimpressed with my choice to do nothing about it.

My eyes shot over to the now-empty table Maci had stood at a few seconds ago. I must've just missed her when I took that shot. I slammed my drink down and brushed Lindsey off of my chest.

"The fuck she is," I said sternly.

I jogged across the balcony and weaved my way through the crowded club until I was at the exit. I got stuck behind a few slow people going down the stairs, but I was out on the sidewalk in just a few minutes.

I looked to the left first, just in case she decided to go in the opposite direction of her place. I started walking to the right and spotted her only a few bars down.

Douchebag's arm was draped around her shoulders, and a fire ignited in my chest.

I cupped my hands around my mouth and yelled, "Mace!"

Chapter Seventy

MACI

March 2016

Even with music from the bars and conversation flowing from the crowd walking down the street, I heard his voice clear as day. It helped of course that he yelled my name, but there was only one person who said my name like that.

When I turned around, he stood only a few feet in front of me. His face was calm, and his dark-green eyes centered on me. His white Henley hugged his shoulders and chest, and his hands were tucked into the pockets of his jeans. It was like I wasn't even standing with another guy—he paid him absolutely no attention.

"Give me a second, Adam," I said to the guy from the bar.

Adam shrugged and walked ahead to give us some space. I turned my attention back to Jaxon and pursed my lips.

"You going home with him?" A cocky grin spread across Jaxon's face, and he took a step toward me.

I swallowed at the thought of him getting any closer and crossed my arms in front of my chest. I honestly hadn't gotten that far in my thinking. I just knew that Adam gave me an out from watching Jaxon get hit on from all different angles. I didn't want to stay and see if he decided to make a move on one of the many girls who would buy him shots all night. Just the thought of it made my stomach turn.

I cleared my throat and shrugged. "We're just going to another bar."

"Is that other bar your place or his?" he teased.

I shook my head and glared at him. "You're unbelievable."

"You would have me thinking otherwise since you're leaving with someone else," he snapped but kept his tone calm.

I smiled condescendingly. "I wasn't sure I could fit at the table with you and your groupies."

He licked the center of his bottom lip and looked at me in a way that made me weak in the knees. "They're just girls, Mace."

I sucked my teeth and rolled my eyes.

"You told me you wanted a night out with your friends," he reminded me. "I'm just having a good time and giving you your space."

"I didn't ask for space!" I exclaimed. It was the same phrase Katie used back at the apartment, and I was tired of hearing it.

I caught him off guard, and his eyebrows knit together. He took a few more steps toward me but kept a safe distance between us. "I told you I wasn't fuckin' around with anyone else."

"Right now, you're not."

He leaned back on his heels and straightened himself out again. "I told you I would tell you if that changes."

I took a few steps toward him, and his dimple dug into his cheek. "What happens when one of us is done, and this doesn't work?" I protested. "You don't worry about me being with other guys?"

"No," he answered quickly.

"You don't worry about it," I repeated. "Not at all."

"I don't worry about it, Mace, because the entire time you're talkin' to him . . . I know you're thinking of me," he said confidently and extended his arm toward Adam. His gaze never left mine, and he continued, "I know because you haven't let me have you since we got back, and I've thought about you the entire time I've talked to girls tonight."

My breath caught around the lump in my throat, and I drew in a shaky breath.

"Tell me I'm wrong, and I'll let you go with him," he threatened calmly. He shrugged and came closer so he was an arm's length away from me. "I'll walk away and let you go right now."

People started to slow as they passed us to try and catch a glimpse of what was going on. I stared at the man in front of me and felt all of my walls come crashing down. My face relaxed, and I ached to run my hands down his chest and wrap my arms around his waist.

The skin around his eyes softened, and he saw right through me. He waved over my shoulder, and I squeezed my eyes shut. "She's good, man. I'll walk her home."

I didn't turn around to face Adam. Instead, I stared up at Jaxon as he closed the remaining space between us. My stomach did a somersault as his cologne flooded my senses.

"Are you serious right now?" I asked defensively.

"I did some thinking when I was at home." He sighed. "You're clearly not the hookup type."

I opened my mouth to speak, but he held up a hand.

"Not a *Fun Dip* kind of girl," he teased, putting emphasis on the term from the night this all began.

"No, I'm not." I sighed, growing angrier. "Is that what you want to hear? That I've been kidding myself since day one?"

"I need you to tell me what you want," he said softly.

I knew that what I said next would decide everything. He was giving me an opportunity to be transparent—to leave no questions unanswered, and to have no more confusion moving forward. We had been on a broken path of communication since we met, and he was trying to help me pave a new direction for us to take together.

My shoulders relaxed, and I decided to trust the man who won me over the moment he gave me his Cotton Candy Blizzard. I knew what I wanted.

"I want to try this with you," I confessed.

Jaxon peered up at the sky like he was pondering my request. He smiled shyly. "Like a trial run?"

"Yeah." I grinned. "Like a boyfriend trial."

"A *boyfriend* trial," he repeated and slipped his arms around my waist.

"If that word is too scary for you, we can call it something else."

"I'll get used to it," he assured me.

Before I could say anything else, he kissed me. I wrapped my arms around his neck and pressed myself against him.

"I'm gonna take you home now," he murmured against my lips.

"You better," I threatened playfully before I pulled him in for another kiss.

Chapter Seventy-One

JAXON

March 2016

"Cheers, my man," Bryson yelled over the bass in our apartment. He smiled at me from the other side of the living room and raised his shot glass. "And happy fucking birthday!"

"Happy birthday!" the rest of the room yelled.

I smiled back at Bryson and took my sixth shot of the night. It was Saturday, and we were about a half hour away from going to the bars. The pregaming was still in full swing, and I felt pretty good.

So far, turning twenty-two wasn't half bad. On Thursday, I spent my actual birthday with Maci in a much more private setting. After we went out for dinner and a few drinks, we came back to her place and didn't leave her bedroom until noon the next day. Maci made it clear that we weren't just celebrating my birthday, but also acknowledging that I had made it through my first week as her official boyfriend.

It was completely worth missing class and taking an absence. If being a boyfriend meant being with Maci whenever I wanted and sharing her bed every night, then I was all for it.

"Heather has asked me three times tonight if you're really dating Maci." Jared shook his head and handed me another beer.

"She shouldn't even fuckin' be here," I murmured and clinked the neck of my bottle to his.

He laughed halfway through his sip. "They're just leeches, man. You know that."

"Fuckin' leeches!" I shook my head and grinned proudly at him. "Bro, you've spent way too much time with Kennedy."

"Oh, absolutely," he agreed right before he turned and got the attention of a cute blonde in a bright-red sundress.

Unfortunately, his disappearance invited a very unwanted guest into my personal space. Heather ran her fingers down the length of my arm and bit her bottom lip. "Happy birthday, Jax."

"Nope," I deadpanned and brushed past her.

I spotted Maci over at the beer pong table with Katie. They exchanged a playful high-five, and Maci caught me staring at her as Katie took the winning shot. My mouth curved into a half-smile, and I waited until they finished celebrating to approach the table.

"Hey, pretty girl." I drew her close to me so I could kiss her temple.

"Hey, birthday boy." She slipped her arms around my waist and rested her chin on my chest. The makeup around her eyes made her bright-blue eyes pop even more than usual, and the rest of the room immediately tuned itself out. "Having trouble avoiding your usuals?"

"Not at all." I read into her sarcastic tone and ran my thumbs above the waistband of her jeans. Her stomach was completely exposed in her long-sleeve crop top. "This boyfriend thing isn't that bad."

She grinned. "You're only saying that because of how I rewarded you for it."

I shrugged and rolled my eyes. She laughed and pulled away to rest her hands against my chest. She looked me up and down until her eyes landed on mine again.

"Just imagine how I'll do it if we last, like, a month," she said slowly in a voice that threatened to make me hard on the spot.

I blew an exaggerated breath from my chest, and her mouth curved into a satisfied grin.

"What will I get for two months?" I prompted.

She shrugged. "I guess we'll just have to wait and see."

"Three?"

"Well, I'm not gonna see you for three," she reminded me.

I halted my stream of questions and realized that month three would put us in June. I didn't recoil at the thought of still being with her in the summertime or having to make things work until we both returned to Bowling Green.

"What if you did?" I asked in a low voice.

She cocked her head and looked at me like I had made a mistake. "We'll be on break."

I shrugged. "So."

Her eyes studied my face and looked for any signs of hesitation. She blinked a few times and crossed her arms in front of her chest. "What are you saying to me, Jaxon Hayes?"

My teeth scraped my bottom lip as my full name left her mouth. Her dimple dug into her cheek, and she waited for me to continue. Butterflies dipped into my stomach, and the words came to me without warning. "Come visit me over the summer."

Her eyebrows shot up toward her forehead. "In North Carolina?"

I grabbed her hand and pulled her back into my chest. My fingers traced along the freckles on her stomach, and she shivered at my touch. I had to keep reminding myself that we were in the middle of my living room—surrounded by a shit ton of people. The end of the night suddenly seemed so far away.

"Why not?" I asked and returned my focus to our conversation. "As soon as I tell my mom about you, she's gonna wanna meet you anyways."

I could tell that the thought of meeting my mom made her nervous. I wasn't going to tell her that she had nothing to worry about. Maci would be the first girl I ever brought home to meet my family. There had been plenty of unfortunate run-ins my mom experienced with randoms, but as soon as I told her that Maci was my *girlfriend* she would probably offer to fly her out first class.

It was exactly why I hadn't said anything to my family yet. I decided to wait until I was officially home for the summer to break the news.

Maci searched my face for any signs of hesitation. "This is a lot for a trial run."

"I'm not gonna be able to go that long without seeing you," I admitted. "Let me fly you out to me."

She stretched up on her toes and pressed her lips to mine. I fisted my hand in the hair at the base of her neck, and she smiled against our kiss. I pulled her to me again, and when she sucked softly on my bottom lip, I knew I had my answer.

I wasn't sure how summer break would work between us. I still had two months left of school to see Maci as much as I wanted before I had to let her go for a little bit. I still had no desire to be temporary, and when I kissed her again, I knew that was no longer even an option.

Without warning, I fell for one of my best friends. I just hoped I could survive the trial period.

Author's Note

Since I was in middle school, I had a passion for creating stories. I wish I could say that I have a bunch of drafts to show for it, but unfortunately that isn't the case. You see, I had a bad habit of talking myself out of an idea before it could become something bigger. Many writers can resonate with that—scrapping an idea because you're afraid of what the rest of the world will think about it. It took becoming a mom for me to realize that the entire concept of waiting for someone else's approval is bullshit, and that the only person who will make or break your passions is yourself.

The idea for *The Hookup Type* came full circle back in 2020. The characters of Jaxon and Maci have been with me long before then. I knew I wanted a story for them, and I had scenes filed away for when I was ready to get it all on paper. But I was afraid to begin another unfinished draft and toss aside another set of characters I knew deserved better.

Among the COVID craziness, I was rocking my son around three in the morning—as all new parents do as we try to navigate parenthood for the first time. While my son, Noel, stared up at me with the most alert pair of blue eyes and no plans of falling asleep anytime soon, a lightbulb went off. I told my four-month-old the secret ending to Jaxon and Maci's story, and it was at that moment I knew I had something different.

I spent the next two years mentally back at Bowling Green State University. There were no hesitations when I chose my alma mater for the setting of *The Hookup Type*. There is something special about that place. Like Maci, I learned about myself through great friends, a cozy college apartment, and a guy I ran into at a bar called Brathaus. I'm proud to say that the guy who asked me to arm wrestle at two in the morning is now my husband, and while he's nothing like Bryson, I couldn't think of a better way for Maci to meet her attempt at a Fun Dip.

I often get asked if anything from *The Hookup Type* actually happened or if any of the characters are supposed to be real people from my time at Bowling Green. Most of the locations are real, the fantastic bar scene is *definitely* real, and I believe that everyone should have Campus Pollyeyes at least ten times in their lifetime. Plenty of scenes in *The Hookup Type* draw from personal experience, but it wouldn't be fun if I gave everything away now, would it?

After eight years in education, in February of 2022, I transitioned out of teaching high school English. I knew I wanted to write and wanted a job that allowed me to be more present at home. Public school teachers are superheroes, and after I had my son, I had to hang up the cape.

So I got a corporate job creating learning materials for a small company in Cleveland. To this day, I'm still convinced it's the most boring position ever created. In a nine-to-five role, I was done by eleven and twiddled my thumbs for the remainder of the day. My boss was an unpleasant woman who couldn't understand why I would want to be at home with my son, and the rest of the staff made me feel like I was in an episode of *The Office*. Now don't get me wrong, I'm a massive fan of Michael Scott. But when you live in Dunder Mifflin, I can promise you it isn't actually funny.

The whole scene was interesting, to say the least. But I truly believe that everything happens for a reason, and it's because of this role I had so much time to work on *The Hookup Type*. I went from having no time to write because of teaching and motherhood—to gaining half a day, five days a week, in a quiet office where I was paid to invest in a story I believed in. It was a blessing in disguise and the push I needed to see the book come to life.

Fast forward thirty more days and throw in a change in childcare, and I was working from home in a role that I loved. I spent the next six months writing whenever I could and balancing working from home with a toddler. Late nights with some wine and my *Sex and the City* girls in the background, weekends spent with my husband on the couch—both of us working late into the night on dreams we both believed in. The constant reels playing in my head of possible plot lines and dialogue I couldn't wait to get on paper.

Everything from that point on came easy, and when I finished *The Hookup Type* in August of 2022, the real work of self-publishing began. It took a little over two years to complete the story and about a year to get things finalized and the book published. This entire process has been a journey, but I'm proud to say that I'm officially a published author at thirty years old.

Thank you to everyone who has made it this far and to everyone who has read *The Hookup Type*.

Thank you to everyone who has supported me this far in my writing career. Your kind words and support did not go unnoticed and mean more than you will ever know.

Thank you to friends and family who had to answer my endless questions when they agreed to be beta readers.

Thank you to my husband, Noel, who was my first official reader and the first person besides myself to meet Jaxon and Maci. He brought up solid points about male banter and the importance of having a fresh cut from their go-to barber. He has been my biggest support system and number-one fan since day one, and he cannot wait for everyone else to read the rest of the series.

To answer the question I get most often, yes, there will be a sequel. I always saw three books in the series for Jaxon and Maci (gasp), and I promise, with some time, I'll deliver them.

I found myself again through writing this book. As mothers, wives, and employees, losing ourselves to those labels is easy. It's necessary to find a spark again and invest in the talents and passions you were meant to pursue. No one is going to create your dreams for you, and we never know how much time we have to make them a reality.

Believe in yourself and your goals, and keep your distance from those who say you can't do something. I'm not done exploring, and I'm not done creating. There are still a lot of unwritten stories floating around in my head that I can't wait to share.

With love,

Brittany

About the Author

Brittany Wilson began her author journey with the release of the first book in her college romance series, The Hookup Type. By balancing real-life with smutty scenes, she hopes her readers can relate to her messy yet lovable characters.

Before she was an author, Brittany taught freshman and sophomore English Language Arts at a small high school. She graduated from Bowling Green State University with a degree in education and the college serves as the setting for many of her books!

While Brittany has always had a love for writing and a passion for telling stories, she is also the wife to her Falcon Flame and the mom to a crazy and creative little boy. You can find her watching a good comfort show, cuddling with her dogs and brainstorming her next book idea. Or possibly her next tattoo.

TikTok and Instagram – @brittanywilsonauthor
www.brittanywilsonauthor.com